WHEN THE LION ROARS

The true story of Dr. James Allen, the world's leading authority on dioxin, a chemical used to defoliate the jungles of Vietnam during the Vietnam War.

GIL BOGEN

ALSO BY GIL BOGEN

FROM MCFARLAND PUBLISHING

Tinker, Evers, and Chance: A Triple Biography

Johnny Kling: A Baseball Biography

Copyright © 2013 Gilbert Bogen
ISBN: 978-0-9884024-4-7
Registration Number / Date: TXu000922735 / 1999-11-12

Published by
DRAGON TREE BOOKS
1620 SW 5TH Avenue, Pompano Beach, Florida 33060
(954) 788-4775 | editors@editingforauthors.com

Jacket Design and Layout by Elijah Meyer.
Cover photos © 2012, Robert Hodierne. Reprinted with Permission.

All rights reserved. This book or parts thereof
may not be reproduced in any form without permission.

Dedicated to Paul Reutershan,

Frank McCarthy, and other Vietnam veterans

who died to keep America safe and free.

ACKNOWLEDGMENTS

Maude DeVictor was invaluable. She started unraveling the mysteries surrounding the maladies befalling Vietnam veterans and was tireless in pursuit of the truth. She led me along several trails that resulted in not only information but in meeting important people who played key roles in the Agent Orange story.

This is to acknowledge the cooperation of Frank McCarthy and Dr. James Allen, who gave freely of their time and knowledge, without which this manuscript would never have been completed.

Christie Allen, Dr. Allen's wife, allowed me to visit their home in Ashville, North Carolina. While there, I had access to the family gravesites and listened to stories about Dr. Allen's ancestors, who were brought into the story. In addition, a visit to the nearby town allowed me to meet members of the community, who became real characters in the story.

My darling wife, Hana, edited the manuscript and was responsible for a great many changes that brought visual effects and depth to the story. In addition, she also rendered opinions when I needed answers to questions. And as a rule, Hana was right on the mark.

Last but not least was my wonderful grandson, Michael. This amazing young man performed major surgery numerous times upon my recalcitrant computer and brought it back to life. Thank you, my WONDERFUL grandson.

CONTENTS

Chapter One 1
Chapter Two 7
Chapter Three 12
Chapter Four 18
Chapter Five 22
Chapter Six 26
Chapter Seven 33
Chapter Eight 39
Chapter Nine 45
Chapter Ten 51
Chapter Eleven 57
Chapter Twelve 67
Chapter Thirteen 70
Chapter Fourteen 76
Chapter Fifteen 81
Chapter Sixteen 88
Chapter Seventeen 95
Chapter Eighteen 98
Chapter Nineteen 102
Chapter Twenty 111
Chapter Twenty-One 114
Chapter Twenty-Two 118
Chapter Twenty-Three 123
Chapter Twenty-Four 128
Chapter Twenty-Five 131
Chapter Twenty-Six 138

Chapter Twenty-Seven	145
Chapter Twenty-Eight	150
Chapter Twenty-Nine	155
Chapter Thirty	158
Chapter Thirty-One	165
Chapter Thirty-Two	171
Chapter Thirty-Three	179
Chapter Thirty-Four	186
Chapter Thirty-Five	193
Chapter Thirty-Six	197
Chapter Thirty-Seven	202
Chapter Thirty-Eight	209
Chapter Thirty-Nine	213
Chapter Forty	217
Chapter Forty-One	224
Chapter Forty-Two	229
Chapter Forty-Three	235
Chapter Forty-Four	242
Chapter Forty-Five	249
Chapter Forty-Six	256
Chapter Forty-Seven	264
Chapter Forty-Eight	271
Chapter Forty-Nine	276
Chapter Fifty	281
Chapter Fifty-One	286
Chapter Fifty-Two	291
Chapter Fifty-Three	295
Chapter Fifty-Four	299
Chapter Fifty-Five	305
Chapter Fifty-Six	313

Chapter Fifty-Seven	318
Chapter Fifty-Eight	325
Chapter Fifty-Nine	331
Chapter Sixty	337
Chapter Sixty-One	340
Chapter Sixty-Two	345
Chapter Sixty-Three	349
Chapter Sixty-Four	354
Chapter Sixty-Five	358
Chapter Sixty-Six	367
Chapter Sixty-Seven	375
Chapter Sixty-Eight	379
Chapter Sixty-Nine	385
Epilogue	387
The Disposal of Agent Orange	389
Chemical Warfare: Agent Orange	391
A Final Word on Agent Orange	393

ONE

For the umpteenth time, Linda Evans, secretary to Dr. James Allen, held the phone tight to her ear. She dialed the number to a one-bedroom apartment at 1219 Sweeney Court, Middleton, Wisconsin. It was ringing, ringing. Still no answer.

It was March 8, 1977. Rickey Marlar had not shown up for work. Nor had he called. It wasn't like him. Even when running a high fever, he'd show up and hurry to the lab. He would break out in a sweat and his whole body would ache, but going home was never a consideration. Rickey would slip into a long, white lab coat, pop two aspirins, grab his notepad and hurry to the Biotron, where his macaque monkeys waited for him. On one occasion, Linda pressed him for an explanation.

"Why are you working? You're sick."

"I don't have time to be sick," Rickey said, brightening as he reflected on the privilege of working for Dr. James Allen, the world's leading researcher on environmental toxins. "This work is exciting. Every day is a real experience," he went on. "We're in an unexplored area, and I know, I just know we're gonna find that the deadliest chemical made by man will never be safe. Never! No matter how small the amount. What a tremendous breakthrough! It could lead to a worldwide ban on dioxin. I know it'll happen. Just think...clean air, pure water, safe food. The way it was a long time ago."

When Rickey first saw his name on a published paper alongside that of his esteemed mentor, he became ecstatic. He whistled the entire day while he worked. He talked to his monkeys, who grabbed and shook the bars of their cages. He waved the latest scientific paper at them as if he had just won the Nobel Prize. Proof, that he was on his way to becoming a real scientist.

"Only one more year," Rickey said to the monkeys. "And a thesis, of course. Then I'll be a PhD."

It had a ring to it, and he loved it.

But today, for the first time ever, Rickey had not shown up for work.

Linda put the phone down, her hand still on the receiver. Her pale green eyes held a worried look. She glanced at John Cartwright sitting in an old but sturdy wooden chair in front of her desk, looking at and fingering a loose button on his white shirt. His round, chubby face and pot belly suddenly annoyed her. For several moments, there was silence.

"Something's wrong," she murmured.

As John looked up, strands of blond hair fell over his brow. With a flick of his hand, he quickly brushed them back in place.

"We went to the Checkerboard Tavern last night," he said. "Then we went back to his place for a beer. We talked some, but other than being a little tipsy, he was fine. He even remembered to call his father to wish him a happy birthday."

Linda took her hand away from the phone. Shaking her head, she frowned and locked eyes with John as if she was laying down the law to a mischievous teenager.

"When are the two of you going to lay off that stuff? The way you guys drink, Rickey must have some hangover."

But beneath Linda's outburst, she sensed that the problem was more than the aftermath of an alcoholic binge.

"C'mon, we've handled it before," John said, waving Linda away. "I was with him until after eight. He was fine."

"If only Dr. Allen were here," Linda replied. Sitting upright in her straight-backed chair, she took a deep breath and exhaled slowly. The old-fashioned Remington on her desk reminded her of typing to be done, but she didn't feel up to it.

"I know I'm a worrywart...but I can't help it. Let's drive over to his place."

John lifted himself up and grabbed his coat and wool cap from a hook on the wall behind him. "Oh, stop worrying," he said. "There's a good reason why he didn't come in. We'll drive out to his place, but first I'll finish up his work. Dr. Allen wants the research paper ready for mailing by next week."

He paused, and to satisfy Linda's concerns, he said, "Let's leave around five, I'll pick you up."

Linda tried to smile gratefully. "Thanks, I'll feel better once I know he's okay. I'll wait for you here."

John wrestled his arm into a sleeve and hurried out.

CHAPTER ONE

Linda reluctantly rolled a sheet of typing paper in place. She tugged at the collar of her red wool sweater and shifted uneasily in her seat. Work had to get done. She stretched her fingers over the keys, cracked her knuckles, and began pecking away. In seconds, the clickety-click-click of the keys and the rapid shifting of the carriage fell into a rhythm. One typed line followed another. The pattern was never broken until Linda reached the end of the page. She pulled the sheet from the roller and examined it.

She never ceased to marvel at the efficiency of the old Remington. She loved that typewriter, especially its jet-black color and gold trim. Her feelings were the same about her job at the Primate Center, and about her office, a small space adjacent to a slightly larger area occupied by Dr. Allen. The furnishings were hand-me-downs from other offices at the University of Wisconsin: wooden desks and chairs with scratches and nicks, a matching beat-up credenza behind her desk, gray metal filing cabinets with stubborn drawers that had to be coddled and coaxed back into place once opened. These old relics spoke volumes about the frugality of the man in charge. But for Linda, these antiques, as she called them, held a sweet nostalgia. They held memories of her grandfather's office. The cluttered book-lined shelves, his wooden roll-up desk, and the scent of his pipe tobacco. As she thought about this wonderful old man, she glanced at the phone and had an urge to call Rickey again.

Two corridors away, John Cartwright was in an alcove off one of the concrete-block corridors. He sat on the edge of a gray metal folding chair, arms resting on white Formica. He was examining pages in an open, hardcover, three-ring notebook. The bright light from above glared down on the blue-lined pages that displayed hundreds of handwritten numbers and letters, looking like a code that could only be deciphered by those who belonged to a secret society.

He flipped from page to page, running his gaze down a long list of data for each monkey in the experiment. As he examined the records, he could hear yelling and screeching from the monkeys in cages out in the corridor. He was glad he worked elsewhere and not in the Biotron, even though it was one of two such buildings in the world.

The environment allowed monkeys to live as they did in the forest—the lighting, humidity, temperature were all controlled and necessary for breeding. The experimental monkeys lived in cages on either side of the wide corridor. They were not by nature the most agreeable animals. They were difficult to work with, and when sick, they became hostile and aggressive. They would yell and scream, just as they were doing now. They would reach out and grab anything if it were close enough. And they smelled. As the effects of the dioxin diet became apparent, the monkeys became visibly sick and aesthetically ugly. Hair fell to the bottom of the cages. Their complexions became spotty. They drooled and spit. That's what he hated most.

John focused on a page. He checked numbers on another page, flipped back, forward, and back again. Data was missing. Raw data. Pre-experimental platelet data. It had been recorded in the paper about to be published. But it wasn't in the records. He closed the notebook and hurried out. It was nearly five, and Linda would be waiting.

Driving along University Avenue, heading out to the Brittany apartments in Middleton, John pushed hard on the gas pedal. The car sped along the avenue, and a silence prevailed as Linda gazed out the window. They passed upscale stores: fashions for women, trendy clothes for men, a furrier with a display of full-length mink coats, a chocolate shop, and children playing hopscotch on the sidewalk. Linda saw none of this. It was as if she was in a misty fog that had settled in around her.

John finally turned left at Parmenter and took another left at Hubbard. The engine roared as the car lunged forward, rounding a bend in the road. Linda was startled as she was thrown against the door.

"Hey!" she yelled. "Do you have to take those turns so hard?"

"Sorry."

Up ahead and to the right, giant oaks circled the water of a quiet pond; its branches were bare. The ground below held grass waiting and eager to turn green. As they sped past this serene setting, Linda said nothing about this one small piece of Wisconsin landscape she fell in love with years ago, when she first saw shrubs and flowers explode into full bloom on a sunny, spring day.

John eased his foot up. The car slowed. He made a sharp right and an almost immediate left. The street had two-story brick buildings on either side and a cul-de-sac at the far end. John killed the engine alongside a straw-colored grassy incline that led up to Rickey's ground floor apartment. John left the car on the side of the road and they both hurried up the small

CHAPTER ONE

stretch of lawn. They made their way into a wide, dimly lit hallway and stood before apartment #3. Linda fingered the metal doorknocker and tapped. No answer. She tapped louder and longer. No answer.

"Listen to the TV," Linda said. "It's loud!"

Linda hurried outside, pressed her nose against the bedroom window, and rapped loudly with the knuckles of her right hand. No answer. She peered inside at the bed just beyond the white, transparent curtain. Light from the living room settled onto a sky-blue bedspread with decorative rose petals. The bed had not been slept in.

John came and stood alongside Linda to squint through the window.

"Let's try the sliding glass door in back," he said.

Linda felt her heart pounding as she followed John around to the concrete patio. The kitchen was dimly lit from light in the living room. John tried the handle of the glass door. Locked. He made a fist and rapped loudly. Intuitively, Linda knew there would be no reply.

"What do we do now?" she asked plaintively. "Let's find the building manager."

Once inside the hall again, John knocked on the door of apartment #4, across from Rickey's apartment. A heavyset man with a bald, shiny head and red suspenders opened the door.

"Yeah?" he said, eyeing the two with a look of annoyance.

"Where's the building manager?" John asked. "Something's wrong with my friend in number three. We gotta get in."

"I'm the manager," he replied brusquely. "Have t'call the police for that, wait here," and he slammed the door, leaving John and Linda in the hall.

Sergeant Jennings and Detective Subra of the Madison Police Department soon arrived, and John and Linda began talking at once.

"Hold it," the sergeant said, holding up his hand. "One at a time." He nodded to John.

"Our friend didn't show up for work," John began. "We've called all day, he doesn't answer. And he doesn't answer the door. Listen to the TV. It's loud."

"His bed hasn't been slept in," Linda chimed in.

"We'll check it out," the sergeant replied. "Where's the guy who called?"

The door to #4 opened. "I called," the manager said. And pulling a ring of keys from his hip pocket, he walked to #3, inserted a key, and turned the lock.

"You two wait out here," Detective Subra said. The two policemen and the manager went inside, shutting the door behind them.

In the glaring light of the living room, the nearly nude body of a young man protruded from the bathroom. He was kneeling, his head touching the floor, angling inward beneath his chest. His bare ass was high in the air. He was dead.

TWO

"OH MY GOD," THE MANAGER WHISPERED.

He pulled open the door and ran out of the building wearing a white undershirt and coveralls held up by his red suspenders. He paid no attention to his stocking feet as he ran toward a tree on the other side of the street.

Linda put a hand over her mouth as she watched Sergeant Jennings close the door. She knew it was bad and took hold of John's arm. He put his hand on hers and said nothing.

Inside the apartment, Detective Subra hung up the phone.

"They're on the way," he said, "including the coroner."

In twenty minutes, four men in plain clothes barreled into the building, one holding a Cannon FTB 35mm camera in his right hand and a strobe light in his left. They glanced at John and Linda leaning against the wall.

The youngest of the four said, "Where's...?" and before he could say another word, John pointed.

Young One knocked on door #3. It opened, and the four men went inside.

Linda's face turned ashen. With her back against the wall, she slowly slid down to the wooden floor. John lowered himself beside her. She closed her eyes as tears ran down both cheeks and wiped them away with the back of her hand.

What seemed like an eternity was really less than ten minutes. The door opened and Detective Subra came out.

Looking at John, he said, "I'd like you to identify the body and then both of you can leave."

Although Linda had known it, the revelation that Rickey was dead jolted her.

"No!" she wailed and began crying as children cry—deep, shuddering sobs with both hands covering her face.

John reached out as if he were going to touch her, then slowly lifted himself up from the floor. He looked down at Linda and watched as the spasms subsided.

"He's my friend. I want see him," Linda sniffed, rising up slowly and reaching out for John's hand.

"It's not a pretty sight, young lady, and the smell is bad."

"I don't care!"

"Well..." Subra hesitated. "Just for a second. Identify him and out. Understand?"

They nodded and followed the detective across the hall, pausing inside the open doorway. Linda stood aghast, staring at Rickey's lifeless body.

"Is that Rickey Marlar?" Subra asked.

John nodded.

"Okay! Out!" Subra said, waving them away.

The invigorating rush of fresh air allowed Linda to regain some composure. She pulled up her coat collar as John looked at the police cars in front of and behind his car.

"They didn't leave me much room to get out."

Linda opened the door and got in. She felt drained.

"I'll call Dr. Allen," she said as John settled in behind the wheel. "He's in New York. He'll want t'call Rickey's parents. He was their only son."

"I'll call staff," John said.

As John inched his car out of the tight squeeze and drove off, six men busied themselves in Rickey Marlar's apartment.

Detective Subra, the coroner, and the other officers huddled around Rickey's body. He was kneeling on the floor between the bathroom and living room. He had on a pair of multicolored socks. His boxer shorts and blue Levis were pulled down around his knees. He was naked from the knees up, his buttocks raised high in the air. Rickey's right arm rested on the floor beneath his head; his left arm lay atop his head. His feet pointed to the toilet bowl while the remainder of the body extended into the living room. The toilet bowl was free of any material.

"He's been dead for at least twenty-four hours," the coroner said. "He's covered with purple spots, and there's rigor from the base of the neck all the way down."

Two Siamese kittens darted into the living room, one chasing the other then stopping and meowing as if greeting the visitors. One cat rubbed up against the coroner, who gently nudged it away. The other cat sat on its hindquarters, meowing, as if bemoaning the plight of its master.

CHAPTER TWO

Detective Subra pointed a finger, almost touching the left buttocks. "Look," he said, "dry blood. Two puncture marks. Could one of the cats have clawed him after he was dead?"

The coroner shrugged. He had no answer. "Let's get some shots so we can turn the body on its side," he said.

Subra bellowed. "Over here. Get some close-ups."

The man with the camera left the coffee table in the living room. The strobe light began flashing from every angle. The cats raced into the kitchen, no longer meowing. Sergeant Jennings and Detective Subra could be heard in the kitchen with barely audible mutterings.

"Make sure you shoot everything in the apartment," Subra directed, "anything that seems unusual or out of place."

The coroner took hold of the body and gently turned it on its side. Dark red liquid spewed forth from the nose and mouth while small pieces of solid yellow material dribbled out of the mouth. A foul, acrid odor instantly rose and reached out into the apartment.

"I've smelled worse," the coroner said, flaring his nostrils and making a face.

"Me too," Subra said, coming in from the kitchen. "But I never saw one like this. It's weird. What do you make of the kneeling position with his butt in the air? His shorts down could mean he had a bowel movement As far as one of those cats clawing him and making those puncture wounds, I can't buy it."

"Hmm," the coroner said, running his fingers through his thick black hair. "The toilet bowl was clean, but he could have wiped himself and flushed it. But why did he just drop down and die? I'll draw some blood. Maybe he was using alcohol or shooting up drugs. I'll get my bag...it's in the car."

Subra examined the puncture marks. "They're more likely from a needle," he said.

Sergeant Jennings agreed. "That's more likely than the cat theory," he replied as his gaze shifted to the far end of the living room. "And those two glasses on the coffee table, I examined them. One has remnants of a Bloody Mary, and the other is partly filled with tea. They could have been shooting up drugs, and maybe this guy keeled over after his friend left."

"Hey guys!" one of the officers called as he came from the kitchen holding a vial. "What's ketamine?"

"Ketamine? I don't know," Subra said as he looked at Jennings, waiting for an explanation.

"Never heard of it," Jennings said.

"This vial is nearly empty," the officer went on. "Where's the coroner?"

"Went for his bag," Subra replied. "He's going to draw blood." Subra didn't like the stench and motioned for Sergeant Jennings to follow him to the bedroom. "Let's talk in here. I'll open a window and let some air in."

"Hold it, Al," Jennings said, "window's unlatched. Check it out before you disturb it." They sat on the bed.

"Whaddya think?" Subra asked.

"If those are needle marks, I don't see how he could have injected himself in the rear that way. But who knows? I also noticed needle marks on his right arm. Maybe he was a junkie. We'll know after the autopsy."

"What about the position he was in?"

"Could be a homosexual affair. We'll know more when we check for semen."

The coroner opened the door carrying a black bag, strode across the living room, put the bag down, and took out a syringe and rubber tubing.

"Lou," an officer called from the kitchen. "I found drug paraphernalia." He walked into the living room holding a syringe, a capped needle, and rubber tubing–just like the tubing the coroner had wrapped around Marlar's arm.

"Put it in the evidence bag," Subra said as he walked out of the bedroom and back to the body. He watched the coroner withdraw a syringe full of blood. "Get another twenty in case we decide to do special tests." He walked back to the bedroom to finish his discussion with Sergeant Jennings.

The coroner was on the phone talking to the forensic pathologist. "It's bizarre," he said. "Could be sodomy, but the puzzling thing is the needle marks on his butt. I don't think he could've given himself injections in the rear that way."

As the coroner and the forensic pathologist continued their conversation, Detective Subra was busy examining the unlatched window in the bedroom that looked out to the front of the building. He pulled a notepad from his hip pocket. As he scribbled notes, he was aware of the full moon in the March sky and wondered when he'd make it home for dinner. But even as he thought of eating, he realized he wasn't hungry. Cases like this always made him lose his appetite.

CHAPTER TWO

The coroner put the phone down. "He'll do an autopsy tomorrow."

Detective Subra nodded.

"The ambulance is on its way," the coroner went on. "The body is going to the morgue. Anything more, Al?"

"No, can't think of anything. Let's wrap it up. I got a long day tomorrow," Subra replied.

Detective Subra sighed. He knew this case was going to be a tough one. Before long, a Medi-Tec Ambulance Service vehicle pulled up, flashing its lights and stopping alongside the police cars. Two men in white hurried inside carrying a gurney. They hoisted the body onto the cart and covered it with a white sheet.

"Where to?" one said.

"County morgue," the coroner replied.

They wheeled the stretcher out and down the grassy incline, lifted it into the rear of the ambulance, and with red lights flashing, whisked the body away.

Watching the activity was a figure sitting at a distance on the grass, with his back against a sturdy oak. It was the building manager. No one saw him. He sat forlornly, hands folded as if in prayer, watching the flashing lights fade away as the chilly, dark night settled in.

Rickey Marlar had been like a son to him. For an old bachelor, their relationship had been something special, something he had cherished. But now all he had left were memories wracked by guilt. If he had only checked on that noise last night, maybe Rickey would still be alive.

THREE

Dr. James Allen eased out of his Olds Ninety-Eight and swung the door closed. He took a few steps and stopped. He wondered if he had locked the door. Retracing his steps, he took hold of the handle and tried to open the door. It was locked. He turned and headed toward a walkway, shaking his head in disapproval of his inability to remember.

Dust from the parking lot settled on his shiny black shoes. Predictably, this would have annoyed him. But today it didn't matter. He climbed a concrete stairway, took hold of the ornate, brass handle of a large teak door, and went inside.

Dr. Allen forgot his customary routine—stopping at the bottom of the stairs and acknowledging the sign above the door:

Madison Regional Primate Center
Funded by NIH Building 7

He felt so lucky about having a place to do research for the rest of his life. He trudged upstairs to the library, one hand on the black railing. The news of Rickey's death had hit him hard. He had tossed all night. Finally, sometime before dawn, he got out of bed, put on the coffee, and downed three cups. It did nothing more than make his stomach growl. When his wife put a plate of scrambled eggs, bacon, and two slices of rye toast in front of him, he stared at it and pushed it aside. His insides were already doing flip-flops. Even now, as he reached the top of the landing, he still felt queasy.

The lights were on and the room was in order. Three walls of books and journals, neatly arranged on shelves, rose from floor to ceiling. Except for faint sounds from the janitorial service down the hall, it was quiet. No one had yet arrived for the morning meeting. So Allen dropped into a padded chair at the head of a rectangular, wooden conference table and closed his eyes.

His usual attempt at relaxation was to think back to his childhood. Happy days, when his mother sat at his side telling him stories about his forefathers. How they came from the British

CHAPTER THREE

Isles in the 1600s. How her great-great-grandfather fought in the Revolutionary War. How he became a legend in 1775 as a Minute Man of a rifle company that marched to Massachusetts and fought in the battle of Bunker Hill. How grandfather was captured by the British. How he escaped. The story portrayed the things the family believed in: fighting for the things they considered important and priding themselves on accomplishments.

He remembered moving from the family farm in North Carolina to the big city. Depression days. He was only three. Papa had to find a job. Papa had to support not only his own family, but his mother, father, and sister. Although times were hard back then, he remembered being happy. There was food on the table. He never went hungry like some of his friends.

"Good morning," a voice said.

Allen opened his eyes. "Good morning, Linda."

She seated herself near him, put a steno pad and pencil in front of her and stared somberly at the conference table. She wore no makeup. Her black hair, parted in the middle, cascaded below her shoulders. It had a shine like smooth silk. She wore the same red wool sweater and black slacks as the previous day. But now a small piece of black ribbon pinned over her heart announced a time for mourning.

"Sorry for today's meeting," she said. "Staff thought Rickey would have wanted it this way. He was always eager and willing about getting all the work done."

"I wish they had canceled it," Allen said. "The deadline for the paper could have been changed, but let's finish it."

"When are the funeral services?" Linda asked.

"Don't know. The autopsy will be done today, and the body will be released to the Anderson funeral home. I called his parents. Mrs. Marlar fell apart. I could hear her screaming in the background. Mr. Marlar said he'd fly in and take Rickey back to Texas. He'll be buried in Lubbock."

Linda let out a deep sigh. Allen noticed her bloodshot eyes. "Are you all right?"

"It's been a bad night, Dr. Allen..." Linda's voice trailed off.

Softly, he said, "Yeah, it sure has."

Staff filed in from downstairs. They dropped into chairs around the conference table while one staff member walked around, putting a copy of the research paper in front of everyone.

"Well," Allen said, "let's get started. I promised Mr. Marlar I'd attend the autopsy. Any comments on the title?" There were no replies. "If everyone agrees, the paper will be titled, 'Morphological Changes In Monkeys Consuming A Diet Containing Low Levels Of 2,3,7.8 – Tetrachlorodibenzo-p-dioxin.'"[1]

Raising a finger in the air, a staff member said, "It's such a long title. What about changing it to just dioxin?"

Another said, "There are so many different dioxins, we have to be specific. But we should indicate the dosage was five hundred parts per trillion. After all, our work is designed to show there are no safe levels of dioxin. Even in miniscule amounts. Five hundred sounds like a lot, but it's a low level. And when we report on our fifty, twenty-five, and five parts per trillion, I believe we will have proven Dr. Allen's theory."

"I'll accept that," the staff member chimed in.

"Any objections?" Allen asked. "If there are none, so be it. We will indicate the dosage in the title. What about acknowledgements?"

A woman's head poked itself into the room. "Dr. Allen, a call from Ida Parker, CBS in Chicago. She said she works with Paul Harvey."

"Would you take a message?" Allen asked.

"I tried, but she persisted. Says it's important."

Allen picked himself up. "Excuse me."

The others continued to examine and discuss the paper. One member, a distinguished gentleman with gray hair, appeared troubled as he listened to the discussion about acknowledgements.

"I don't like it," he said. "We should not recognize Dow Chemical. We can't trust them."

The staff did not disagree. One member moved her head from side to side as if weighing a yes or no, but found it hard to arrive at a clear reply.

The door opened and closed quietly as Allen returned. He eased out of his gray suit jacket, hung it over the back of his chair, and lowered himself into his seat.

"CBS is getting phone calls from Vietnam veterans with questions about dioxin. I told them it was perfectly all right to refer the calls here. Where were we?"

"We were on acknowledgements," the gray-haired man said with an obvious show of irritation. "I'd like to bring up something we've talked about, but we only talk! We keep on

CHAPTER THREE

doing the same old business-as-usual thing. I believe it's a mistake to acknowledge Dow in our future publications. I have an internal Dow document, and you can bet it was sent by one of their employees. Allow me to read what was prepared by their top scientists," the gray-haired man went on as he held a letter in the air for everyone to see. "It says, 'Dow Chemical first became directly involved in the toxicology of dioxins in 1964.' Just think of it!" he went on, his gruff voice suddenly bouncing off the walls. "Dr. Allen published articles in 1966 after feeding toxic fat to chickens. He reported liver damage. Other experiments with toxic fat showed other kinds of pathology. When Dr. Allen was calling it toxic fat, Dow knew the deadly chemical was dioxin. They kept it secret. And listen to what they said about findings in their own employees." The elderly gentleman turned several pages, and with a rising anger, he said, "Listen to this! 'The signs of intoxication are characterized by a chronic illness and liver damage. Half of the deaths occurred more than two weeks after treatment.' They also found fetuses with intestinal hemorrhage and severe maternal toxicity. This was in rats. And if you think their reports are only about rats, this other document tells of liver damage in humans. It tells of medical problems with their own employees. I think it's a big mistake to acknowledge a company that keeps information like this secret while telling the public how safe their products are. In my opinion, they care only about making money. I don't think they give a hoot about public safety! You can't trust people like that!"

A young lady with a gentle tone in her voice spoke up. "I understand and agree with most of what's been said, but Dow is supplying us with free dioxin. And we need Dow right now. Until we are able to make other arrangements, we need their dioxin to continue our work. An acknowledgement at the end of the paper doesn't seem like a big deal."

"Oh, no!" the elderly gentleman jumped in, his nostrils flaring. "It shows the scientific community and the public that we have a tie-in with Dow! It's no different than a gang of thieves robbing a bank! If that's the kind of business the gang wants to be in, so be it. But please don't ask me to drive the get-away car."

"That's ridiculous!" the young lady shot back. "How can you make such a comparison?"

They realized the confrontation had the makings of a real brouhaha, and they both looked at Dr. Allen.

"I don't like the way Dow conducts their business or their research," Dr. Allen said. "Scientists at Dow do what the company wants, or they'd have to find another job. Those men have pension plans, and they must follow orders. We're fortunate. We have grants. That gives us freedom to do research and publish our results. No secrets. No dictates from above. And as such, I'd like to put it to a vote with a show of hands. All those in favor of acknowledging Dow in future publications? Those against? Fine. This is their last acknowledgment."

"Why do we have to put it in this publication?" the elderly gentleman persisted.

"We promised. If we break our promise, Dow could cut off our supply of dioxin immediately. Our ongoing work would be ruined. I'll have to find another source of dioxin as quickly as possible."

The elderly gentleman grimaced but said no more.

Allen glanced at his watch. "Before I leave," he said, "let me share something with you. I was in Niagara Falls. The Love Canal Homeowners Association asked me to visit their community. People there have been living on a time bomb that's already gone off. Dioxin was dumped there years ago. It's seeping up from the ground into their basements, into vegetable gardens, and into their lives. I saw what it's doing. One family has a boy and girl, both born with brain disorders. Both have severe learning disabilities. The father's symptoms are similar to those we see in our monkeys. The wife told of going to church every day and praying for answers. She would like to see a total ban on all dioxin chemicals. Everyone living there wants the government to buy their homes so they can get out. Many have come down with cancer. They asked for my help, and I promised to return. And another thing! This is something Rickey wanted to devote his life to. A healthy environment: clean air and water, healthy food. The work we do here may someday help the world achieve just that. It's a long haul, and it's not going to be easy. But maybe, just maybe, we can pull it off."

Allen suddenly realized he had gone off on a tangent. A man on a soapbox, preaching.

"I don't know why I'm talking like this," he said, shaking his head. "I'm sorry. Maybe it's because I've been thinking a lot about Rickey. Maybe he's up there keeping an eye on all of us, and I want him to know we'll keep trying to make this world a better place."

"Wait a minute," the gray-haired man shot back. "What do you mean you're sorry? I'd like to know stuff like that instead of all the scientific baloney."

CHAPTER THREE

The room erupted in laughter.

"Thank you," Allen said as he lifted himself out of his chair. "Now that we have that out of the way, any comments before I leave?"

"Yes," John Cartwright replied with an uneasy look on his face. "When Rickey didn't show up, I finished his work and found that the pre-experimental raw data for platelet counts were not in the records."

Allen stood at the end of the conference table wondering how data could not be in the clinical records. Rickey had gathered it, checked it, organized it, and recorded it in the paper now being prepared for publication.

Allen looked at John. "Are you sure?" he asked.

"Yes," came an unequivocal reply.

"We need that data. It shows the platelets to be normal before starting the experiment. Without it, our findings could be questioned. Two years of work could go down the drain. Could someone check Rickey's apartment?" Allen asked. "Maybe he took it home and didn't bring it back."

"I'll check," Linda said. "But should I mail the paper in to the journal for publication even though raw data is missing?"

"Does anyone see a reason not to send it?" Allen asked.

Everyone looked for some sign of dissent. There were none.

"It's bound to turn up," Allen said, lifting his jacket from the back of his chair. He draped it over his left arm and headed for the door. He hated going to the county morgue to watch the autopsy on Rickey Marlar.

FOUR

The forensic pathologist, a tall man, stood under a piercing light that shone down on Ricky Marlar's lifeless body. It lay stiffly on a white porcelain autopsy table, which was supported by a white pedestal anchored to the floor with heavy, stainless steel bolts. Rickey's arms were at his side. Eyes closed. A silver wire wrapped around a big toe held an ID tag. A stainless steel sink, at one end of the table, held large glass jars containing formaldehyde, a solution used to preserve tissue. Smaller jars lay atop the table near the sink, all filled with a clear liquid and covered with white screw caps.

The pathologist's assistant was a smaller man with an obvious nervous twitch in the muscles around his left eye. He appeared to be constantly winking at no one in particular. He nervously looked at people in the gallery, and then jerked his gaze upward at the high ceiling that made the amphitheater look extremely spacious. He lined up instruments on the table, realigned them, tugged on a sleeve of his white surgical gown, then tugged on the other sleeve, always fussing, fidgeting with something, even though it was obvious to the onlookers there was really nothing to do. Everything was in order.

The forensic pathologist, on the other side of the table, was a huge man, reminiscent of Bronco Nagurski, a player for the Chicago Bears who could never be brought down by a single tackler. What set the pathologist apart from the hulk of the football player was the white gown that wrapped itself around him. And the fact that he wore rubber gloves and had a scalpel and other surgical instruments on the table in front of him.

As the pathologist looked at the gallery, he recognized Dr. Allen seated in the first row, next to detective Subra, who was talking to the coroner. People in the middle section chatted with one another while uniformed police officers in the upper section rested their arms on the black railing in front of them and looked down, waiting for the autopsy to begin.

"Quite a crowd I've got today," the pathologist thought to himself. He checked the small microphone fixed to his gown, eyed the corpse on the autopsy table, and began.

CHAPTER FOUR

"This is the body of a well-developed, well-nourished, Caucasian male who appears approximately his stated age of twenty-nine years." The drone of his voice stirred everyone to sudden silence. "The body measures sixty-nine inches in length and weighs approximately 170 pounds."

Even before the pathologist started, Dr. Allen's thoughts traveled back in time. He remembered how happy Rickey had been when he learned that his name would appear on a scientific publication. He could still hear Rickey's voice, "Hey," he said, "I really feel like a scientist."

Six months later, another publication. He was especially proud of this one because of the importance of the study. He knew that the effect of long-term, low-level exposure to dioxin was as yet an unexplored area. And he, at the young age of twenty-eight, had been given the opportunity to join his mentor to explore a new scientific world, like an adventurer sailing uncharted waters, not knowing what he would find on the distant shore.

Allen also remembered how Rickey had been so intimidated by those Rhesus monkeys, always wanting to move his office out of the Primate Center. But he hung in there. He worked long hours, seven days a week. He more than earned the right to have his name on that paper.

Allen was pulled back to reality when the pathologist said, "In the upper outer quadrant of the left buttocks there are two approximately fresh needle puncture wounds which will be excised for microscopic study."2

The pathologist picked up the scalpel and held it deftly between thumb and the adjacent two fingers. He made exacting movements at the site of the injections, carefully depositing two sections of tissue into a small jar nearby and waited for his assistant to cap it and mark it.

"Also identified are two fresh venipuncture wounds over the right antecubital fossa," the pathologist went on. "This young man may have been injecting himself with drugs." Again, he put the scalpel to the area and excised two small sections.

Allen wanted to stand and shout, "Drugs? He didn't use drugs! I've known this young man for three years. Beer, yes! Never drugs!" But Dr. Allen merely watched each of the pieces of tissue splash into a tiny jar held out by the pathologist's assistant.

Having completed the external examination, the pathologist made three quick incisions, peeled away skin, and exposed the abdomen. He then cut away ribs and opened the chest. He kept using words, "Normal appearance...normal appearance," until he came to the respiratory tract.

"The nasopharynx contains a mixture of fresh blood and vomitus," he said. "All lobes of both lungs are enlarged, heavy, wet, and show edema and hemorrhage. These features are those of massive bilateral pulmonary aspiration of vomitus."[3]

"My God," Allen mused. "How could he have aspirated? Was he unconscious?" He watched the pathologist cut a large section of lung tissue and hand it to the man with the winking eye, who in turn took several steps to the sink and dropped it into a large jar. It landed with a loud splash. Droplets of formaldehyde settled on the bottom of Rickey's feet, and a few drops ran down to his heels.

The pathologist rolled his eyes upward, furrowed his brow, as if appealing to the Almighty to find him another assistant. The assistant returned to his place alongside the autopsy table, his eye winking with much greater frequency.

"We now come to the gastrointestinal tract," the pathologist announced. He again used the words, "Normal appearance... normal appearance," until he said, "There is hemorrhage and tearing of the rectum."

Some of the officers who had their eyes closed from boredom suddenly became alert. They took hold of the railing and leaned forward. Dr. Allen also leaned forward. The pathologist looked up and spoke to the gallery.

"Up until now, one could theorize that all of the findings were self-inflicted. But the hemorrhage and tearing of the rectum is difficult to explain without suspecting foul play. You might argue that Rickey Marlar found it pleasurable to sexually stimulate himself by inserting something into his rectum, but taking into consideration the four injections and the massive aspiration, I find it unlikely that he was enjoying self-induced activities. This is an extremely interesting case. We should have the lab results in a few days, but the microscopic sections will take about a week. Any questions?"

"Will you be able to tell if the tearing of the rectum was due to homosexual activity?" Detective Subra asked.

"I'll do a microscopic exam," the pathologist replied, "but I don't expect to find anything. The small amount of stool in the rectum would have destroyed any trace of semen."

"If you find evidence of homosexual activity," Allen asked, "would this be sufficient to rule the death a homicide?"

CHAPTER FOUR

"I can't answer that at this time. Most important will be the tissue sections of the four injection sites, other tissue sections and the results of the laboratory tests. But homosexual activity remains a possibility. Any other questions...? None? Thank you for coming."

Walking out of the morgue into the City-County Building parking lot, Dr. Allen got into his car. He felt uneasy about picking up Rickey's parents at the airport. Their plane was due shortly past noon. For the past day, he had been thinking of questions they might ask and how to reply, how to offer proper condolences. He had never met them. To meet them under such agonizing circumstances would be very difficult. What does one say to parents who suffer the tragedy of losing an only son? Parent who might ask how it happened?

Dr. Allen had no experience with the situation he now found himself in. He had devoted the major portion of his adult life to research. All he had ever wanted was to work in his laboratory and explore new frontiers. There he knew what or what not to do. But he was Rickey's supervisor and mentor. And as such, it was his responsibility to attend to the situation that now required his attention.

For the moment, Dr. Allen completely forgot about the missing data.

FIVE

March 11, 1977. Three days after finding the body, the coroner closed the file and ruled the death of Rickey Marlar accidental.

"But why?" the deputy coroner asked.

He knew he had been too aggressive in asking the question, wishing he had kept his mouth shut. This was his boss, someone who didn't like being questioned. So he expected a tongue lashing. But there was none.

The coroner leaned back in his rich, brown leather chair, his hands laced across the back of his head and his eyes fixed on his deputy, who sat on the opposite side of the desk. After thirty seconds of silence, the coroner rolled his swivel back, eased himself up, and turned to three large windows that looked down on the city.

"It's going to be a nice day," the coroner said, staring off into the distance. "No haze. Clear sky. I can see the university buildings."

He surveyed the landscape surrounding the City-County Building, something he loved to do, especially on a clear day. The university campus lay in the distance, its tall buildings stretching high. He prided himself in knowing every important building on every street. He also took pride in being able to call and talk with every influential person in Madison. He turned away from the windows, dropped into his swivel, and faced his deputy.

"Look," he said. "I want to keep the day pleasant. So don't keep asking me why I'm getting rid of this damn case. I don't like being asked to explain myself. Understand?"

The deputy bit his lower lip to keep himself from a quick retort. He wanted to lock eyes with his boss and reply. He wanted to recite the duties and responsibilities of the coroner. He wanted to recite all of them, including the treatment of subordinates. He really wanted to shout it right through the paneled walls into adjacent offices. He wanted everyone to hear and to know about the shenanigans his boss was engaged in. He wanted to, but he was afraid. He was also stirred by a sense of propriety. After all, he was only a deputy coroner, an underling.

CHAPTER FIVE

"I don't mean to offend you," he said gently, "but this case is only three days old. The autopsy clearly shows evidence of homosexual activity. Somebody was in that apartment the night of Rickey's death. The evidence says so. The case is still under investigation. How would it look if you suddenly closed this case without giving Detective Subra time to follow up on all the evidence we found at the crime scene? How could you justify that? What would you say as to the cause of death?"

With a tone of irritation, his boss said, "In this business, there is always something one can say. Since I am the coroner, it's my call. Detective Subra can complete his investigation, but I'm issuing a death certificate and I am ruling this death as an accident. If any evidence turns up that is convincing to the contrary, this case can always be reopened."

Emboldened, the deputy replied, "Why the rush? I'm your deputy. I'm entitled to know."

With rising impatience, the coroner said, "You are my deputy. You certainly are. You're also a pain in the ass! Always asking questions. If you had it your way, we'd have a hundred or more cases still open. How would it look if the coroner's office couldn't close a case? It would make me look bad. And if I looked bad, I'd have my butt kicked out of office."

"So how are you closing it?"

"Pulmonary aspiration, alcohol, and ketamine intoxication. Accidental. Any more questions?"4

"What should I do with the body?"

"Release it to his sister. She called. Her parents couldn't get on the plane. Too upset. The body's still in the morgue. She's flying him back to Lubbock, Texas, for burial."

The intercom buzzed. The coroner grabbed the phone.

"Detective Subra on line one."

"Hi, Al. How goes it?"

"Just wanna keep you informed. I'm pursuing the theory that the tearing and hemorrhage of the rectum was due to homosexual assault on an involuntary basis."

"How do you plan to prove it?"

"He frequented the Back Door Tavern, a gay bar. The owner gave me names to check out. I have a photo of Rickey posing in the nude and other nude photos of people who as yet remain unidentified. You never know what will turn up."

"Even if he was homosexual," the coroner replied, "that's not sufficient reason for me to say he was murdered. We have no proof to say that someone was with him after Van Miller left his apartment."

"I don't agree. There's proof to say that someone may have spent hours in the apartment after his death. As far as Van Miller's story, I have to check it out. He was the last known person to see Rickey alive."

"Too much speculation. Rickey was depressed because of legal and financial problems. His friends say he filed for bankruptcy. He had access to ketamine. It was used in his work. He probably couldn't sleep. So he injected himself with the monkey tranquilizer. I could go on and on. In my opinion, it was an accident. I'm closing the case."

"But I've got leads to follow up on. Evidence at the scene. Further questioning of Van Miller, who agreed to take a lie detector test. Maybe polygraph testing of others. It'll take time."

"I agree. Take all the time you need. Stay in touch. The case can always be reopened."

Putting down the phone, the coroner shook is head. He looked at his deputy.

"Detective Subra is okay. He wants to do a first class job, but it will not happen in a town like Madison. The police department doesn't have the money or the resources for a top-notch investigation. They didn't even dust for prints."

"How about checking with the forensic pathologist? His findings might make you change your mind."

"You sure have spunk even if you are a pain in the butt," the coroner replied. He picked up the phone and punched in numbers.

When he hung up the phone, the coroner pondered the information he had just received: small hemorrhages in the brain could have resulted from a blow on the head or the fall. Extensive scarring in the wall of the rectum, showing he had been involved in homosexual activities more than once. But what really impressed him was the inflammation at one injection site while the other site had none. And since a ketamine injection takes seconds to render a person unconscious and a half-hour to stir up an inflammation, Rickey had to be unconscious when given the second injection of ketamine. And the concentration of ketamine in the blood was lethal.

The coroner did not share this information with his deputy because he still had every intention of closing the case.

CHAPTER FIVE

He turned to his deputy and said, "Rickey Marlar had legal and financial problems causing him to become depressed. He had access to drug paraphernalia and ketamine, a monkey tranquilizer. On the evening of his death, he was constipated, intoxicated, and unable to sleep. He injected himself with ketamine. While having a bowel movement, he strenuously forced himself, causing rectal tearing and hemorrhage. Upon completing the bowel movement, he rose from the toilet, and with the amount of ketamine and alcohol in his system, he collapsed, causing trauma to his head. He then vomited, and in all probability, with his head and neck bent under his chest, he could not project the vomit outward. This caused his death by aspiration."

"You're the coroner, it's your call," the deputy said.

On the following day, the coroner was not at all pleased at the way the news media reported his news release. His statement was exactly as he had prepared it, but it became part of a long article. It portrayed the death of Rickey Marlar as still mysterious.

It reviewed aspects of the case that contributed to the mystery and hinted at foul play. Detective Subra touched upon the possibility that Marlar had been sexually violated.

The article ended by saying, "Marlar was responsible for collecting and summarizing clinical data in a study by Dr. James Allen. At the time of Marlar's death, experimental data was found to be missing."

SIX

Rickey Marlar went home. His sister accompanied the casket on a flight to Lubbock, Texas, where family members stood at the graveside and cried as the coffin was lowered into the ground.

Dr. Allen thought about attending the burial of his student, but decided not to. He had a more immediate responsibility. The men, women, and children of Love Canal needed him. They were living on top of a cesspool filled with dioxin. People were dying of cancer. Children were born with ungodly birth defects. The entire town was filled with anger and despair. He had agreed to help them prepare a report, arguing in favor of the government buying their homes so they could move.

Although depressed and not in the mood, Dr. Allen forced himself to return to Love Canal the day after the coroner ruled Marlar's death accidental. He had promised to return as soon as possible.

While Allen was gone, the Madison police department halted its investigation. Although Van Miller agreed to take a polygraph test, none was given. Although two shirts found in Marlar's apartment were identified as not belonging to Marlar, there was no follow-up. The two glasses on the coffee table, one half filled with tea and the other containing the remnants of a Bloody Mary, had not been fully explained. Marlar drank the Bloody Mary, but Van Miller, the last known person to see Marlar alive, did not drink tea. Who drank tea?

The police had evidence that Marlar had frequented a gay bar. They had photos of others frequenting that bar who may have known Marlar, and nude photos were found in Marlar's apartment, but there was no follow up on any of this. And even when the findings clearly demonstrated that the rectum had been penetrated, the police did not challenge the coroner's ruling that there was no evidence for homosexual activities.

Unknown to Dr. Allen, Marlar's death attracted the attention of the FBI. Two agents arrived on campus and questioned the small band of researchers. Their questions attempted to link the missing data and Marlar's death to Dr. Allen. His staff knew the boss was being

CHAPTER SIX

investigated, but they were afraid to talk about it and decided not to tell him. Their fear was alleviated when the federal investigation suddenly disappeared.

Dr. Allen finally returned to his lab with a sense of accomplishment. His work at Love Canal had gone well. And he found his lab with a semblance of normality, except for the added responsibilities everyone shared from doing Marlar's work.

They were three weeks into the new fifty-parts-per-trillion dioxin study, and a rigid and demanding schedule had to be followed. An endless number of things had to be done. Added to the intensified demands on Dr. Allen was the incessant ringing of the phone. It never stopped. Vietnam veterans kept calling with questions about dioxin. People begged to see him, and he couldn't say no.

When a mother called from New York on Thursday, he agreed to see her on Saturday. Allen's wife, Christie, convinced him to combine Saturday's business with a bit of recreation, knowing it would help him relax. He agreed, but only because he loved the idea of strolling around campus in cowboy attire and going horseback riding afterward.

Saturday rolled around. Allen ambled into the Hampton Inn near campus, holding a pocket book edition of *Dracula*. People stared at his white, ten-gallon hat and blue jeans and jacket. They admired the old, lovingly polished, high-heeled, brown leather boots. He glanced around the lobby and saw two plump sofas sitting at right angles under a row of narrow windows. He walked over and dropped into a cushioned seat and thought about Rickey Marlar and the missing data. Linda couldn't find it in Rickey's apartment. Detective Subra couldn't find it. This troubled him immensely. He needed that data to support his findings. Suddenly, his attention was drawn to a wisp of a woman walking rapidly toward him.

"Are you Dr. Allen?" she asked.

"Yes, ma'am," he replied, standing up and looking down at a fashionably dressed woman with hair done up in a stylish coiffure. "And you're Mrs. Reutershan."

"All one hundred five pounds of me. You don't at all look like a scientist. When you said, you'd be wearing a white hat, I had no idea you'd look like a cowboy. I like it!"

"Well, thank you, ma'am. Won't you sit down," Allen said, motioning her to the sofa. As they seated themselves, she cocked her head to a side to see the title of the book he was reading.

"*Dracula*," she said softly. "A scientist, a cowboy, and *Dracula*. That's interesting."

Allen saw her wide-eyed expression and said, "It's easy to explain, ma'am. On Saturday, I sometimes dress this way. It's comfortable, and I like it. My neighbor owns a horse farm, and on my way home, he lets me ride one of his horses. It's a nice way to relax. As far as this book, I collect sci-fi. Been doin' it since I was five."

"But *Dracula*? Is that something a scientist like you should be reading? You have many scientific publications, an international reputation, and you are the authority on dioxin. And... and...*Dracula* is nothing but a horror story about a count who drinks people's blood."

"There's more to it than that, ma'am. *Dracula* is a powerful myth because it allows evil to remain mysterious. All the scientific skill in the world couldn't change the dreadful power of Count Dracula. A crucifix could. It was the only effective weapon against evil, and it still is. We call it faith. Or belief in God."

"I never thought of it that way. You've been collecting books like this since you were five? How many do you have?"

"With this one...one thousand eight hundred two, but many are duplicates and in different languages. I saw this one in the window of a thrift shop for twenty-five cents and grabbed it."

"Isn't that something," she replied. "When you agreed to see me, I had a completely different picture of you."

Allen smiled. "Now that we've met, what did you want to see me about?"

"My son, Paul," she began with a slight hesitation. "He was a helicopter crew chief in Vietnam. He told me about chemicals he sprayed, how his hair and face and body dripped with the stuff day after day. How the military told him the chemicals were safe, told him they were not at all harmful. But I have proof the government lied! My son...is dying of cancer."

She choked with emotion. Tears ran down her cheeks. People in the lobby stared. She turned away, opened her handbag, and took out a kerchief. Allen put a hand on her shoulder.

"I am so sorry," Dr. Allen said.

Mrs. Reutershan raised her head, eyes closed, sniffed, dabbed at her eyes and said, "I'm sorry. Please excuse me for behaving like this."

"You have nothing to be sorry for," Allen replied as he put his hand back on his lap.

With her handbag still open, Mrs. Reutershan took out two envelopes and held them out to Dr. Allen. "I want to give you this before I tell you why I came."

CHAPTER SIX

Allen unsealed the flap from one of the envelopes and took out a number of letters. The top one, dated July 20, 1965, was stamped "Dow CONFIDENTIAL." It was a letter from D. P. Roland to Tom Needham. It said, "Dioxin is exceptionally toxic. It has an enormous potential for producing systemic injury...under no circumstances may this letter be reproduced, shown, or sent to anyone outside of Dow."

Allen glanced up, said nothing, and fingered the next letter. It was dated 1957. It was from the Boehringer Company to Dow. It described the results of their research on chloracne. It said, "In making 2,4,5-T, the temperature should not go higher than 150 degrees Centigrade. Otherwise, the contaminant [dioxin] would be present in large amounts."

Dow replied and thanked them for the information.

Allen had heard rumors that Dow made 2,4,5-T with a temperature of 215 degrees Centigrade because it was cheaper. He vaguely remembered another rumor that had to do with medical problems with Dow employees. But the one thing that stuck in his mind was the fact that an employee could die from exposure to 2,4,5-T.

Dr. Allen now fingered an internal Dow document dated September 7, 1967: "We are formulating to a specification by the government on a formulation established by the military and are producing a weapon. It has no use in civilian business. It presents a serious health hazard in our plant if not properly controlled." It was signed by E. A. Hickman and sent to J. H. Gowell.

Dr. Allen looked at Mrs. Reutershan. She had her gaze riveted on him, waiting for a reaction. He turned to the next letter. It was from G. J. Williamson, vice president at Dow, to Melvin R. Lang, Secretary of Defense, dated June 15, 1970. "There is abundant evidence that dioxin occurring as an impurity in 2,4, 5-T is highly toxic. We at Dow are convinced that 2,4,5-T containing less than one part per million can be used safely. Certainly, such a product is safer to use than one containing larger amounts. Dow again recommends strictly that the government set appropriate specifications and controls to insure that no 2,4,5-T be used if it contains more than one part per million of dioxin."

Allen again looked at Mrs. Reutershan, who still had her gaze fixed on him. "Where did you get these?" he asked.

"My sister, Millie, in Michigan. She dates a man who works for Dow. She told him about Paul, about his wanting to sue Dow and the government before he dies. He agreed to help, but he wants his name kept confidential. The other envelope has information from our government, our military leaders!" she said with anger and agitation.

Dr. Allen unsealed the envelope and took out many pages. He scanned page one, a report on children born in North Vietnam. "Children with no eyes, a three-year-old with a stump for a left forearm, and extending below the elbow, tiny appendages, like small fingers coming out of the skin..." The people who reported this told of "A white spray from American planes."

Page two, the military's response prepared by Captain Charles V. Collins of the SEAsia Team, was titled, "Herbicide Operations July 1961–June 1967." It told of crop destruction operations, citing rice and beans. It went on to say, "It should be emphasized that these chemicals are nontoxic and generally not harmful to any form of human or animal life. The air crews are exposed to it daily and, in the US, defoliants of this type are used on over four hundred million acres annually. Defoliants are nonpoisonous, and food and water may be consumed without fear of resulting effects."

Page three was a copy of a page from an army manual dated 1964. As Allen read, Mrs. Reutershan watched the shaking of his head, the squinting of his eyes, and the expression on his face. She knew he did not agree with the government's report.

When Dr. Allen finished, he said, "The military said the chemicals were safe when used in concentrations as low as one-half pound per acre. But I happen to know they used Agent Orange at a concentration of over thirteen pounds per acre. What Collins did not say is that the military used this defoliant in Vietnam in totally undiluted form. This made Agent Orange more deadly. It should have been diluted. Domestically, it is often highly diluted with oil or water."

"Read the next one," she said loudly with an attempt to control her agitation. "It mentions the name of a scholar, an American statesman, a man who helped establish a cease fire in Vietnam, a Nobel laureate. It mentions the name of Henry Kissinger."

The letter was dated November 20, 1970, from Edward David Jr. to Dr. Henry Kissinger, assistant to the president for national security affairs. It was marked "CONFIDENTIAL."

It told of a meeting whereby evidence would be presented to the Fulbright Committee (at the hearings of the Geneva Protocol). It said the US used a herbicide that contained impurities greatly exceeding those permitted in herbicide operations in the US. It said the impurity (dioxin) was known to cause fetal abnormalities in experimental animals and was believed to be causing

CHAPTER SIX

malformed children when ingested in adequate quantities by pregnant women. It said that Agent Orange contained 25 parts per million (ppm) of dioxin while current regulations of the U.S. Department of Agriculture only permitted 1 ppm for herbicides used commercially in the US.

Allen could feel a rising inner tension. He was not as depressed as before. He saw what the government had done and knew it wasn't right. He went to the next letter. It told of even higher concentrations of dioxin. Shaking his head, Dr. Allen leaned forward, and fixing his eyes on Mrs. Reutershan, he asked somberly, "How can I help?"

"My son and the veterans need you. These letters prove what our government and Dow did. You're an expert. People respect you. They listen to what you say. It would help my son win his case. Others also need you. Wives who can't have children. Babies born deformed. Veterans dying of cancer. You are the only person I know who can help reveal the truth."

"These letters," Allen said. "Your son's lawyer has them?"

"Oh, yes. That's why he agreed to take the case. My son has no money. Neither do I. The lawyer said that with your research findings and your testimony, he had a good chance of winning. I beg you...say yes."

Dr. Allen knew that eventually he would have to become involved. He knew what dioxin could do. He knew that one day it would have to be outlawed. But he wasn't ready to do battle. Dow would immediately cut off all shipments of dioxin. Their help with tissue analyses would be terminated. This would destroy ongoing research. Grant money would have been wasted. The consequences would be devastating.

He took a deep breath. "Mrs. Reutershan, tell Paul I'm willing to help. But I need time. Tell him that Dow must not learn of my future involvement in his case. It's important that his lawyer keep this confidential. If Dow or the government knew of my intention, it would destroy my research. When I'm ready, I'll let you know."

Tearfully, she clasped his hands. "God bless you," she said. "If your sister sends more documents, would you send me copies?"

"Absolutely. And can my son call or write you?"

"Anytime."

"You're a nice man," she said. "You've taken time to talk with me. It's not often one finds an important person like you doing that."

Allen's face turned crimson. He laughed. "I've never considered myself an important person," he said, "but it's nice of you to say that."

"You're just modest. I checked up on you. I know about your work. It's important. If our governmental leaders were like you, they would have protected our men. And my son would not be dying of cancer. So many others would still be alive. That's important. You're important. People like you are hard to find."

Allen had listened to the strength in her voice, saw the fire in her eyes, felt the pain of a mother trying to provide for the needs of a dying son, and he sensed her determination.

Gently, he asked, "How's Paul doing?"

"He's in and out of the hospital. Doctors don't give him much time."

"I see...when are you flying home?"

"Tomorrow morning. And I want to thank you so much for caring."

As Allen drove home, his thoughts were not on the road. Much had happened. Rickey was gone. Data was missing. He was loaded with work and not enough time. And yet he felt obligated to help others.

His staff depended on him to obtain half a million dollars in grant money yearly. Writing grants and paperwork for each trainee took endless hours. Besides paperwork, he had to find time to make arrangements for all future tissue analyses in his lab, but never again by Dow. He also had to find another source for dioxin. This was crucial. He had to put in more than his seventy hours a week, additional time away from family. But they would understand.

As he neared his farm in Baraboo Bluffs, overlooking Lake Wisconsin, he did not stop at his neighbor's ranch. He wasn't in the mood for horseback riding.

SEVEN

Paul Reutershan knew he was dying and that he didn't have much time. Days passed. But every morning, he would open his eyes and watch the rays of sunshine stream through the window onto his bed. They were comforting.

Weeks passed. Slowly, to his delight, he began to feel better. Stronger. Soon, he was even well enough to leave the hospital, and he had a faint glimmer of hope that the doctors were wrong in their diagnosis. Soon, he felt well enough to go back to work.

Shortly thereafter, to everyone's amazement, he made his way down the aisle enjoying the rush and sway of the rapidly moving train, punching tickets and chatting with familiar faces. His new uniform, with a smart looking cap, gave him a look of distinction. The women passengers thought he was handsome as he handed them back a ticket with a hole punched on its side. Everyone knew, just by looking at his every movement, how much he enjoyed his work as a Conrail commuter train conductor. His smile never changed. Not even during the frantic pace of the rush hour run.

"Good morning," a passenger said, holding out his ticket. "I heard you were back in the hospital. Nice seeing you again."

"Thanks," Paul replied, punching the ticket.

"If you think I'm getting too personal, Paul, just tell me to mind my own business. But you've been in and out of that Madison hospital since last year. Anything serious?"

Paul looked down at the middle-aged man with the navy blazer and a white button-down shirt and said, "It started with a bellyache. I thought it was food poisoning. After a couple of months, my doctor ran tests. It was cancer." Paul marveled at how easy it was to say cancer, no longer getting choked up, no longer fighting back tears.

"Did they catch it in time?"

"No such luck. It wrapped itself around the main artery. I'm told it's inoperable."

"I'm sorry to hear that. You're such a young man, a health nut, always telling folks about eating right and staying in shape. Does cancer run in your family?"

"None I could find. It must've been those chemicals we sprayed in Vietnam. I was told it was safe. So were a lot of other guys. But too many have died, or are dying like me. The one thing we all have in common is Agent Orange."

"Agent Orange?"

"Yeah, a chemical. I was a helicopter crew chief. We sprayed it every day. Sometimes several times a day. It killed everything...trees, insects, animals, crops, everything. Some of the guys poked fun at the natives who wouldn't go into sprayed areas. The natives called it the land of the dead. Those natives were right. That's why I'm dying of cancer. I'm sure of it."

Paul had momentarily diverted his attention from the shifting movements of the train to the jungles of Vietnam. The rapid forward movement of wheels on tracks curving to the right threw him off balance. His cap flew into the air, and he fell into the lap of a middle-aged lady who had been eavesdropping. Someone snickered, but they quickly smothered the sound. The lady, in whose lap Paul found himself, was seemingly pleased with the young man who had suddenly selected her as the object of his affection.

"Please excuse me," Paul said, lifting himself upright into the aisle. "I'm so sorry. Did I hurt you?"

"No," the lady replied, smiling. She held the brim of his conductor's cap, patted off a smudge, and handed it to him.

"You'll need this too," said the man on the other side of the aisle. He handed Paul the metal punch that had fallen to the floor. "Let me give you my card," the man continued. "I'm a cable TV talk show producer. I would like to put you on the air for an interview. Tell your story. Not many people have heard of Agent Orange."

Paul slipped the card into his pants pocket. "I'd like that," he replied, and then he hurriedly proceeded down the aisle, punching tickets. He still felt somewhat sheepish about his misadventure.

Later that night, as was his custom, he pushed his dinner plate aside, blew a kiss to sister Jane, and proceeded up the stairs to his room to be alone and sit quietly on a soft cushioned rocker to record the day's events in a large, leather-bound diary. He opened it to a fresh page.

CHAPTER SEVEN

Paul recorded his conversation with the TV producer, as well as the phone call later that day, setting up an appointment for an appearance on national television. He recorded his feelings and his excitement about finally getting the word out to fellow veterans.

Putting his diary aside, Paul picked up a large scrapbook from the stack on a round table next to his chair. It was titled *Me and My Buddies*. Turning several pages, he reviewed the past.

Photos of the Vietnam War splashed across pages from newspapers and magazines. Terrible scenes he had lived through, scenes of wrenching cruelty. A letter from Alan Wall, a friend and helicopter pilot stationed with C Company, Phuc Vinh, South Vietnam, who told how after a spray mission, his clothing was saturated, his hair and face wet, and that sickening sweet smell of Agent Orange. And how he'd lost weight, how his muscles had deteriorated, and how an abdominal mass had been found at Parkwood Hospital in Covington, Louisiana, that was inoperable.

Paul flipped to another page, a newspaper article about Paul Blitt, another friend and Vietnam veteran who had been a conductor for Conrail. The story Blitt told left no doubt in Paul's mind that Agent Orange killed. Blitt was a sentry dog handler. He roamed the jungles sprayed with Agent Orange. He told of sentry dogs dying of cancer. He told of government documents that described severe medical problems in military working dogs. Glossitis, or red tongue as it was popularly termed, was a prevalent disease in Vietnam during the late 1960s and early '70s. The condition occurred within one week after arrival in Vietnam, the documents said, and the changes indicated a toxic irritant.

Another document told of large numbers of malignant tumors found in dogs.[5]

Paul reasoned that if it caused cancer in dogs, it could cause cancer in him and others. Besides cancer, a document described an army study where twenty out of twenty-two dog-sentry platoons had epidemic deaths due to internal hemorrhage. And Paul knew that within his stack of scrapbooks, there was a Dow document stamped "Confidential" that told of gastrointestinal hemorrhage as being a unique anomaly caused by dioxin. He also knew from Dr. Allen's publications that besides cancer, Allen had found the same kind of hemorrhage in monkeys that had been fed dioxin.

Dow knew this. So did the military. So did the government. And he still pondered that burning question as to why he and others were exposed, knowing dioxin would kill. As he thought about it, his anger flared up, not only at the US government but at himself.

At seventeen, he had volunteered to fight for his country. But his country had betrayed him. Lied! He now had proof. He now knew about the pure fabrication perpetrated by the Secretary of State. He now had the communication sent to the American Embassy in Canberra, Australia.

"If asked, you can say there were no special precautions taken for medical reasons to preclude the exposure of ground troops to aerial spraying since there were no known hazards from such exposure. Precautions were taken to alert ground units to clear the immediate area prior to large-scale USAF spray missions. These precautions were not based on chemical hazards, but were to enable aircraft escorts to return freely any ground fire directed at the spraying aircraft."

This information was to be passed on to the Australian Embassy so the position of the US would be known.

The Australian government knew the US position was a lie, but they went along with it.

The only men protected were the Australian teams who sprayed Agent Orange.6 Nothing, however, was done to protect the Australian combat troops even though their military leaders knew protection was needed. Paul had read the story hundreds of times.

And he remembered how he and his crew flew through clouds of Orange. He remembered flying without cargo doors so ground fire could be returned. He also remembered the whir of the rotary blades as they kicked up little tornadoes of spray into the faces of his men. He wanted to sue the government, but his lawyer told him the government was protected under something called the Ferris Doctrine. And this was connected to something else called sovereign immunity. So the government was off the hook.

Paul would have to be satisfied suing Dow. Aunt Millie was his secret weapon, and he loved her for sending him documents. How her boyfriend obtained them remained a mystery, as did his name. But he sure knew his way around Dow.

As Paul was about to turn the page, a gentle knock on the door diverted his attention. The door opened and his sister Jane wheeled a serving cart into the room.

"Time for hot cocoa and cookies," she said.

"Hi, Sis," Paul replied, taking the scrapbooks from his lap and putting them back on the stack.

"The cocoa is hot, just the way you like it. I brought myself a cup too." Jane pulled up a chair, took a cup, and took a sip of cocoa.

CHAPTER SEVEN

"It's nice of you to fuss over me and let me live here," Paul said, holding the cup to his lips with both hands. "Free room and board isn't easy to find."

"We're family. What's family for?" Jane replied, reaching for a cookie. "Try one, they're still warm. You always liked fresh baked cookies."

Paul looked at his sister's beaming face and listened to her voice. "You should have been an actress," he said.

"Me? An actress? Why do you say that?"

"Well, I'm dying. You know I'm dying. Sooner or later, it's going to happen. Yet you look happy. I know how you feel. I heard you on the phone the other day talking to Aunt Millie. You were crying."

"It was your aunt's fault," Jane said. "Whenever she bawls on the phone, I join her. It's contagious."

"She's a nice aunt," Paul replied. "Did she tell you any more about the guy she's dating?"

"He's a widower whose son was killed in Vietnam. Millie said that every time he steals a document, it's not only for you. It's also for his son. He wants the truth to come out."

"But if they catch him, he'll get fired."

"Your aunt told him he could move in with her. Since Millie's got a good income, she can support him. I think she'd like that. But she told him they'd have to get married first. I think he'd like that too. Millie wanted to know if you received the last document mailed three days ago."

"Yes, I did. I owe her a letter. I want to thank her and tell her how much I love her."

"She knows that."

"I know she knows. But I want to tell her anyhow, just like I always tell you how much I love you."

"There you go, getting mushy on me."

"Sis," Paul said, looking at her with a tear running down his cheek. "This lawsuit will take a long time. Years. I won't be around that long. I'd like you and Mom to help the vets carry on. If we win, there are thousands of veterans out there who need help. Their families need help, especially the kids with birth defects. The money can be used to establish a foundation, something that could last forever or...for however long the veterans and their families need help."

37

"Oh, bite your tongue. I expect you to be around for a good while yet. Those doctors don't know everything." Jane's voice faltered. "But if you do go before the suit is over, I promise to make those bastards pay! Excuse me, I think I'm going to have a good cry." She hurried out of the room, leaving Paul with his thoughts.

How long would he live? No one knew. But he knew that for as long as that was, he had to get the word out. He had to reach hundreds of thousands of Vietnam veterans. He had to tell them about the government and Agent Orange, about dioxin and cancer. About why they were sick and why their kids had birth defects. About everything the government had done. As long as he had one breath left in him, he was determined to get the message out. Veterans would listen because he was one of them and he was dying.

EIGHT

A SHADOWY FIGURE BLENDED INTO THE EARLY MORNING ON GREENBAY DRIVE. It changed direction, moved rapidly across the grass, and stood facing the door of the Madison Regional Primate Center. A slender object slid into the lock, and in seconds the door clicked open and then closed.

Fifteen minutes later, Dr. Allen eased his car between two white lines, killed the engine, and turned off the headlights. An orange-yellow glow peeked over the horizon as he walked briskly toward the building that housed his monkeys.

At seven in the morning, a thin, elderly woman with a gray wool cap and a matching button down sweater walked quickly toward the Primate Center, one hand holding the sweater tight to her neck. It's May, she thought, hurrying along and wondering when it would warm up. She hated cold, and she hated going inside Primate Center even though it was warm. Those monkeys just gave her the jitters. All that screeching, and those hands reaching out through the bars. Working at her best, it would take an hour to clean up, and it was a job. She went inside.

In seconds, the door flew open. A high-pitched cry broke the silence on the campus, and the cleaning lady ran across the lawn waving her arms and shrieking.

"He's dead, he's dead!" she screamed.

Men and women carrying books in the distance stopped and turned. They watched the lady as her wobbly, bony legs carried her helter-skelter across the roadway and onto open ground, where she slipped and fell headlong on wet grass. Lying flat on her belly, with her arms stretched out in front of her, she began to cry. People gathered from around a bend in the road and nearby buildings, some on bicycles, others on foot. Some of the onlookers seemed to appear out of nowhere. As the crowd assembled, several onlookers knelt beside her. One held her hand, spoke softly, and finally helped her up. Her cries became a whimper.

Distant sirens sounded. They grew louder. Flashing red lights came into view as two police cars rounded a turn and stopped in front of the Primate Center. The front doors of both vehicles opened, and four uniformed officers hurried into the building.

They found Dr. Allen sitting on the floor, his legs drawn up and the palm of one hand holding the top of his head. His black hair had matted together and blood still oozed from an ugly gash.

"Are you okay?" one officer asked.

Allen nodded and held out a bloody hand with a finger pointing upward. A monkey lay dead at the bottom of a cage. Another officer was already looking into that cage, shining his flashlight on the silky, yellow-hair of a two-foot monkey whose tail hung down from between the bars.

Allen attempted to rise, but slid back to the floor. He looked at his bloody palm, then at the officer, who helped him to his feet.

"We're taking you to the hospital," the officer said.

"No hospital," Allen replied.

Allen wasn't concerned about the blood on his hand or the injury to his head. Someone had broken in. One of his monkeys in the 50 ppt dioxin study was dead. "What's going on? What the hell is going on?" Allen kept wondering to himself.

Later that morning, Allen sat at his desk holding a Styrofoam cup of steaming coffee with Linda sitting to a side, also drinking coffee.

"What happened?" she asked.

Allen put his coffee down. "I...went to the Primate Center early to check on yesterday's data," he began. "When I went to Marlar's office, drawers were open and in disarray. I knew someone had broken in and was looking for something." He picked up the Styrofoam cup, leaned back in his swivel, and took several large swallows as Linda looked on, waiting. "My concern was for the monkeys, so I hurried to the cages. A control monkey in the first cage was dead and its tail was hanging down from between the bars. As soon as I touched it, someone hit me over the head. The next thing I knew, police were there. The University Health Service cleaned me up and bandaged my head."

"A dead monkey?" Linda asked.

"A control monkey from the 50 ppt study we started nine weeks ago. Whoever broke in killed it. We are nine weeks into that study, and suddenly I've got a problem. We need security around the clock. If someone breaks in again, I want the

CHAPTER EIGHT

university police here in minutes. Good thing I came in early. He could have killed all the monkeys."

"Good thing you came in early? He could've killed you!"

"I can't worry about that. We've got work to do. I have to see that it gets done. That dead monkey requires an adjustment in our overall protocol. Otherwise, the study may never get published."

Linda nodded disapprovingly at her boss's remark. "If you're killed," she said, "there'll be no publication. You better worry more about yourself...any idea how someone got in?"

"Police said someone jimmied the door."

Linda remained quiet for a number of seconds, then asked, "Could this tie in with the missing data?"

Allen seemed startled by the question. He shrugged and said, "I don't know, but if the missing data was stolen, someone is out to ruin our work. And Rickey's death could be part of it."

"Hmm," Linda murmured. "I still wonder why the coroner ruled his death accidental."

"Me too," Allen replied. "I was at the autopsy when the forensic pathologist pointed out that Rickey had been injected four times, twice in the buttocks and twice in a vein. I don't see how Rickey could have given himself two injections in the rear that way. He would have to be a contortionist to reach around behind his back, plunge a needle into his butt, and inject the liquid in using one hand."

Linda nodded. "I agree," she said, "but we'll probably never really know what happened."

"We'll probably never know," Allen agreed. "But there is one thing I do know. Unless we finish our work, the country's food supply will continue to be sprayed with dioxin. Kids will continue to die of leukemia. And humanity will continue to see birth defects, abortions, stillbirths, many forms of cancer, and all kinds of medical problems. Just ask the people in rural Louisiana, especially those living near soybean and rice fields. Dioxin is killing them! Their cancer death rate is the highest in the country. And nobody is doing a damn thing about it except us and a few others. Unfortunately, we have to use monkeys to prove it."

"You talk as if it bothers you to use monkeys," Linda said.

"Absolutely!" Dr. Allen's pent-up emotions came out as he went on, "I hate going to the Primate Center! I don't like watching monkeys lose their hair, lose weight until they are skin and bone. It's horrible watching their fingers turn gangrenous. And when they hemorrhage throughout their body and infections spread, how do you think I feel knowing they are going to die! Then cutting them open and seeing their bellies full of fluid. It has always bothered me. It always will! But it goes with the job whether I like it or not."

"I never heard you talk that way. It's good to get it out of your system."

"It's always in my system. I felt bad today when I saw that dead monkey, killed by that bas...that person who hit me on the head."

Linda had never heard her boss swear and realized how important it was for him to maintain a proper decorum. "Are you okay?" she asked.

"I'm fine," he replied, waving the question away.

"I wonder if they'll catch him," Linda said.

"It's unlikely unless he's a junkie and gets caught breaking into another place. But if he was a junkie, I would not expect him to kill a monkey. I'll feel a lot better with a security system."

"I'll arrange for it," Linda said, easing herself up and walking out of the office.

Dr. Allen had no desire to move. He stretched his legs under his desk, closed his eyes, felt the peaceful silence of his office and began to drift off. Suddenly, the phone rang and startled him.

He leaned forward and grabbed the phone. "Dr. Allen," he said.

"Dr. Allen, my name is Paul Reutershan, my mother said I could call."

"Yes...anytime."

"Can I ask you some questions?"

"Go ahead."

"Before my lawyer files suit, he'd like to know if I have dioxin in my system. Is there a test for it?"

"Best man for that is Dr. Gross, University of Miami. He's good at checking body fat for dioxin. From what your mother said, your level should be high."

"Is it expensive?"

"I don't know. Tell your lawyer to call me. I have Gross's number in my files. What's his name?"

"Peter Reilly. He's a lawyer for the Railroad Worker's Union. He's great! He knows I have no money and is getting paid only if he wins."

CHAPTER EIGHT

"Any idea when he'll file suit?"

"No, he said it will take a while to put it all together. But he knows I'd like to see it filed before I die."

"Paul, I'm no psychiatrist, but I know it's important to think positively. Keep making plans. Have something to look forward to. Don't let yourself get down."

"I know, but it's hard. I lie awake at night wondering why our government didn't protect us. They knew how deadly dioxin was…why did they decide to destroy their own men?"

"It was US policy," Allen replied. "The government refused to admit it was engaged in chemical warfare. They told the world the chemicals were safe. Did you know the military have their own dictionary, put out by the Joint Chiefs of Staff? They define words to suit themselves. The definitions make it hard for the world to prove they engaged in such deadly warfare. How would it look if our government told the world Agent Orange was safe and then turned around and gave you protective clothing, a face mask, and gloves?"

"You're saying the government was willing to sacrifice hundreds of thousands of its men for the sake of policy?"

"It seems like it."

There was a brief silence. Paul felt his anger rising. He wanted to do something. Something more than just filing suit and waiting to die.

"Dr. Allen," he said.

"Yes, Paul."

"I know you need Dow's help at the moment, so you can't attack them. But at some point, you'll have to tell the world what happened."

"At the right time, I will. Dioxin should be banned forever. Otherwise, our children and grandchildren will pay the price. But don't minimize your suit! It will attract media attention, especially if you sue for a large amount."

"My lawyer said seventy million, ten for each of seven counts."

"I'm not a lawyer, Paul, but with the documents I've seen, you have one heck of a case. They show that Dow knew they had provided the military with a deadly weapon but sold it anyhow. They knew US troops would be exposed and knew the consequences. It was their product, and they must be held accountable."

"My lawyer takes it a step further. He said those bastards shouldn't have made a deadly product even if the government wanted them to. But their main concern was making a buck. And what's really tragic," Paul went on, "is the government's attitude. Lying! Covering up! Something has to be done about this sovereign immunity crap! Why should the military or even the president do whatever they want...and get away with it? Are they above the law?"

"Take it easy, Paul. Getting worked up will not help."

"I know! But I get so damn mad! I wanna do something! I want to make a difference before I die! But I'm just one person!"

"There are many like you, Paul. Tens of thousands. Hundreds of thousands. Try to mobilize them. Form an organization. You will have a platform from which you can speak out. Use the news media, get them behind you."

There was a momentary pause. "Yeah, I like that. I like talking with you. Someday I'd like to meet you. I'd like to shake your hand."

"And I yours," Allen replied. "In the meantime, we both have a lot of work to do."

When the conversation ended, neither Allen nor Paul knew about a young woman in Chicago who had set out to solve a mystery. She wondered why so many Vietnam veterans were dying years after they had returned home from war. She was struggling with the idea of going public, of letting the world know what she had found.

NINE

M‍AUDE DEVICTOR WAS IN HER MAKESHIFT OFFICE SPACE IN A CORRIDOR ALONG an orange wall eight feet tall. Two matching orange, cloth-covered partitions, each six feet tall, staked out her territory. From front to back, her office measured six feet, four inches and not one inch more. Her desk? Four silver legs and a brown, metal surface. Her chair? A relic pulled from storage. Her filing cabinet? A box on the floor under the desk. But she loved it! She had a space of her own, connected to the world by a phone. There it was! A new thing! Right out of the AT&T box. Shiny white and all hooked up, waiting for its first call in the VA Regional office, a stone's throw from the Madison University campus. On her desk was a pad of paper and a black, Paper-Mate pen, both eager for business, just waiting for the phone to ring.

"Maude DeVictor," she said. "May I help you?" Her voice was animated with perfect articulation. The caller knew he was talking to a pro.

"How do I go about getting disability benefits?" the caller asked.

"Give me your name and address. I'll send out forms. If you have any difficulty, I'll be happy to assist you. Just ask for Maude."

"Well...thanks, Maude."

"You're very welcome."

So it went for some time. Maude took calls from veterans seeking monetary benefits. As a VA benefits claims counselor, she was determined to do all she could to help her fellow veterans.

Maude remembered the day she joined the U.S. Marines in 1959 at the age of nineteen. She served two years and then decided to leave. But she left with a fondness for her brothers.

Other counselors recognized her ability to connect with veterans, and some began sending her problem cases.

In 1976, Maude took a call from a woman in tears. Doctors informed her that her husband, Albert Cohen, had terminal cancer and didn't have long to live. He wanted to apply for disability benefits. Maude told Mrs. Cohen she would send her the standard forms. Before she hung up, Mrs. Cohen told Maude that her husband once said that if he ever got cancer, it would be because of those chemicals in Vietnam.

Within weeks, Albert Cohen died. His widow filed for survivor benefits, but in October 1977, her claim was denied. The VA said her husband's cancer was not service connected. Mrs. Cohen begged Maude to help with the appeal. Maude agreed to try.

She looked at the Cohen's case as a mystery, something to solve. All she knew was that Albert Cohen had served in the air force. She wanted information, so she called the office of the Air Force Surgeon General and talked with Major Holloway, a specialist in herbicides.

Major Holloway gave Maude detailed information about the herbicides used in Vietnam. Maude learned about Agent Orange and dioxin and was briefed on the medical symptoms associated with dioxin poisoning. She was told about chloracne and other possible medical problems, including cancer. As he talked, Maude took notes, putting down every word, even long technical terms that Major Cohen spelled out for her.

Maude thanked him and put the phone back in its cradle. She reviewed her handwritten, five-page report titled, "Report of Contact." She dated and signed each page, then hurried to the far end of the corridor, passing a dozen makeshift offices. The copier stood idle, its green light on. In seconds, Maude had a copy for her boss.

Boss was an older man in a long-sleeved, white shirt and navy blue tie. He pushed his bifocals tight to the bridge of his nose, studied Maude's report and was highly impressed. From the very beginning, he had recognized Maude as a stickler for details.

"Interesting," he said. "But Albert Cohen was a finance clerk, never in the field."

"I'd like to study his military record," Maude replied. "I'm not satisfied. There has to be something there. Why would he have said 'those chemicals'?"

Boss looked up at Maude, saw the sparkle of enthusiasm in her eyes, smiled slightly, and nodded his approval.

At first, Maude found nothing in Cohen's record to show he had been involved in fighting, until on the back of one page, Maude found a notation, "Counter-insurgency experience, Vietnam, July."

"Cohen was in the field," she said, holding the copy of the notation out to Boss.

CHAPTER NINE

"Well, well, what have we here?" he replied, glancing at the one line of information. "Send it and your report to Washington. And," he hesitated, "good job."

The VA was skeptical about the connection between Agent Orange and Cohen's death, but granted benefits to Mrs. Cohen. They asked Maude to send more information.

Maude gathered evidence and kept documents in the box under her desk. She visited a VA Hospital in Chicago and found forty sick veterans she believed were made ill by Agent Orange. They were between twenty-six and thirty-two years of age. Young men! Men with cancers found in men over sixty. Maude kept her supervisors informed, but they refused to accept the idea of a connection between dioxin exposure and the medical problems she had documented. Nevertheless, Maude was convinced she was right. She knew she had to do something because the facts she had gathered told a chilling story.

The evidence was there! She knew it! She struggled with the idea of contacting Bill Kurtis, a top reporter for CBS-TV in Chicago. She was afraid she'd be fired for going public. She needed the job to support herself and her son.

She struggled with her dilemma. She couldn't sleep. She tossed and turned in the darkened bedroom, pondering her choices. One morning, as Maude sat on the side of the bed, she decided to go public. Later that morning, she contacted Bill Kurtis, and he agreed to meet with her.

For six weeks, Kurtis and his investigative team traveled the country, trying to weave a pattern of the dioxin poisoning that emerged in so many widely scattered areas: sick people and dead horses in Missouri; sick people and deformed goats and ducks in Globe, Arizona; sick residents of national forests; and sick Vietnam veterans.

Kurtis found common symptoms: skin problems, hair loss, joint problems, headaches, nausea, fatigue, blood disorders, psychological changes, cancer, and birth defects. On March 23, 1978, Bill Kurtis ran an hour-long documentary called, "Agent Orange: Vietnam's Deadly Fog."

Vietnam veterans, visibly sick and dying of cancer, came before the American public. They told of the deadly legacy they had inherited as a result of the war: medical problems that made it impossible for them to work; the prospect of an early death from cancer; wives who had spontaneous abortions; and children born deformed.

The nation's experts participated: Drs. Woodward, Messelson, Moore, Commoner, Selicoff, and Allen. Their indictment of dioxin was unanimous. It was the most deadly chemical made by man.

Dr. Allen showed photographs of monkeys that had been fed low levels of dioxin. He pointed to growths on extremities and gangrene that had set in before they died, as well as early spontaneous abortions in female monkeys...no different than what occurred in people who were exposed to dioxin throughout the world.

Bill Kurtis reported, "The amount of dioxin sprayed in Vietnam was a hundred thousand times greater that that used by Dr. Allen's work with monkeys."

Kurtis interviewed an air force captain, an expert on dioxin. He refused to acknowledge the deadly effects of dioxin. He cited his own work with beach mice at Eglin Air Force base, but other experts claimed he had misinterpreted his own data.

Kurtis reported that dioxin had been found in beef cattle and mother's milk. He was filmed in Globe, Arizona, where he explained how the U.S. Forest Service made a helicopter run in June 1969, spraying a mountaintop to get rid of foliage. The women in the canyon had vaginal bleeding. Eighteen had miscarriages. Goats and ducks were born with deformities.

A picture of Billy Shoecraft, a poet, captured everyone's attention. She wrote a book called *Sue the Bastards*. And she did. She sued Dow Chemical. Her physician, Dr. Granville Knight, told of finding high levels of dioxin in her body fat. She died of cancer.

Dr. Barry Commoner was interviewed. He expressed the opinion that dioxin was stored in body fat and remained there for years. Should that person lose weight, the dioxin would be released into the system, causing medical problems. This explained why countless numbers of veterans died of cancer years after the war.

Bill Kurtis next interviewed Judy Piatt and Frank Hampel in Moscow Mills, Missouri. They told of the spraying of waste oil on the dirt floor of their horse arena. This was done to keep dust down when the horses were being trained. The waste oil contained dioxin. Dogs, cats, birds, and sixty-seven horses died. Judy and Frank still had medical problems, seven years later.

Kurtis reported on the Veterans Administration position. The VA claimed there was no evidence linking Agent Orange to the medical problems complained of by the Vietnam veterans.

CHAPTER NINE

Then Maude was interviewed. And her phone never stopped ringing. Dying veterans even called her at home, desperate for someone to talk to. Nurses at local VA Hospitals often asked her to visit patients in despair. By April, she was receiving so many calls at work that the VA decided Maude had to go back to her regular job. She had to be a benefits counselor. Nothing else! Other counselors handled the calls at work, but Maude continued to take calls at home. She talked freely to researchers and reporters and attended a "whistle blowers" convention in Washington, DC.

Two months after the DC meeting, she received a call from ABC television in New York. It was about a Vietnam veteran named Paul Reutershan who wanted to talk with her. Maude agreed.

They talked on the phone often and long, usually at night, four to five hours at a stretch. Even though they never met, it became a rare, intense relationship. Paul told Maude about Agent Orange Victims International, an organization he had started, and of his suit against Dow Chemical. He wanted to talk about Dr. Allen, but he remembered his promise to keep Allen's offer of help confidential. He also wanted to talk about his wonderful aunt and her boyfriend, but he knew this too had to remain secret.

They shared stories told by veterans and Paul would say, "There are a thousands of scared veterans out there. The government keeps handing them a lot of crap instead of telling them about the time bomb going off in their bodies. We must open up people's eyes."

Maude agreed.

Meanwhile, a flood of disability claims and Congressional inquiries poured into the Veterans Administration. The VA hastily formed committees to deal with the mounting pressures. A hotline was established, directives sent out to all VA Hospitals, position papers drawn up, and top officials selected to deal with issues that demanded immediate attention.

An ad hoc meeting was held at the VA central office in Washington, and the Bill Kurtis expose was the topic of conversation.

"The fat biopsy issue has taken center stage," Dr. Hobson said. "In the CBS presentation, there was a scenario showing a physician extracting a fat sample from a patient. The physician stated emphatically that he could obtain confirmation of dioxin poisoning through such biopsy specimens. Veterans and action groups speaking for the veterans are demanding that the

49

VA test them for dioxin. They believe they are walking around with a chemical time bomb in their tissues. The VA has no option. We must know if there is any proof that dioxin remains in fat for eight years after the last exposure in Vietnam. If no dioxin is found, if no reliable data can be obtained in the best laboratory in the country, the validity of the CBS statement can be challenged!"

The VA was convinced that, after so many years, dioxin would never be found.

TEN

Mid-April, 1978. At precisely four in the afternoon, a black stretch limo pulled into the driveway and stopped in front of the Washington, DC Watergate Hotel. A doorman decked out in a white top hat and white gloves bounced to the rear door and held it open. A grim, tight-lipped man in a black suit eased himself out. He stood upright, slowly turned his head, checking his surroundings like a general checking out the terrain. The trunk sprang open. A bellhop stood close by. In seconds, the bellhop followed General inside, pulling a cart with three pieces of black, fine-grained calfskin luggage. General headed straight for the elevator. The bellhop hesitated, glanced at the registration desk, saw a hand signal from the manager, and pulled the cart a little faster.

As the elevator began its ascent to a top floor, General mentally checked off details for which he had been given a cool million. All sixty attendees to be checked in by seven; two floors reserved; no individual registration; everyone in a private room overlooking the Potomac River; dinner in the Brasserie at eight; room service for late arrivals; all expenses to be billed under a Bahamian corporate name; secrecy mandatory.

As the elevator came to a smooth stop, doors slid open, and General followed his baggage, knowing he would be in a magnificent suite. He'd been here once before, and everyone had enjoyed elegant and comfortable surroundings. They had raved about the cuisine and the indoor pool, nautilus, sauna, and steam room. Everyone would be satisfied. He had attended to everything, down to the last detail.

General remembered the lecture he received as his check was being signed. "These are very important people. They are to have red-carpet treatment, whatever it costs. But remember one extremely important fact. The Watergate Hotel is host to the highest level of political gatherings and important executive conferences, and under no circumstances are any of our attendees to discuss what they are there for. If they meet friends or if someone asks, their replies are to be noncommittal. As far as we are concerned, tomorrow's meeting never took place. All billing will be in the name of the offshore corporation. The importance of secrecy cannot be overemphasized."

Even as that lecture was being delivered, General knew that everyone was keenly aware of his reputation. He had always delivered without a hitch. He knew his job. Who in the hell were they to lecture him? But a million bucks, less expenses, was a nice piece of change.

At nine the following evening, coats and ties came through two massive open doors. They looked well rested and content. Some branched out in pairs, others gathered in small groups, selecting chairs facing a lectern where General held a mike. And behind General was a wall of windows overlooking the Potomac. A stunning view of the nation's Capitol lay in the distance. The sun was shining.

In five minutes, all sixty attendees were seated facing General. Some looked up at the high curved ceiling with its ornate design, waiting for the meeting to begin.

"Gentlemen," General said after the doors to the room had been closed. "Thank you for coming. Our three days will consist of morning meetings, and the rest of the day is yours. The only request I have is that our discussions be kept confidential. There will be no minutes. But everything will be recorded, and I will have the only tape. Any questions or comments?"

An arm shot up from a young man with a blue bowtie in the second row. "If the emphasis is on secrecy, will any of our names be on the tape?"

"No," General said emphatically. "I will not call anyone by name, and I ask you not to identify yourself. Thank you for that question."

"I have a question," a man with a black goatee said, raising a finger in the air. "What about phone calls?"

"Make them. Any of us can be here for whatever reason, as long as your name is not connected to what goes on in this room. Any other questions?"

General allowed ten seconds for contemplation, waiting for a response. He had been embarrassed by the question of names on the tape. He had not considered that aspect of security, but he had answered well.

"If there are no other questions," he began, "let's start with the Bill Kurtis production on CBS. You all received a video. Any comments?"

CHAPTER TEN

A man with horn-rimmed glasses in the first row, directly in front of General, said, "It was well presented, compelling, and believable."

"And one-sided," a voice from the rear called out. "Six so-called experts for their side and only Captain Collins on ours. Six to one would make it look compelling."

"Gentlemen," General chimed in, "I think we would all agree that it made us look bad. But the Kurtis show should be put in the context of other events. Allow me to tape an ongoing conversation."

Everyone watched General as he leaned forward and fussed over a small table three feet behind the lectern. He punched a button, stood upright, tossed a sidelong glance at the group, and waited. In seconds, voices came out of a black box.

"Dr. Allen, my name is Paul Reutershan. My mother said I could call."

"Yes...anytime."

"Can I ask you some questions?"

"Go ahead."

"Before my lawyer files suit, he'd like to know if I have dioxin in my system. Is there a test for it?"

General punched a button, the voices went dead. "I played this to make a point," he said. "We've taped Allen before. Five years ago, it was Bonnie Hill in Oregon. Allen was involved. Now it's Paul Reutershan. Allen is involved. Last month, Allen was involved with the Bill Kurtis production. You saw him mouthing off as usual. This guy has been on a crusade for years. And for those of you who may not know it, Dr. Allen will testify when Reutershan's case goes to trial. He is determined to prove how deadly dioxin really is, even at extremely low levels. If he is successful, it will have a devastating effect on our entire industry! Gentlemen! He is twenty weeks into his 50 parts per trillion dioxin study. He is close to proving there is no safe level for dioxin!"

"What can we do about it?" Horn-rimmed glasses in the front row asked.

"That's why we're here," General replied. "How do we destroy Allen's credibility and invalidate his life's work? As you know, several steps have already been taken, but how do we proceed at a more rapid pace, considering the mounting pressures?"

"Kill the son-of-a-bitch," a voice in the back called out.

All heads turned to the man in the back who had voiced a simple solution. Many had toyed with this idea. It was simple, quick, and easily accomplished. One pull of the trigger, and it would be over. Why not do it? Moments of silence prevailed.

"Any comments?" General finally asked.

Continued silence. One man, with his legs stretched out in front of him, one ankle crossed over the other, puffed on a good cigar and blew smoke rings into the air. He watched them rise, grow larger, and slowly disappear. He inhaled, blew more rings, and said, "Bad idea, won't work."

"Why?" the man in the back asked.

"This man has one hundred and two scientific publications. When he sounds off, people listen. When he publishes, the world knows. He is in constant demand as a speaker for national and international meetings and a consultant to foreign governments. His membership on committees has placed him in a position of influence and power. He has been the single most important person in the scientific community influencing public policy on environmental toxins. Allen is the world's leading authority on dioxin. I mention this to let you know why this man must be stopped. But killing him is not the solution. His work would live on. Killing him would not invalidate what he has already accomplished. Someone would pick up his work and run with it."

Another voice in the back row said, "When Dr. Allen's articles were published, each one underwent peer review. Three experts in the field scrutinized each article and accepted it as valid. Only then did the journal's editorial board agree to publish it. How can you possibly invalidate a body of work when experts have already accepted it?"

"You may be right," General said, "but we have with us today an individual who agreed to address that question." General nodded to an elderly man in the front row.

The man stood and faced the audience. He had a certain presence, a persona that commanded everyone's attention. He looked every bit like a man who was familiar with success. He gathered his thoughts and began. "I'm familiar with Dr. Allen's paper published in 1977 when he fed small amounts of dioxin to monkeys. It was reviewed by three scientists who found the research valid. But if I could review the entire experiment from the inception to its very end, it may be possible to invalidate the 500 ppt dioxin study."

CHAPTER TEN

Everyone sat upright, fully attentive.

"I would want," Success went on, "the original slides of all the tissues, photographs of monkeys at various stages, all the pre-experimental and experimental data. Also, the manner of preparation of the monkey chow and a history of every monkey used in that experiment, including any illnesses incurred during the experiment. This would be most important. I would also want to know if the monkeys had ever been subjected to PCBs."

"PCBs? Would you explain that?" General asked.

"PCBs are ubiquitous," Success explained. "They are everywhere. Even in the monkey chow Allen fed to the monkeys. Normally, there is a background level of PCBs. Small amounts are normal and of no consequence. But if the amounts are large, PCBs can cause medical problems similar to dioxin. It is therefore important to know if the monkeys were exposed to this contaminant in the past and during the experiment."

"Tell me," General asked, "can you recommend someone for such an evaluation?"

"Absolutely!"

"It doesn't make sense!" a voice in the back blurted out. "Why would Allen be dumb enough to let someone examine his slides and all of his work? How could anyone force him to turn everything over?"

"It could be arranged," Success replied, taking his seat.

"Any other questions or comments?" General asked.

"I fully subscribe to that idea," another voice in the back said. The remark came from an old man who now stood holding and leaning on the chair in front of him. "But I would like to toss out an additional idea. I remember when it was easy to dig up dirt on anyone. A word here, a word there, and the news media would have a jolly time. What about digging for something juicy? Allen must have a past."

General ran his left index finger under his starched white collar and undid the top button of his shirt. On loosening his tie, he said, "We have tried that, but his background has been exemplary. We could find nothing."

"Exemplary!" Old Man shouted. "Are you saying he has never done anything wrong?"

"Judge for yourself. Family background is one of hard work and patriotism. He grew up on the family farm, led an uneventful life, and graduated high school in 1944. He joined the

55

navy, and his military record was spotless. Allen met his wife at the Portsmouth Naval Hospital, and after several years of courtship, they married. While she worked as a psychiatric nurse and supported the family, he went to school. When they had four kids, he was still going to school. He was never a problem in service nor in school, has never been arrested, doesn't smoke, drink, or use drugs. There is no evidence that he ever had an extramarital affair, and his conduct at the university has never been questioned. He now puts in an eighty-hour week and enjoys the respect of male and female colleagues."

"Look," Old Man replied, his voice weak but rising with indignation, "there isn't a person alive who's clean. And I am not impressed with your information. Did he ever steal anything? Or did he ever knock a gal up in high school or college? Allen is handsome. And he has hormones like everyone else. What has he done when his sex drive was in full gear, turn off his chemistry? He receives a half-million dollars a year in grant money! Has he ever used a single dollar in a way for which it wasn't intended? That kind of money invites temptation! And I believe that if you dig, you will find something. And when you say he enjoys the respect of his female colleagues, I don't know what you're talking about. What do they respect him for? And what about female students! There are a lot of gorgeous women where he is. Are you telling me the only thing he looks at are those monkeys?" Old Man hurriedly sat down, still holding onto the chair in front of him, breathing hard.

General scratched his head. He never experienced such an attack. "Who in the hell does that old fart think he's talking to?" he thought. Yet he knew he couldn't reply the way he would like to. His job was to obtain information from some of the most influential men in the country. Big money was involved, and he could not afford to antagonize anyone. He looked at Old Man and said, "We'll keep digging."

"Do that!" Old Man replied in a whisper, still breathing hard.

ELEVEN

Dr. Allen opened his eyes in the darkness of his bedroom. A soft pillow against the side of his face was like a sedative, pulling him back into a deep sleep. He was tired, with no desire to move, just to lie there and drift off again.

"Better get up," he told himself forcefully, urging himself to fight the feeling of serenity and sheer contentment. Grudgingly, he surrendered and forced himself to turn on his back. Instantly, pain grabbed him, froze him to the spot. He was afraid to move. He clenched his teeth and tried to ease himself back to his former position, but the slightest movement brought on excruciating pain in his lower back, forcing himself to remain perfectly still. It was the only thing he could do.

"This is stupid," he muttered. "It's time to get up. I've got work to do." He had to free himself from this ridiculous situation. But he couldn't move.

He tossed a glance at the chifforobe against the wall in front of him. The clock on top showed 6:51 a.m. VA Hospital nurses changed shifts about now, and Christie would be coming home. But if Christie's night had been a hectic one, she might nap for an hour or two before leaving. She didn't like to drive when she was all worn out.

He knew he had to wait for her, she'd know what to do. But lying there bothered him. The 50 ppt study had shown results similar to the five hundred study. It had to be carefully followed to avoid problems. The dead monkey was enough of a problem. It had been replaced with another control monkey, and fortunately the results of the experiment would be valid. But he could not forget the autopsy findings on that monkey. The cause of death could not be found. The monkey just died.

Preparation for a 25 ppt study was underway, and planning for the final study, the 5 ppt experiment, had already started. What he had desperately needed in the final phases of his work was an administrative assistant, someone who would take the responsibility of doing the nitty-gritty paperwork so as to allow him to do the research. Fortunately, a young lady appeared in his lab, having been sent to him by personnel.

At first, for some unknown reason, he had been reluctant to hire her. But Linda urged him to do so...it would take a load off his back, she had said. So he hired Kathryn Anderson. But this young lady didn't get the work done no matter how many times he explained it to her. So he still found himself entangled in tedious paperwork. And he had been patient. But when she walked out of an important meeting and didn't come back, that was it. He knew she was on probation the first six months, and he offered her the option of resigning or being fired.

As Allen lay there thinking, he heard the closing of a door and footsteps below. Christie was home.

"Christie!" he hollered.

She rushed up the stairs. "What's wrong?" she asked, seeing her husband flat on his back, still in pajamas.

"I can't move, my back."

"I'll call a doctor."

"No! No doctor. You be my doctor."

"I'm a psychiatric nurse! What do I know about backs?"

"It's from too much work, stress, probably muscle spasm. Please get me a heating pad and some aspirin. No doctor."

Later that morning, Allen was still in bed, a red-checkered quilt pulled up below his chin. He was comfortable but clearly grouchy over his sudden incapacitation. Two pillows were propped beneath his head, and he guarded the phone that had been put alongside him. It was his only contact with the outside world, and he had to keep in touch.

"I'm not giving up the phone. I'm not going to nap. I'm not," he said, looking at Christie sitting in a rocker near the side of the bed still wearing her wrinkled white uniform.

"You wanted me to be your doctor," she argued. "So, it's doctor's orders. Stop acting like a child. Having a tantrum because you can't go to work doesn't become you."

With nothing more to say, he raised his hand and waved her away.

Christie smiled. "You know," she said, "we haven't been together in the morning this way for years. We're always working. You all day, and me all night."

He threw her a sideways glance. "There's been too much to do," he replied, knowing she was correct. "I enjoy my work, but being a university professor means living in dignified

CHAPTER ELEVEN

poverty. If not for your salary, we couldn't manage. The boys couldn't go to college! I know it has been hard for you working full time, raising four boys, and putting up with me, but—"

"Putting up with you? Whaddya mean? I don't see much of you. You're always somewhere. Working or traveling or speaking or attending meetings or something. We've jokingly attributed our long marriage to the fact that our jobs have kept us apart. We've never had a chance of growing tired of each other."

"True. But when we do get together, it's been fun," Allen replied with a sheepish, boyish grin.

Christie laughed. "It's funny," she said. "We've been married all these years. We have four sons, and you still get embarrassed when we talk sex. It's amazing...a grown man, it's just amazing."

Allen nodded, looking at his toes sticking out from under the covers at the foot of the bed. "I've always been that way, even in high school. All the guys were making out and bragging and poking fun at me for being shy. You knew that about me when we were dating. Remember how long it took for me to give you that first kiss! I wanted to, but something held me back. Maybe it was my mother, always talking religion, fire and brimstone stuff. I don't know."

"Maybe that's why I fell in love with you. The others were always trying to take advantage of me. But not you. Never!"

Allen smiled and locked eyes with his wife. "But look where it got you. Always working to make ends meet. It started as soon as we were married. You never knew what you were letting yourself in for when you agreed to let me go to school as long as I wanted."

"I never thought I'd survive," Christie replied with a chuckle. "Fifteen years and four days later, you were still in school. It was really something to watch four boys and their father doing homework and cramming for exams. Good thing there was always a shortage of nurses. My five kids had to eat. You were like one of the kids."

"I remember. You've been great, and I love you."

"I know. I love you too. In spite of the hard work, we've had a good life together. Lucky us. We have wonderful boys who take after their father. They're all still in school preparing for life. But their parents should be spending more time together because they are getting older and they don't know how many more years they will have together."

"I'd like that. I could interview students and find someone to replace Rickey Marlar. It would free up some time for me. And I would like to replace this new administrative assistant, Kathryn Anderson. She doesn't get the work done, and I'm always doing what she should be doing. I'd like to take Saturday off and be with you. I'd buy you a cowgirl's outfit, and we could go horseback riding together."

Christie reached out and held his hand. "Sounds good to me," she said. "Can you see the two of us in town with cowboy hats, blue jeans, and high-heeled boots?"

"Why not?" Allen replied enthusiastically. "But right now, you better get some rest. You're on duty tonight. I'll get out of this bed somehow and turn it over to you."

"You cannot get up! I'll sleep on the couch in the other room. But first I'll get the mail. It should be here by now."

Dr. Allen was pleased at the stack of mail. It gave him something to do. The top letter was from Paul Reutershan. It read:

Dear Dr. Allen:

It's best we not talk on the phone anymore. Aunt Millie wrote and said Dow knows you are going to testify on my behalf. They also know that some of their documents leaked to the outside. Her friend has to lay low for now. My phone has been bugged, so check yours. I hope this hasn't created a problem for you. From now on, I'll write.

When you read this, my suit will have been filed. You will receive a copy, along with information I've received from veterans. It's wonderful to see guys all over the country digging up documents. We have an invisible army out there looking for the truth.

Your idea about an organization was great. We already have thousands of members, and applications are pouring in every day. We have thirteen chapters with Regional Directors in different parts of the country. Our Board of Directors include five lawyers, the most famous being Victor Yannacone. He was the lawyer who was successful in banning DDT.

CHAPTER ELEVEN

I still haven't raised that $1,000 for that fat biopsy. Since the VA plans to do some testing, I volunteered. But they'll say no because I've been fighting for disability benefits, and if they find a lot of dioxin in me, it would make it harder for them to keep turning me down.
I'll keep you informed.

Sincerely,
Paul Reutershan

Allen put the letter down and marveled at the spirit and enthusiasm of a young man like Paul who was dying of cancer, fighting it all the way, speaking out, mobilizing veterans, and gathering information.

Allen opened a large brown envelope and pulled out documents. The top one was Paul's suit filed July 20, 1978. He set it aside. Photographs and stories of veterans and their children captured his attention.

Rickey DeBoer, an infantryman with the 17TH Air Cavalry, told how he and his unit searched for and engaged the enemy in the central highlands of South Vietnam. He humped across land that appeared to have been bombed and napalmed with such ferocity that the earth lay barren. Entire sides of mountains were scorched away. The vets filled their canteens and washed themselves with water in pools and streams as they continued doing their job. For months afterward, DeBoer had terrible headaches. And his skin, as well as that of nearly every member of his platoon, was hideously discolored with what they called the "creeping crud." He learned that the entire area had been defoliated, but he didn't worry. The army had told the men that Agent Orange was "nothing to worry about." Ten years after he came home, DeBoer discovered he had testicular cancer. He tracked down six of his former platoon members. Five had cancer. They also had dead or deformed children.

Allen looked at photographs of Daniel Loney's daughter, Jennifer, one and a half, born without a right arm. He looked at Michael, eight, and Chad Jordan, ten, of Austin, Texas, born with missing fingers and missing bones in their wrists and arms. A note on the back of Chad's picture was from Dan Jordan, father of the two boys. It said: "In Vietnam, we had no idea our own government was using something that would cause our death and deform our children."

A letter from Mrs. Thomea Welter cried out as she told of her son, Jack, who recently learned he had cancer. He was a medic on the front lines in Vietnam. Mrs. Welter also told of two grandchildren born with deformities.

Another document was a news item. It told of mounting pressures being put on the government to do something and of its response. The Veterans Administration issued a directive and orders to the directors of all VA Hospitals. It said: "It is essential that all concerned personnel be given copies of this Circular. It should be understood that there is no positive evidence for deleterious effects on the health of individuals exposed to these herbicides which is of a permanent nature."

Allen stopped reading. He knew the statement was false. His research with monkeys showed dioxin would kill. And monkeys were so close to humans, and the VA knew about his work. And if that wasn't sufficient for them, what about the women in Seveso, Italy, who were exposed to dioxin and died of cancer. The VA knew that too! Allen remembered the letter from Dr. Gehring, a scientist for Dow, to Dr. Reggiani. The letter discussed the death of this woman. It told of the large amount of dioxin found in her body fat. How could the VA say there was no evidence for harmful effects of a permanent nature? What could be more permanent than death?

Dr. Allen turned back to the VA circular. It said, "In order to resolve this controversy, a study will be conducted that will measure dioxin levels in fat tissue from veterans with a history of exposure to herbicides and from an unexposed control group. Until this study is completed, no VA Hospital should attempt to measure tissue dioxin levels in any of its patients without prior consent from VA Central Office."

Dr. Allen put the document aside. He wondered what the VA would do if a physician refused to follow such orders. He wondered if there was one VA physician in the country who would have the courage to disobey this order, to take a small sample of fat from one of his patients and order a dioxin determination.

Allen picked up another document, minutes of a meeting at VA's central office in Washington, DC. It was a meeting of a newly formed Advisory Committee on Herbicides. Col.

CHAPTER ELEVEN

Johan Bayer, Office of the Surgeon General, U.S. Air Force, was at the meeting. He said: "In response to various questions, the DOD never contracted with chemical companies to have components of Agent Orange made specifically for DOD. The available production of the chemical industry in the U.S.A. was used."

"That's nonsense," Allen muttered to himself. He knew the DOD never used the same Agent Orange as was used in the U.S.A. He clearly remembered a two-line statement in one of the documents that said, "We are formulating to a specification by the government on a formulation established by the military, and we are producing a weapon. It has no use in civilian business."

Another document was a letter from Dow to Melvin Laird, Secretary of Defense. It said, "There is abundant evidence that dioxin occurring as an impurity in 2,4,5-T is highly toxic. We at Dow are convinced that 2,4,5-T containing less than 1 ppm of dioxin can be used safely. Certainly, such a product is safer in use than one containing larger quantities. The Dow Chemical Co. again recommends strongly that the government set appropriate specifications and controls to insure that no 2,4,5-T be used if it contains more than 1 ppm of dioxin." Allen knew the military had never followed this recommendation.

Allen put the mail down. He didn't feel like reading anymore. He had read enough for one morning. But thoughts of the other documents would not allow him to rest. He picked up a front-page article by Robert Hatzell in the *Stars and Stripes*. It said,

"The responsibility for the effects of chemical warfare places the government in a compromising position. To admit that the long-term effects are real opens the administration to costly testing and outreach for afflicted veterans. The VA has already called it nothing more than North Vietnamese propaganda, attempting to ridicule away symptoms complained by veterans. Action from the VA, albeit slow, was forced upon them by Vietnam veterans and media reports.

"The newly established committee to investigate defoliant poisoning may have been completely compromised from the beginning. Dow Chemical is represented on the Advisory Committee, but notably absent from the Committee to investigate defoliant poisoning are such recognized experts as:

"Dr. Selicoff, Mount Sinai Hospital, New York

"Dr. Allen, University of Wisconsin

"Dr. Messelson, Harvard University

"Dr. Commoner, Washington University, St. Louis

"Professor Woodward, University of Minnesota

"All have extensive background in dioxin poisoning," Hatzell wrote, "but none of them are on the Advisory Board."

Allen remembered that he and the other four had participated in the Bill Kurtis documentary. They had all been honest and above board. He knew this was something the government frowned upon. They needed men who would do their bidding. Little men. Toadies! Men who would lie! Men who would sell their soul for a promotion, for a raise in status with an ever-increasing salary, even for a word of praise.

Dr. Allen was tired. Reading the documents was stressful. He closed his eyes and tried to relax, but the phone would not allow this.

"Hello," he said, speaking softly, trying to talk in a relaxed demeanor.

He became fully alert when he heard Paul Reutershan's voice. "Dr. Allen, I had to call. I've got a problem," Paul said hurriedly. "Lenny Laviano, a vice president of our organization, just learned he has cancer that can't be treated. When he heard the news, he called three buddies, all dying of cancer. They are going to the Dow plant to kill as many executives as they can find. They especially want to get their hands on David Rooke, president of Dow. They blame him for everything."

"Talk him out of it," Allen said, "do something to change his mind."

"One of our guys is trying to do that, but Lenny is hollering that he and his friends are dying anyhow, so why not do it. He wants to give Dow a message, and thinks this is the best way to deliver it. These guys know how to kill, and they have some heavy duty weapons."

"Lenny's on the board, call the other board members."

"I did! Some agree with him and may even join him. Would you talk to him?"

"Will he talk to me?"

"I think so. Except for Vietnam veterans, you're one of the few people he'll trust. Hold on."

As Allen anxiously waited, he could feel his back acting up again. He didn't know what to say. But he knew that if Lenny went on a killing spree, it would destroy everything Paul and the board had worked for. It would destroy their organization.

CHAPTER ELEVEN

"Yeah," came a voice over the phone.

"Mr. Laviano, we've never met, but you know me, right?"

"Yeah."

"What you want to do will hurt a lot of people, mostly your friends."

"Whaddya mean my friends? I'm not hurting my friends."

"If your organization is destroyed, think of what it would do to thousands of veterans who've joined. It's the only place they can go for help. Your group is the only group they have, the only group they trust."

"I don't know what you're talking about."

"Think about it! If you, as a member of the board, went on a killing spree, the government would say you were part of a terrorist organization. The FBI would step in. Your organization would be destroyed."

Lenny Laviano was silent. Allen knew he had touched a sensitive chord. This was a man who would do anything to further the cause for his fellow veterans for as long as he lived. Lenny thought about the dilemma he suddenly found himself in.

He finally replied, "I never thought of it that way. But whaddya do to the sons-a-bitches who have the power to do any damn thing they want and get away with it? Whaddya do? Look at what our country did to us! They had us fight a fuckin' war we didn't want. They sprayed that shit on us, and that war is on my mind day and night. I dream about it! I wake up screaming! And now I'm dying."

"The war is over," Allen said.

"The war isn't over!" Lenny screamed. "For me, it'll never be over until I'm dead! If God would grant me one wish before I die, it would be for me and my buddies to put on our combat uniforms, take our weapons and attack the Pentagon. I'd like to get me one general, tie him down, and hose the hell out of him with Agent Orange, and then put a tube down his gut and pump him full of it. I'd like each of my guys to do the same to other asshole generals. Let those bastards find out what dioxin will do. Let them know what it feels like to die from cancer. Let them die by inches, a little at a time! Let them have kids who are born dead or kids without arms and legs, or kids with faces that are twisted and deformed. Let them suffer like we are suffering. Let them! Let them! They deserve to know what it feels like! Those bastards."

"Lenny, calm down. Lenny."

"Look, Doc, I came home glad to be alive. I wanted a small piece of land where I could grow things, a wife to love, a son to play with, a daughter to hug. But I've got nothing! No life, nothing. I'm so damn mad, all I want is to go out and kill. Maybe I'll get killed in the crossfire, but that would be good. I wouldn't have to suffer anymore. I wouldn't have to wait so long to die."

There was silence. Lenny was crying. Paul had his arms around him. He too was crying. Dr. Allen was in bed, holding the phone, knowing there would be no further conversation. He too had tears running down his cheeks. For the moment, he forgot about his backache.

TWELVE

Dr. Allen was in the kitchen, sitting on a straight-backed wooden chair with a red throw pillow in the small of his back. He could not remember ever being home, barefoot, in pajamas and robe, sipping orange juice at ten in the morning. He looked out at the stretch of sunny farmland. Rows of corn, eight feet tall with its long, narrow green leaves were swaying in the breeze. A large section of alfalfa and grazing cattle were in the distance.

"I should've been a farmer," he said to the window.

There on the table in front of him, letters and documents and unopened envelopes, one of them from Paul. The top of a set of documents had a warning: "This material contains information affecting the national defense of the United States within the meaning of the espionage laws, Title 18 U.S.C., Sec 793 and 791, the transmission or the revelation of which in any manner to an unauthorized person is prohibited by law."

Here he was, a scientist, a mere mortal, a man with a backache who suddenly had the urge to grow corn, dirty his hands with soil, throw feed to the chickens, talk to his cows, visit his neighbor, and go horseback riding wearing his white cowboy hat and high-heeled boots. He didn't want documents with a warning about espionage laws.

Allen gingerly fingered the corner of each page as if he were touching glowing cinders. As the last page came into view, there at the bottom it said, "The United States made no attempt to educate people about herbicide spraying, to warn them of attack or assist those who had been affected." Allen pushed this aside.

Another document was a communication from the American Embassy in Wellington, New Zealand to the Secretary of State in Washington, DC. It had been classified, but at least it had nothing to do with espionage. He downed the rest of his juice, put the glass on the table, and read: "Press stories concerning Agent Orange and its possible harmful effects on veterans exposed to the spray in Vietnam continue to appear in New Zealand newspapers." The most recent headlined article stated that Vietnam War commanders told New Zealand troops that the harmful defoliant Agent Orange was to kill mosquitoes. The *Dominion* reported letters from thirty veterans detailing their illnesses and deformities of their children.

Stapled to this report was a page from the Federal Supply Catalogue. It listed Agent Orange as one of its products under number 06 00-075-9749. The government said it was being used as an "Insect and Leech Repellent."

"Astounding! Simply astounding!" Allen said to the documents on the table. He marveled at the way Paul's guys dug up this stuff. But his admiration for them became boundless when he saw how they proved that the US government lied.

The military brass could deny newspaper allegations. They could deny the claim about telling troops that the spray was being used to kill mosquitoes. It was their word against the word of veterans. And allegations would soon become old news. But Paul Reutershan's guys had dug up proof! And the government could not deny what they had published in their own Federal Supply Catalogue.

"What am I to do with this information?" Allen thought. He had the urge to grab the phone off the wall and call Paul. But that impulse was quickly stifled by the thought that Paul's phone was bugged, and he wondered about his own phone.

"How's your back?" Christie asked as she came bouncing into the kitchen wearing a green jogging outfit and holding a two-pound black iron weight in each hand. She stood looking at her husband, flexing her arms and demonstrating her commitment to physical fitness.

"Better," Allen replied. "You're running in this heat?"

"Only two miles, I must stay in shape."

"You work all night, you're busy all day. How do you manage with such little sleep?"

"I'm in shape! Try it! You make time for your sci-fi books, and now all that mail. You should exercise, you know you should. Well, my dear, I'm off," Christie said as she walked to the screen door, nudged it open with her elbow, and took off on a run.

Allen pushed his mail together in one pile, eased himself up slowly, and with a slightly forward bend, hobbled up the stairs to the bedroom. As he settled back in bed with three pillows propping him up, the phone rang.

"Hello."

"Hi, Doc, it's me, Lenny Laviano. I hope you don't mind my calling."

CHAPTER TWELVE

"Not at all. How are you?"

"Fine, Doc. I called to thank you."

"For what?"

"For bein' there when I needed you. For listening to my foul mouth. For helping me think straight."

"And I'd like to thank you, Lenny."

"Me!"

"Yes. You, Paul, and the others who are showing me what the world is like out there. I'm amazed at how naïve I've been. I knew Vietnam was bad, but I never realized how bad. I never realized there was a cover up. When our government came out with a news release, I believed it. But these letters and documents tell a different story. For that, I thank you."

"We were naïve too, Doc. And it has cost us nothing but grief. By the way, I hope you don't take offense if I give you a bit of advice."

"Go ahead."

"Well, we sit around and talk about you. And we all agree that you oughta be more careful about what you say and do. Dow and the government will come after you, maybe even kill you."

"Why would they do that? I'm a scientist. Dow may not like what I say about dioxin, but that's the way it is in research. There's always a difference of opinion, but eventually the truth comes out. In fact, Dow has been helpful. Their scientists and I have gotten along well for a number of years." Allen did not want to tell Lenny over the phone that he was desperately trying to find a new source for dioxin. And he did not want to let on that he was afraid his phone had been bugged.

"Regardless of what you say, Doc, don't trust them! They know we need you. You're the world expert on dioxin and the only guy we trust. We don't want anything to happen to you. And if you need us, call me. I'll put Plan B into operation."

"Plan B! What's that?"

"Don't ask, Doc. Telephones have big ears. Let's just say it's classified."

THIRTEEN

August 1, 1978. A black Chevy Malibu sedan crossed the Michigan state line into Ohio towing tin cans on a string tied to the rear bumper. The clinking and scraping at forty-five miles an hour forced motorists to smile. One driver pushed down on the accelerator, pulled up alongside the Chevy, gave the occupants a thumbs-up, and with a short toot on the horn, passed them by. Drivers going in the opposite direction glanced at the red lettered sign on the side of the car reading "JUST MARRIED" and tooted their horns too. Millie sat close to the driver, marveling at all the well-wishers on the road.

"Herb," she said, "we've been traveling three hours. When are you going to get rid of those tin cans? And...the sign? It's attracting too much attention."

"You know you love it," he replied, smiling.

"Well, yes, but so much attention. We're not youngsters, you know."

"We sure are! You know the old expression, you're as young as you feel."

"Well, yes, but...I don't know." She snuggled closer and closed her eyes.

The clinking of the cans had a hollow tinny sound. Millie picked up a rhythm. If she could put the words to music, she'd compose a love song about two older people finding happiness after years of living alone. She'd name it "Love Again Live Again."

"It's so exciting," Millie said, hugging his right arm, "a honeymoon in New Orleans. I've never been there but I heard about the French Quarter and Basin and Bourbon Streets. Dixieland jazz is still played there, right?"

"Oh, yes. You're not going to hear Joe 'King' Oliver or Louis Armstrong, but you will discover some fantastic jazz, real jazz with a trumpet, sax, trombone, tuba, snare drum, and percussion."

"My goodness, where did you learn all this? And who is King something or other and Armstrong?"

"I read a lot. King something or other and Armstrong are the two men who pioneered jazz."

"I can't wait to get there."

CHAPTER THIRTEEN

"It's a beautiful place. Picturesque houses on narrow streets, exquisite food that is an adventure in eating. You'll love the hotel, Dela Monnate. It's one of the finest."

"As long as I'm with you, Herb, I'd love anything. I'm glad we got married."

"Me too, but it happened so fast. It was fine with me, I have no family. You do. They probably feel bad about not being invited."

"I couldn't call, their phone is bugged. They'll get my letter in a few days. It would've been nice to have them at the wedding. They're the only family I have, but it was nice to do it quick like. No fuss. No bother. Just you, me, and the preacher."

"It's nice to have family," Herb said. "It is something I've missed for years. My wife died twenty-three years ago when our son, Michael, was four. And he died eight years ago. I think about them every day."

"I know you don't like talking about how your son died," Millie replied, "and if I shouldn't be asking, just say so. I'll understand."

"It still tears me up, but I want you to know. In 1970, he was on a spray mission. Another helicopter was downed by enemy fire, so Michael landed, and he and his crew ran to the wreckage and pulled the men out. The damn fool then tried to extinguish the fire. Why did he try to put out a lousy fire? If he had taken off, he might not have been killed."

Millie tightened her grip on his arm. "I'm sorry," she said, "I shouldn't have asked."

"You should! I've got this all bottled up! It's time it came out! I can still see two military men standing at my door. I can still hear them. They told me what a hero he was and gave me his Silver Star. I didn't want a medal! I didn't want a dead hero! All I wanted was...my son." Herb choked up and said no more.

The clinking of the cans rattled along the highway. Millie remained quiet, allowing her husband quiet time to regain his composure. She thought about Paul dying of cancer. She thought about Herb and all the documents he had somehow pilfered. She wondered if anyone would ever find out.

"Would you like to stop for food or to use the restroom?" Herb asked.

"I'm fine, unless you would like to stop."

"Well, we've come two hundred miles, and we still have another one fifty before we stop for the night. I'll get off at the next stop, fill 'er up, and we can get a bite to eat."

"Fine," Millie replied. "What about the tin cans? Are we going to drag them all the way to New Orleans?"

Herb did not reply. He was gazing into his rearview mirror. Suddenly, his foot eased off the accelerator. The needle dropped down to thirty miles per hour.

"What's wrong?" Millie asked.

"Maybe nothing. There's a car back there. I saw it an hour ago. The driver has kept the same distance, as if he's following us. I'm slowing down to see if he will pass us."

"Oh, my!"

"He slowed. Now he's speeding up. Here he comes, even faster. See if you can get his license."

The white car zoomed by. "That's a 1977 Chevy Caprice," Herb said. "Did you get his license?"

"I couldn't, there was something covering the plate."

Herb gunned the engine. The clinking of the tin cans became louder. Herb's foot pushed to the floor, and Millie was in a frenzy.

"Don't chase him," Millie begged. "Let him go."

"I'm not chasing him. I'm trying to estimate his speed. When I had it up to ninety, he was still pulling away. I know his car. It won the Motor Trend's Car of the Year award. It couldn't reach the speed he was going unless he had it souped up. That car is special."

"I'm glad he's gone."

"I think he was following us," Herb said.

Millie said nothing. She was worried. Herb kept vigil in the rearview mirror. Now and then he'd speed up, then slow to a crawl, always checking the mirror.

"That sign. One more mile for food and gas," Millie said. "I guess we have to stop, we're running out of gas."

"Don't you want to stop?"

"Not really. If that guy was following us, he could be waiting. He must've known we were running low on gas."

The car and the tin cans veered onto the exit ramp. A Texaco sign, a McDonalds, and a diner surrounded by trucks was seen in the distance.

CHAPTER THIRTEEN

"I'll drop you off at the diner and join you after I fill it up," Herb said as he swept his gaze from an old pick-up truck parked at Texaco to the last six-wheeler at the far end of the diner. He saw no sign of the souped-up job. But he was troubled. His gut told him something was wrong.

"I'll go with you," Millie said, her arms folded across her flowery, cotton blouse as if nothing in the world could move her.

The clinking became softer, then stopped. Fourteen beat-up Coke cans lay spent on the ground, still joined together by a sturdy long string entwined with wire. Herb pushed open the door and put one foot on the ground, and an explosion erupted with a violent, deafening roar. The black Chevy Malibu was a blazing fireball, doing somersaults twenty feet in the air. It smashed down on the old pick-up, already ablaze and on its side. Fiery debris flew helter-skelter, raining down on everything. The tops of two trucks began to smolder. Thick black smoke bellowed upward. Another explosion, from where the gas pump had been, tore through the Texaco station, engulfing and devouring it with one swoop and creating a massive firestorm.

The engine had torn away from the Chevy, and the red-hot mass of metal smashed into the golden arches, forcing them to the ground. Doors and tires and bumpers flew in all directions, into the windshield of a six-wheeler and onto a side road heading to a town four miles away. Twisted metal, shattered glass and patches of burning gasoline covered the ground for a hundred yards in every direction. Every window in the vicinity had been shattered.

Fortunately, McDonalds had not been busy. Nevertheless, the manager, his crew, and two customers were killed. But the diner was packed, and thick-chested truckers, sipping coffee and roaring with laughter at obscene jokes, were flung from their counter stools to the floor. Their cries and screams added to the chaos that surrounded this small oasis off highway I-75.

Slowly, some of the more fortunate limped out of the diner with blood on their arms and faces. Two injured truckers managed to climb onto the roofs of their trucks and were working their fire extinguishers. Sirens could be heard in the distance.

August 4, 1978. Paul Reutershan was in his room sipping hot cocoa and nibbling on an Oreo. He knew it was America's favorite cookie, but he preferred home-baked, especially when fresh from the oven.

Jane was busy downstairs, opening mail, setting aside checks and sending out membership cards to Vietnam veterans. Agent Orange Victims International had grown in number.

A tally showed 58,892. The organization now had a sizeable bank account and political clout. Paul was glad he had followed Dr. Allen's advice. He had something to live for.

A loud shriek startled him. Al ran out of the room, down the stairs, and into the kitchen where Jane sat sobbing.

"What's wrong?" Paul asked, leaning down and putting an arm around his sister, who had always been so easygoing.

She held up a letter and continued to cry. It was from Aunt Millie. She was married, and as he finished the letter, he still could not understand the reason for the commotion.

"I don't understand," he said, "why are you crying?"

"She's dead!" Jane replied, erupting into another bout of sobbing.

"What do you mean, she's dead?"

"The fourteen tin cans," Jane replied, taking the letter from Paul and pointing to a line in the center of the letter, still sobbing.

"The fourteen tin cans?" Paul was still confused.

"The news report three days ago," Jane said. "The explosion, people killed. The police found fourteen beat-up Coke cans still tied to a bumper on a side road. Remember? Aunt Millie and Herbert were in that car."

Paul looked again at the letter. The middle paragraph said, "He's so cute. He tied fourteen Coke cans to the back of the car and posted a sign on the side. I never told you that he was an all-state football player in high school. His jersey number was fourteen. So he adopted that as his lucky number. He's nice. Romantic and real sentimental. You'll like him."

That evening, Paul sat in a booth at Harry's Pub, a small neighborhood tavern. He, Lenny Laviano, and Frank McCarthy, another Vietnam veteran, were huddled together sipping cold beer and talking softly about the death of Aunt Millie.

"If not for the tin cans, we'd never know she was dead," Paul said.

Frank held the handle of his frosted mug tilted to his lips and took a sip. "Yeah," he murmured, "she and Herb would have just disappeared and you'd never know why."

"Why no bodies?" Lenny asked. "You'd think there'd be some bones."

Paul lifted his mug, downed the lager, and thought about Lenny's question. "I don't know. Police said they were cremated. But in Nam, when a chopper exploded or a plane crashed, there

CHAPTER THIRTEEN

were bodies, black as coal, but there were bodies. Gasoline never cremated nobody. The fire wasn't hot enough. It doesn't make sense."

"It doesn't make sense if you believe the cops," Frank said. "How the hell do they know Herb was smokin' when he pumped gas? They don't know if he even got out of his car. The whole damn place was a hole in the ground. Two truckers said there were two explosions. I believe it! But the cops shrugged it away. The second explosion would have been gasoline. What about the first?"

"I'll be damned if I know," Paul replied, forcing himself to keep his voice down as he felt a sudden rage. "What kind of explosion was it that cremated my aunt?"

"I sure as hell don't know," Frank said. He looked toward the bartender and raised his hand, signaling for more beer. "Maybe we'll never know, but my gut tells me Dow arranged it. Herb leaked out company secrets, and they had to get rid of him. If I'm right, Dow has to get rid of Doc Allen. He's a real danger for them, and they can't afford to let him go on doin' research. Bad things are going to happen to that man. Mark my words, maybe another explosion. Or maybe somethin' just as bad."

FOURTEEN

Kathryn Anderson kneeled on the floor of her apartment, resting her buttocks on the backs of her legs. A Smith Corona on a beat-up wooden coffee table was in front of her. Leaning forward, she fingered a white sheet of paper, held it in place, and rolled it into her typewriter. She sat back on her haunches chewing bubble gum. She puckered her lips and began blowing. A bubble appeared. It became larger and larger. She watched it grow until, bang! It burst, and gum lay all around her mouth. Her tongue shot out and lapped it all up in under a second.

Her boyfriend, sitting on a couch across the room, laughed. But beneath the laughter, he harbored irritation. He hated the smacking of gum, but he was living in her apartment, with free meals, TV, and a piece of ass any time. Not a bad deal.

Kathryn wiggled closer to the typewriter, positioned her fingers over the keys, and began pecking away. She was typing a simple message to her boss but stopped and stared at her boyfriend. "The jerk's a distraction," she thought. "Look at him in boxer shorts, a shiny bald head, mean eyes, staring into that stupid TV. What do I see in him? He's a moocher, always grabbing me. All he wants is more. But he serves a purpose."

She turned back to pecking away, and in no time, she completed a polite, business-like letter, notifying Dr. Allen of her resignation. A turn of the knob, and it was ready for her signature.

September 22, 1978

Dear Dr. Allen:

This is to officially inform you that I will be resigning my position as Project Specialist with the Department of Pathology effective as of Friday, October 6, 1978.

CHAPTER FOURTEEN

Sincerely,

Kathryn L. Anderson

cc: *Department of Pathology*

October 4, 1978, twelve days later, Kathryn was in an administrative building on campus, giving a young lady a letter about Dr. Allen, listing horrendous allegations against her former boss, the top three being camouflaged sexual advances, racial slurs, and violation of federal grant regulations.

"Jim," Dean Smith said into his speakerphone, "please come to my office immediately. It's important."

Allen sat holding a letter, his eyes racing down the page. Dean Smith sat behind his desk. He saw Allen's jaw drop open, the look of disbelief, the narrowing of his eyes as he neared the bottom of page two, the red flush of anger on page three, and total outrage at the end, flinging the letter on the desk in disgust.

"Do you believe this?" Allen asked.

"No, but she didn't just send this letter to me. She routed copies to the University Committee, the Departmental Chairman, Chancellor Shain, and Rob Fixmer of the *Capital Times*."

"It's a pack of lies!" Allen exclaimed. "I never sexually harassed this woman, not verbally or physically. And I did not misuse even one dollar of grant money. Every penny can be accounted for."

"She says she was sexually harassed in many subtle and oblique ways."

"Subtle and oblique ways? What the hell does that mean? Ask any of my staff! If I patted, petted, and hugged her and continually pried into her sex life as she claims, don't you think someone would have noticed? I know you've been dean for less than a year, but you know me by now! What kind of person do you think I am? A sex freak! A thief!"

"Calm down. We have to figure out how to deal with this. She's making a lot of noise, and Chancellor Shain is heavily involved."

"What does that mean, heavily involved?" Allen angrily replied.

"You know the rules. There are no unemployment benefits if a resignation occurs in the first six months unless the resignation is due to employer misconduct. And Shain told the Payroll Office to pay her and not ask questions."

"Not ask questions!"

"That's right! Shain doesn't like the newspaper publicity. So he told the *Capital Times* that the university felt there was enough validity to the charges and recommended granting unemployment compensation."

"The university? Chancellor Shain is the university! Am I to conclude that Shain believes I'm guilty?" Allen yelled. "Who the hell does he think he is? Judge, jury, and executioner! I resent this!"

"Look, Jim, I'm on your side. Calm down. The thing that's bothersome is the university's premature involvement. I don't understand why Anderson was granted compensation before the University Committee had a chance to look into the charges. Tell me about this woman. Who is she?"

"I really don't know. I needed help and talked about hiring an assistant. One day, she showed up and said she'd been hired as my administrative assistant. I didn't think anything of it and was glad to have her. But after a month, it was obvious to everyone that she either couldn't or wouldn't do the work. She was impossible! She'd walk out in the middle of an important meeting without any explanation. I finally gave her the choice of resigning or being fired."

"Where did she come from?"

"I was told she worked at another university, had proper credentials, and a good academic record. I never saw any references and assumed she'd be a valuable member of the team. I sent her a letter of acceptance on what I was told and spelled out all of her responsibilities. As I think about it, I really knew nothing about her, and I had very little contact with Miss Anderson. As you know, my schedule is a hectic one with a great deal of traveling. I never discussed sexual matters with her, and the only thing that she may have misconstrued was when I told her I was invited to Hanoi and would need someone to assist me in my work in North Vietnam. I asked her if she would be interested in going. The matter was never further discussed. And as you know, I did not go."

"Did you ever touch her?"

CHAPTER FOURTEEN

"Never! Except for...one time when I saw her walking stoop-shouldered. This was something our staff joked about when they called her a hunchback. When I saw her walking that way, I put my hand on her shoulder and told her to straighten up. She gave me a look, and I realized immediately that I shouldn't have been so blunt."

"What about the other charges?"

"Ask staff. I never told anyone to falsify records or make false statements. Her charges are pure fabrications. The idea that I would misuse money! Staff knows I swap money from one pot to another like everyone else, but that's because of my frugality. I hate giving money back. So I'll use it and replace it either with money from another grant or from my personal discretionary account."

"Any idea why she would say this?"

"Maybe she's angry at my decision to get rid of her. Maybe she wants to get even. Maybe she's just a nut. I don't know."

"One other question. How could she get such detailed information? The dates these events occurred were before she started working here."

"She had access to my files. Her job description called for it."

"Well, as it stands now, Chancellor Shain asked me to investigate the charges. I'll talk to Dr. Inhorn. Since he's the departmental chairman, he can talk to staff. I'll be guided by his findings."

Dr. Allen found it impossible to work. He would pick up a report from his desk and throw it back down. He pondered his dilemma. What would Christie think? Would she believe any of this rubbish? What about his sons? Everyone at the university? Students and colleagues? Surely they would know it was a pack of lies! But the newspapers were going to carry the story. Everybody would talk. Point fingers. He could already feel the disgrace.

Dr. Allen leaned back in his swivel and felt a twinge in his lower back. "Let the pain come," he said to himself. "I'll go home and become a farmer. Once and for all, I'll grow alfalfa, carrots, and whatever else I want. I'll raise more cattle and breathe fresh air. I'll get as far away as I can from this university."

Linda rapped twice on the door before coming in with a letter in hand. "Got a minute?" she said.

"You don't have to knock," Allen replied, waving her to a chair.

"Have you ever seen this?" she said, holding the letter out to him. "I was looking for a manual in John's desk and saw this letter from Dow Chemical to Dr. John Van Miller. I know he's not a doctor, so I glanced at it and saw they had sent you a copy. I know I never saw it, and if I didn't see it, you never got it."

Allen took it. "May 8, 1978?" he said, with a tone of disbelief. "That's five months ago! I never received this. I'll be damned! Dow claims to have found high levels of PCBs in my tissue samples. If true, it would destroy the entire study! But it's not true! I checked for PCBs, and there were none!"

"Why would Dow check for PCBs?" Linda asked. "When I typed your letter to them, you never asked them to do that."

"That's right. They were to check for dioxin, only dioxin."

"The letter says," Linda replied, "Dr. Kociba talked with you about PCBs in your tissue samples and you thought it proper to find out where they came from."

"He never talked to me! Remind me to talk with Cartwright and Kociba. Right now, I have to deal with these outrageous charges against me. Have you heard what's being said?"

"I've heard, and everyone knows about those bitch's charges. Everyone knows it's just a lot of hooey. Who'd want to snuggle up to her?"

"Did you ever see her going through my files?"

"All the time. And I feel responsible. When she suddenly appeared, I urged you to hire her. Too bad you didn't send her back to Personnel."

"It's not your fault. There was too much work, and I was glad to have her. Now I've got a hell of a problem."

"Don't worry, we all know it's baloney. When we talk to the University's Committee, they'll know it's nothing but a pack of lies."

Dr. Allen felt grateful for Linda's loyalty. Her words gave him hope that it would somehow work out. He knew his colleagues would speak out on his behalf. When the University Committee had finished its investigation, the newspapers would have to print a retraction. His wife would know the truth. His sons would know the truth. Everyone would know. He would be able to walk on campus with his cowboy hat and boots and not feel ashamed. But at the moment, he had an empty feeling inside. At the moment, he was afraid.

FIFTEEN

Allen was in the barn sitting on a bale of hay, his feet dangling above the floor. He held kernels of corn in his outstretched palm. A large black and white Holstein stretched its neck forward and nibbled at the kernels, obviously enjoying the early morning offering.

Tending to the less taxing needs of the farm had been Allen's only activity for the past week. He was not physically able to take on the more demanding responsibilities. These were left for his sons. But if he had to, he'd get in shape: start running with Christie, do sit-ups, push-ups, and weight lifting. In a few months, he'd be able to do anything, even pitch hay! Or grab hold of the pitchfork with both hands and break ground for new plantings.

Becoming a farmer suddenly seemed wonderful, an opportunity to free himself from the gossip and wild speculation that had become the craze on campus. The *Capital Times* fueled the rumor mill, and the public just gobbled it up.

The latest story reported that Allen had invited Kathryn Anderson to his Colorado retreat for a weekend getaway. It said he had made similar suggestions to another woman who had come forward, but the damn paper gave no name. And no other woman had as yet been identified. The paper claimed Allen told this anonymous woman he could use government money for such holidays. It said other outrageous things! But no reporter from the *Capital Times* had ever called him, talked with him, or asked for his comments.

Kathryn Anderson must've been called every day. She made the news. One word out of her mouth, and off it went. Another headline! They called it First Amendment rights! Freedom of the press! But what about his rights, the presumption of innocence until proven guilty!

Allen found himself numb to the daily events that had been his life for so many years. He had no desire to go to the lab. His energy and usual exuberance were gone. In its place he found a disinclination toward any effort to carry on with his research and frequent episodes of utter despair.

The loud clang-clang-clang of a bell vibrated through one side of the wooden barn.

"Jim!" Christie shouted, "breakfast!"

He put one hand on Holstein's snout, gave it a pat, eased off the bale of hay, and strolled out of the barn. Once in the kitchen, Allen wondered why he was sitting there.

"I'm not hungry," he said, staring at the platter of scrambled eggs, bacon, and rye toast.

"You hardly ate anything yesterday, nothing the day before. You have to eat, even a few bites," Christie replied, recognizing his depression. She saw it every day at the VA Hospital. Her psychiatric training told her she had to somehow intervene.

She had to give him hope.

Allen nibbled at a corner of his toast while his wife poured coffee into a mug. She slid the butter dish and a jar of strawberry jam to the side of his plate. He glanced at it and shook his head.

"I know those charges are false," Christie said, inching her chair next to him and looking into his face. "Your friends know it too. And so does the dean. He said there was no evidence."

"But the newspaper won't let go. Those stories sell papers, and it's not going to stop. Everyone's talking. I hate going to work. I can't face people. I'm ashamed."

"It has to end," Christie said with more vigor. "The dean wrote to Personnel and told them there was no evidence to support the charges. He asked for a meeting with you, university officials, and that woman. It could do away with the problem."

"That woman refused. She'll not meet with anyone, and the university accepted her decision. I know the chancellor believes the sexual charges against me because, even though she worked less than two months, he gave her unemployment benefits. This means he accepted her charges as true."

"What about hiring a lawyer? You can sue Anderson and the newspaper."

"I thought of that. I even talked with an attorney. He wants a five thousand dollar retainer. Where would we get the money? We have four boys in college. We can barely make ends meet now."

"We can mortgage the house and farm!"

"A mortgage? We could lose everything and still not have enough to pay a lawyer. I think I'd be better off dead!"

Christie was taken aback. "If you were dead, who would help those people out there who need you, the veterans and their families? They need your testimony! You saw pictures

82

CHAPTER FIFTEEN

of those horribly deformed kids! They need operations! That takes money! You must finish your work! You could help them win millions. Without that money, they will have nothing but misery."

"I know, but I can't shake off this feeling. It goes from bad to worse. When I talked to the dean, he told me about this woman's live-in boyfriend who swore at the dean, shook his fist, and carried on while students and faculty listened. This madman demanded to know why the dean wasn't punishing me for sexual harassment. The dean said that no one had ever accosted him that way. And it didn't take long for the entire campus to hear about it. I'll bet that even my colleagues must wonder if it's true."

"That's ridiculous!" Christie exclaimed. "They all came to your defense! They've been with you for years! Even as you sit here, they are carrying on with your work. You have a staff of twenty people, and ten are graduate students. They all want you to succeed!"

Allen was startled by the ring of the phone. Christie picked up the receiver. "It's Linda. She said she has something exciting to tell you."

Allen took the receiver. "Yes, Linda?"

"Dr. Allen!" she exclaimed. "The monkeys in the 50 ppt study are showing the same signs we saw in the five hundred. They are beginning to look like the other monkeys. We saw it this morning when they began to lose their hair. You must see it! It proves your theory!"

Linda's excitement aroused a twinge of curiosity in her boss. He could envision the way the monkeys looked, but he just wasn't up to getting excited.

"I'll try to come in tomorrow," he said. "How's everything else?"

"Everything else? Oh, you mean the gossip. When anyone asks, I tell them it's nothing but a pack of lies. All of us have signed a letter to the chancellor telling him the same thing, but that bitch and her boyfriend keep on talkin' and the *Capital Times* continues to print those horrible stories. But the truth will come out! It has to!"

"I hope so," Allen replied, and without saying good-bye, he put the phone back on the wall. He eased himself out of his chair and shuffled out of the kitchen. He was tired and wanted to rest.

When Christie heard his footsteps trudging up the hall stairs, she took the receiver off the hook and punched in numbers.

"Agent Orange Victims International."

"Mr. McCarthy," she said in hushed tones. "This is Mrs. Allen. I'm calling about Dr. Allen. He would never approve of my calling but…"

Frank McCarthy immediately sensed the concern of a woman who had to speak softly. "What's wrong?" he said.

Christie filled him in quickly and brought him up to date. "You are someone he admires and trusts. Maybe a call from you would help."

"Okay. And I won't tell him you called."

"Thank you," she said as tears choked off communication.

In seconds, the phone rang. Christie ran into the bathroom and hollered, "I'm in the bathroom! Get the phone!"

Allen lay flat on his back, fully clothed except for his shoes. He was tempted to let it ring. But more from habit, he reached out to the bedside stand and lifted the receiver.

"Yes?" he said, determined not to carry on much of a conversation.

"Hi, Doc, it's me, Frank."

"Hi, Frank."

"I called to bawl you out, Doc."

"Why's that?"

"I told you to let me know if you needed help. Why didn't you call?"

"What makes you think I need help?"

"Hey, Doc! You know I've got a lot of guys out there. And when I say out there, I mean everywhere. Including the university campus. My guys keep me informed. And you haven't been showing up for work."

"I've been depressed, Frank."

"Well, you better get over it, fast. My guys have been busy getting information on this woman. I know that neither you nor anyone else interviewed her before you agreed to hire her. I know your university is a state school, and that job had to be posted but never was. I think this whole thing was a well-planned set-up. And I'm determined to dig it all up."

"I sure hope you do, Frank."

"Let me ask you something, Doc. Has anything happened to you that was out of the ordinary?"

CHAPTER FIFTEEN

"Well...yes. Not long ago, someone broke into the Primate Center, and one of our monkeys was dead. I never found out why it died."

"Anything missing?"

"No. File drawers were open and desk drawers had been broken into, but nothing was missing."

"You're sure?"

"I think so. Maybe I prevented a theft by walking in. I was knocked unconscious."

"Were you hurt?"

"No, I was okay. But that forced me to install a security system in both of our buildings."

"This monkey. Was it in one of your experiments?"

"Sure was. The 50 ppt dioxin study. It's the latest and one of our most important."

"Anything else happen?"

"No, not recently."

"Whaddya mean not recently?"

"Well, not since over a year ago. One of my students was found dead in his apartment."

"How did he die?"

Allen started with the finding of Rickey Marlar's body. Then he told about the autopsy findings supporting the possibility of homosexual activity, and four injections of a monkey tranquilizer rendering the victim unconscious, a lethal amount being found in his system. After that, vomiting and the aspiration of the vomitus. The coroner's ruling of accidental death just three days after the body was found.

"Doc, the way you said that, it sounds as if the ruling bothered you."

"It still does. First of all, I was amazed that a ruling was handed down in three days. I was at the autopsy. The findings pointed to homosexual activity. The four injection sites raised questions that left me wondering about the possibility of homicide. I've never mentioned this to anyone, but I still think about it."

"Did the death interfere in any way with your research?"

"Not really," Allen replied with some hesitation. "Some data from the study was missing, and we never found it, but the paper had all the data and it was published."

"You gave me three big ticket items, Doc. How about little things?"

"Little things?"

"Yeah, something that may have seemed insignificant but troubling."

Allen suddenly remembered Linda reminding him to call and talk to Dr. Kociba and to talk to Cartwright.

"Well," he said, angry at himself for letting it slip his mind. "Dr. Kociba, a scientist at Dow, sent a letter to Cartwright, one of my students. Kociba claimed that Dow found high levels of PCBs in tissue samples from my 500 ppt experiment. That bothered me. That kind of letter should've been sent to me, not a student. And that letter showed that I had been sent a copy. I never received a copy. And Dr. Kociba never talked to me about finding high PCB levels as he claimed in his letter. Even now, it still makes me mad."

"Doc, what would it mean if there were high PCBs?"

"It would destroy the study. High PCBs can cause the same kinds of medical problems as dioxin. Dow could argue that it was the PCBs and not dioxin that did all the damage. But there were no high PCB levels. I know because I checked. There were only background levels that occur everywhere and are of no significance."

"Did Cartwright ever show or talk with you about the letter?"

"No."

"Do you trust him?"

"I always have. He's bright and a hard worker. I never had reason not to trust him. I even gave him permission to use my work for his PhD thesis."

"Is Cartwright gay?"

"He can't be. He's married."

A roar of laughter forced Allen to hold the receiver slightly away from his ear. "Please excuse me for laughing, Doc," Frank said apologetically, "but where've you been living? He's married doesn't mean he's not gay. Some people like variety."

"I see. Well…I was troubled by his excessive drinking, but there was never any indication he had sexual preferences other than his wife."

"Did he know the student who died?"

"They were the best of friends. In fact, Cartwright was the last person known to have seen Rickey Marlar alive. They were drinking together the night before."

CHAPTER FIFTEEN

"Drinking where?" Frank Carter asked.

"In some bar. Afterward, I believe they went to Marlar's apartment. Oh, stop it, Frank, Cartwright had nothing to do with Marlar's death."

"Whatever you say, Doc. But I learned something a long time ago. As far as I'm concerned, there are times when a person should be viewed as guilty until proven innocent. I'll start pokin' around. I've got an excellent guy in your area, and take it from me, Doc, he's the best."

"Frank!" Allen said as he swung his legs off the bed and sat upright, "thank you."

"I'll do everything I can, Doc. I'll be in touch."

"By the way, Frank, how is Paul Reutershan getting along?"

"Not good. His aunt's death hit him hard. He blames himself and tries very hard to get the message out to other vets. His talks on radio and TV are great, but he's not the same. The fight and the fire in his voice isn't there anymore."

"What about the lawsuit?"

"That'll go on. Victor Yannacone has taken over and is goin' to expand the lawsuit into a class action, with groups of lawyers all over the country. That will involve a lot of guys, Doc. And we need you. You are the only one doing long-term studies on dioxin. That makes you the only one who can prove the damn stuff is killing us all and causing those damn birth defects. Without you, Doc, we could lose our case."

"God willing, I'll be there Frank."

SIXTEEN

Filled with a semblance of hope, Dr. Allen backed his car out of the driveway. Frank had touched him and brought back the enthusiasm that had gone awry. The hatter had blocked and cleaned his ten-gallon hat. It was new again. His jeans had been freshly laundered and creased. His boots sparkled when rays of sunshine angled in through a window as his foot pushed down on the gas pedal and the car sped away.

First stop, the Primate Center. Allen slid his key into the slot and the door clicked open. He hurried inside. A shrill sound went off, and he quickly punched four numbers and the pound sign into a lit up keypad on the wall. The high shrill ceased.

Monkeys screeched and shook their cages, and Dr. Allen felt good about being back. As he visited the first cage, a hand reached out. He took it, held it, and smiled. He didn't know that his phone in the other building was jumping off the hook.

The residents at Love Canal were calling. They were frightened. They felt that their lives were at stake and the lives of their children were at stake. One resident, Robert Kott, was standing on a makeshift scaffold held up by two sturdy wooden crates. His right fist worked a hammer, pounding a nail into a sheet of plywood. He had spent thousands of dollars and hundreds of hours painting, insulating, and caring for his precious property. But the time had come to shutter up his house before fleeing with his wife and kids, the youngest being seven, the oldest fifteen. He feared for their safety and finally had to call it quits.

"I don't mind telling you," Robert said to his neighbor, who stood on the grass, holding a box of nails, "we've been scared for a long time, scared for our lives."

Kott's neighbor was also scared. They had been living a nightmare of noxious odors leaking into their homes, a sinister sludge seeping into their basements, and their children playing in potholes filled with chemicals containing dioxin.

The residents cried when women had miscarriages, when children were born with birth defects, and when the townspeople came down with cancer. The homeowners were

CHAPTER SIXTEEN

angry and shaken. A federal study found eleven of thirty-six residents with chromosome damage. Everyone demanded to be moved out, and they wanted to be moved immediately. "The neighborhood is contaminated!" they shouted. "Declare a federal emergency!" they screamed. They asked that Dr. Allen be appointed to the Ecumenical Task Force to address the Love Canal disaster. They wanted Allen, and they wanted him now!

When EPA officials said, "A final decision on the evacuation of seven hundred ten residents will not be made at least until next Wednesday," those at the meeting reacted with outrage.

"Why Wednesday? Why not today?" demanded Lois Gibbs, president of the Love Canal Homeowners Association. James Clark demanded to be moved out instantly. Ann Hills shouted, "We don't want any more testing. I want money for my house so we can move!"

Phyllis Whitenight told of her bad news. She had six abnormal cells in her blood sample. "They said it could be cancer!" she cried. "I had breast cancer five years ago, and three of my neighbors had cancer too. What is this? An epidemic?"

The testing of the residents was done to gather evidence for the federal government's $124.5 million lawsuit against Hooker Chemical and Plastics Corporation. Both companies had used the Love Canal area as a chemical dump twenty years earlier. When D. L. Baeder, president of Hooker, saw the chromosomal findings, he issued a public statement.

"The company is concerned for the health and well-being of all residents of the Love Canal community," he said. "We are however, concerned that these preliminary and uncorroborated medical results, if not properly understood, could cause unnecessary anxieties. To draw any conclusions or take any precipitous action based on these inadequate findings would be unwarranted and a disservice to the residents of the Love Canal area."

The residents saw it differently. They prepared a document titled, "Love Canal, Public Health Time Bomb. A Special Report To The Governor and Legislature, September, 1978."

It read, "The profound and devastating effects of the Love Canal tragedy, in terms of human health and suffering, and environmental damage, cannot and probably will never be fully measured. The lessons we are learning from this modern-day disaster should serve as a warning for governments at all levels and for private industry to take steps to avoid a repetition of these tragic events. They must also serve as a reminder to be ever watchful for the tell-tale signs of potential disasters and to look beyond our daily endeavors, and plan for the well-being of future generations..."

Frank McCarthy, Lenny Laviano, and Paul Reutershan sat on a couch watching television, each holding a can of Schlitz.

The TV newscaster slammed the Carter administration. "Reliable sources tell me," he said, "the president is considering the appointment of a blue-ribbon committee to evaluate the Love Canal controversy. Some residents of Love Canal have boarded up their homes and fled the area. Others are demanding there be no more studies. They claim the deadly chemical is a danger that requires immediate attention, and they want that attention addressed now."

Frank, Lenny, and Paul were holding empty Schlitz cans, thinking about the news.

"Another beer?" Frank asked, looking at his buddies.

"I'll have one," Lenny said.

"No, thanks," Paul said. "One's my limit."

"Let's shut the tube off," Frank called from the kitchen as he checked shelves inside the refrigerator, pushing aside a gallon of milk and reaching for beer.

"I've got an idea," Frank said, handing a Schlitz to Lenny. Paul leaned back on the couch, eyeing the ceiling, waiting to hear to hear more about Frank's idea.

"Those Love Canal people are dyin' from dioxin," Frank went on, "and kids are deformed. It's one hell of a disaster. We know what it's like. Maybe we can help and get some PR for our organization."

"How do we do that?" Lenny asked.

"Let's call Doc Allen. He's pretty naive about some things, but when it comes to dioxin, he knows his stuff. The residents of Love Canal want him on the task force. With the noise they're makin', they will get him. Maybe he can give us an idea on how to help. And at the same time, we might get some PR and get the word out about dioxin."

"I'm for it," Paul said. Lenny nodded.

CHAPTER SIXTEEN

Frank took a long swig and tossed the empty Schlitz across the room into a trashcan...a three pointer! He walked to one side of the room, picked up phone off the floor and returned to the couch, the extension cord slithering along the floor behind him. Dropping into his seat, Frank punched familiar numbers.

One ring. "Hello?"

"Mrs. Allen! Frank. Is Doc in?"

"He left for his office a while ago, try him there. And Frank, thanks for calling the other day. He felt much better after talking with you."

"Anytime, Mrs. Allen."

"Frank! I'd prefer you call me Christie. If you don't, I'll call you Mr. McCarthy."

Frank laughed. "Thanks, Christie."

"Thanks for what?" she asked.

"For being so friendly."

Frank rang Allen's office, but got no answer. Thirty minutes later, no answer. Frank began to worry. "His wife said he went to the office. He should be there."

"It's Saturday," Lenny said.

"He's a workaholic," Frank replied. "He's always in the office, always working, unaware of what's going on around him. One of his students was found dead a while back and experimental data was missing. For me, there's a connection."

Frank punched in numbers. Still no answer. "We oughta talk to McKitrick," Frank said. "It'd be a good idea to keep an eye on the doc."

"He's important to our case, isn't he?" Lenny asked.

"Crucial," Paul replied, "his work proves dioxin kills. Without him, I don't think we've got a chance."

"What if he was bumped off?" Lenny asked.

"It could blow our case. He's the only one in the world doing long-term studies on dioxin."

"Why's that?" Lenny's eyes narrowed.

"It's a lifetime of work. When Allen started with 1,000 ppt of dioxin, it didn't take too long for monkeys to die. When he fed 'em 500 ppt of dioxin, it took a few years longer before they died. Now it's 50 ppt, then 25 ppt, and the last study will be 5 ppt. All this means a hell of a lot of years of working, watching, and waiting. It costs millions. He's been lucky, the government kicks in half a million a year."

"Wow!" Lenny exclaimed. "How long's he been at it?"

Paul thought a moment. "I'd say about sixteen or seventeen years. He also has one of the only two Primate Centers in the world. Think of it...that building took millions to build. It's near impossible to put a package like that together."

"That's why he's called the Dean of Dioxin," Frank chimed in. "I worry about that guy. A lot of people would like to see him disappear."

Frank picked up the phone and tried again. No answer. Fifteen minutes later, a cheerful, "Hello?" found its way from Wisconsin to New York.

"Hi, Doc," Frank said in an easygoing, friendly manner.

"Hi, Frank."

"Where've you been gallivantin' around?"

"I was at the Primate Center. There was a lot of work to do. Oh, by the way, thanks again for talking to me the other day, you're a real friend."

"Anytime, Doc. You know that."

"I certainly do. Anything I can do for you, Frank?"

"That's why I'm calling. Lenny and Paul are here and we were wonderin' what we could do to help those folks at Love Canal."

"Hmm..." Allen pondered the question. "Those folks want me on the Ecumenical Task Force because they know I am in favor of moving them all out. It might help if you found out how that mess developed. Dig up as much as you can. Turn it over to TV, newspapers, and radio so all of the news media will have it. It will make a real splash and help those people move out of Love Canal. The power of the press can do anything. I should know! It got me so depressed, I had the crazy idea of killing myself."

"Good thing you didn't, Doc. We need you." After hanging up, Frank turned to his buddies and said, "We've got work to do. We've got to find out how that mess at Love Canal got that way."

CHAPTER SIXTEEN

In ten days, the information was ferreted out, put together, and turned over to the news media. Three days later, the trio sat on the floor against the couch, knees drawn up, each holding and sipping a Schlitz. The CBS evening anchor was on.

"In the late 1950s, home building began next to the Love Canal landfill. More than one hundred homes were built. An elementary school opened. Thus were sown the seeds of a human and environmental disaster.

"The problem surfaced when chemical odors in basements became noticeable. This followed prolonged heavy rains and one of the worst blizzards ever to hit that section of the country. The events that followed were an environmental time bomb gone off. The bomb was dioxin.

"Paul Reutershan claims the same time bomb exploded in his body and is now killing him. Paul has inoperable cancer. Doctors do not give him much more time. Mr. Reutershan has been the spokesperson for a Vietnam veterans' organization that now boasts a membership of over eighty-nine thousand veterans. These brave men share the same tragedy as the residents of Love Canal."

"Whoo-ee!" whooped Lenny, "we're on national TV!" He jumped up from the floor and raised a fist in the air. "Yes!"

On the following day, Frank and his buddies lay on the floor with the newspaper stretched out in front of them. A column on page two read, "The rising crescendo of publicity reverberated in the Oval office and in the halls of Congress. Studies completed to date are sufficiently suggestive of a threat to public health. President Carter has therefore declared the region a disaster area. The state of New York purchased 239 abandoned homes from residents nearest the Love Canal dump site at a cost of $10 million. The state health commissioner came out with a recommendation that all pregnant women and children under age two evacuate the region immediately."

"Have you heard from the VA?" Frank asked.

Paul shook his head. "I don't expect to. They're not going to grant me disability benefits. They haven't given benefits to anyone."

"Even with this publicity," Lenny asked.

"That's right!" Paul replied, "even with this publicity. The VA keeps on saying, 'There is no scientific evidence that dioxin causes anything other than a rash.' Hell will freeze over before the VA changes its policy."

"Somethin's screwy," Lenny said, looking at Paul and then at Frank, waiting for an explanation as to why the government recognized the danger for Love Canal residents and not for Vietnam veterans.

"It's the same dioxin," Lenny said.

"That's right!" Paul replied. "It's the same dioxin, and it doesn't make sense. But it's been that way for a very long time. And I'm afraid it's not goin' to change."

SEVENTEEN

A BALD, ELDERLY GENTLEMAN SAT IN HIS OFFICE IN WASHINGTON, DC GOING through mail with his sleeves rolled up and tie loosened. A light blue cardigan hung on a hook on the wall behind him. His thoughts were on retirement. He'd been with Health Education and Welfare (HEW) for almost thirty years. Soon, he'd be living in sunny Florida in a Miami Beach condo with an ocean view. He planned to golf, swim, fish, or just plain loaf.

He was about to toss an envelope into a box on his desk when the name "Senator Proxmire" caught his attention. He opened it, read it, fixed his tie, rolled down his sleeves, and with one arm wrestling its way into the cardigan, hurried out and immediately carried Proxmire's letter to the Justice Department.

In one week, a team of auditors landed in Madison, Wisconsin. They piled out of the plane, were picked up by a van and taken to the University of Wisconsin. They stopped at Bascom Hall and went into the chancellor's office.

"We're from HEW," the team leader said, "our agency funded Dr. Allen's research, and we are here to audit his books."

They were escorted to the Office of Legal Affairs, where a command post was set up and managed by the head honcho who issued orders. The team fanned out and parked themselves in various offices. They began pouring over ledgers, records, phone logs, invoices, canceled checks, receipts, requests for reimbursements, and anything else they could find that showed Dr. Allen's expenditures.

"Good gosh!" one auditor exclaimed to the director of fiscal, "Allen's been here for going on eighteen years. His grants total five hundred thousand a year, and his research operation looks very complex. This audit will take months! It's hard to know where to start."

"Start anywhere. What would you like first?" the fiscal officer asked.

"Let's start with travel expense records," the auditor replied, already resigned to the tedious task ahead of him.

As auditors pulled records from files and carried them off, telephone lines hummed. Opinions flew around campus. Speculations surfaced, and rumors ran rampant. The talk was about the investigation of Professor Allen.

Allen felt devastated. Work was difficult, but he carried on with an outward pretense of composure. He followed the progress of monkeys in the 50 ppt dioxin experiment, started a new study using 25 ppt, and made plans for the 5 ppt to begin March 23, 1979. He kept up with the nitty-gritty of everyday work in addition to tending to the needs of his graduate students.

Meanwhile, Allen's colleagues kept long hours. When they became excited over a finding, he could not share their joy. He'd look at them, listen, and nod with a troubled, far-away look in his eyes. He was depressed again. On some days, he would wake up so fatigued that he couldn't make it into the office. He'd sit at the kitchen table and stare with dismay at headlines, wondering if it would ever come to an end.

Today's paper trumpeted another story. As usual, Rob Fixmer was the reporter. Old charges were repeated. Fixmer was not going to let his readers forget. He continued to call the mystery woman "Liv" because she had asked that her name and address be kept confidential.

"What kind of a name is Liv?" Allen wondered, "and why did she want her name kept secret?" As he read on, Allen was aghast at Fixmer's report.

"She had stuck it out long enough. Not one person, from the school dean to Allen's coworkers would agree to rock the boat. All seemed to feel it was better to look the other way. She went to Senator William Proxmire, who immediately turned her complaint over to the Department of Health Education and Welfare."

Allen tossed the paper aside and stared out of the window. The sun was shining, and Christie had urged him to get out of the house, sit on the verandah, take a walk down the road, do something, anything. But he didn't feel like it, and he just couldn't shake off this feeling. The phone rang. He looked at it with irritation, but picked up the receiver. It was Linda.

"Dr. Allen!" she said. "I'm hearing that doctors at the medical school are under investigation. A union steward filed a complaint about fraud and theft, but the rumors keep changing. I don't know what to believe, but the U.S. Attorney is calling for a grand jury investigation."

"Maybe Rob Fixmer will have something else to write about," Allen replied, scowling at the mouthpiece. He suddenly felt a bit more energetic.

CHAPTER SEVENTEEN

In spite of the added energy, Allen found it hard to get going. But he forced himself to shave, shower, and dress, get into the car, and head toward the university. As he drove along, he wondered why it was so hard for him to put up a fight when he found the going tough. Why wasn't he like his great-great-great-grandfather who fought in the battle of Bunker Hill, or his great-grandfather on his father's side, Colonel Lawrence Allen, who commanded the 64TH Regiment in North Carolina during the Civil War? They fought for what they believed in. He tried to carry on the family tradition by volunteering for the Naval Air Corps in World War II, but the navy no longer needed pilots, so he ended up a hospital corpsman. He never had to go through the hell of living in a foxhole or trying to take a beachhead with heavy enemy fire overhead. He had lived a more or less sheltered life in the navy.

His entire life had been sheltered. Growing up on a farm, working in a lab doing research, going to universities and getting degrees, moving up the ladder to a full professorship, giving lectures, publishing, building a team of professional staff, supervising students, attending conferences, being on committees, and overall living in an ivory tower, never really being exposed to the hard knocks of life.

"Maybe that's why I have this feeling," he said out loud, "that I'm being ganged up on and I don't know what to do. Oh well, better get going." As he pushed down on the accelerator, the car picked up speed and sped down the highway.

Unknown to Dr. Allen at the moment, there was talk at the university about many tenured professors going to jail and the possibility that without an adequate number of teachers, the university would close.

EIGHTEEN

The HEW auditor, with severe myopia, eyed the secretary's shapely ass as it wiggled by his cubicle on its way to the ladies room. He craned his neck out of the small space in which he was working, squinting hard, trying to keep the wiggle clearly in view. It began to blur! He watched it disappear behind the fuzzy outline of a swinging door.

He felt like chasing it! But what would his wife do if he got caught? Get a divorce? Demand custody of the kids? Fight for alimony? Would that really be bad? He could spend the rest of his life auditing professors like Dr. Allen. University life could be fun. Either way, he knew one thing for certain. He had to get glasses. Being nearsighted was a bitch.

Reluctantly, he turned his attention back to a long sheet he held in his left hand. His two hands worked the sheet, moving it downward while he scanned each phone call. The completed list trailed down to the floor and under his wooden chair. As the sheet neared its end, he suddenly stopped and drew a red circle around one of the numbers.

"That's it," he said to stacks of records covering every inch of his desk, "finished." He hurried out to join his comrades for a night on the town.

The team leader and his four cronies piled into a black limo in front of Bascomb Hall and were whisked away to the heart of downtown Madison. After two months of painstaking work, an evening out was something they looked forward to. It would help them unwind before pulling their findings together.

They sat around the table: white linen, heavy silverware, fine crystal, dim lighting, and a waiter in a tux taking orders. Martinis and scotch on the rocks settled them in. Caesar salad in wooden bowls and hot dinner rolls in a basket introduced the filet mignon, baked potato, asparagus, baby carrots, and peas that were about to be served. They downed everything with gusto, and everyone was in a festive mood. The table was cleared. A young man in a tux holding a small whisk broom brushed crumbs off the table into a silver receptacle in preparation for coffee and dessert.

"Okay," the team leader said, "what have we got?"

CHAPTER EIGHTEEN

"Nothing," said one auditor.

"Yeah, nothing," said another.

"Ditto for me," said a third auditor as he loosened his tie. The team leader looked at the man to his right. "I found something," he said. "Allen has been here for years. He receives five hundred thousand each year, and every dollar was accounted for, but from March 21, 1978, to March 21, 1979, there were four irregularities. He misused $892. It all occurred in one year, that seems strange."

"What did he do with the money?" one asked.

"Trips, four trips. On one, he took someone along."

"Was it business?" another auditor asked.

"I don't know. But even if it wasn't business, we've been here two months, and the only thing we found was a possible $892 theft and one illegal phone call to a friend. But for a guy with this kind of budget, we didn't find much of anything compared to what we usually find."

"Seems so," the team leader said. "But do you see what's going on at the school? They have an army of state and federal investigators stokin' the fire. Everyone from the chancellor down are shittin' in their pants, trying to keep the lid on. The entire school is on pins and needles, worried about the massive theft that is being uncovered. And here we are, investigating Dr. Allen and talking about a possible penny-ante theft. This guy must have some enemies out there who are really determined to get rid of him. Oh, here's our dessert, hot apple pie and chocolate ice cream. Dig in, guys."

The first heavy snowfall dumped six feet of snow on the central lowlands of Madison. Cars stalled in the middle of the streets. People shoveled valiantly, trying to free their vehicles. Snowplows moved through thoroughfares, piling snow curbside. School closings were reported on television. Most businesses shut down.

But some people made it in to work. After three hours of inching along, Dr. Allen finally pulled into the plowed parking lot adjacent to the Primate Center. Bundled in a fur-lined coat, he hurried inside, where the controlled temperature began to take the chill out of his bones.

Once inside, he disarmed the security system, hurried to Rickey Marlar's old office, and hung his coat in a closet. Picking up a clipboard, he strolled into the corridor where monkeys shrieked and cages rattled. The jarring sounds bounced off the concrete walls, traveling the length of the corridor. As he neared cages, hands reached out between the bars, eager for contact.

Allen inspected every monkey in the 50 ppt dioxin study, a sickly, pathetic group. He made notes of hair loss from the entire body, dry flaky skin, eyelashes thinning out, and small hemorrhages on the gums and on the inner lining of the mouth, just as he had anticipated. It was happening! The fifty group was no different than the five hundred. So far, his theory held up. There was no safe level for dioxin. It was deadly in any amount.

Allen then checked the new group, three and one-half weeks into the study: happy monkeys, eating their chow with an appetite, getting 25 ppt of dioxin. Hands reached out for him. They wanted to be touched. Allen stroked their smooth skin and pictured how it would look years from now. His heart ached for all of them.

Having finished, Allen donned his coat, armed the security pad on the wall, pulled his collar up, and went from a tropical rain forest environment to a freezing snowstorm.

He knew the HEW audit was over and worried, as did other grim-faced professors who had already been called before the grand jury.

Allen trudged through the snow to the next building, carefully climbed up the snow-covered stairs, pulled open the doors, and headed toward his office. Once inside, he unbuttoned his coat, threw it over a chair, and dropped into his swivel. He stared at the paperwork and mail in the inbox on his desk. Since Linda couldn't make it in, he decided to open the mail and do whatever needed attending to.

Allen pulled open a drawer and picked up a silver-bladed letter opener. He began opening envelopes: bills for monkey chow, syringes, and latex gloves. The last bill was for ketamine. It reminded him of Rickey Marlar.

A soft rap on his partly open door interrupted his thoughts. One of the auditors poked his head in. "Got a minute?" he asked, stepping inside.

Allen was annoyed at the sight of the man with the potbelly hanging over his belt. This man had been tight-lipped for the past two months, never a friendly word, not even a hello. He'd barge in, ask for something as if it had been hidden, and now he politely says, "Got a minute?"

Without waiting for a reply, the auditor continued, "We're catching a morning flight." He paused and carefully chose each word. "After such an audit, we normally sit down and talk. We

CHAPTER EIGHTEEN

ask questions to better understand some of our findings. In your case," he hesitated, "we didn't do that. You have enemies in high places."

Allen's eyes widened. "Do I need a lawyer?"

"If it were me, I'd seek counsel. And one more thing," he said, opening his right hand, "I found this bug in one of your files. Here, take it."

Allen was stunned. He dropped the letter opener on his lap, took the bug with the tips of his fingers, and watched the auditor go. He stared at the small metallic object. He remembered Frank telling him about bugs. They were always planted in groups of three. Was this the fool's bug? Who planted it? Enemies in high places? If only the auditor had told him more.

Lenny Laviano and Frank had warned him. Someone was out to get him. He desperately needed a good lawyer. The only one he knew was a tax attorney who did his yearly tax return. Allen felt his heart pounding as fear and anxiety welled up inside him. He fingered the button-like microphone. Was someone listening at the other end?

NINETEEN

Paul Reutershan opened his eyes. The light was dim. A siren was screaming. He felt rapid movement, twists and turns, and knew he was strapped down in an ambulance. He looked up at the man in white who sat beside him, checking his pulse. He could not remember what happened, and he was hurting all over.

The paramedic saw his eyes open. "You've been in an accident," he said, "try not to move."

Paul nodded. He tried to remember something about the accident, but all he could think of was the excruciating pain in his body and his throbbing head. He closed his eyes.

"We're almost there," the paramedic said.

The ambulance began to slow, then came to a stop as the siren went dead. Doors opened, and Paul felt himself being lifted out into the cold air. He heard a snap and click, the cart was moving, a swish of doors, a brightly lit corridor, men and women in green, with stethoscopes hanging from their necks, running alongside him, talking and issuing orders.

"Start an IV, 5 percent saline," someone shouted.

Paul wanted to scream, "I've got cancer! Incurable cancer! Why bother? End it now!" He opened his mouth, but nothing came out.

Memories swirled in his head. He remembered home. His medication was low, and his sister Jane had her coat on, telling him to rest. He refused because Dr. Allen told him to keep busy, keep going, do things. If he slowed down, there'd be too much time to think. He remembered getting on his motorcycle, and his thoughts were suddenly jarred back to the emergency room.

Paul was being wheeled out, head done up in bandages, his right leg and body bound up in a cast. A bottle of fluid hanging from a hook, dripping, and tubing angling down to his arm. An elevator going up, wheeled alongside a bed and lifted onto it, and his mother and sister standing beside him.

"How do you feel?" Jane asked.

"Okay," he said, not wanting to complain. "What hospital is this?"

"Highland Park," Jane replied. "When the police called, I told them to bring you here."

CHAPTER NINETEEN

Wanting to cheer him up, his mother piped in, "I've got a letter from the VA. They sent you a disability check. It's in my purse."

"VA, a check?' Paul murmured. "They agreed I was poisoned by Agent Orange?"

"No, they didn't say it was from Agent Orange, but it's your first check. You will get one every month."

"What happened?" Paul asked, turning to his sister.

"A car hit your motorcycle. You have a few broken bones and a concussion."

"I don't remember. I do remember those two men following me again, they had a camera. By the way, what day is this? I have to meet Yannacone on Friday. He's turning my case into a class action suit."

"It's Tuesday," Jane said, "twenty-two days before Christmas. Meetings will have to wait. You are not going anywhere."

Paul knew she was right. He felt totally exhausted. He closed his eyes and began to doze, leaving his mother and sister standing at his bedside.

The next day, Paul was pleased when Lenny Laviano and Frank McCarthy walked into his room.

"Hi, guy," Frank said, "you're gonna need a new motorcycle. The old one's a smash."

"Ha ha," Paul replied "a one-liner, pretty good."

"We brought you a copy of the newsletter," Lenny said.

Paul fingered it fondly. The AOVI motto stood boldly at the top of the page. It said, "With Dignity, Self-Respect and Solidarity."

"Nice," Paul said.

Paul looked at a photo of C-123s flying in formation over the jungles of Vietnam. Sheets of white mist shot out of spray nozzles anchored beneath each wing. He remembered his helicopter days, his men, and the agony they had all shared since leaving Vietnam.

"Jane told us you were followed again," Frank said.

"Yeah," Paul murmured.

"I'll bet those guys are from Dow," Lenny said angrily. "I'd like to do a number on 'em. What have I got to lose? I'm dyin' and it would feel good to take a few along with me."

"No violence," Paul reminded him. "Remember our motto."

"Yeah, yeah, I remember. Dignity and all the other stuff. But there's a lot of guys out there who'd vote for Plan B. How much crap do we have to take?"

A nurse walked in. "You'll have to leave now," she said.

December seventh. Paul found himself breathing more rapidly, heart racing, tired. All he could do was sleep.

"Hi, sleepyhead!" Jane stood beside his bed looking down at her brother. "Got some interesting news."

Paul opened his eyes. "Hi, sis."

"Read this from President Carter."

Paul wondered if the president would ever respond to his claim that Agent Orange had caused his cancer. National television and radio had carried his message. He had been successful in getting the word out. But the president had remained silent—until now. He reached out and took the letter. It read:

Dear Mr. Reutershan:

President Carter has asked me to respond to your message and convey his thanks. You can be assured that careful consideration is given to all suggestions from those who share his concern for the well being of the nation.

Landon Kite, White House aide

"It's a BS letter," Paul said with disgust, handing it back to Jane.

She crumpled it in her hand, wanting to offer a word of encouragement. What could she say? She stood there thinking about her baby brother. His appearance on TV and radio, his outspoken stance against the military, the VA, the government, and Dow chemical, his fight to uncover the truth, his concern for all Vietnam veterans and his ongoing accusation against Dow and the U.S. government regarding its responsibility for his murder. Jane could still hear his cry, "I died in Vietnam and didn't know it!"

CHAPTER NINETEEN

Jane marveled at the organization he started, the friendships he had made, and his burning desire to establish a foundation to help Vietnam veterans and their families. Jane knew he would soon pass the baton to someone else. She knew the end was near. His doctor gave him less than a week.

December eighth, Paul was feeling better. He asked that the head of his bed be raised so he could talk more comfortably with Lenny and Frank.

"Great article," Paul said as he read about the formation of a new Agent Orange Victims International Chapter in Ohio. It told of Russ and Ann Humphrey of Sugar Creek Township and the problems they and others encountered from exposure to Agent Orange. It told of the typical governmental brick wall they'd run into: medical records destroyed, records that proved the link between Agent Orange and the health problems of an alarming number of Vietnam veterans and their families.

"We wrote Russ a letter on your behalf, thanking him for starting a new chapter," Frank said.

"Thanks," Paul said. "When I'm gone," he went on, "I'd like you to take over, Frank. Lenny's got cancer. You're the best one to head up the organization."

"I'd be honored," Frank said, "but who told you it was time to check out? Do you have a pipeline to God?" Frank found it hard to deal with this good-bye. There had been so many tearful good-byes over the years…heart-wrenching good-byes.

Paul smiled. "Absolutely! I talk to God every day. I know he is listening, and sometimes… God talks back to me. This morning, he told me to ask you guys to put my sister and mom on the organization's board of directors. Give them something to do. I know the organization is for vets, but Jane would be a good secretary. Mom would be an excellent treasurer, she's good with money. She can turn one penny into two."

Lenny and Frank forced a smile, nodding their approval while fighting back tears. "One other thing," Paul said. "That check on the dresser, I'm not endorsing it. Return it to the VA with a note saying, 'Shove it.'"

"Do you really want me to say that?" Lenny asked. "You of all people. The one who lectured me about dignity, self-respect, and solidarity."

Paul grinned. "Touche."

December tenth.

Muriel Reutershan and Jane Dziedzic held hands as they faced the doctor. "It will happen any time now. I'm so sorry," the doctor said.

He explained that following the accident, the cancer no longer responded to medication. The malignant cells had been set free, rapidly invading Paul's body, destroying everything.

They watched as Paul lapsed in and out of consciousness. They watched him grow weaker. All they could do was be with him, hold his hand, cry, stroke his forehead, and cry again. They sat all day and into the night, waiting. In the early morning hours on December 14, 1978, Paul died. Burial arrangements were made in Peekskill, an upstate New York town. Family and friends gathered, listened, and participated in the ceremony. Tears flowed freely as the casket was lowered into the ground. As Frank wiped his eyes, he noticed a distracting presence on a hilly slope in the distance: two men with cameras, taking pictures.

"Look," Frank nudged Lenny. Other Vietnam veterans also looked.

"Let's get those bastards," Frank said angrily.

They chased the intruders all the way to their car, but the men sped away as Frank jotted down the license number. Frank called a friend, a cop, a fellow Vietnam veteran. The car was traced to a detective agency. Days later, Frank saw the same two men on his tail. He discovered that others had been following Lenny and all the other AOVI board members.

Frank had had enough. He drove to Victor Yannacone's office. "I've had it!" he shouted. "Our guys are not gonna put up with this shit. There's going to be violence, and I can't stop it. Those two men followed me here. If you look out the window, you will see their car half a block away."

"That's it!" Victor exclaimed, slamming his hand on the desk. "Maybe it's time for Plan B." He picked up the phone and called Lenny Rifkin, one of Dow's attorneys in New York who was involved in defending Dow against the Vietnam veteran's lawsuit. "Lenny," Victor said, "if your guys from the detective agency aren't called off in fifteen minutes, I am going to distribute the photographs, names, and addresses of every Dow executive, from the president down, including the board of directors. Vietnam vets dying of cancer know how to kill. And if I give the okay, they'll kill." Victor slammed the phone down.

Frank stood by the window. In minutes, the car pulled away.

CHAPTER NINETEEN

On the following day, the AOVI board members met in the Greenwich Village basement apartment that doubled as Frank McCarthy's office. He named it the Bunker. It was below ground level with two small windows that looked out at a patch of grass, a sidewalk, and a two-lane street. Beyond the street was a long stretch of park with scrubby grass, trees, and shrubs.

The apartment was a small space, hidden from the sun but comfortable. Walking down a short flight of stairs, a door opened into the living room-den of sorts, lit by a bare bulb screwed into a socket on the ceiling. The room housed a mismatch of used furniture: a tan leather couch pushed against the far wall, a black, wrought iron stand holding a small TV against a side wall, its rabbit ear antennae spread apart. At the other end of the room, pushed tight to the wall, stood a fiery red thing. It was four feet long with a high, curved, and padded back, soft velvety seats and armrests. It stood on ornately carved wooden legs. Except for its threadbare appearance, it was fit for a king or queen.

Frank and Lenny carried folding chairs from a bedroom closet into the den while members stood in small groups talking quietly. No one had yet taken a seat. No one was in the mood for a board meeting. Many of them, including Muriel and Jane, were looking at a framed photo on the wall. It was Paul, kneeling on the ground in front of Frank and other buddies, some in uniform, others in wheelchairs.

Muriel nudged Jane and motioned her to a wall above the couch. Two wooden frames hung side by side. In one was a Bronze Star for valor, in the other was a Purple Heart for wounds received in action. Muriel and Jane had never been in Frank's apartment and knew nothing of his Vietnam experience. It was something he never talked about.

Suddenly, Frank shouted, "Hey, guys! There's cold drinks and food in the kitchen. Help yourselves."

Jane and Muriel hurried over to Frank, who was sitting on the edge of his red thing, legs crossed in front of him. Muriel wondered where this unusual piece of furniture came from, but decided not to ask. She was concerned about the delay in starting the meeting.

"What are we waiting for?" she asked. "Why don't we start?"

Frank looked up. "Nobody's in the mood. I'd like to call the meeting off. We can meet next week."

"Don't you dare, Frank McCarthy!" Muriel said in a feisty tone. "Jane and I have something to say!"

Frank acknowledged her request by standing and hollering, "Would everyone please take a seat? Some will have to sit on the floor, there's not enough chairs."

He waved Muriel and Jane to the folding chairs next to the card table. They were secretary and treasurer of the organization, and as officers, they were entitled to sit at the head of the room with him. Frank leaned forward, arms on the table, and looked out at the group.

One member on the floor looked up at Frank and said, "This place really looks like a bunker, Frank, especially with those two narrow windows with a ground-level view to the outside."

"Yeah," Frank replied. "This place has a real feel. I love it."

Muriel raised her hand high in the air after some hesitation.

"You don't need permission to talk," Frank said softly.

His gentle reassurance gave her what she needed to speak her mind.

"Well," she said, "it's so dark in here. That bulb on the ceiling is the only light in this room. A sixty-watt bulb would brighten things up. A one hundred–watt would be better. And I'd like to plant some flowers in that scrubby lawn on the other side of those windows." And after reflecting for a moment, she went on, "Tulips would be nice."

Frank stared at this tiny woman who had never been to his apartment, who suddenly had the audacity to come up with a plan to change the Bunker into a who-knows-what kind of place.

"Muriel, I like it this way," he said. "It feels like a real bunker."

"Well, I haven't ever been in a bunker, but if I were in one, I would not enjoy looking out at a patch of grass, a wrought iron fence, a cracked sidewalk, and a two-lane street with lots of traffic. Tulips would hide all that. Tulips would be beautiful."

With Paul still in everyone's heart, the solemnity of the moment was somewhat lifted by this gentle, yet forceful woman who seemed determined to get her way. But Lenny, who reclined on the couch, was irked. Even if she was Paul Reutershan's mother, who was she to suggest changing the bunker? Flowers would block the view to the outside! A bulb with more light would allow someone to see inside more easily! A sharpshooter could easily pick off anyone who popped into view at the window. Everything about the bunker was part of a larger

CHAPTER NINETEEN

plan that he, Frank, and Paul had talked about. They agreed upon it soon after Victor Yannacone changed Paul's suit into a class action case.

Everyone recognized the power of the chemical companies. They had billions! They were firmly entrenched with influential politicians. What if Vietnam vets didn't receive justice, what could they do? Long discussions ended with an agreement on Plan B. It was perilous, but there were times people had to die in order to get change. The veterans could kill many Dow executives if necessary, even if it meant they too would ultimately die. The bunker would be their stronghold. It would allow them one last battle, one last stand. It would send a powerful message.

To prepare for such a contingency, Frank pulled his uniform out of storage as well as his helmet and an M-16, a fully automatic weapon that had saved his life on more than one occasion. He bought army surplus ammo and other weapons. The M-16 would soon be on display in the Bunker.

Lenny wanted Muriel to mind her own business. "Frank," he said, interrupting Muriel, "none of us are in the mood for business. Let's call the meeting off."

Frank glanced at Muriel. Before he could reply, Muriel looked at Lenny and gently said, "I agree. Neither Jane nor I feel like talking business. But couldn't we all plan for Paul's gravestone? You were his friends. It would be nice if we did it together, Jane and I would appreciate it, we really would."

The room was silent. "I'd like that," Frank finally said, looking around, checking for consensus.

"Me too," someone said. Heads nodded, including Lenny's.

Weeks later, Jane and her mother found themselves at the gravesite, surrounded by members of the Board. They came to unveil a simple gravestone. It read:

Paul Reutershan
March 24, 1950–December 14, 1978

Unselfishly You Gave In Your Time Of Suffering So That Others Might Be Saved. This Gift Shall Stand As A Testament Of Your Courage, Strength and Faith.

Friend Of The Earth, Lover Of Life
You Know The Joy Of Being One
With God.

"I'd like to say a few words," Frank said, kneeling down and touching the polished brown stone. "Paul was a friend who talked about a foundation, one that would provide for Vietnam vets, their wives, and their kids. He knew it would take a lot of money. Millions. Let us bow our heads and pray for what we are about to undertake, a class action suit that could raise those millions. Victor Yannacone will soon be going to court to file that suit. As we stand here, I know Paul is listening. I know he is up there talking to God, getting the word out."

TWENTY

Dr. Allen was in a Bagel Place, a busy cafeteria, facing a heavily trafficked street. He sat on a padded barstool with his face to the window, waiting to report to the grand jury at one in the afternoon. The soles of his shoes rested on the middle rung of the stool, and his knees were under the counter. He felt tense and apprehensive. He felt as if his life was unraveling. He sat there, staring at the slushy street, the piles of snow that had been pushed curbside, and the slow, bumper-to-bumper traffic.

Christie sat next to him, breaking off pieces of banana-nut muffin, sipping coffee, chewing and waiting, the interminable waiting.

People spun their way through the revolving door for a quick lunch while wall-to-wall people and long lines of those waiting to get seated buzzed in low-key conversations. Waitresses jotted down orders and hurried off while busboys carried away dirty dishes with half-eaten leftovers, then wiped off tables at a furious pace. It was a jovial crowd carrying on business as usual.

But Dr. Allen saw none of this. He was deeply lost in thought, fearful of what might happen when he walked into the U.S. District Courthouse, a gray stone building down the block with a wide, intimidating stairway. What was he being accused of? What had he done wrong?

He poured himself another cup of coffee from the pot on the counter, took a flask from his hip pocket, and poured a generous second helping of Kahlua into the brew. He sipped it, smacking his lips, It was tasty, just what he needed. Tension was starting to ease.

It was a typical cold January afternoon with heavy traffic, horns honking, and people walking rapidly, their heads bent, protecting themselves from the sudden gusts of swirling snow. He watched a lone jogger hugging the curb, moving along at a steady pace, seemingly oblivious to traffic and the elements around him.

"I need to be like that," Allen thought, "just got to keep on going despite all the challenges around me." But Dr. Allen was not accustomed to fighting.

"What am I doing here?" he said to his wife. "I should be at the Primate Center, drawing blood, photographing the monkeys, meeting with staff to prepare the abstract for the 50 ppt study. It's ready for publication and...look at me. I'm in front of a U.S. Courthouse pumping alcohol and caffeine into my body."

"It'll be over soon," Christie said, trying to reassure him. "You've done nothing wrong. How can they do anything to you?"

"I know I've done nothing wrong, but I'm here! I'm testifying before the grand jury. They could indict me. Look at what's happening to other professors. There's talk of criminal charges and of prison. You know, Christie, I'm really afraid."

"But you know you've done nothing wrong. And not everyone is being indicted," Christie replied. "Folkert Belzer, the chairman of the Surgery Department, and Professor Bach received letters of reprimand. Nothing happened to them, so don't start talking of prison."

Allen filled his cup and added more Kahlua. Sipping it, he felt better, more relaxed. He could think more clearly. It was true. Others hadn't gone to prison; they were still at the university. Maybe his situation would amount to a slight infraction of some bureaucratic regulation. Maybe it would all come to nothing.

"I'd feel better if Kessler was here telling me what to expect," Allen said, "and giving me advice. Even though he's a tax lawyer, he must know something about the grand jury. He did tell me that he would not be allowed in the courtroom because grand jury hearings are secret. He also told me that Frank Tuerkheimer, the U.S. Attorney, would be in charge."

Christie frowned and spoke up strongly. "I don't feel good about Kessler, he's a tax lawyer. You should have a criminal lawyer, like Frank said."

"I told that to Kessler," Allen replied, "and he recommended Jim Robbins, an attorney in his office, in case something bad happens."

"Stop with the bad! Please," Christie said.

The Kahlua had calmed him. It was 12:40 p.m., only twenty minutes to go. "I should eat something," Allen said, glancing at the half-eaten banana nut muffin. "Are you going to finish that?"

"I'm not hungry," she replied, pushing the muffin over to him. "Do you want me to go in with you?"

"You're not allowed in the courtroom, and I don't know if there's a place for you to sit in the corridor. Wait here."

CHAPTER TWENTY

Sitting on a barstool, Christie watched her husband hurry down the block, up the stairs, and disappear inside the courthouse. She drained the last cup of coffee from the pot and sipped it slowly even though it was no longer hot.

She sat, watching the traffic and the crowd. Across the street, a tall man, thin like a beanpole, stood laughing at a cabbie who held his arm out of the window, shaking his fist at cars in front of him. The traffic stalled, and the cabbie kept shaking his fist without let-up. Beanpole thought it was funny. Christie saw nothing funny about it. She was in no mood for humor. She suddenly wished she had some Kahlua.

TWENTY-ONE

Two hours later, Christie was still sitting in Bagel Place. The lines were gone except for stragglers still talking and draining coffee from pots. Tables were empty, and seating was plentiful. But Christie remained perched on the barstool, her black leather shoes dangling eight inches from the floor. With her face to the window, elbows on the countertop, and fingers laced under her chin, she dozed.

The owner angrily hollered for a busboy, pointing to a corner table in disarray and then hurried over to Christie while wiping his hands on a dirty white apron that hung down to his knees. The scowl on his face gave him an ominous look. Leaning his sweaty, balding head close to Christie's face, he saw her eyes closed and listened to the slow, rhythmic breathing.

He drew himself up to his tallest, most commanding demeanor and shouted, "Hey, lady! Wake up!"

She opened her eyes with a start, blinked, and focused her gaze on a man with a scowl on his face. For an instant, Christie did not know where she was.

"Oh," she said, yawning, stretching her neck, rubbing fog from her eyes with both hands. "I'm sorry, I must have dozed off."

"What you think this is!" he went on. "My establishment is not for sleeping! Eat or get out!" The scowl stayed in place.

"I said I'm sorry," she replied, easing herself off the barstool and tossing a quick glance out the window. "I'm waiting for my husband. He's still in the courthouse."

"You can't wait here!" his voice rose, and he reached out with the intention of taking Christie by the arm and showing her to the door, but she had had enough.

"You put one finger on me," she yelled, "and I'll haul your ass into court and sue you for every cup and saucer in this dump."

Bald Head pulled his hand back, and the scowl on his face vanished. He stood speechless. He glanced around, wanting assistance from a waitress who was chatting with two women at a far table, but his silent call for help went unanswered. He backed away, bowing and extending

CHAPTER TWENTY-ONE

his arm toward the door. He decided to extend her courtesy and respect, but he wanted the bitch out.

Christie threw him an up-and-down glance, stopping momentarily to look down at his sweaty, bald head, and then sauntered out. As the door closed behind her, she saw Bald Head through the window wiping his brow with the apron, growling at the waitress, who stood looking at him with eyes and mouth wide open.

The sun was no longer high in the sky, and sidewalks began to freeze up again. Walking was hazardous. Traffic had thinned out and was flowing smoothly. Christie crossed the street at the intersection a half-block away, taking care not to fall. With small steps, she made her way toward the courthouse.

The sidewalk near the courthouse was still busy with people rushing in and out. An old man bundled in rags, bearded and dirty, sat on an orange crate near the bottom step. He looked up at men hurrying down the steps.

"Change for a hungry man?" he said, holding out a tin cup with a dollar bill and change inside.

As Christie approached, she looked up at the American flag flapping briskly in the breeze, then lowered her gaze to the old beggar. Opening her purse, she took out a handful of change and dropped it into his cup.

The beggar smiled, his grateful blue eyes looked up at her. "Thank you," he said.

Christie's gaze followed the flow of men, some disappearing behind the revolving doors while others suddenly appeared, coming out. It was turning colder, and she began shivering. She thought of going inside and finding a place to sit, but she had already clocked over two hours on that barstool and hadn't jogged for a week. Walking up and back would be good exercise, and she would be there when Jim came out.

An argument between two bystanders, cars honking, a dog barking, and the wind howling in downtown Madison did not distract Christie from her thoughts. They were on Jim and the day they met.

It was 1943. She was on surgical ward number six at the Portsmouth Naval Hospital. Dr. Allen was delivering newspapers to men back from Okinawa. These were men who had been badly wounded. The GIs paid for a paper, but the amount was so small, it was almost free. She wanted a paper. The previous sailor had given it to her at no charge, and she wanted Allen to continue with the same free service. After all, Christie was a hard-working nurse, and an officer with the rank of ensign.

"You have to pay for this, ma'am," Allen murmured with some trepidation.

Allen was a lowly enlisted man talking to a superior, and he felt uncomfortable being asked to break rules. He had been told to collect three cents for every paper, and three cents it had to be.

"The other man gave me a free paper," she firmly replied, taking full advantage of her superior rank.

"I understand, ma'am, but rules are rules."

"It's only three cents," she retorted.

"That's right, ma'am," Allen persisted. "It's only three cents."

Ensign Christie Smith let him have it. "You are just a cheapskate!" She grabbed a newspaper from a stack under his arm and held it tight.

James Rex Allen didn't know what to do. How could the lowest man on the totem pole say something nasty or make out a report on a superior officer? She would probably file charges and have him court-marshaled for refusing to obey an order. Insubordination would not look good on his record. And who knows what else might happen?

"Ma'am," he said. "Can we settle this?"

"Explain yourself," she replied, maintaining a superior attitude.

"Ma'am, could we come to an amicable agreement?"

"Explain yourself!"

"I'll pay the three cents every day if you go out with me now and then."

"That's against the rules! It's not allowed. Officers can't socialize with enlisted men, you know that!"

"Well, ma'am," James Rex Allen said, "I'm paying for the newspaper instead of you. That's kind of breaking the rules, and if I'm willing, how about you?"

Christie remembered how funny it all was, how she smiled, and how they both laughed.

Her thoughts were interrupted by a police officer scurrying down the steps with a walkie-talkie in his hand. "Excuse me," he said, "you've been up and back so many times and you keep looking at the door. Can I help you?"

CHAPTER TWENTY-ONE

"Yes. My husband was called before the grand jury at one. It's now four forty-five and I'm worried."

"They started on hour late, somewhere around two. Would you like to come in and wait?" Christie exclaimed gratefully, "I would like that. Thank you."

She followed the officer through the revolving door. She was awed by the magnificence of the lobby, a spacious hall with banks of elevators on both sides, marble walls and floor, tall pillars, and winding stairs circling up to different levels and wide corridors branching off in all directions.

"You can wait over there," the officer pointed to a stone bench against a wall. "Everyone comes out this way, you can't miss him."

"Thank you," she replied. Turning, she moved away from the security area that guarded entry to the courthouse. Christie welcomed the opportunity to sit and thaw out. Her toes had become numb.

Again, her thoughts drifted back to the naval hospital. Jim was tall and thin. He looked like a teenager ready to try out for baseball. He was handsome. Soon, they were on their first date without reprimands from higher-ups. The dating continued, and she had fallen in love. They continued seeing each other until that awful day when she was handed a transfer to the Norfolk Naval Hospital.

Her thoughts were suddenly interrupted. She saw him bouncing down a staircase that wound its way from the second landing. He was smiling, energetic, and looking good, head erect. Yes, he was himself again.

As he neared the first landing, Jim saw Christie and waved. She hurried to the bottom of the landing, and in seconds, he threw his arms around her, for a hug and a long kiss. With his arm around her waist, they walked past the officer who nodded in recognition. The revolving door held each of them for only a second, and they were outside, going down the steps. The beggar sat at the bottom with his tin cup.

Christie opened her purse, took out a five dollar bill and dropped it in. The beggar stared at it, his eyes open wide. He looked up at them and said, "God bless you."

117

TWENTY-TWO

By mid-January 1979, Frank's apartment began to take on the look of a real bunker gearing up for a war. Before, it had qualified for a fortification of sorts, but after Victor Yannacone filed the class action suit, Frank pulled his uniform, helmet, and M-16 out of storage. Army surplus ammo and other weapons were brought in: an M-14 rifle with a twenty-round magazine, a semiautomatic assault weapon, a bazooka and two rockets, two semiautomatic handguns, and an M-60 machine gun. Should Dow cause trouble, Frank and his guys were ready.

Victor Yannacone and his consortium of lawyers also prepared for battle. But their fight was to be waged in a courtroom. Their ammunition would be evidence showing the deadly effects of dioxin.

They filed class action suits in U.S. District Courts in twenty cities. The plaintiffs were Vietnam veterans who asked for compensation for damages caused by Agent Orange. The defendants were Dow, Hercules, Thompson-Hayward, Diamond-Shamrock, Monsanto Chemical, and Uniroyal.

"These companies destroyed our lives," the veterans said, "we're sick and dying because of dioxin. Our wives and children are going through hell."

Almost overnight, more than six hundred veterans joined the suit. Victor Yannacone took pride in being the lead attorney for some of the most prestigious law firms in the country. He took pleasure when he pointed to U.S. District Courts in twenty cities, knowing his suit had suddenly become the largest product liability case ever filed. Billions were at stake.

"We're going after them big time," Yannacone told Frank.

"Great!" Frank replied. "It's gonna be a dream come true. And it's not just the money, but at last we are going to be heard. That's what is so great!"

Frank McCarthy and all the board members whooped it up when Yannacone served notice on the chemical companies, forcing them to come up with documents. Among them were memoranda going back fourteen years. The Dow memoranda told of surprisingly high

CHAPTER TWENTY-TWO

amounts of toxic impurities in their own and in competitive products. Dow also revealed tests done on rabbits and reported, "Liver damage is severe, and a no-effect level, based on liver response, has not yet been established. There is some evidence it is systemic."

The Vietnam veterans were ecstatic. This showed that Dow had knowledge about the danger of dioxin and kept it secret for years. The same document told why.

Donald Baldwin, a Dow vice president, was afraid the situation might explode. He knew his competitors were marketing 2,4,5-T with alarming amounts of dioxin, and if the government heard about it, the whole industry would suffer. A Congressional investigation on the manufacture of herbicides and restrictive legislation was something they had to avoid.

Jubilation faded when the veterans were told, "Dow refused to turn over twenty-five studies." They were locked in a vault and their self-righteous claim was national security. It was then that Frank thought about Plan B. If the suit turned sour, Frank would talk with his guys and maybe take a trip. The knew about vaults.

One week later, Frank and Lenny were in the Bunker. "Let's give Doc a call," Lenny said as he sat on the floor, rubbing a soft cloth on the barrel of the M-16. "Maybe he knows something about this national security crap."

Frank was at a table, sipping a Fresca and watching Lenny put a shine on the fully automatic rifle. "Good idea. We can see how he's doing," Frank said, picking up the receiver and flicking a switch on his new speakerphone.

He loved it because everyone in the room could get their two cents worth in during a conversation. They could bring Victor's booming voice into the room to settle heated debates about the lawsuit. And now and then, they could all talk with Dr. Allen.

"Hello...?" came the voice out of the speakerphone. It was loud, bouncing off walls. Frank adjusted volume control.

"Hi, Doc! Just wanna touch base with you and ask a question," Frank said, taking aim and tossing the empty Fresca can across the room, missing the basket. "Lenny's here too."

"Hi, Doctor Allen! I've got the answer to all of our problems," Lenny hollered, holding up the automatic rifle with both hands.

"Don't mind him, Doc, he's always clowning around," Frank said, motioning and shaking his head vigorously.

The finding of a bug in Allen's office continued to be a real worry. Frank did not want it known that he had an M-16. His own place was clean, but Allen's home and office had not yet been completely checked out.

"Hi, guys," Allen replied, savoring the use of a term he had acquired from Frank.

"Sounds good, Doc," Frank chuckled. "It's about time you started using real English instead of all that scientific jargon that nobody understands. The word 'guys' has a nice sound to it."

"It does, Frank. I like it."

"Doc, I'd like to ask a question, knowing your phone could still be bugged. Feel free not to answer. In your line of work, could there be a scientific study where the results are legally denied under the claim that the release of the findings would jeopardize national security?"

"I'm not afraid to answer questions," Allen said firmly. "If someone wants to listen, let them! As long as I'm not doing anything wrong, why should I care? As to your question, it reminds me of Senator Hart's hearings in 1970 on the hazards and dangers of dioxin. Testimony by Wellford and Turner called for a total ban on the use of 2,4,5-T on food crops. Their data was overwhelmingly convincing. They pointed out the ridiculous situation where the FDA recommended that marketing of unsafe products be stopped while the Department of Agriculture rejected this advice nearly all of the time."

"But why would Agriculture not ban unsafe food?" Frank asked. "And what would that have to do with national security?"

"Doctor Byerly from Agriculture cited a study by Velmar Davis and went on to say that without herbicides there would be an added cost of more than two billion a year to grow crops. And we could grow them only if we had enough hoes and people to do the hoeing. That was in 1970. What would it cost today? And if we didn't have people to do the hoeing, what would happen to our economy? Could there be mass starvation? Possibly, and this could apply to national security."

"Wow! That's really something!" Frank exclaimed, watching Lenny rub a little faster, putting more shine on the side of the stock. "What kind of studies could Dow be hiding?'

After a pause, Allen replied, "Dow has a large number of scientists. They know how deadly dioxin is. Their studies in the vault may show that our government should have banned those

CHAPTER TWENTY-TWO

herbicides years ago. But you know the government, Frank. You and your guys know those bastards better than anyone else."

"That's the first swear word I've heard you use, Doc."

"I know. There's a first time for everything, Frank."

"Let it out more often, Doc. There are a lot of bastards out there, and they're tryin' to do you in, I'd bet on it."

"I've been wondering. Any word on the whereabouts of Kathryn Anderson?" Allen asked.

"Not a trace. That gal just disappeared. And believe me, she did not do it on her own. And she didn't get hired the way she did without someone pushing the right button and calling the shots. And that bug in your office didn't just crawl in. And the missing data didn't just walk away. And Rickey Marlar's death wasn't an accident. I could go on and on, Doc. All of it was planned! Don't you see? They're out to get you. By the way, what did Cartwright say about the letter from Kociba?"

"He thought I knew about it. He felt there was no reason for him to show it to me. Kociba supposedly sent me a copy."

"Did you ever reach Kociba?"

"I tried, but he never returned my calls."

"And that letter was about PCBs. You said high levels could flush your work down the drain. Seems to me Dow is trying to discredit you. I can't see it any other way. And with the government breathing down your neck, you've got real trouble. You know, Doc, if those two have joined forces, it would explain everything that's happened: the missing data, the Anderson gal, the break in, the bug, and the auditing of records. Oh! How did the grand jury go?"

"I explained everything, and from the looks on their faces, I think it went well. When the U.S. Attorney asked me about the one illegal phone call, some jurors smiled, as if it was a funny kind of question. Imagine! One illegal phone call in seventeen years. If I wasn't so nervous, I would have pointed out how ridiculous that question was. And as far as the swapping of $892, they seemed to understand why researchers swap money from one program to another. But I have to believe that the U.S. Attorney wants to send me to prison."

"One of my guys checked him out, Doc. He's been a full professor at the law school since 1973. I'm waiting to hear if he's coming down as hard on the medical school profs he is on you.

Personally, I think he has a conflict of interest. A full professor investigating other professors in his own school just doesn't seem kosher."

Suddenly, a shrill, continuous alarm sounded. Allen tightened his hold on the phone. "Frank, do you hear it?"

"Yeah, what is it?"

"The security system! When everyone left, I armed it. Someone's breaking in!'

"Lock the door to your office! Now!" Frank hollered.

Allen dropped the phone, sprang from his swivel chair, slammed the door, and fingered the lock and the dead bolt. He stood with his ear to the door. From below, the alarm kept ringing. His heart was racing. How long would it take for the police to arrive? For the moment, he forgot about the receiver dangling from his desk, six inches about the floor. Frank was on the other end, waiting.

TWENTY-THREE

It was early Tuesday morning, and Frank McCarthy was in the Bunker popping a can of Mountain Dew. He needed energy. He always had a few cans of Dew on hand for those times when night was a tug-of-war between thinking and sleeping. And last night was a bummer. Frank was convinced that a noose was slowly being tightened around Doc's neck. But it was hard to find proof.

But something was going on! The security alarm went off! The police came and found nothing. No sign of forced entry. "Must've been some quirk in the alarm system," they said.

Larry "Bull" McKitrick had examined all entry points to the Primate Center and held a different story. He was an expert with a proven track record, a member of an elite group of men who understood the art of defeating locks and burglar alarms. Everyone in the trade referred to Larry as a "surreptitious entry specialist." After an hour-long phone call, Frank knew why his friend had been given that impressive and lofty title.

"The intruder had a key," Larry said.

"There's only four keys, and they were accounted for," Frank replied. "Everyone swore their key had not been out of their possession. So a copy could not have been made. Why couldn't someone have picked the lock, entered, and left as soon as the alarm went off?"

"Impossible. The locks have six tumblers. A four tumbler is a piece of cake. Not so with six. It would drive me nuts trying to pick a six tumbler lock."

"Then how do you explain it?"

Larry chuckled, "Easy. You pick up a blank key, grab the end of it with a pair of pliers, slip it into the lock, and twist it back and forth a few times and pull it out. Now you will see bright brass showing through where flecks of carbon rubbed off. Then it's a matter of filing. It's a tedious job, but it can be done."

Frank marveled at this explanation. During the night, he thought about McKitrick's theory. He also thought about a phone call from one of his guys, a Vietnam veteran with pipelines into governmental agencies. His guy reported, "The EPA had issued an order for an audit of Allen's rat study."

"What the hell's going on?" Frank wondered.

Throughout the night, Frank thought about everything that had happened to Dr. Allen, starting with Rickey Marlar's death. By morning, he was firmly convinced that a conspiracy was the only reasonable answer, and he decided to call Doc first thing.

As the street outside his Bunker came alive, Frank swallowed another mouthful of liquid energy, and still trying for a half-court shot, he aimed a one-hander at the wastebasket. The can curved down, bounced off the rim, and lay on the floor.

"Almost," muttered Frank as he turned to his speakerphone and punched in numbers. Allen's office phone rang and rang. No answer. He called the Primate Center, and Linda picked up. The screeching of monkeys could be heard in the background.

"Hi, it's Frank. Is Doc in?"

"He left for Oregon on Sunday, Frank. On a farm with a family in Alsea. He hasn't called in, and I don't know how to reach him."

"What's he doing there?"

"Some kind of meeting about an EPA study."

"Thanks."

Frank popped open another Mountain Dew can and thought about Allen leaving on Sunday with Spencer, an investigator arriving on Monday. How convenient! He dialed information, and in seconds he was talking to the Chamber of Commerce in Alsea, Oregon. Frank fired off two questions.

"Yes, there is a community meeting in Alsea. Yes, I do have the number."

In less than two minutes, Dr. Allen was on the phone.

"It's Frank, Doc!"

"Hi, Frank."

"What are you doing in Oregon?"

Allen quickly explained the six-year battle between the women in Alsea and Dow Chemical. The women wanted 2,4,5-T and Silvex banned because they contained dioxin, both chemicals having been made by Dow. After the forestry service

CHAPTER TWENTY-THREE

sprayed the chemicals over vast acres of land, an epidemic broke out. Women miscarried. It happened in the first trimester just like in the monkey experiments. Studies by the EPA had been completed, and a decision about banning the chemicals would soon be handed down. The people asked Allen to review the data. They did not trust the government.

"I understand, Doc," Frank said, "but do you realize the trouble you've got back home? As we talk, a Doctor Spencer is auditing your lab. The EPA ordered him in, and he's there. While you're in Alsea, someone's attacking your rear. Doesn't it seem odd that as soon as you leave town, this guy moves in? I don't think it's a coincidence. Someone seems to know when you're out of town."

Dr. Allen was silent for a moment. "Any idea what he's auditing?"

"A rat study."

"I don't get it! How can they legally audit my lab, or why would they want to?" Allen paused to consider his question. "It's only a preliminary study," Allen explained. "Any idea who let him in?"

"I heard Cartwright is assisting him and showing him around. There's that name again, Doc, Cartwright."

"If Spencer came with some kind of order, Cartwright would have to let him in."

"But who decides the legality of an order, Doc?"

"The university's lawyer. But I don't understand. That rat study is nothing. Why would they want to audit it?"

Frank's gut told him there was a damn good reason. As far as he was concerned, anything Dow did meant trouble.

"Look, Doc," Frank began, "when Rickey was found dead, data was missing from a study that had just been finished. Dow knew your findings. They also knew that three weeks earlier, you had started another study. That gal suddenly appears for a job that is not posted, and someone hires her. This woman makes allegations and quits. Your records are audited, there's a break-in and a Kociba letter about high PCBs. You're before a grand jury. The security alarm goes off, and now Spencer is auditing your lab. Come on, Doc! It's a conspiracy!"

"Maybe so, but what would you have me do? Stay home and guard the door with a shotgun? Dare people to step over the threshold? Wage some kind of war? Refuse calls from people who ask for my help?"

"Why not?" Frank asked, guzzling down the remnants of warm Mountain Dew.

Allen spoke with conviction. "You have to understand my background! My ancestors never shirked their duty. They sacrificed their lives for what they believed in. One fought in the Revolutionary War, another the Civil War. During the Depression years, my father had a hell of a time putting food on the table, but yet he helped the whole family. He taught me about hard work and sacrifice from early on. And you're no different, Frank! You're helping thousands of Vietnam veterans. You may not admit it, but you are your brother's keeper."

Frank knew he was right. "You touched a tender spot in me, Doc. But I wasn't always like this! I was a wild kid, a fighter who didn't take nothin' from nobody. I was expelled from school for punching out the principal. Looking back, it's a miracle I survived, but I think it prepared me for Vietnam. There too, I survived. The most horrendous experience for me was being blown up in the middle of an ambush at a place called Trung Lap. Shrapnel tore into my body. I've got to tell you, Doc, I was an angry and bitter young man who at heart was still a kid who would become nasty for no reason."

"What turned you around?" Allen asked.

"What turned me around was meeting Paul Reutershan, joining him when he formed Agent Orange Victims International, watching him travel around the country, getting the word out, wanting the world to know what the government did to us. Watching him die was awful. but that's when I somehow changed and began helping others. You too are busy helping others when you should be helping yourself, especially when your work and future are at stake."

Dr. Allen was grateful for Frank's obvious concern. But what could he do? It was his nature to help. "You're right, Frank. But when someone needs help, I can't say no! When I first met Paul's mother, I felt her pain, and I had to reach out. When Paul asked me to talk to Lenny, I had to. And I don't like what's happening all over the world. Dioxin must be done away with! I have to go, Frank, they're calling me."

"When will you be back? I've got to talk to you."

"Tomorrow evening. Let's talk on Thursday."

CHAPTER TWENTY-THREE

"Okay, Doc."

Frank clicked off the speakerphone. The thought of Spencer arriving at the lab the day after Allen left town gnawed at him. Someone knew when to rush in and when to rush out. Someone was listening in on Doc's phone calls. Something had to be done. He'd call McKitrick. Maybe he'd know what to do.

TWENTY-FOUR

Frank McCarthy and Lenny Laviano were in the Bunker playing checkers when the TV newscaster came on the air.

"The Veterans Administration has issued a news release announcing the start of its fat biopsy study. They are convinced that once and for all it will prove that dioxin is not the cause of veterans' problems. In a Telex circular to its hospitals, the VA suggested that all available data shows that this chemical is not retained in tissues for prolonged periods of time. The VA, therefore, expect negative findings in the newly launched study to be conducted by Doctor Michael Gross at the University of Nebraska."

Red and black checkers fell to the floor as Frank pushed himself away from the card table. He hurried into the bedroom, picked up index cards and a ballpoint pen from the top of the dresser, and came back to the den.

"You get the kitchen phone, I'll use the speakerphone. We'll have to arrange for transportation for three guys for sure," Frank said, shuffling out index cards to Lenny. "Find out what hospital each one goes to and make sure they have a way of getting there."

"I need a pen," Lenny said.

"There's one next to the phone on the kitchen table," Frank said. "Oh! Another thing. Besides putting down the hospital, get the name of a brother or sister or a close friend in case something happens. Better they get a call from one of us than from some insensitive asshole in the VA."

"We're going have to stay on top of each guy, Frank. Once we know which hospital they're goin' to, we can get one or even two of our guys to be there and stand watch."

"Yeah, start calling."

Lenny took off for the kitchen. Frank dropped into his soft-cushioned seat in front of the card table, and switching on the speakerphone, he dialed up numbers.

"Just heard the news, Verlin. I'm sure glad the VA is moving it along. I was afraid they would call the whole thing off. Which VA hospital do you go to?"

CHAPTER TWENTY-FOUR

"Hines," Verlin Belcher said with disgust, obviously disinclined to embark on his newly announced journey.

Frank tried to reassure him. "Hines ain't so bad, not like others. Wish ya luck, buddy. We'll have someone there when you wake up. Anything you want, just ask. You're all set for a ride home, right?"

"Right, but whaddya mean Hines ain't so bad? Not bad for who? I'm the one goin' in. I'm the one bein' worked on. You oughta give Doctor Greenlee a call and wish him luck. He's the surgeon, and he'll have to find thirty grams of fat. I don't know where he's gonna find it because I'm skin and bone."

"I know. How ya been doin'?"

"Not good. These boils go from bad to worse. A lot of 'em ooze puss. And if I try layin' in the sun, the damn rash gets worse. I also got this numbness in my fingers and...it never goes away. I'm so tired, all I do is sleep. I'm sleepin' my life away. The other day, I called my mom, and when she answered, I didn't know what to say. My head was empty. I sat there, holdin' the phone, feelin' like a damn fool. It was weird, and it scared me. Seems like I'm really losin' it, Frank. And I still have no appetite and still losin' weight. As far as sex, I might just as well cut it off."

"So many guys say the same thing, Verlin. And a lot are worse, like Lenny. He's dying from cancer, and it wont be long before he joins Paul. And it makes me so damn mad. He's here now, in the kitchen, manning the other phone."

"Say hi for me. Do you have a list of all the guys getting' a biopsy?"

"Not a complete list. I don't know who the air force officers are. The VA first said there would be three officers who did research on dioxin for years. Now they say the officers will be three guys who flew C-123s and who were heavily exposed to Agent Orange while sprayin' the stuff. There's something fishy about that. How in the hell does the VA know they were heavily exposed? I think they're stacking the deck just in case dioxin is found in you and the other guys."

"I don't understand!"

"Well," Frank explained. "You are sick as hell! The VA will pick three officers who aren't sick at all. If you've got a lot of dioxin in you and you're real sick, and if the officers have dioxin in them and are not sick, the VA will point to those officers and say, 'If dioxin is bad, why aren't these officers sick?' But I know that pilots who flew C-123s weren't exposed to Agent

Orange when they sprayed it. One of the pilots told me. If Gross finds dioxin in them, he is not going to find a heck of a lot."

"I see why none of our guys trust the VA," Verlin replied. "It's a good thing we got Doctor Gross doin' the test. Everyone says we can trust him."

"That's what Allen said when he recommended him. And what Allen says is good enough for me. He also said that you better get yourself in a hospital and get takin' care of."

Verlin Belcher lay in a bed at the VA Hospital in Hines, Illinois, feeling the effects of an injection. Two women dressed in white fussed over him. He watched with one eye half open as one of the women carefully ran a razor over his belly, wiping off hair from the blade and returning for more.

"She's gentle," he thought, "and cute. She can shave my belly anytime."

The other woman had wheeled in a bottle of fluid hanging upside down on a hook. She was poking his arm with a needle, pulling it out and shoving it in again.

Verlin felt like saying, "Bug off bitch. If you can't do the job, get someone who can." He knew that if he wasn't doped up, he would have given her a mouthful. Finally, thank God, after five sticks, she hit pay dirt. The fluid was dripping, a drop at a time.

The gentle lady covered him with a white sheet and a white blanket. He had been feeling cold and was thankful for her kindness. He would have hugged her if he could.

Verlin felt himself quickly lifted and shuffled to a flat, firm, and not-so-roomy cart. He could feel the cart moving, people talking, someone in the distance laughing, the clang of metal hitting the floor, the cart turning, moving in a different direction, stopping, and again he was lifted and shuffled onto a slightly more roomy, softer surface.

He opened his eyes slightly. Bright lights forced him to shut them tight. He began to drift off; his thoughts were about thirty grams of fat. Did he have that much? Didn't care about losing it, but cared about what might be in it.

Verlin now felt himself slipping away...slipping away...slipping away.

TWENTY-FIVE

ALLEN WAS IN HIS OFFICE, ROCKING BACK AND FORTH IN HIS SWIVEL, FINGERS laced behind his head. He felt listless and downcast.

Frank's call had forced him to hurriedly conclude his business in Alsea and rush back to Madison. After landing, he headed straight for the Primate Center. After disarming the security system, he looked into every nook and cranny in his office and found no bugs. It was late when he finally locked up and drove home. He then began turning the house inside out looking for the damn things. When Christie asked him to sit down and have dinner, he shook his head and continued searching. When she suggested he go to bed, he refused and continued searching. A little past midnight, Christie heaved a heavy sigh and went to bed. Dr. Allen continued searching most of the night. He found nothing.

In the early morning, he returned to the office. He picked up the phone and called Frank. He told him about the horrible all-nighter. Frank said that even though he found nothing, there could still be a well-hidden bug in his house or office. Or perhaps the tap could be at the phone company. It would be difficult to check up on Ma Bell, but McKitrick would try. To play it safe, a public phone had to be used to keep information secret, such as when he was going out of town. After several minutes of talking with Frank, Dr. Allen hung up.

Frank had again reminded him of unanswered questions starting with the death of Rickey Marlar, because it could not have been a coincidence that his death occurred when his research had just shown dramatic results. And where was the missing data? And what about the unanswered questions about Kathryn Anderson? And the comment from the auditor: "You have enemies in high places?" Did he mean here at the university? Was Dow Chemical influencing the university to be his enemy? Too bad he had not yet found another source for dioxin.

His thoughts were suddenly distracted by Linda walking into his outer office in wintry wraps, carrying a box of Dunkin Donuts.

"Good morning," she cheerily said as she passed his open door. In minutes, she sauntered in.

"They smell delicious, have one," Linda said, holding the box close to his nose, hoping the aroma would entice him. She tried to appear in good spirits but was really dismayed and fearful for her boss.

Allen glanced into the box and lifted up the wax paper with the thumb and forefinger of his left hand. They smelled good. A chocolate Bismarck filled with custard, cinnamon rolls, and a Boston crème lay on top. And the corner of two apple croissants peeked up from the bottom.

"What's the occasion?" he asked.

"You're always bringing in peanut butter, jam, and bread. Now it's my turn."

"That's sweet of you. Thanks." Nudging the Bismarck aside, he reached in with two fingers of his right hand and wiggled out the apple croissant.

"Would you like coffee?" Linda asked.

"No thanks, but I would like to ask a question."

"Okay." Linda smiled.

"So much has been happening," Allen said. "What are your thoughts about it?"

Linda sat down on a chair at the side of Allen's desk. In a lowered voice, she said, "It's obvious that someone is trying to hurt you. It scares me."

Allen bit into the croissant and chewed. He wanted to ask about Cartwright, but was reluctant to do so even though there was a possibility that he was sabotaging the lab, as evidenced by his helping Doctor Spencer.

Instead, Allen asked, "What did you think of Doctor Spencer?"

"I saw him briefly. He left quickly with John. I don't have an opinion...except, it seemed strange that he suddenly showed up a day after you left for Oregon. Someone should have let me know he was coming."

"How was it decided that John would show him around?"

"I don't know. Someone from Legal Services brought Spencer here and asked for Cartwright."

Doctor Allen was still in his swivel, chewing another mouthful of croissant when two men in suits and ties walked in from the outer office. Allen froze. Linda muttered, "Excuse me," and hurried out.

"Doctor Allen," the tall, thin one said, "my name is Thomas. I'm with the FBI."

CHAPTER TWENTY-FIVE

Allen quickly swallowed the croissant and dropped what he was holding into a wastebasket next to his desk. He locked eyes with the intruder and remembered seeing this man during his testimony before the grand jury. It was the same man who followed him in Salt Lake, Denver, and Telluride, Colorado. It was the same man who had been gathering information on him for the past year. Why? And who was the other one?

"And who are you, sir?" Allen asked, turning his gaze to the short man with a round face and a full head of black hair.

"I'm an attorney for the university."

"I thought Ed Krill was the university attorney."

"Ed's not in today. The university has several attorneys."

Allen tried to relax. He took a deep breath. "What can I do for you?" he asked.

"Before I say anything," Thomas said, "I am obliged to give you your Miranda rights. You have the right to remain silent. Anything you say can and will be used against you in a court of law. You have the right to talk to a lawyer and have him present while you are being questioned. If you cannot hire a lawyer, one will be appointed to represent you before any questioning if you wish."

Doctor Allen's mouth dropped open. He felt terrified, as if he had suddenly been put on the FBI's most wanted list. He swallowed hard. His mouth was dry. He felt numb and devoid of all thought. In less than thirty seconds, he had been transformed from a respected member of the community to a criminal. He just sat there saying nothing.

"Doctor Allen, do you have an attorney?" Thomas's question hit him hard.

"Oh...yes," Allen nodded. "Bill Kessler, he's a tax attorney."

Thomas hesitated, "I mean a criminal attorney. The one who advised you prior to your grand jury testimony."

"Advised me? No one advised me. I never talked to anyone except Kessler, my tax attorney. He did say there was another attorney in his office, but I have not talked to him."

"Do you understand your Miranda rights?"

"I...I think so."

Thomas rolled his eyes as if to say, "Is he putting me on or is he really this stupid?" He tried again.

"Doctor Allen! This is a criminal case. Do you want an attorney present while I ask questions, someone who specializes in criminal law?"

The word "criminal" was like a stick of dynamite tossed into his lap, ready to explode. Tiny drops of moisture gathered on his brow, his palms, and under his arms. He felt drops of sweat falling from his armpits to his chest. A few drops rolled down his brow and into his eyes. He wiped them away with the back of his hand. He closed his eyes for several seconds, trying to take away the sting. His heart was racing and thumping wildly against his chest wall.

He was innocent! He wanted to prove it! He'd answer questions! He had done nothing wrong and had nothing to hide. Yes! He would answer questions, even though he really didn't want to. He would answer just as he had done before the grand jury.

"Would you excuse me for a moment?" Allen asked. He rose and brushed past the men heading down the hall to the men's room, a momentary sanctuary. He turned on the faucet and, with both hands cupped, leaned over and splashed cold water into his face. He pulled down a paper towel from the dispenser on the wall and wiped his face and hands, and then he studied himself in the mirror.

"They're trying to say I'm a criminal," he said to the mirror. "Me, a criminal!" He cracked his knuckles and grimaced, urging himself to go back and answer the damn questions. But he was afraid. Why was he facing the FBI? When he finished up before the grand jury, he was certain it went well. From the attitude of the foreman, he felt certain there would not be an indictment. And yet…he now felt like a criminal. He walked out of the men's room wishing a hole would open up so he could fall through and disappear.

On arriving back at the office, he dropped into his swivel with both feet flat on the floor, his arms on the armrests, and looked his accuser squarely in the face and waited.

"As I was saying, Doctor Allen, do you want an attorney present?"

Shaking his head, he said, "No."

"Okay. How do you explain the $892 discrepancy and the illegal phone call that the auditors found?"

Allen was irked. That question had already been covered. "I answered that at the grand jury hearing, Mr. Thomas. You were there. My answer is the same now as it was then."

CHAPTER TWENTY-FIVE

Round Face, the attorney, reached into his inside suit pocket, took out a small notepad and a Bic pen, clicked it, and began jotting down notes. Allen felt intimidated.

"I repeat my question, Doctor Allen, if you don't want to answer, say so. That's your right."

Allen took a deep breath and exhaled slowly. Leaning back in his swivel, he began. "I've been doing research for nearly eighteen years. My grants total a half million a year. If I made one illegal phone call in eighteen years, I'd say that's a damn good reason for saying that I'm an honest guy. Why am I being accused of theft for a two dollar phone call? As for the $892, it represents a training grant due to expire. If the money wasn't used, it would have to be returned to the granting agency. It's common practice to swap money from one pot to another. Everyone does it. In this instance, Walter Hargraves, a trainee, agreed to let me use his training grant money with the understanding that when he was ready to attend a national meeting, I would reimburse him from my discretionary account. If you check the dates of my four trips, you will find they all occurred within one year, between March 21, 1978, and March 21, 1979. That's because the grant was due to expire."

The FBI agent decided to get nasty. "But when you took a trip on June 8, you put down the name of Walter Hargraves and pretended that he accompanied you when in fact it was your son!"

"I couldn't put my son's name down. The money belonged to Hargraves! His name had to appear on the reimbursement request!" Allen shot back. "My son works in the lab, and I wanted him with me. But that's not theft! My discretionary account would've paid for Walter's trip. He knew he wouldn't be able to attend the meeting he wanted to go to if the money in his account was returned to the granting agency. I could have returned the $892 and used the money in my account, but my frugal nature got in my way."

Round Face scribbled away. Allen realized he had talked too much. He pressed his lips tightly together as if to remind himself to keep his mouth shut.

FBI pressed on. "Doctor Allen..."

"Stop right there," Allen blurted out, sitting upright. "I'll answer no more questions without a lawyer."

"That's your right," FBI said. Round Face scribbled two more words, and in seconds, they were gone.

The clock on the wall said 9:59 a.m., Linda was gone, and the Dunkin Donuts box still rested on her desk. He had a course to teach in seven minutes. Graduate students would be waiting. And he was drained. Nevertheless, he forced himself to go on with the lecture and struggled through it. One hour later, after class, Allen retreated to a green Naugahyde easy chair in a corner of the student union lounge. He hadn't seen Linda or anybody else other than the students. And he was glad to be alone to think.

How could he be so learned in one field and completely ignorant in another? A real moron in law. When he had to interact with law officers, he was a blubbering idiot, an imbecile. He didn't know how to keep his mouth shut when confronted by the FBI.

Allen thought about every minute before the grand jury. Sitting in front of them, three tiers, one higher than the other. The foreman asking questions. One woman in the second row, about fortyish, wearing a blue two-piece knit outfit, keeping her eye on him, never blinking, always watching. But he had felt in control, answering honestly. Everything he had said made sense...or so it seemed.

Until today, when Thomas said something about Kessler advising him before testifying. But Kessler didn't advise him about anything. He remembered Frank's advice about needing a lawyer versed in criminal law, someone with a good track record, someone who could do battle with the U.S. Attorney and the FBI, even if it meant mortgaging your home.

A thought suddenly occurred to him. Why hadn't he seen it before? The date was February 1979. Kathryn Anderson had resigned on October 5, 1978. She went to Senator Proxmire after she quit, but the FBI was already following him in September 1978, before she resigned, before the allegations, and before the audit of his records.

"Bastards!" Allen said aloud.

His outburst lifted him out of his contemplation. He looked around, wondering if anyone had heard him. Two male students were sitting not too far away on a couch. They buzzed with speculation about a newspaper article that had just come off the press. The loud one gestured with his hands while the quiet one listened and replied softly.

"Professor Snowden was charged with a fifty-five count indictment," Loud One said, holding up five fingers of one hand and five from the other. "It's five years in the pen and a ten thousand dollar fine for each charge. He'll die in prison." He turned both thumbs down.

CHAPTER TWENTY-FIVE

"That's bad," Quiet One replied.

"I never did like his course," Loud One said, raising his hands and gesturing as if he had just pushed away the entire university curriculum.

Doctor Allen heard enough. He headed for the exit door, sidling his way between small groups of students, some with their noses in books. Exiting the building, he forced himself to confront the hard question.

Kessler had recommended an attorney with criminal law experience. Who was he? What kind of experience did he have? Was he good? He had to know, and he had to know now.

TWENTY-SIX

For what seemed like the hundredth time, Allen threw an impatient glance at the stairway going up to the second floor. He sat alone in a nicely furnished waiting room, a large hall that had once been the foyer of a stately home. The desk, twenty feet in front of him, was vacant. A placard said, "Debra, Receptionist." The credenza behind the desk held a large silver urn and Styrofoam coffee cups. The red light at the bottom of the coffee maker was on. Debra had been here earlier.

To his right, the law library boasted a large conference table and chairs. This room had also remained vacant since his entry into the law offices of Bill Kessler & Associates. "Where's everybody," he wondered, "where's Kessler?" Every two or three minutes, he'd shift his rear in the soft leather armchair, not from discomfort but from his inability to sit still. He had already paged through every magazine, glancing at articles, but nothing held his attention.

The antique clock on the wall above the credenza showed 3:30 p.m. "I've been waiting an hour and a half," thought Allen. "Ridiculous!" He had an urge to get up and leave. After waiting this long, he wouldn't consider it objectionable to slam the door on his way out.

If he left, where would he go? He had no other lawyer. But what the hell! Would he really have a lawyer, someone versed in criminal law? Kessler was a tax attorney who did corporate, business, and high-tech law, whatever that was. Is this why he had not received advice about the grand jury prior to his testimony? Maybe this young whippersnapper knew as much about advising as he himself did. Nothing!

Allen tried to relax by studying the décor of the room. Oversized padded colorful chairs. A dark brown leather couch. Sky blue textured wallpaper. Ornate golden frames proudly displaying floral motifs, trumpet shaped lilies, purple and yellow magnolias, sunflowers, pink zinnias, and other flowers whose names he did not know. The carpeting underfoot was as soft as playground sand and about the same shade. It blended nicely with the receptionist's desk and the credenza, both the color of caramel corn.

CHAPTER TWENTY-SIX

The ringing of the phone jarred him. He felt like answering and saying, "No one's here," and then slamming it down. It would serve Kessler right! Imagine! Leaving the office unattended with a coffee urn holding hot coffee and no one to offer him a cup.

What a way to run a business. It was February, a busy time for tax attorneys. The phone kept ringing; clients were calling.

As he contemplated leaving, the door opened. Bill Kessler hurried in and closed the door behind him. He patted his straw colored hair back in place and tossed a quick glance in the general direction of the jingling phone. He tried to mask his perturbation.

"My receptionist must've had an emergency. She's always here," he said. "I didn't know you were coming." He waved Allen up the stairs. "First office to your right, I'll be right there."

"Humph," grunted Allen, still miffed. He climbed the stairs with his hand on the railing. Upon entering Kessler's office, he dropped into a soft leather couch in front of Kessler's desk.

"Sorry you had to wait," Kessler said, bouncing into the room. He dropped into a high-backed chair and rolled himself closer to his desk. "It's best to make an appointment," he said.

"Didn't have time. I had a visit from the FBI this morning, and I'm worried," Allen replied, trying to lock eyes with his attorney, who was glancing at a memo on his desk.

Kessler's eyebrows raised, "Tell me about it."

Glad to have captured Kessler's attention, Allen continued. "Well, this Mr. Thomas came in, gave me Miranda rights, and in five minutes he made me out to be a thief!"

"Did you answer questions?"

"I told him about the arrangement I had with Hargraves and about swapping money."

"Did he mention the $892?"

"He did, and the one illegal long distance phone call."

"Did he go into your four trips?"

"No. I stopped talking."

Allen waited for Kessler to advise him, to come to his defense. Instead, Kessler leaned forward shaking his head. "Do you realize how difficult it is to justify those trips, especially with your written requests for reimbursement?"

Allen was confused. "Why is it so difficult?"

"Well, look at the trip with your son."

"Okay."

"You used grant money, right?"

"To be paid back from my personal account!"

"But you used grant money."

"So?"

"You can't do that."

"The grand jury accepted it."

"You don't know that."

"What are you saying?" Allen could not believe what he was hearing.

"The facts speak for themselves. They say you're guilty."

"Guilty!" Allen exclaimed. "I haven't been tried! I'm innocent until proven guilty. You are supposed to defend me! Whose side are you on?"

"Calm down, I'm on your side. I want the very best for you, but I have to take the law into consideration. I have to think like Frank Tuerkheimer, the U.S. Attorney who is prosecuting this case. I need a way of getting you off with the lightest possible sentence."

Doctor Allen sat with his head down, looking at the floor. He thought about Professor Snowden and the fifty-five count indictment. Fines and jail time. "He'll die in prison" is what one student said. Then he remembered what the FBI man said.

He looked up at Kessler. "The FBI asked me if you had advised me before my grand jury testimony. What did he mean?"

Kessler shrugged. "I don't know, maybe Robins will know."

"Who's Robbins?"

"Jim Robbins. He's the lawyer I told you about, the one with expertise in criminal law. He and I will be working together."

Allen went numb. He was being tried as a criminal. "When will I meet him?"

"I'll set up a meeting and let you know."

Later that evening, Allen had not yet arrived home. His wife, Christie, was sitting at the kitchen table holding a cup of tea with both hands. She took small sips, staring aimlessly out of the window. Darkness abruptly settled in after the full moon vanished behind a cloud.

CHAPTER TWENTY-SIX

She had planned to go to work. A fresh, lightly starched, white uniform and white shoes lay on the bed. Her photo ID had been pinned over the left breast pocket, and her hair had been done up in a bun. A touch of red lipstick and she was ready, but Linda's call had alarmed her.

"Where's Doctor Allen?" Linda asked. "I came to say good-bye because I've quit. I don't like working here anymore. Someone is out to harm Doctor Allen, so I'm not going to stay and watch it happen. But I wanted to say good-bye, and I've been waiting. He was in this morning, but since then, no one has seen him, and I'm worried."

Christie too began to worry. She called her boss at the VA Hospital and feigned illness, claiming to have a sore throat and a high temperature.

"I'll make it in tomorrow," she promised.

She started making phone calls. Her son at the university had not seen his father. Doctor Smith, the dean, had not seen him. Dr. Inhorn, chairman of the department, had not seen him. Nine other phone calls. No one had seen him. This had never happened. What should she do? It was now 10:05 p.m. She'd wait one more hour before calling the police.

Trying to keep calm, Christie set her cup down and went out on the front verandah. A full moon had reappeared. The road was visible for more than two hundred yards before it began to fade away and disappear into darkness. She peered hard at the darkness, hoping to see a faint glimmer of headlights. Walking down five wooden steps, she stood there momentarily, still searching. She moved down to the walkway. It was quiet except for the hooting of an owl somewhere behind her.

"Where is he?" Christie cried out to the darkness. She last spoke with him early in the morning when he called from the office. He told her about Spencer's audit of his lab, about his all-night search for a bug, and of Frank's warning to be extra careful when talking on the phone. And with the problems he was having, she worried about his safety.

She thought about their life together. She remembered their first date. Summer 1946. A movie in Portsmouth. Soft whisperings in the balcony. Two bags of popcorn. She'd throw a few kernels into his mouth, and he'd reciprocate. Then both of them allowed a sprinkling of popcorn to fall to the seats below. They were like two mischievous teenagers. Naturally, they didn't see much of the movie. When he took her home to the nurse's quarters, she was hopeful for more. Boy! Was she disappointed. Not once did he ever take advantage of her. It was she who tried to subtly seduce him...without success. That's why she knew the sexual harassment charges against him were vicious lies.

As far as him stealing money...nonsense! It was contrary to everything he stood for. When old man Shaw took an order for cattle feed and summed it up $163 short, Jim asked Shaw if he was giving away a Christmas present in the middle of June. Shaw looked up at him with his mouth half open and a dumb look in his eyes and puckered his lips as if to speak, but nothing came out. When Shaw found out what he had done, he glanced down at he floor, shook his head and admitted that his ol' noggin was sure gettin' forgetful. Her husband was not the kind of man who stole money. He was a wonderful man.

Waiting for him to come home had become unbearable. She wanted to call the police, but she was hopeful that he would soon show up. Finally, she decided to make the call. She started up the stairs, and before opening the screen door, took one more look into darkness. She thought she saw two points of light in the far distance. Her breathing quickened. She craned her neck, trying to better discern the light. Definitely...two pinpoints of light growing larger. Either him or a trucker.

Christie started to hurry down the stairs, but stopped midway. She didn't want to greet him with alarm. "Be natural," she told herself. He'd wonder why she wasn't at work. She'd lie. Hurrying inside and closing the front door, she scooted back into the kitchen.

"Thank you God," she whispered as she turned on the range for more hot tea, then sat by the window, watching two bright lights.

They soon made a right turn onto the driveway and came to a stop in front of their two-door garage. The lights went out, and the engine quit. The car just sat there, waiting for Doctor Allen to open the door. It took a full thirty seconds.

The tea kettle whistled. Christie took her eyes away from the window, lifted herself up, turned off the stove, and busied herself with setting the table and a package of cookies. When her husband walked in, he found his wife in the kitchen, a cup of hot tea, a white sugar bowl, and a plate of Oreos waiting for him. Christie turned, and one look into his eyes told her that something was terribly wrong.

He pretended badly. "Why aren't you at work? Are you okay?" His voice choked.

CHAPTER TWENTY-SIX

"Sore throat," she whispered with a pretense of forced effort.

He reached out and touched her forehead, "Fever?"

She shook her head and waved him to a cup of steaming tea. He lowered himself into a chair and heaved a heavy sigh.

"How was your day?" she asked, trying to start a casual conversation.

"Horrible," came the instant reply.

"Do you want to talk about it?"

He shrugged and seemed to be on the verge of talking, but nothing came out.

"Remember Virginia Beach?" she tried again. "Wasn't it nice walking barefoot in the sand, listening to the waves? I always wanted to be with you. I cared a great deal about you then...and I still do."

Tossing her a sideways glance, his eyes immediately overflowed with tears. He tried fighting them back, but his entire body trembled and shook as he burst forth with loud incessant cries of anguish and despair. He covered his face with both hands to hide his shame. Christie bit her lip, but refused to cry. She inched her chair alongside his and wrapped her arms around him. He buried his face in her bosom, sobbing.

After what seemed like an eternity, she asked, "What happened?"

He tried to compose himself. "Sorry," he mumbled. "I'm crying like a baby."

"That's okay," Christie said softly. "What happened?"

He told her about Miranda and the $892, swapping money, Kessler's comment about the facts, saying he's guilty according to the law, and about Jim Robins, the expert in criminal law he had yet to meet.

"Where have you been all day?"

Doctor Allen again fought back tears. His mouth moved, but as soon as he tried to speak, he choked up. He swallowed hard to keep from crying.

"I," he began through tears, "I drove to Lake Mendota to think. If my own lawyer sees me as guilty, what chance do I have?" His body shook again with uncontrollable sobbing.

"I believe in you, Jim," Christie said gently. "I know you are innocent."

She went for a box of tissues and put it on the table. He took a handful and dried his eyes.

"Professor Snowden went to prison. He'll probably die there. Is that what's in store for me?"

143

Christie held him and pressed her lips to his tear-streaked cheek. His body still trembled and she wanted to calm him, but she didn't know how.

Allen continued. "I've been thinking all day...trying to unscramble the last year of my life. But as I look back, it's easy to see that my life has been a horrible nightmare. Kessler is talking about the lightest possible sentence. That could mean jail time. I'm humiliated! How could I ever live it down? I'd be better off dead. I wanted to kill myself. But the lake was cold and dark. And I was afraid...so afraid..."

TWENTY-SEVEN

At 4:35 A.M., THE PHONE RANG WITH STARTLING SHRILLNESS. CHRISTIE AWOKE with a jolt and jumped out of bed. No one ever called this early unless someone in the family died. She hurried around to the nightstand at the other side of the bed and grabbed the phone.

"Yes?" she said softly, turning away from her husband, who lay stretched out on his back.

"It's Frank, Christie. Can I talk to Doc?" His voice conveyed urgency.

She wondered what to do. "He's sleeping. I hate to wake him."

"Well...don't. One of our guys in DC called. He talked about a loudmouth who was guzzlin' beer and braggin' that he finally done-in a world famous scientist. 'It's up the river for Professor Allen,' this loudmouth was tellin' some broads. What's goin' on?"

"Frank," Christie replied above a whisper, "Jim thinks he's going to prison. He thought of killing himself last night."

"Oh my!" Frank exclaimed. "He's gotta have a good lawyer...with experience! I'll talk to Yannacone. Maybe he knows someone. I'll get back to you."

"Thanks, Frank." She put the receiver down.

Christie lowered herself to the floor. She folded her arms across her chest, feeling the warmth of her flannel nightgown. She sat there, looking at the man she had married more than thirty-one years ago, on June 17, 1948, to be exact. She thought about the ceremony at the Baptist church in Mars Hill. His sister and brother-in-law were the only ones there. She remembered Reverend J. R. Owen, a retired minister who conducted the ceremony. She remembered being happy. This handsome young man who had refused to give her a free newspaper was finally hers. To love and to cherish until death do us part. And yesterday, death was a moment away. A jump from a large rock formation into Lake Mendota would have ended it all. Her eyes filled with tears that ran down her cheeks. Alone, she allowed herself the luxury of letting it all out. She was frightened. Jim was going through hell and on the verge of suicide and she had nobody to turn to...except Frank. But he was so far away. What to do? She could call Jim's parents in North Carolina and invite them over. They would do anything to help their son. Maybe they could convince him to mortgage the farm. Or force him to accept some of their savings. She knew they would gladly give it up. She also knew her husband. A proud man who lived by principles. But maybe...just maybe he would accept their help now that he was having such a difficult time.

He could then hire a good attorney, one with a proven track record, one who could do battle with the U.S. government. That could really be the answer to all of her prayers. She liked the idea. It could help her husband resolve his frustration in trying to convince the world that he was not a thief.

She agreed with Jim's reasoning about the $892. Not because he was her husband, but because what he said made sense. His trips were paid for with grant money that was going to expire. If the money wasn't used, it would have to be returned. So he used it.

But he promised to replace it with money from his discretionary account. That wasn't theft! It wasn't even stupidity! It was frugality. For him, watching every penny was a way of life.

Christie felt like sitting on the porch swing. She couldn't sleep anyhow. So she lifted herself up, tip-toed from the room, down the stairs, and out.

Her rigid routine as a psychiatric nurse demanded that she work nights and sleep days. Off duty at 7:30 a.m. and a leisurely breakfast at the hospital. When she was exhausted, a five-minute drive to the graveyard, where she parked and napped. Everyone joked about her sleeping with the dead.

"But there's one advantage," she would say. "No intruders."

When she tried returning home without her graveyard visit, her eyes rebelled. They closed, and she remembered a time during pea harvesting season when she pulled over to the side of the road and conked out. The next thing she knew, police were shaking her. The operator on the harvesting machine, chugging along between rows of sweet peas, had come from the far end of a field over to her car. He saw her sitting at the wheel, head back and mouth open, and called police.

"There's a dead woman in a Mustang," the farm worker reported.

CHAPTER TWENTY-SEVEN

As she rocked on the swing, thinking about the past, the screen door creaked.

"What's wrong?" Allen asked.

"Couldn't sleep. Come sit," she said as she patted the spot next to her.

"I'll get a robe and slippers."

"Pajamas are fine. I think we have an early spring."

He padded over and eased himself onto the swing. With feet dangling above the floor, rocking up and back, they listened to the rhythmic squeak of the chains.

"Frank called."

"Oh...why?"

"He wants to help. He's going to talk to Yannacone about finding a good lawyer." She thought it best not to mention the "up the river" remark by a loudmouth drunk.

"I've thought a lot about lawyers," Allen replied. "We have very little money. With the way lawyers charge, we would be broke in no time. I can't mortgage the family farm. It was handed down by my ancestors, and I have to pass it on. It belongs to our children, our grandchildren, and their children. How could I violate such a sacred trust?"

Christie decided to tell him of her idea to call his parents. "How about refinancing the farm?"

"It would bother me, but I might be willing to do that."

"Good. The most important thing right now is not money. It's fighting for your reputation. Nothing else matters."

Automatic sprinklers came on. Water shot out in all directions with long circular arcs, reaching as far as the white picket fence surrounding the front and side lawn. The water cascaded down on a two hundred foot stretch of new grass, dotted with beds of sprouting flowers and towering trees.

Dawn threw a golden haze across the sky. "Look at that," Allen said. "It's beautiful. It would be a shame to increase the mortgage on all this. It would prove how much of a failure I've been all my life."

"A failure? How can you say such a thing?"

"It's true. In high school, I liked football and basketball, but could never make the team. I enlisted in the navy wanting to be a pilot, but they didn't need me. All I did was scut work in a hospital. Never saw combat like my ancestors. They were fighters in the American Revolution, the Civil War, but me, nothing."

"Ridiculous! You are a world-famous scientist. Nobody does the kind of research you do. No one! World leaders call on you for help! When there's an accident with dioxin, the phone starts ringing, And it's been ringing for years."

"But look at the price I've paid. I'm a workaholic. My sons grew up without seeing much of their father. You've been without a husband. And what do I have to show for it? Publications? I had my priorities mixed up!"

He drew a deep breath, shaking his head. "Publications don't support a wife and four kids. They just add to my prestige, my glorification. I enjoyed being in the limelight, but it's all vanity and selfishness. I've been a failure even in providing for my family! If not for you working all of our married life, we couldn't make it."

Christie sat upright and nudged her husband hard. "That is pure nonsense! I've worked all my life because it made me feel needed. Everyone has a niche. My salary helped, but nursing has always been important to me."

Christi's thoughts and emotions came tumbling out. "Last week, I watched a Vietnam veteran die. Michael Francis Smith died from cancer of the pancreas. He kept saying, 'Please God, let me die.' It broke my heart every time he'd say it. I would sit with him, talk to him, and try to make him comfortable. He died with me and his mother at his side. He had both hands through the guardrails, one on each side of the bed, and we held them. When he closed his eyes and took his last breath, he seemed to be at peace. I'll never forget the squeeze he gave me just before he died. It was as if he was saying goodbye and thank you."

"Was he exposed to Agent Orange?"

Christie shrugged. "The information he gave said so, but the doctor wanted to do a fat biopsy to prove he was loaded with dioxin. But the VA officials said no. That's why your work is so important. It will prove what dioxin did to all the Michael Francis Smiths out there. Then the government will have to admit to its culpability in killing these men."

Doctor Allen looked at the rising red glow in the east and thought about his need for a damn good lawyer. He thought about his wife, who had always stood beside him.

CHAPTER TWENTY-SEVEN

"Honey," he said, "you are much stronger than me. I fall apart, and you slug it out. I could use some of your toughness."

"Must be the genes," she shot back. "By the way, I forgot to tell you, Linda called. You left your cowboy hat in the office."

Allen shook his head in disbelief. "It shows where my mind is. I hope something good happens soon. Maybe Yannacone will find a good lawyer."

"From your mouth to God's ears," Christie said.

As the morning sky grew brighter, Doctor and Mrs. James Allen listened to the rhythmic squeak of the chains as they kept swinging, she in her flannel nightgown, he in his pajamas. She leaned her head on his shoulder. He put his arm around her and drew her close. They looked like a Norman Rockwell painting.

"Hey," Jim whispered. "When did I last tell you how much I love you?"

"You don't have to tell me," she whispered back. "I know."

TWENTY-EIGHT

MARCH 1, 1979. DONALD ROONEY, PRESIDENT OF DOW CHEMICAL, WAS IN HIS OFfice at the Bennett Building in Madison, Wisconsin. He had anticipated drastic EPA action against his company, and the ax fell early that morning with the emergency suspension of Silvex and 2,4,5-T. But the ban was not a complete one.

Dow had positioned itself well to deal with the painful blow. This would not go unanswered. The most prestigious law firms in the country had been hired to plan and plot strategy. An unlimited budget had been set aside to deal with every possible contingency. The battle was looming.

Two thousand five hundred twenty-three miles away, the townspeople of Alsea, Oregon, no longer needed a strategy. After years of fighting, they had won. It was over! The forestry service could no longer drop deadly chemicals on their community. Silvex and 2,4,5-T had been outlawed.

The EPA issued a lengthy statement proclaiming to the world, "Studies completed days ago show a high miscarriage rate immediately following the spraying of 2,4,5-T in the forests around Alsea, Oregon. This alarming correlation comes at a time when seven million pounds of chemical are about to be used to control weeds on power line rights-of-way, in pastures, and in forest lands across the nation. These uses will be halted immediately."

Barbara Blum, deputy administrator of the EPA, told of studies showing that the chemicals were concentrated with dioxin. She pointed to Allen's studies. She pointed to other studies where very low levels caused birth defects and tumors.

"These chemicals pose a carcinogenic risk to humans," she went on to say, "at any level of exposure. Any level."

It was the Allen Principle. It was his life's work. The EPA then announced plans for cancellation hearings. If these plans were successful, dioxin-containing chemicals would never again be manufactured, never again cause miscarriages, never again cause tears and heartaches for so many families. It called for a celebration.

CHAPTER TWENTY-EIGHT

Within days, people throughout Oregon and neighboring states crowded the streets of Alsea. Cold wind blew through the town, but no one cared. They were warmed not only by clothing, but by dancing and singing and hugging and kissing. And by clapping along with the drum and tuba as the band and the schoolchildren marched in parade.

Long tables stretched the length of an entire block on one side of Main Street. Platters were piled high with crispy fried chicken, pot roast with carrots and peas, barbecued spare ribs, fat kosher hot dogs, thick and juicy hamburgers, hot corned beef and cabbage, spicy meat balls and spaghetti, French fries, mashed potatoes, candied yams, coleslaw, and dozens of other savory dishes. Then dessert! There was an array of homemade pies and cakes, bread pudding, and gingerbread men adorned with red, white, and blue frosting, each holding an American flag. Hot cocoa and hot coffee in large silver urns was provided by shopkeepers on the other side of the street.

Politicians joined carolers. They sang and shook hands as if there was an upcoming election. Television sound trucks, cameramen, and reporters roamed about, mingling with folks and gathering news. A reporter interviewed a woman activist as she sipped hot cocoa in the drugstore.

"This celebration is phenomenal," the reporter said. "How do you feel about it?"

Morosely, she muttered "Sad."

"Sad?" he exclaimed. "You should be happy!"

"No. It's sad because it took so long for the truth to come out. It's sad that so many babies were lost. But thank God it's over."

"But how do you feel about winning? You just beat up on a multibillion dollar company."

"Well," she answered slowly, "that part makes me feel good."

The reporter paused as if to give emphasis to the next question.

"So...what was the most important thing in helping you win this fight?"

"Well, I'd have to say it was Doctor Allen. His work with monkeys got us started."

The news media ran with the story and carried it nationwide. On the morning of March 2, 1979, Doctor Allen's phones kept ringing. They rang all day in his home and his office, but no one answered. Both he and his wife had gone away. The decision had been a spur-of-the-moment thing, a glorious idea.

Just two days earlier, they were sitting on the verandah steps feeling drained by the pent-up fears and anxieties. Christie fingered the *Ladies Home Journal* while her husband sat forlornly with images of prison life running through his head. The brilliant orange sun was finding its way down on the distant horizon.

"Look," she said, pointing to an ad.

Doctor Allen glanced at the page. "Forget Spring Cleaning. Get Away For Romance Instead," it said.

"Let's run off," Christie pressed on, "just you and me. A honeymoon. We haven't been away together for years. It'll be fun."

"Run away? Where to?"

"The Dells isn't far. No tourists this time of the year. It'll be deserted. We'll have the place to ourselves. I'll pack a lunch and dinner, a thermos, and we can enjoy the rock formations. And if you're in the mood, we can make love."

That seemed to shake Allen to his old self. "Hey," he smiled mischievously, "what if I don't want to come back? What if I find a cave and decide to become a hermit? What then?"

"Well," Christie paused, "no problem. It's close enough to home. I'll keep you supplied with food and water. No one will know. And when I bring supplies on weekends, we can make love again. How about it?"

Her husband nodded, feeling uplifted by his wife's upbeat mood. "Let's go," he said.

Early next morning, the only car seen was a red Mustang heading out of Madison, traveling west.

Fifteen hours later, the Allen's were back. Mentally refreshed, Christie had just turned out the light and had snuggled up close to her husband. They had just put their arms around one another when they were startled by the ringing of the phone.

"It's close to midnight!" Allen exclaimed, rolling on his side to pick up the phone.

"Hello?"

"Hi, Doc! Where've you folks been?"

"We just got home, Frank," Allen replied, mildly irked at the lateness of the call even though he knew there had to be a good reason. "Anything wrong?"

"No, but I had to talk with you about today's news."

CHAPTER TWENTY-EIGHT

"What news?"

Christie edged in close behind her husband. Taking hold of his hand that held the phone, she moved it slightly away from his ear so she could listen.

"The EPA's ban. You two must've been down some coalmine away from the world. The news media ran the story all day, about the people in Oregon, how they won their fight against Dow. The people thanked you on national television. Politicians talked about your service to the country in helping to establish a sound environmental public policy. There's a rumor of you being invited to the White House for a personal thank-you from the president. But don't get sucked in, Doc. If anyone invites you to DC, don't go. The government and Dow might want you to leave town for some damned reason. I would not trust them."

"Right now, I don't care about publicity. I've got this jail thing hanging over my head."

"I think you can rest easy for awhile. We had a board meeting. Our lawyers were there talkin' about you. That's why I'm calling at this late hour. Don't talk to any lawyer." Frank's tone was adamant. "Do nothing, let the government make the next move. With the way politicians are praising you, it would be politically unwise for the feds to come after you right now. That is what everyone thinks. Just go on working as usual."

Christie gave her husband a thumbs-up and nodded.

"What if I need a lawyer?" Allen asked.

"Call me. But with the political climate in your favor, and the investigation into the university's medical school professors, the U.S. Attorney may have to back away for now. I'm sure he'll come after you, but certainly not now. He's got his hands full. I think the situation at the university is close to boiling over into a nasty public mess. The doctors have been filling their cookie jars since 1958. That's a lot of cookies. And from what the newspapers are saying, some of the money coming in may not have been legal. I'm reading words like possible fraud."

Christie tapped her husband on the shoulder and silently mouthed, "You need a lawyer."

"I'd feel better if I had a lawyer, Frank."

"Me too, but let's play it by ear. Victor Yannacone does not know anyone in Madison. He can't take you on because he's over his head in work. There's over a hundred suits in different parts of the country. It's mind-boggling, and he's trying to combine it all and file it in federal court. Our guys are tryin' to help by lobbying everyone, but it's going to be a tough fight. There's a lot of powerful people out there who want the Vietnam vets to fall."

Dr. Allen shook his head in wonderment. "Frank, how do you find out things? Like what's going on at the medical school?"

"We have an army, Doc. There were 2.6 million guys in Vietnam...and 57,692 never made it back. Since coming home, all of us have witnessed suffering that never seems to go away. So we've banded together in every city and every town. Our guys have family and friends, like Paul's Aunt Millie. And she had a boyfriend who worked for Dow. That's how it works! People power! They send me records. I keep 'em on file. I've got a six-inch stack in front of me now, came yesterday. The top one says, 'Larry Johnson, age 30, diffuse inoperable abdominal carcinomatosis.' He died at the Fitzsimmons General Hospital in Denver. When I see one of these, I look up at the sky and scream obscenities! Where is God? He must know how we are suffering. And this kind of suffering makes us all brothers, Doc. Digging for information is easy. Doing something about it, making it work to our advantage, is what's really needed."

Christie shook her head, signaling her husband not to discuss such upsetting things. "Sorry I asked, Frank. It got you all riled up."

"No, Doc. I'm always riled up. I'm always screaming on the inside. I scream at Dow Chemical for making a weapon, knowing it will kill. I scream at the military for killing us. I scream at the VA for handing out bullshit, in essence telling us to go to hell. The only hope we have is winning our suit and getting enough money to start a Foundation. Only then can we help ourselves. In order to win, we need you, Doc, just like the people in Alsea."

"You know you can count on me, Frank," Dr. Allen replied firmly.

"I know. In the meantime, play it cool. If you have to be away from the lab, do it quietly. No one need know. You have a crew of twenty people. They'll do the work whether you show up or not. And if you must be away, ask one of your older associates not to let anyone into your lab, like Cartwright did with Spencer. From what I've been able to learn so far, the EPA had no authority to order Spencer into your lab. And I'm sure it's part of a strategy to do you in. One of these days, we'll probably find out. But by then, it may be too late. It's a real worry, Doc."

TWENTY-NINE

MARCH 25, 1979. WHEN FRANK CALLED, DR. ALLEN HAD BEEN AIRBORNE FOR TWO hours, and there was no way of letting him know what was happening.

"Just make sure nobody gets into your lab," Frank had said.

"My closest associates are standing watch," Allen had replied reassuringly. "It will be over their dead bodies before anyone gets in. There will be no more unannounced intrusions, no more audits." And to top it all off, Linda had come back.

She had been watching the news when the story came on the screen about the momentous EPA announcement along with the jubilation and festivities in Oregon. She loved the praiseworthy comments about her former boss. Linda didn't take long to reconsider her decision. She jumped in her car and hastened back to the university where she withdrew her resignation.

Things began to look up for Allen. A seventy-hour workweek instead of eighty proved to be a blessing for him and Christie. The extra ten hours allowed for weekend romantic jaunts to the Dells. Work was proceeding nicely. The 50 ppt study showed results as predicted. The 25 ppt was on track. The last and final 5 ppt project had just started, but it would take years for a definite conclusion that would, once and for all, settle the debates about the deadly effects of dioxin. It could be the last nail in the coffin for this deadly chemical.

Best of all, there was no further word about prosecution, no break-ins or alarms going off. There were no sleepless nights and no thoughts about jumping into Lake Mendota, where in a moment of quiet desperation, the dark waters could have ended it all. For the first time in a long time, Doctor Allen felt in control. He looked forward to meeting Frank, that intriguing guy who called him Doc. And he wanted to renew his friendship with Mrs. Reutershan, that charming wisp of a woman who met him in a motel lobby. He remembered how she cocked her head to see the sci-fi book he had just acquired, how she looked at him with a sparkle of admiration in her eyes and said, "A scientist, a cowboy, and Dracula. That's interesting."

She too was interesting. The treasurer of AOVI who guarded every penny of a meager budget, a frail thing who could easily be carried away by a strong gust of wind. But beneath the veneer, she was a dynamo. A hard-driving woman who mustered up an abundance of energy in pursuit of her son's goal: to create a nonprofit foundation that would tend to the needs of Vietnam veterans and their families.

Dr. Allen knew that his testimony was crucial to achieving those goals. He knew that billions were at stake. He also knew that under discovery, Victor Yannacone had forced Dow to turn over documents. The chemical giant relinquished every scrap of paper except for twenty-five studies that had been exempted under "national security." Each document had been scrutinized, examined, re-examined, discussed, and organized as to topic and relevance and importance. This was the largest product liability case ever. And Allen was a major witness.

His opinion could determine the outcome. His past and current studies proved that dioxin killed, deformed, and dehumanized veterans and families who had come in contact with it. By examining confidential and secret documents, Allen would now have a chance to compare Dow's data with his own. He could then testify under oath that Dow knew its product would kill even before they sold it to the military. This one fact could make Dow liable for billions.

At 10:15 a.m., Robert Aberg, a round-faced, distinguished man with the firm of Aberg and Jorgensen was in his law office in Madison, Wisconsin. He was busy.

People from the university had hastily carried in a microscope, slide projector, screen, and a box labeled "slides." These items were dropped off in the reception area without thought of where to put them. They cluttered up the floor.

Mr. Aberg required order. So, very quickly, the objects were moved from the waiting room to the conference room, which was rapidly transformed into an orderly classroom setting.

Doctor Allen's microscopic slides, color Polaroid photographs, projection slides, and photos of gross and histopathologic alterations of tissues, as well as an in-depth review of all data that had been used to publish the 500 ppt dioxin study, was to be gone over in every detail.

Earlier that morning, Aberg had received a call from the legal affairs office at the university. The caller informed him that two Dow employees, doctors J. D. Burek and T. J Bell, had arrived. They were ready to conduct their review of Allen's work that resulted in the publication of a scientific paper in 1977. Aberg had agreed to be available throughout the day after being told that Mr. Cartwright, coauthor of the study, would be available by phone should the reviewers need assistance or information.

CHAPTER TWENTY-NINE

When Burek and Bell opened the door to suite 1001, they were greeted by Mr. Aberg, who showed them into the conference room.

"Very nice," Bell said, nodding with obvious approval.

Burek opened a large brown envelope, slid out sheets of data, and turned to Aberg, who had his hand on the door.

"Before you leave," Burek said, "would you call Cartwright and check these data sheets for us? They were sent to us by Kirkland and Ellis, Dow's attorneys, prior to our coming here. Ask him if these copies were made from the originals."

A quick phone call affirmed the origin of the data sheets in question. "Yes, Cartwright said they were made from the originals."

Throughout the day, Burek asked questions and Aberg called Cartwright, who provided answers. By the end of the day, Cartwright agreed to copy any records in the pathology lab that would support or verify the accuracy of the preparation of the tissues that had been examined.

Upon his return to the university, Dr. Allen found everything in order, nothing out of place and no unusual occurrences. The lab was intact. He never knew that an audit had been conducted in the law offices of Aberg and Jorgensen. He never knew it had been ordered by Dow's attorneys. He never knew that Cartwright had cooperated. He never knew that Dow's attorneys had copies of his data sheets from a 1977 experiment, the year Rickey Marlar died, the year other data from the same experiment was found to be missing.

THIRTY

Edmund Janiszewski stood in Frank's Bunker, his legs apart, both hands in front of him, firmly gripping a flagstaff bearing an American flag. It was a customary procedure for members of the board to stand during the invocation prior to a meeting. All heads were bowed.

"We pray God's presence will be with us," Rev. Trees began, "and help us to understand how best to help our brethren. We pray for those who are ill and unable to be with us and for those in the community. We pray for a blessing for our leaders, may God grant them wisdom and grace."

A chorus of "Amens!" arose.

"Okay, guys!" Frank said with exuberance. "There's soft drinks and pretzels in the kitchen."

The flagstaff was returned to its base. The flag stood against an eight-foot wall and contrasted nicely with a trophy case holding an M-16. The flag bearer looked up at the weapon and heaved a heavy sigh. A flash of terrifying moments still dwelled inside him.

The crowd shuffled in and out of the kitchen, chatting and joking as they snacked and pointed to changes in the Bunker. Frank moved from group to group, welcoming them. As president of AOVI, he felt it his duty to create an atmosphere of camaraderie and kinship.

"Frank!" a vet called out across the room, pointing to a large map on the wall, "I love it! Great idea!"

Frank nodded. He too was pleased with the dozens of colored pins in cities and towns on the map, each pin boasting of an AOVI chapter. The organization had really grown.

"Over here, Frank!" Jane called. She and Muriel and three other board members were admiring the M-16 in a clear plastic case fixed to the wall. Beneath it, a gold metal plate held the words "MY BABY."

"What does that sign mean?" Jane asked. Muriel wanted to ask, but she had the feeling Frank had been irked by her excessive chatter. So she decided to let her daughter do the talking.

CHAPTER THIRTY

Frank was pleased at her question. "That really was my baby," Frank said. "When I roamed the jungles of Vietnam, that heavy weapon never weighed me down. It felt as light as a baby, and it kept me alive."

"Interesting," Muriel said, immediately pressing her lips together to remind herself to keep her mouth shut.

"Hey, Frank! Over here," a veteran hollered.

"Excuse me," Frank said, sidling his way toward his friend, who disappeared into the kitchen. Once there, Frank saw his friend and three others huddled near the fridge, all holding Cokes. "What's up?" he asked.

"We've been talkin'," the man replied. "We even made a little bet."

"What kind of bet?"

"It's about that red thing you sit on during the meeting. Tell us about it."

Frank wondered what they were grinning about. "What do you guys want to know?"

"Where'd ya get it? That's what the bets about. We each put up a buck and took a guess where that red thing came from."

Frank was amused. He decided to keep them guessing. "Where do you think it came from?"

"We got four picks. One, it's a hand-me-down from your great-great-grandma. Two, a piece of junk you picked up at a garage sale. Three, a relic from an antique shop that went outta business because they couldn't sell such trash. And four, a chair from a whorehouse that the madam sat on when she greeted guests."

Frank threw his head back and laughed. "I'm not telling," he said, shaking his head. "No one's going to win this bet."

"C'mon, Frank," his friend said. "You gotta tell! What is that thing?"

"Well...for your information," Frank replied, "that piece of furniture is a settee. It was popular in the eighteenth century and was owned by rich and powerful aristocrats. It was a status symbol. If you didn't have one, you didn't belong."

"How do you spell that word?" the friend asked.

"It's spelled s-e-t-t-e-e and pronounced set-tay."

"I'm impressed!" he said with mocking jocularity. "Really impressed!"

Knowing the meeting had to get started, Frank waved them away with both hands, hurried back, and seated himself on the settee. He checked a tape recorder on the card table in front of him, saw that Muriel, seated to the right of the table was ready, and Jane to the left was also ready with pen and notepad in hand.

Everyone had taken a seat or a space on the floor except his friend and the three others. They emerged from the kitchen and were inching their way toward Frank, who eyed them with suspicion. He knew they were up to something.

They surrounded the settee and began examining it. They ran their hands over the padded back and sides, fingered the smoothness of the carving on the wood frame, pushed down on the padded seat cushion, all the while pretending to examine it in a professional manner. Nodding to one another, they stroked their chins as if contemplating their find. It was an act everyone enjoyed, including Frank.

Friend suddenly dropped to the floor, rolled on his back, and shimmied himself under the seat. "Aha!" he hollered, "I knew it." He eased himself out from under, stood, looked at the crowd, pointed, and said, "You know what this is? It's a settee!" He shook his finger at it and said excitedly, "A real settee! Believe me! I know what I'm talking about. Frank owns a genuine settee."

"Where did he get it?" a voice asked.

"He won't say! He did say it goes back to the eighteenth century and that back then it was a status symbol. But let me say this. I grew up with Frank. We went to school together. We enlisted and went off to war together. We've been friends from day one. And I know my buddy. He has more status today than anyone ever had in the eighteenth century no matter how many settees they owned. What he's done. And what he's doing is nothing short of incredible. He's devoting his life to our guys and their families, and that is real status."

Friend and the three other turned to Frank and put their arms around him. "We love you, Frank," they said and then found a seat on the floor.

The room erupted into thunderous clapping while Frank sat on his settee, tears running down his cheeks. The clapping subsided, and then stopped. Everyone waited. Frank was all choked up and found it difficult to start the meeting.

He cleared his throat, took several deep breaths and said, "Thank you for coming. Let's begin."

CHAPTER THIRTY

"I move we dispense with the reading of minutes and reports," a voice quickly said.

"I second it," shouted someone from the back of the room.

"Any objections?" Frank asked, pausing and looking around. "No objections noted, the motion is passed."

Jane busily jotted down the flow of conversation.

"We have one item of business," Frank went on. "I would like to introduce it by playing a tape. It came two days ago from one of our guys in Michigan."

Frank fingered a button on the tape recorder, and a voice came out of the speaker.

"Did you participate in the EPA audit of the Allen and Schantz laboratory?"

"That's Dow's attorney," Frank rapidly explained.

"Yes, I did."

"That's Spencer," Frank added.

"What study did you audit?"

"I audited the rat study."

"Dr. Spencer, have you heard testimony by Dr. Gehring, a Dow scientist, which referred to PCB contamination with respect to the Allen and Schantz study?"

"Yes, I have."

"Was PCB contamination found in the food used in the monkey study?"

"Yes."

Frank pushed stop. The speaker went silent. Jane caught up with her notes. "Who is Spencer?" someone asked.

"He works for the EPA," Frank replied. "He barged into Allen's lab not long ago when Doc was away and audited a rat study for PCBs."

"What gave him the right?" Mrs. Reutershan asked indignantly.

"He had no right," Frank replied. "And even though he managed to get into Allen's lab, all he did was audit a rat study. And yet you heard him testify about a monkey study that Doc did more than two years ago. How could Spencer testify about a study he never audited? But he answered questions about it. Listen."

Frank pushed play.

"To clarify matters, you said there were two studies at different dose levels with monkeys."

"That is true, yes."

"Which dose levels?"

"Five hundred parts per trillion and fifty parts per trillion."

"With respect to the finding of high PCB contamination, was this found in the 500 study?"

"Yes, it was."

Frank pushed stop.

"What don't we hear?" Frank asked.

"This is a trial!" Murial Reutershan asked. "Why doesn't the EPA lawyer object?"

"That's right!" Frank roared. "Spencer is answering questions about a study he never audited. He is mouthing his answer based on testimony by Dr. Gehring, a Dow scientist. And even though Spencer's answers are based on hearsay, there was no objection. This is not a trial! It's a sham, a deliberate attempt to put into the court record the fact that it was PCBs that killed the monkeys, not dioxin. That kind of bullshit testimony can destroy Doc's work. And if Doc goes down, our suit could also go down. That's how I see it."

Lenny Laviano was on the floor in the middle of the group, glaring at his empty Coke can. "I'm sick of listening to all this crap," he thought. Slowly, he began squeezing the can. It gave a little and formed a slight bend. As hard as he tried, the flimsy can refused to yield any further. It refused to be crushed. Lenny picked himself up and held the can out for everyone to see.

"Look!" he said. "I used to crush this miserable thing with one squeeze. Now it's invincible. I don't have strength. Soon, I'll be leaving you guys forever. I've got weeks or months at the most. What's the point of my going out this way? Wouldn't it be better for me to leave with a bang, giving some of those bastards a message? This motto we have about dignity, self-respect, and solidarity is fine for all of you. You're gonna be around for a while. It would be better for me to resign from the organization and become a renegade. I'd love it! I would die happy! I would go knowing I left my mark."

Mrs. Reutershan stood up, gingerly weaved her way into the group, and parked herself in front of Lenny. She deftly snatched the Coke can out of his left hand and tossed a one-hander against a wall. It clinked and dropped into trash.

"Come with me, young man," she said in a no-nonsense tone. Taking his right hand in hers, she led him to the settee. "Move over, Frank," she said, "you are taking up all the room."

CHAPTER THIRTY

"Yes, ma'am," Frank replied, sliding his rear to one side.

"Sit," she ordered.

They both squeezed themselves in. Everyone watched with astonishment. Some were amused. But no one dared laugh, not even smile. What Mrs. Reutershan had done was a welcome relief to the tension that had suddenly erupted by Lenny's plea for permission to return to the days of Vietnam. The hushed silence in the room lingered.

Mrs. Reutershan took Lenny's hands in hers and said, "You remind me of my son. He was my only son, and I loved him dearly. He'd finish dinner and go to his room to write in his diary. But there were times when he'd just sit in the dark, alone with memories. I remember hearing him cry in the middle of the night. I would tiptoe my way to his room. No light shone under the door, but I'd listen to his sobs and mutterings. He'd use profanity and talked about killing a few bastards. But by morning, he was his old self again. I think he talked to relieve some inner craving that was always with him. Talking became a way of letting out anger at his country. But deep down, he knew he'd never pick up an M-16 and go out in a blaze of so-called glory. I knew he couldn't do it. And I know you won't do it."

"But I want to," Lenny said through his tears.

"I know you do," Muriel replied tearfully. Everyone was crying or dabbing at their eyes with a sleeve or the backs of their hands. Frank, who usually tried not to show emotion, called for a brief recess.

In ten minutes, the meeting resumed with three people now sitting on the illustrious settee: Frank, Lenny, and Muriel Reutershan. Her natural instincts had diffused a dangerous situation. Frank shifted his position on the crowded settee, placed the speakerphone on the table in front of him, and punched in numbers.

"Hello?"

"Hi, Christie! It's Frank. Is Doc in?"

"Hold on, he's in the barn."

As everyone waited, Mrs. Reutershan wondered what her cowboy was doing in the barn. Jane doodled on her notepad. Frank glanced at the doodle, not knowing what to make of it. Lenny sat there thinking about Paul, who had sobbed and muttered in the dark, something he had been doing for a long time.

Dr. Allen's voice came into the room. "Hi, Frank!" he said, trying to catch his breath. "What's up?"

"I'm in the middle of a board meeting, Doc. I've got you on speakerphone. And first off, I'd like to thank you again for going over Dow's documents."

"Anytime, Frank. What's up?"

"Our board just listened to a tape of Spencer testifying in court about your 500 ppt study."

"He had nothing to do with that study! What was the trial about?" Allen asked.

"When the EPA banned Silvex and 2,4,5-T, Dow filed suit to have the ban lifted."

"What's that got to do with me? Those chemicals were banned because of the EPA's findings in Alsea."

"The EPA cited your work, Doc. They used it to justify the ban. I think the trial is part of a Dow strategy. They're trying to prove your work was flawed, that it was PCBs that killed the monkeys, not dioxin."

"That's ridiculous! Dow can't discredit the 500 study. It was published in a scientific journal. It was reviewed by three scientists, and they recommended publication. This business of high PCBs reminds me of that Kociba letter to Cartwright, claiming high PCBs in the 500 study. If Dow found it, they would have shown it to me. But so far, I've seen nothing."

"You've seen nothing because they have nothing." Frank replied. "But Spencer testified that Dow did the work and found PCBs because you weren't able to do that work."

"What a lot of bull," Allen replied. "Ask Mrs. Reutershan. She has a copy of every one of my publications. I was publishing studies on PCBs for years. Those analyses were always done in my lab."

Mrs. Reutershan nodded. She wasn't going to say a word with Frank in the room. She saw the way he rolled his eyes, asking God for assistance when she talked too much. And although she didn't give a hoot about what Frank thought, she cared a great deal about the Lord's opinion. Her son was up there, and she wanted him to be proud of her. Bad PR from Frank to God was something she definitely did not want.

THIRTY-ONE

June 10, 1979. Doctor Allen was on a flight to DC, sitting next to the window, tormented by his thoughts. All around him, life and events went on as usual.

To his left, billowing white clouds floated in the blue sky. Next to him, a male passenger flipped the pages of *Sports Illustrated*. Up front, a stewardess wearing Delta wings pushed a cart, stopped, and passed out drinks. But Allen saw none of this.

He was in deep trouble. A letter from the U.S. Attorney informed him that an arraignment had been set for October 17. He worried about his legal representation. Yannacone could not find an attorney who would take him on without a ten thousand dollar retainer. The large sum was absolutely essential. The theft charges would have to be investigated. Colleagues would have to be contacted and depositions taken. A defense would have to be planned. And at two hundred an hour, money would quickly disappear.

How could he afford it? He pondered the question of increasing the mortgage on his home and farm. This idea didn't particularly disturb him. But the unthinkable did.

What if there was a prolonged court battle? What about possible appeals? Additional money would be needed. The amount could become astronomical! He could lose his property! And worst of all, there was no guarantee he would go free.

Ending up in prison was a horrifying nightmare. What would happen to his family? His sons were in college, tuition was high, and Christie could not make it on her own. If she and the boys had to, they could move in with his parents and live on the family farm in North Carolina. It was free and clear of all encumbrances. But then what?

Doctor Allen looked up at the sound of a voice. "Would you like something to drink, sir?"

"No, thank you."

The fasten seatbelt sign lit up. "We're encountering a bit of rough air. Please remain in your seats," a voice from the intercom said.

Allen clicked his seatbelt and tightened the strap. The plane suddenly dropped, moving with up, down, and side movements. Passengers looked about with a sense of alarm at the thought of a possible calamity. Allen too had a fleeting thought of disaster but was not unduly alarmed.

"I'm worth two hundred thousand...dead," he thought. "It will pay off the mortgage and put the boys through school. And if Christie sues..."

Allen adjusted his seat to a reclining position and closed his eyes. He tried to relax, but the reason for his flight to DC bounced around in his head.

The VA had invited him to become a member of the Advisory Committee on Health Related Effects of Herbicides. He was puzzled. Neither he nor his wife could explain it. Frank was certain it was an attempt to get him out of town and advised him to stay put. However, by nature, Allen was curious. He wanted to find out why the VA had invited him. They knew his position on Agent Orange. It was totally opposed to their own. They had seen him on the Bill Kurtis documentary more than a year ago.

When he finally decided to accept the invitation, he relished the idea of going dressed like a cowboy. He took his ten-gallon hat down from a closet shelf, put it on, looked in the bathroom mirror, and liked what he saw. Clint Eastwood! But Christie shook her head. Her face told of absolute disapproval.

"The VA meeting is not for cowboys. It's for scientists," she said.

Reluctantly, he returned the hat to its resting place. But deep down, he was sorry he had not followed his instincts. He would have loved to walk into the VA meeting with his high-heeled boots and all, a symbol of a cowboy's arduous way of life. A life that tended to develop rough-and-ready virtues, full-blown manliness. It would feel good to deliver that kind of message.

"All attendants prepare for landing," the captain said.

June 11, 1979. The next day, at 9:55 a.m., a security officer pointed Dr. Allen toward room 119. In moments, he came to an open doorway. He paused and quickly counted twelve men at one end of the room, sitting around an oval conference table. Facing the distinguished panel, elbow-to-elbow spectators sat quietly on metal folding chairs.

No one said hello as Allen found an empty seat near one end of the table. "Why haven't they acknowledged my presence," he wondered. "They would sure pay attention if I looked like Clint Eastwood, unarmed of course."

CHAPTER THIRTY-ONE

"I'd like to begin promptly," Dr. Haber said, sitting on a straight-backed chair at one end of the table.

The meeting moved forward. Dr. Haber called upon members to introduce themselves and to explain their particular area of interest. Allen listened to each speaker attentively.

Finally, Haber looked at Allen and said, "The potential link between exposure to herbicides and long-term pathological effects is something that has seized the public interest. We must not establish such a link until it has been made clearly evident through scientific inquiry. Dr. Allen, will you please tell us where you are in your research and what your plans are?"

"They are digging for information," Allen thought. "Is this why I was invited?"

He moved himself to a more upright position. The words flowed effortlessly.

"We have found that a low level of dioxin is extremely toxic." He quickly glanced around, all eyes were on him. "At 500 ppt in the diet for nine months, over 50 percent of the animals died." The word "died" elicited an expression of uneasiness on the faces of two members sitting opposite him. "After the first three months, monkeys began to lose their hair, they had swollen eyelids, dry, scaly skin, and hematological abnormalities. At six months of exposure, the animals developed a severe decrease in white and red blood cells and a marked decrease in blood platelets. We then attempted to breed the eight animals. Three became pregnant and two aborted early. At seven months, we lost our first experimental animal due to excessive bleeding. By the ninth month, we lost our second animal due to widespread hemorrhage. By the tenth month, we took the animals off the diet."

A man next to Dr. Haber glanced at his watch. Allen didn't care. He wasn't about to stop halfway through his talk. He shifted in his seat, pulled himself up, and kept right on talking.

"During the next three months, we lost three more animals. Five of the eight animals died from dioxin intoxication." Allen was on a roll and moved along. "Some of the lesions we found, in addition to loss of hair and eyelashes, swollen eyelids and dry scaly skin, including thickening and ulceration of the gastric mucosa. We then started new studies and reduced the dioxin to 50 ppt. After six months, we attempted to breed them. Of the eight, six became pregnant. Four aborted early, just like the first group. This showed the effect of dioxin on the reproductive capability of nonhuman primates."

One member at the far end of the table looked at Dr. Haber with an impatient expression that asked, "How long is he going to talk?" He knew Allen posed a threat to his own beliefs about dioxin. He had heard enough. In fact, too much. He thought it best for Haber to call on another speaker, but Doctor Allen kept on going.

"This 50 group has been on the diet for two years, and they are showing the same signs as the 500 group. When the levels of exposure to dioxin are higher, changes occur more rapidly than when the level is low. It appears that the same effects develop in experimental animals regardless of time, whether it be three months at 500 ppt or two years at 50 ppt. We now have new studies. We are feeding 25 ppt of dioxin to monkeys."

Several members cleared their throats. Others closed their eyes. Some looked at Haber, clearly annoyed. They did not want to hear any more. If Allen was allowed to go on, he would be talking about 5 ppt and would be on the verge of saying there was absolutely no safe level for dioxin.

Everyone knew, except Allen, that the committee was mandated to put the minutes of the meeting into the Federal Register. This was a requirement for all formal, governmental committees. They did not want Allen's words in print for the world to see. "Shut the guy up," is what they wanted, but Allen decided he had something else to say, something very important.

"I would like to mention our preliminary work with rats fed dioxin diets with a level of 3 parts per billion and 5 parts per trillion. Thirty-seven percent had lung and liver tumors, and the same was found by Dow Chemical at somewhat higher levels of dioxin. The Illinois Institute of Technology also showed that dioxin caused cancer, and at recent meetings of the American Association for Cancer Research, they agreed! Dioxin does promote cancer."

Dr. Haber tried to silence him. "Thank you," he said. "I'm sure there will be questions about it this afternoon."

But Allen didn't want to keep quiet. It was his turn to speak up, and talk he did. He described work done at the National Institute of Environmental Health Sciences. Tumors were produced at a dioxin level of 70 micrograms per kilogram of body weight. The only difference? It took longer for tumors to show up when the amount of dioxin was low. Allen hit a homer. It was at the heart of his theory. It was what the Vietnam veterans would prove when their suit wended its way through the court system and stood before the bar. Allen would testify

CHAPTER THIRTY-ONE

that low level exposure over long periods of time produced cancer in addition to everything else the veterans complained of. He had not found a no-effect level. There was no safe level for dioxin. Doctor Allen had one more thing to say. It concerned the ill effects of dioxin on people.

"I have received unofficial reports—"

Dr. Haber quickly interrupted him. "Thank you, Dr. Allen. We certainly appreciate your statement. I'd like to move on. Dr. Erickson, would you please tell us what your laboratory has been doing and can you shed any light on this problem for us?"

"The rates have remained fairly stable. Birth defects have been around for a long time," Dr. Erickson said.

Dr. Erickson went on to talk about the thalidomide problem in the 1960s, a birth monitoring program, and the epidemiology of birth defects...

As he talked on, Doctor Allen felt as if he had been slapped in the face. He listened as Dr. Haber called on other speakers and not once did he forcefully shut any of them up. Allen was now certain he had been invited because the VA wanted to know where he was with his work. And he gave them a mouthful, and now he wondered if it would have been more prudent to have kept his mouth shut. He remembered Frank's words of caution, "Be careful, Doc. They are out to get you."

As the morning dragged on, his thoughts wandered back to his early days. He had been happy just doing research. No requests from foreign governments pulling him away from home. Only the joy of working in his lab and discovering something new.

Suddenly, the name of Frank McCarthy pulled him out of his mental wanderings, and he saw a tall, thin and young spectator speaking at the far end of the room.

"I saw Frank in Kansas City last week," the young man said. "And he didn't think it was worthwhile coming to this meeting because he believed the purpose of this committee was to whitewash the entire issue."

The young man went on to tell of endless medical problems experienced by veterans: cancer and tumors in men twenty-five to thirty-five years old, difficulty in conceiving children after returning from Vietnam, multiple miscarriages by wives often followed by the birth of a child with severe physical deformities.

"So what was the VA's response?" the young man asked. "No firm evidence exists to incriminate these herbicides. Men were brutally turned away with the statement that their problems couldn't be from Agent Orange, that it was all in their heads. And they were then sent to a shrink. Each time the news media carried the reported symptoms, calls from Vietnam vets poured in to our office. A document came to our organization showing that VA central office called for the destruction of tumor and cancer registry records. At the same time, spokesmen from VA central office assured us that all medical records would be preserved and sent to the National Cancer Institute. In addition, vets from all over the country have called in to tell us of the run-around, red tape, and outright malpractice in the VA healthcare system. The VA seems to have lost all credibility with this country's Vietnam veterans. Until the VA gives vets their rightful first-class medical care, courteously, sympathetically, and with dignity befitting their status as warriors of our society, vets will stay away."

Doctor Allen was impressed by the young man's eloquence. The way he spoke his piece. Gesturing with his hands to emphasize a point. No hesitation. No fear. Looking at Dr. Haber with fierce determination in his eyes. Raising his voice at the proper moment. Lowering it to ease emotional tension. The young man's complaints were damning, and one could now believe anything about the VA. Dr. Allen was glad he came.

On the flight back to Madison, Allen took time to reflect on the meeting and events of the past. He knew the VA wanted information about his work. Haber asked for it, and he foolishly gave it. They now knew his studies would prove the deadly effects of dioxin. They now knew he would prove there was no safe level of dioxin. To stop him, they would have to discredit his work. He remembered the Kociba letter to Cartwright that told of finding high PCBs even though he had never asked Dow to check for PCBs. That Kociba letter established a false record. It could be used to invalidate the 500 ppt dioxin study. Spencer's testimony could also be used to invalidate the 500 study. Taken together, they could lead to the destruction of his life's work. Years of effort down the drain.

"It's a damn neat little plan they've cooked up," he mumbled to himself. "Why have I been so blind?"

THIRTY-TWO

As the Summer months of '79 blended into Fall, the medical school issue dominated the news. Two hundred fifty professors from every department had reportedly been raking in tens of thousands of dollars, in addition to salary. And they absolutely refused to provide a complete and detailed financial report to Dean Smith.

"The doctors don't necessarily like outsiders, including the dean, to know what they're doing," Dave Pritchard said in his *Capital Times* article. He went on to report, "Right now, behind closed doors, a federal grand jury under the direction of the U.S. Attorney Frank Tuerkheimer is investigating how money flows to and from the professors through the clinical practice plan."

Capital Times articles forced Dr. Allen into a daily ritual. He'd leave home at sunup, pick up a paper on his way to the office, sip coffee, and read the news until every sentence in every article had been thoroughly digested. Only then would he throw himself into his work, while still struggling with his own legal dilemma as to who would represent him.

The date for his October 17 arraignment was fast approaching. Logic demanded that he get an attorney highly experienced in criminal law. He had checked into the background of Jim Robins: born 1953, BA degree at the University of Wisconsin, law degree at Chicago-Kent College of Law, and admitted to the bar in 1977. How good was he with only two years of experience under his belt?

In spite of this nagging question, the financial problem dominated his thinking. Christie, his sons, and his parents urged him to increase the mortgage on his home and farm, but he refused. His position was clear. The government had unlimited resources and paid no heed to costs. He had very little. So even if he were to increase the mortgage or sell the property, the money would not last long. Legal fees would mount up, possibly to staggering sums. He just could not do it. Therefore, he would take his chances with Kessler and Robbins. He called and made an appointment.

October 8, 1979, mid-morning. A cloudy day with on-again, off-again drizzle. Allen and his wife eased their car into a parking stall outside a beautiful old home overlooking Lake Michigan.

The news media were waiting, and Dr. Allen and Christie immediately faced a minicam. Photographers and reporters surrounded their car. Bulbs flashed even before they exited the car. Allen felt devastated at the thought of being in the news again.

Christi's door flew open. She stood upright, leaned on the open door, and pleaded for the press to leave. "There will be no statements. None," she said, using both hands to emphasize the fact that not one word would be forthcoming. Bulbs flashed again and again.

Allen's door slowly opened. The crush of the press would not allow for a wide opening of the door, but Allen lifted himself out and found a hand reaching out toward him, holding a mike. Questions were thrown at him. "Were you indicted by the grand jury? How will you plead? Will this affect your research?"

Dr. Allen and Christie ran for the building. Entering and breathing hard, Christie closed the heavy oak door behind them. The news media lingered outside like a pack of wild dogs waiting for its prey. Allen marched straight up to a dark-haired, young receptionist who bore a demeanor of impeccable efficiency. The placard "Debra—Receptionist" reminded him of his last visit when nobody was here to greet him.

"Mr. Kessler is expecting you," she said.

Allen motioned with his head to Christie. She came forward and whispered, "Go up alone, I'll wait down here."

Bill Kessler and Jim Robins were waiting. The introduction was brief, and Allen looked Robins over: young, slim, round-faced, clean-shaven, neatly trimmed hair, and would present himself favorably to a jury. But how much experience did he have in criminal law?

"The auditors reported," Robins said, "that in four instances, you submitted vouchers for trips where no business was conducted. They said you went skiing."

"They misrepresented the facts!" Allen exclaimed. "I did go for business, but on two occasions, the people I was supposed to meet weren't there. I couldn't just wait around, so I returned another time and completed the business on my own time and at my own expense."

Robins raised his eyebrows, seemingly skeptical.

CHAPTER THIRTY-TWO

"Look," Allen said, "taking a few hours off for skiing was within my rights. I subsequently paid for the trips with my own money."

"Hmm..." Robbins murmured, studying his notes. "What about the other two trips? One included your son."

"My son was on that trip because he worked in the lab and was in part responsible for the research on pulmonary hypertension in monkeys. I wanted him to participate in the future planning of that project. So we went to the Colorado State University to discuss it. After the working session, he and I went skiing. My personal discretionary account paid for that."

"And Fort Collins?" Robins asked.

"My son and I went to the airport to go to Fort Collins," Allen replied with vigor. "Flights were delayed because equipment problems and bad weather. We could not get there, but I went at a later date and completed the work at my own expense and on my own time."

"Did you combine business with pleasure using federal grant money?"

"I combined business with pleasure. I explained it to the grand jury, " Allen went on more strongly. "A training grant was due to expire. If it was not used by Walter Hargraves, it would have to be returned to the granting agency. Walter wanted to present a paper at a later date and needed money for the trip. With his approval, I used the training grant money for my trip with the understanding that he would use my discretionary account money for his trip. I swapped money like that all the time."

Robins asked no further questions. Kessler had listened without comment. Doctor Allen felt good about his explanation because it was logical and made sense. But he now wanted to hear the opinion of someone versed in criminal law. He waited.

"One other point," Robins said, "the auditors mentioned a long distance, private phone call, paid for with federal grant money."

"You must be kidding!" Allen exclaimed. "One illegal phone call in seventeen years! So what! Who remembers? Did it cost a dollar? Or two or three? For that I'm a thief?"

Robins remained silent. Kessler jumped in.

"Dr. Allen," he said, "I would like to dispense of this matter as quickly as possible. In doing so, Jim and I have to consider the legalities of the situation you find yourself in. The legal issues involved are foremost in the mind of the U.S. Attorney. I'll call him. Maybe something can be worked out. It's Tuesday. Let's meet Friday, the eleventh, same time."

Jim and Christie lunched in a booth at the Olive Garden. The minestrone soup was hot and delicious and eased some of their tension.

"From what you told me, you did well," Christie said. "I don't see how you can be accused of theft. You didn't steal anything."

A waitress and busboy turned a corner at the far end and came toward their booth. He held a round tray balanced on the palm of one hand. The waitress kept pace with him and said a few words to him as they neared Allen's booth. A wooden stand was quickly put in place and the tray set down. The busboy left and the waitress placed thick eggplant parmigiana, a side order of spaghetti, and long, hot garlic rolls in front of them.

"Is there anything else I can get for you?" the waitress asked.

"Everything's fine," Allen said.

"Looks good," Christie said, cutting into her thick, cheesy entrée.

"Too much food," Jim said as he coiled spaghetti onto his fork.

"Tell me," Christie asked, "why was Professor Snowden given such a long sentence?"

"He used Teacher Corps project money for meals, clothing, and liquor. This was a government program. He also used money for recreation at Stevens Point Country Club. He embezzled thousands."

"Was he part of the medical school?"

"No, he was in the school of education."

"Why haven't there been charges against any of the medical doctors? I read they submitted bills to Medicare and Medicaid when they provided no care. Isn't that fraud?"

"Probably, but the CPP program was started years ago, and rumor has it that if charges were filed against doctors, the university would have to close the medical school. It's a real hot potato."

"What's CPP?"

"Clinical Practice Program. Doctors have private patients and submit bills to the insurance company. Millions come in every year. Medicaid and Medicare pays for the poor and elderly. One fourth of CPP's income is from these patients. There's talk that improper bills were submitted. Only people at the top know what happened."

CHAPTER THIRTY-TWO

"So I have to believe that the grand jury must know, and the U.S. Attorney must know."

"Seems like they should," Jim replied. "But the only thing I know is that the university receives some of the profits, and I get a gift donation from it every year. It's put into my discretionary account. And I'm free to do whatever I want with it. It's not monitored or controlled in any way. The other gift donation I get is from the Food Research Institute. I do work for them, and they've been generous to me. I have well over $20,000 in my account right now."

"That's a nice sum."

"Too bad I didn't use that money for those trips. This mess wouldn't have happened."

Christie speared more eggplant, chewed, and rolled up a forkful of spaghetti, shaking her head, lost in thought of what might have been.

Mid-morning, three days later, Doctor Allen was in the conference room with Kessler and Robins. He waited for someone to start the conversation.

"The best way of settling this is by cutting a deal," Kessler said.

Allen was startled. "Cutting a deal?"

"Yes. Pleading guilty in exchange for a lighter sentence."

"Guilty? Why should I plead guilty when I'm innocent?"

"I talked with Tuerkheimer. He said it's either a deal or he will take it to court and prosecute. It's best to settle without a trial."

Doctor Allen's heart was doing double-time, and his mouth was dry.

"It doesn't seem right! I explained everything! I didn't steal anything!"

Robins spoke up. "If you look at the facts, you did take money from a federal grant and used it for recreational purposes. In one instance you took your son along. When you asked for reimbursement, you made it appear as if Hargraves had accompanied you. From a legal point of view," Robins hesitated, then firmly said, "that's theft."

"What if I plead not guilty?" Allen asked.

"You're guilty," Kessler replied. "The facts speak for themselves. If you refuse to agree to a deal, Tuerkheimer will prosecute, and you stand a chance of going to jail."

This was the hardest punch Kessler could have delivered. It threw Allen into a panic. Guilty? From his own attorney? Was Kessler correct? Did the facts speak for themselves?

Was it better to cut a deal and hope for the best? Or should he take his chances in court? He didn't know what to do, but he remembered what Frank had said, "Go slow."

"I'd like to think about it," Allen said, staring at his hands resting in his lap.

"Fine," Kessler replied. "I'll talk with Tuerkheimer and see what he's willing to offer. We will continue to act on your behalf and do what's best for you."

Although his gut told him to plead not guilty, Allen did not trust his own judgment or his instincts. He was ignorant of the law. So he would take time to decide. He would talk with his sons and close friends.

"Today is Friday," Allen said, "I'll call Monday."

"Good enough," Kessler replied. Standing up, he showed Dr. Allen out of the conference room.

For Dr. Allen and his family, the following two days were hell. Allen decided to hide from the press and stay home. Friends and colleagues called and told him of front-page coverage in Madison newspapers. His story and a photo of him crossed state lines. Papers sold quickly in New York and Oregon where the Love Canal and Alsea battles had been fought.

The phone line was manned by his son, Chris, who filtered out crank calls and those from the press. Christie kept her husband abreast on what had been reported. One bold headline in Madison read, "Top Scientist Indicted. U.S. Attorney to Prosecute." Another read, "Oregon Environmentalists Tell Scientist To Plead Not Guilty."

It seemed as if the phones never stopped ringing, and Allen was no longer talking. He was tired of advice and tired of listening to opinions.

"Hold all calls," Allen said to his son, He glared at the receiver every time it rang and restrained the urge to throw the phone in trash.

The immediate family sat huddled together in the living room. A grouping of chairs sat around a coffee table with cold drinks in tall glasses and a fruit bowl with apples, bananas, pears and oranges, but no one had an appetite.

Dr. Allen's parents had flown in overnight to lend support. Now, all four sons—Rob, Chris, Oliver, and Jim—and his parents, himself, and Christie discussed the dilemma.

"We have savings," the elder Allen said, gesturing with both hands, almost pleading with his son. "It sits in the bank doing nothing. Take it! Defend yourself! Plead not guilty!"

CHAPTER THIRTY-TWO

Doctor Allen's mother nodded approval as her fingers twisted a linen kerchief.

"Your money will go fast," Dr. Allen replied.

"The family farm is worth a fortune," his father said. "We can easily raise more money."

Allen stood up, paced up and back as he spoke with fervor. "I can't do it. I can't sell my heritage. It belonged to my great-grandfather, my grandfather, then to my father. It belongs to our children," his voice rose with the passion of his conviction. "That land must be passed on. It is a legacy, and I refuse to destroy it. It's too precious. I would rather die."

Christie broke in, siding with her father-in-law. "Our house hasn't been in the family! All we have to do is refinance. We could get $25,000. It would last a while."

Dr. Allen shook his head. "It would be a waste. I talked with a friend whose son is a lawyer. He said the time needed to defend this case would be enormous. And with appeals, it would cost at least $250,000, probably more."

Dr. Allen gazed at the faces of his loved ones. He chastised himself for what he had done to them.

"Dad," Chris cut in. "We talked it over. We'll drop out of school. We can save and go back in a year or two." The boys nodded.

Dr. Allen continued pacing.

"No," he firmly replied. "I cannot allow you to pay a price because of your father's stupidity, or sins, or whatever else you want to call it."

"Sins!" Christie shouted. "How can you say sins? You know, we all know you did nothing wrong!"

Doctor Allen dropped into a chair, anxiously staring at everyone's faces. He took a deep breath and sighed. He felt old and tired.

"You're all ganging up on me," he said. "But my mind is made up." He held up his hand to stifle protestations. "I'll do the best I can without interfering in your lives. I do appreciate what you want to do, but my conscience won't allow it. I cannot accept your offers."

The phone rang. Chris picked it up as Allen gestured that he wasn't up to taking calls. Chris smiled at the voice on the other end. "Dad, it's Frank." Dr. Allen grabbed the phone.

"Hi, Frank."

"It's in the paper, Doc. Is it as bad as it sounds?"

"Could be, Frank."

"Doc, you've gotta fight! You must have an attorney with a helluva lot of experience. Someone who knows how to fight the government. I know it costs a bundle, but it is a must. Everything you've worked for is at stake. And people want you out. As far as I'm concerned, the university is in on it. You cannot let it happen!"

"You're probably right, Frank. Before the HEW auditors left, one of them said, 'You have enemies in high places.' That could be the chancellor of the university."

"Your problem right now, Doc, is not the university. Your problem right now is deciding which way to go. You seem to have lawyers who believe you're guilty. You say you're not guilty. So, what's it going to be, guilty or not guilty?"

THIRTY-THREE

Larry McKitrick was the most famous Vietnam veteran in Wisconsin and the one person feared most by the press.

Growing up in southern Kentucky, Larry was a gawky kid with skinny legs who dreaded going to school. While hurrying along, books cradled in his left arm and a brown paper bag clutched in his right hand, local bullies surrounded him. They would grab the bag and laugh as he frantically looked for a way to escape. They would push, jab, and taunt him, all the while biting into his Oreos and passing around his two baloney sandwiches. One time, a brown mutt ran over from across the street and stood on its hindquarters, looking up, mouth open and tongue lapping at air.

The taller bully tossed a scrap of meat to the mutt. "Here, Brownie," he said, "skinny legs don't wan' it." Brownie snapped it up and begged for more.

Poor Larry laid on the ground and cried. Only then did the bullies leave, laughing all the way. Larry's father, Mr. McKitrick, a muscular bricklayer, tried to teach his son to fight using a punching bag, heavy bag, weights, jump rope, and boxing gloves. Lessons were given every day in the basement, but the bullies still overpowered him. Larry struggled to the twelfth grade with skinny legs and skinnier arms.

In his last year of high school, he stood before the mirror one morning, bare-chested, looking himself over. He flexed his right arm, making a fist as tight as he could, straining every last piece of flesh in that skinny thing. With his left hand, he touched what looked like a rise in his right arm. It was firm! A muscle! It was there! He wasn't a wimp!

Graduation. Vietnam war. Larry wanted to be a fighter. He volunteered with his father's blessing and his mother's tears. Larry had no siblings, and Father always said that one was enough. But now, Father was hopeful. Maybe the military could do what he had never been able to do.

It wasn't long before Larry Mckitrick shipped out. Then something happened that was almost magical. Larry filled out. He had muscular arms, legs, chest, back, and neck. He became a big man with baby blue, twinkling eyes. Mother said it was God, but her lady friend called it hormones. Either way, his buddies nicknamed him Bull.

Overseas, Larry "The Bull" McKitrick became a terror. He was the youngest soldier in a Special Forces crew of two officers and ten enlisted men stationed in a camp between Na Trang and Cam Rahn Bay, bordering the China Sea. The crew was positioned in an old fortress, once the home of royalty. A moat surrounded the palatial camp. But Larry did not spend much time inside.

His crew was constantly on the attack, killing Viet Cong. Larry would race through the jungle ahead of the others, firing his automatic weapon, charging the enemy like a raging bull. He did this several times a day for almost a year. One day, his crew ran into heavy enemy fire. Larry lost his right ear when a piece of shrapnel sliced it clean off. His fighting days in Vietnam were over.

His parents saw him without an ear. Although Father felt badly, he also felt proud. He bragged to friends of his son's twenty-six medals, all with bronze and silver oak leaf clusters. But mother cried to her friends as she talked about the horrible accident, and although friends tried to console her, their words only brought on more tears.

With time, Larry began looking for a job. He'd fill out applications and put down his name as Larry "The Bull" McKitrick. When interviewed, he answered questions truthfully.

"My experience? None," he'd say. "The only thing I know about is guns and killing Viet Cong. I've never had any other job."

Larry couldn't find work. One day, he received a call from Madison, Wisconsin. A security firm heard about him and hired him over the phone after talking with him for three minutes. Bull loved the work. He never took time off. He was fiercely loyal to the firm and covered for other workers when they became ill. He made good money and stashed it away. Five years later, he quit and opened up his own security firm. He jokingly called it "The No-Bull Security, Inc." His father beamed. Mother smiled, and there were no more tears.

Business was good, and his work force increased. When a new man was interviewed, Bull asked one question, "Did you serve in Vietnam?" If the answer was yes, the man started work immediately. And if the new employee was hard up for money, he received a week's salary in advance.

CHAPTER THIRTY-THREE

When Paul Reutershan formed Agent Orange Victims International, Bull joined. He soon had a Wisconsin chapter of AOVI and became its first director. When Paul died, Bull wrote a letter to Frank McCarthy signed by sixty-one employees, all Vietnam veterans. They pledged loyalty and full dedication to everything AOVI stood for. They vowed to help not only ailing veterans, but also their families and children and anyone else who served the needs of the organization.

On Sunday, October 13, 1979, Frank McCarthy's filled in Bull on Dr. Allen's concerns.

"The news media won't leave him alone," Frank said with a note of alarm in his voice. "They've been playing it up big. The publicity has been awful. He has an appointment to see his lawyer tomorrow, and the media will be waiting. He needs a lawyer experienced in criminal law, but it has to be pro bono. What can he do?"

"No problem with the media, Frank," Bull replied, leaning back in a rickety, wooden swivel. "Free lawyers are hard. None of our guys are lawyers. Sorry to say, I don't know anybody."

When Bull hung up, he knew there would be no problem with the media. His experience with the media began fifteen days after he started his new job with the security firm. He captured a break-and-entry in a large department store. The thug had the getaway car loaded with expensive jewelry. Newspapers carried the story and Bull's picture. Another photo showed the owner of the store posing with Bull, handing him a twenty-four karat Bulova. It was the first time in his life Bull had owned pure gold. He carried it for six days, heard of a buddy whose family was hungry, sold the watch, and gave his fellow veteran $1,450.

A reporter picked up the news. It became a sensational human interest story, and this was the start of many stories about Larry "The Bull" McKitrick. Vietnam veterans loved him. They would die for him. And Vietnam loyalty extended to wives and children, grandparents, uncles, aunts, cousins, more cousins, and an endless number of friends of all these people. This vast array of people added up to votes, and when officials ran for office, one word from Bull could tip an election toward the incumbent or the challenger.

Politicians courted him. They threw money at him, but the money soon went back with a polite note, giving them the address of AOVI. Contributions poured into the organization, but the need was so great, it barely made a dent.

Bull's clients and many contributors to AOVI had difficulties with the news media. Reporters would barge in when not wanted. Photographers would hide behind bushes and jump out, flashing their cameras. People would ask for Bull's help, and it did not take long for him to protect people's privacy.

Newsmakers began having difficulties. Bulbs would not flash. Cameras were accidently damaged, some beyond repair. By coincidence, four tires on a car would be found flat, and reporters could not get to their stories on time. Phone lines died, and some newspapers came out of the presses upside down; time was involved in correcting the problem and deadlines were missed. When a problem became too much of an annoyance, presses broke down, and expensive repairs became an emergency item on the balance sheet for that month.

No one was ever injured unless a reporter took a swing at Bull and connected. That newsman was soon lifted from the street onto a stretcher and rushed to the hospital. And when he was released from hospital care, the unfortunate man collected unemployment compensation. Many times, he would have to apply for permanent disability benefits.

Owners of newspapers and boards of directors tried to get Bull into trouble, but he had too many political connections. News media owners finally waved the white flag.

Because of his experience with reporters, Bull knew there'd be no problem with the news media when he delivered Dr. Allen to his appointment on Monday.

On Monday, October 14, at 8:30 a.m., the Allen clan heard a distant roar growing louder and louder. Suddenly, it moved onto their driveway and died. Startled, Christie ran to the window.

"Oh my!" she exclaimed excitedly, gesturing everyone toward her.

In seconds, the Allen family formed a tight knot of eight heads, peering at three men on red Harley-Davidson motorcycles. They were dressed in black leather jackets, pants, boots, and helmets, and they exuded an air of authority. One of them swung his leg off the bike, adjusted the kickstand with the toe of his high-heeled boot, and strode toward the front door. Helmet in hand, he rang the doorbell.

Dr. Allen warily opened the door. "May I help you?" he asked, somewhat startled by looking at a face with one ear.

"Are you Dr. Allen?"

CHAPTER THIRTY-THREE

"Yes," Allen said quietly.

"Frank McCarthy asked me to escort you to your lawyer's office. He wants to make sure the news media leave you alone."

"Oh!" Dr. Allen replied, pleased at the thought of having an escort. He wondered how the news media would be kept away. "Come in. You and your friends. My appointment is at ten. My wife and I will be ready in time. How about coffee and some breakfast?"

"No, thanks. We'll wait outside. My name is Larry 'The Bull' McKitrick, but my friends call me Bull," he replied, holding out his right hand.

Dr. Allen shook his hand heartily. He had read about Bull and knew of his reputation. "It's a pleasure meeting you. I've heard such great things about you."

Bull smiled and headed back to the waiting Harleys. Allen closed the door, and suddenly he had a wonderful feeling. Bull McKitrick meant absolute safety, at least from photographers and reporters. They wouldn't dare tangle with this man.

Dr. Allen and Christie wanted to leave no later than 9:00 a.m. and had been listless all morning, not having slept much during the night. But with the arrival of Bull, their adrenaline began pumping.

The phone rang. "Hello?" Allen said brusquely, not knowing who would be on the other end.

"It's me, Doc. Did my guys get there?"

"They're here now, Frank! Thanks a million."

"Let me know how things go, Doc."

"I will, Frank."

At 9:00 a.m. sharp, Dr. Allen and his wife were in their car, backing out of the driveway. The Harleys waited on the road, motors purring. In seconds, the motorcycles accelerated and headed toward Madison, two red Harleys in front and one behind the red Mustang. They soared down the two-lane highway, attracting attention. Farmers waved. Cows stopped their chewing and mooed. A lady bus driver in a yellow school bus put her hand on the horn in salute to the mini-presidential caravan.

The entourage arrived in the outskirts of Madison at 9:26 a.m. and found their way to Kessler and Associates by 9:59, with ten minutes to spare. Allen turned off the ignition as the Harleys continued to purr. Christie looked out the windows in amazement. No reporters, no photographers, no minicams or mikes.

"Incredible," Christie said, highly impressed.

Her husband smiled at her. "It pays to know the right people," he said.

Allen opened the door and stepped out. He chatted with Bull for a few moments. "I don't know how to thank you," he said.

Bull gave him his card. "If I can do anything for you, call anytime, day or night. I mean it."

Dr. Allen choked up from gratitude. "Thank you," he said.

Christie waited downstairs, knowing that if she heard Kessler tell her husband he was guilty, she would give him a mouthful. Upstairs, Allen sat facing his lawyers, one behind the desk, and the other seated at its side.

"This is what Frank Tuerkheimer offered," Kessler said, pushing a letter with a three-page attachment over to Allen.

The top of the page said, "Affidavit." The words "theft of money" jumped out of paragraph one and hit him hard. His heart began racing, but he maintained his composure. Taking a pen from his breast pocket, Allen began reading, pondering each sentence, every word, making notes off to the side of every page. After fifteen minutes, he looked up.

"This makes me out to be a thief," he uttered angrily. "They are lies! Every one of the four counts are lies! You know they're lies! I explained everything to you."

"Calm down," Kessler said, holding up the palms of both hands. "You've made notes. Scratch out what you don't want, put down what you want. I'll take it to Tuerkheimer. Let's see what he says."

"You bet I'll put it down!" Allen retorted. "I cannot agree to a pack of lies." He turned again to the letter from the U.S. Attorney and the three-page attachment.

Dr. Allen carefully read each word again, blacked out offensive words and phrases, and substituted others. At times, he would go back to a word and blacken it deeper, until the word could no longer be deciphered. When an objectionable word or phrase was no longer seen, only then did he appear satisfied and slid the document across the desk to Kessler.

CHAPTER THIRTY-THREE

"Tell Tuerkheimer I will not sign anything that is slanted to make me out a thief. Anyone who reads this must know that I did not profit one red cent by doing what I did. How can I be called a thief if I didn't put money in my pocket? It just doesn't make sense. And if it doesn't make sense to me, I don't see how it would make sense to a jury," Allen said as he heaved a heavy sigh.

THIRTY-FOUR

October 15, 1979, three in the morning. Nobody could sleep.

Allen's parents, Mary and James, had the guest bedroom, with a four-poster bed. It had a good spring and mattress, fluffy down-pillows, and nice coverings...good for sleeping. But instead, they talked and decided that no matter what their son said, they would sell the family farm and hand him the money. After it was done, there'd be nothing he could do. They liked the idea and then tried to drift off. However, thoughts nagged at them and refused to let go.

Chris, as was his custom, bedded down in the barn. He enjoyed talking to the cattle and loved earthy smells—a simple life, far different than the frenetic pace of the city, that crazy place where a driver behind him would lean on his horn, wave a fist, and speed around his car at eighty miles an hour, only to end up at the stop light five seconds ahead of him. Yes! He loved the barn, a pile of hay, sleeping in his clothes, and no hassle.

Tonight, though, Chris was worried. Dad was in trouble. Something had to be done to convince his stubborn father that the house, furniture, and all the other things were not important. The only important thing was family, their health and their freedom. And Chris hated the idea of sitting idly by and watching his father go to jail.

The other three sons found tossing and turning and thinking not conducive to a good night's rest. Around midnight, they sauntered out to the front verandah in pajamas. They sat on the floor, huddled together, arms round their knees and shared soft mutterings, expressing their concerns, their anxieties, and their fears.

Dr. Allen and his wife tried to drowse off, but they tossed and turned from one side to the other. Every twenty seconds or so, the mattress would move. They just could not sleep and finally padded down the stairs in bare feet and made their way toward an outside door. Christie pushed the screen door open. Heads turned as the top hinge squeaked.

At three in the morning, they were all together, a gloomy family reunion.

"Well," Dr. Allen said, peering up and down the dark porch, "what have we here?"

CHAPTER THIRTY-FOUR

"I'll fix coffee," Christie said, looking around at everyone. "Okay?" Three of her sons at the end of the verandah nodded. Chris, who sat next to them, said, "I'll have green tea." Christie looked at her in-laws on the swing at the other end of the verandah. "Coffee is fine for Dad and me," Mary said.

As Christie hurried inside, the elder Allen asked, "Still feel the same about not selling the farm?"

"Sure do, Pa," Dr. Allen said as he sat down on the landing with his feet on the steps.

"What would you do if we sold it anyhow? Ma and me are tired of living in the boonies. City life would be fun."

"You wouldn't do it. The farm would never be sold unless it was a unanimous decision. We gave our word. You'd never go back on your word, Pa."

"What if we quit college and got a job?" Chris asked, walking over to his father and sitting down next to him. He put his arm around his dad. "It would free up a lot of money," he said, almost in a whisper.

Dr. Allen glanced at his son and quickly looked down at the step. He struggled to fight off tears, but a few eased out in the corners of both eyes. He quickly wiped them away with the back of his hand. "You boys have to carve out a future for yourselves," he said, "you all have a life to lead. I can't..." Dr. Allen's voice cracked. His heart felt too heavy to continue.

A long silence followed. The three boys sat together as Chris kept his arm around his father. The elder Allen thought about going back on his word because the situation was an emergency. Dr. Allen looked up into the darkness, where only a sliver of moon could be seen. He thought about Rickey Marlar and the missing data, about Kathryn Anderson and her allegations. She had started it all.

And now, here he was, unable to answer his son, but finally said, "Tuition money won't go far. It would disappear fast. Thanks anyway."

"Come and get it!" Christie called, backing out of the open screen door, one hand holding the handle of a white serving cart and other holding open the screen door. She angled the cart to a side and the door slowly closed.

Steam rose from eight white Styrofoam cups. Two paper plates held Oreos and Ritz crackers topped with Swiss cheese. Everyone gathered near the cart except Chris and his father. Chris still had his arm around his dad, who sat looking up into absolute darkness. The sliver of moon was gone. Soon, he and Christie would be heading toward his lawyer's office.

The drive to Bill Kessler and Associates was uneventful. Larry McKitrick had called off the hounds, and Dr. Allen did not have to race for cover, trying to evade reporters and other news people.

Upon arrival, Christie chose to remain downstairs, and as Dr. Allen sat facing Kessler and Robins, waiting for one of them to speak, he wished that his wife had chosen otherwise.

Kessler led off. "Tuerkheimer will not change it," he said as he pushed the affidavit across the table.

Dr. Allen fingered the document, read it again, and let out an audible sigh. "You want me to sign this?" he said.

"We would recommend it," Kessler replied.

"Why?" Allen said with a hint of irritation.

"They're the facts," Kessler replied, "and both of us agree that it would be in your interest to sign it."

Dr. Allen squirmed uneasily in his seat. "They make me out to be a thief."

"The auditors found it and reported it," Kessler quickly replied.

"It doesn't tell the true story. It misrepresents the facts. It makes this whole thing a lie!" Allen felt like getting up and running out.

Kessler leaned back. "Legally, that's the story," he said, "and that's what the U.S. Attorney wants."

Dr. Allen was angry. He felt humiliated and betrayed. "You are supposed to be on my side!" he said, holding down his anger. "What if I plead not guilty?"

"Tuerkheimer will prosecute."

"I'd want a jury trial."

"Do you really think that will help?" Kessler replied.

"Twelve people are better than one!" Allen exclaimed. "What do you think, Mr. Robins?"

"It's always better to cut a deal. Your charges are not felonies, they are misdemeanors with lesser penalties. If a jury found you guilty, it could mean jail time."

CHAPTER THIRTY-FOUR

Dr. Allen felt as if he was facing an execution. He stared at the table and pictured what it would be like locked up in a cell, dressed in prison garb, eating meals at a long table with other prisoners. How old would he be when let out? Maybe he should agree to plead guilty. The arraignment was two days away.

"If I plead not guilty, when would it go to trial?" he asked.

"Hard to say," said Robins. "There's a lot of preliminary work. Contacting witnesses, depositions, motions, picking a jury and other matters. It could take months. Hard to say."

"What would it cost?"

"It wouldn't be cheap," Robins replied. "We can talk about it if you decide to plead not guilty."

Allen felt overwhelmed because of the difficulty in making a decision, "Both of you think it best for me to sign?"

Kessler and Robins nodded.

"If I do, what happens next?"

"We could resolve the entire matter in court on Thursday," Robins replied. "It shouldn't take long. I know. I've been through this many times."

Allen looked at Kessler. "If I plead guilty, do you think I'll go to jail?"

"It depends on what Tuerkheimer recommends to the court. Then it would be up to the judge. The best thing to do is be apologetic. It could lower any possible jail time. You can prepare something in writing and read it verbatim if you wish."

"Get it over with," Allen thought to himself. He nodded and hated his decision.

On October 17, 1979, Dr. Allen was in the United States District Court for the Northern District of Illinois. He sat at the defense counsel table, between his attorneys, staring at the floor. He felt like his life was over. His name on a three-page affidavit had just turned him into a criminal. His attorney, Jim Robins, attested to that fact by signing as notary.

Frank Tuerkheimer was at a table for the prosecution, facing the bench. He surveyed the array of folders and documents neatly arranged in front of him. He mentally checked off each one, knowing he was ready. He glanced up at the bench and wondered why His Honor had not yet appeared. Judge Elmore was always a stickler for being on time.

Tuerkheimer held himself proudly in a curved-back chair. A dark, pin-striped suit hung handsomely on his well-built, thin and trim six-foot frame. His regular haircut and clean-shaven appearance added a distinguished look to his long, narrow face.

Suddenly, a door opened behind the bench. There he was! Judge Elmore in a long black robe. "All rise for the court," the bailiff near the bench loudly called out.

"Please be seated," Elmore said, as he dropped into a high-backed, worn leather chair behind the bench.

"Case number 79-CR-71," the bailiff called out, as if trying to inform people out on the street hurrying past the courthouse. "United States of America versus James Allen. Call for an arraignment. May we have the appearances please?"

The U.S. Attorney rose. "Frank Tuerkheimer for the United States."

Robins stood. "Jim Robins and Bill Kessler appearing with the defendant in person."

"Thank you, counsel," Judge Elmore said as he peered across the courtroom from his high perch on the bench.

With one finger, he adjusted his specs to the bridge of his nose. He focused on seven spectators in the front row, a middle-aged woman with four young men, two on either side of her. One held her hand. Another held his arm around her. And an elderly couple sat next to the youngsters. The elderly man kept shifting in his seat, and the elderly woman next to him was wringing her hands. A bailiff stood at attention at the far end of the center aisle, guarding the door. Other than that, the courtroom was empty.

"Where's the press?" Judge Elmore wondered. "Where's the reporters? What about the artists doing renderings! Where are they?" Elmore enjoyed publicity. He wanted a sketch of himself handing out justice. He had a scrapbook, and needed entries for every event. Yes! Where was the press?

He peered over the top of his metal-framed spectacles and looked down at the U.S. Attorney. "Mr. Tuerkheimer," he said, "do you suggest I direct my inquiries to all of the counts?"

"Yes, Your Honor. That information was filed earlier today. I do suggest that."

"Thank you. Mr. Robins, would you and Dr. Allen come forward to the lectern if you please?"

"Yes, Your Honor," Robins replied.

CHAPTER THIRTY-FOUR

They stood before the judge, with Dr. James Allen looking at the floor.

"Counsel, before we proceed, I would like to direct questions to Dr. Allen bearing on his ability to understand what is being said and done here. While I am doing that, of course, you are free to interject at any time."

His Honor then questioned Dr. Allen as to his age, education, illnesses, and everything that could affect his ability to understand. Allen understood. The judge went on to question both attorneys about information filed, maximum penalties, and proceeded into Allen's plea and the plea bargain that had been agreed upon by both sides. He then returned to the defendant.

"Dr. Allen," Elmore said, again fidgeting with his glasses. "Before I accept your plea, I want to determine if you understand what it is you are charged with."

Each offense, as listed in the affidavit, was read. After each reading, Allen said yes. He pleaded guilty to all four counts. When other questions were thrown at him, he said yes. No matter how it was phrased, the answer was yes. Yes, yes, yes.

When Judge Elmore asked, "Do you understand that if I were to accept your plea of guilty to these charges, you could be subjected to a four thousand dollar fine and four years of imprisonment?"

"Yes," was Dr. Allen's reply. Other questions came. Same answer. Allen understood he had given up his right to a trial by jury.

As he continued to respond in the affirmative, he hoped for a lesser sentence. The thought of prison had caused agonizing, painful, sleepless nights. He was consumed by devastating thoughts of killing himself, but this time it was worse. The thoughts would not go away.

Down deep, he would have really liked to have had a noisy defense and prove his innocence, but now there was no turning back. He had signed the affidavit.

As the judge droned on, Allen was lost in thought until he heard his name. "Dr. Allen," intoned Judge Elmore, "are the facts basically as the United States Attorney has just stated them?"

"Yes," Allen answered softly.

"Thank you," Judge Elmore said. "On the basis of this discussion with all concerned, and upon the basis of the entire record in this case, I find and conclude that the defendant has entered a plea of guilty to each of the four counts of the information filed today. And that he has done so knowingly, with an understanding of the nature of each of the charges and with an understanding of the consequences of the pleas of guilty. I accept that plea."

Dr. Allen heaved a heavy sigh. It was over.

Judge Elmore continued. "I am also satisfied that there is a factual basis for each of the offenses charged in counts one, two, three, and four. I order that a presentence investigation be conducted and that the report of the investigation be filed within thirty days from today."

The judge released Dr. Allen on his own recognizance and asked Robins and Allen to get together with Ray Herje, the court's probation officer who would be in charge of the presentence investigation.

With no further remarks, Judge Elmore banged his gavel and said, "The court will adjourn."

Slowly, Dr. Allen turned and looked at his family. They were huddled together in the first row, shedding quiet tears.

THIRTY-FIVE

THE DAY AFTER THE GUILTY PLEA, THE CAMPUS BUZZED WITH RUMORS, GOSSIP, and wild speculation. Phones rang. Students milled around the Regional Primate Center, wanting to catch a glimpse of the infamous professor. Some of the faculty expressed shock and dismay. By noon, gossip had it that he lost a bundle in Vegas shootin' craps and a little on blackjack, one caller said.

By 1:00 p.m., some said he liked to play the ponies, and Dr. Allen's lifestyle was described as one that required large sums of money. By 2:00 p.m., he had developed an addiction to gambling. But after 3:00 p.m., a tidal wave of rumors swept through the campus, and of the $500,000 in grant money, a sizable chunk must have been siphoned off and stashed. And over a seventeen-year period, Dr. Allen had definitely accumulated a fortune.

"He can afford to plead guilty and go down the tube," one caller said, "from now on, he's going to be on easy street."

By 4:00 p.m., the phone lines went crazy. Wild speculation reported that Dr. Allen had graduated to a top position in the Mafia. He was in charge of an organization that was owned by the largest crime family in the United States. And Madison was a hub for illegal activities, and the Regional Primate Center was really a front for the mob.

In seven hours, Professor James Allen had been chewed raw. He was no longer a graduate cum laude from the University of Chicago, a dedicated scientist, a senior scientist at the Primate Center, a member of fourteen professional and scientific societies, an internationally acclaimed researcher with 216 scientific publications, a teacher and mentor for over fifty graduate and post-graduate students in experimental pathology, a dynamic leader in public policy regarding environmental health, listed in Who's Who in American Universities, a consultant to Italy and Canada, and a loving husband and father. He was no longer any of these. Dr. James Allen was a thug and a hood.

At 6:00 p.m., Dr. Allen finally gave in to Christie's urgings and went outside to tend to flowers bordering the inside of his white picket fence. He had been in the doldrums all day and could not go to work. He was ashamed to face people, especially friends. Sitting inside the house made him feel worse. And tending flowers did not help. Nothing helped. His world had collapsed, and there was nothing left for him to do.

What would happen now that he had a criminal record? Would he be allowed to stay on at the university? What about his research? Would that continue? He was getting older and had given his life to the world of research. It was the only thing he knew, the only thing he had ever wanted.

In his teens, his other desires were childish fantasies. A fighter like his ancestors, a pilot in the navy winning decorations and being hailed as a hero, a postwar political future starting with a run for governor of North Carolina. But as he matured and studied, he gravitated to the world of research, a world where his curiosity was slowly nurtured by thinking, planning, working, and watching, ever mindful of clues along the way. Research was an exciting world where his expectations became reality. It had been so wonderful. But now, after a lifetime of discovery, his career was slipping away.

"Jim!" Christie called from the porch. "Telephone! It's Frank!"

In minutes, Allen kicked off his shoes on the living room floor and lay stretched on the couch.

"Hi, Frank, have you heard?"

"Bull told me. Damn shame your lawyers let you do that."

"They said I was guilty. I don't know the law, maybe they're right."

"Bullshit!" Frank exclaimed. "My guys told me enough, and in my opinion, it was a set-up! It was a conspiracy between Dow, the government, and the university. From what I heard this morning, the chancellor is about to put your head on the chopping block. You are on your way out!"

There was a long silence. Finally, Dr. Allen said, "How could things be happening so fast? And why?"

"You uncovered a bag of worms, Doc. You were about to prove that no matter how small the amount, dioxin kills. That will cut into Dow's bottom line, and they don't like it."

CHAPTER THIRTY-FIVE

"Why the government?"

"C'mon, Doc! Think! Our guys were poisoned! Thousands died! Now you are going to testify for us, and you will point to dioxin as the culprit that killed us. The government will then have to pay for what they did. Billions in benefits are at stake."

"Why the university?"

"It's money! Lots of it! Simple as that," said Frank. "The school officials would kiss Dow's ass if they had to, anything for a buck. So who's Dr. Allen? Who cares? Certainly not the university."

"I never had a chance, did I?"

"Not when Dow can hire every asshole and his brother to do their dirty work. Take that Anderson gal. She was planted in your office to do a number on you. And she was paid by Dow. We've tried to find her, but she has disappeared from planet Earth."

"I never realized what was happening, and now I'm paying a price for being so stupid."

"It's not yet over, Doc! Your enemies are still at it, and some of your own people could be working against you."

Dr. Allen had no reply.

Frank paused and spoke as gently as he could. "Sorry to lay it on you this way, but I have to be up front with you. My guys will do whatever they can to help, and if you want anything, call Bull."

"Thanks Frank, let's stay in touch."

Dr. Allen clicked off and wondered when he would be hearing from the chancellor.

The day after his talk with Frank, Professor James Allen was in the news again. Reporters had not bothered him after his plea of guilty. No attempts had been made to interview him. No minicams, no mikes, and no phone calls from the media. But a flood of information from the university made headlines that again ignited a reading frenzy in the city of Madison.

Everyone was reading about "Ex-Prof's Dioxin Research In Doubt" and "Allen Case Puts University Administration Under Gun."

Newspapers occupied every seat in the Bagel Place. And people stood in line waiting for a seat. The line flowed out the door and wound down the block. Some people sat on the curb and read while others leaned against the walls of buildings, reading the newspaper.

The entire town was reading, talking, and debating, and opinion wavered one way, then back again, and everyone in the Bagel Place took their time eating while a bald man with grease on his apron hurried from table to table.

"Eat!" he hollered, "people are waiting! Hurry up and eat!"

But the crowd didn't pay attention. They merely buried themselves behind open newspapers. Scrambled eggs became cold, and toasted bagels were ignored. Waitresses stood around with pad and pen and nothing to do because there were no new orders. The kitchen talked of closing down while the bald man shook his fist, ranted, raged, and cussed, but finally surrendered from total exhaustion. He sat on the floor with his face in his hands breathing heavily. A waitress threw him a headline and he joined the crowd and read.

The front-page story was written by Whitney Gould, a staff writer for the *Capital Times*. He wrote, "University of Madison's chancellor is expected to make a decision soon on the fate of Professor James Allen, the internationally famed pathologist who recently admitted to the theft of $892 in governmental money."

Chancellor Shain was in his office. After reading the story, he knew the paper didn't have it right. He wasn't going to make a decision. He had already decided. Dr. Allen had to go. He punched in numbers, and in minutes, he had a conference call where arrangements were put in place to remove Dr. Allen from all responsibility related to the handling of grant money. After punching in more numbers, the draft of a letter was being prepared to inform Dr. Allen of two choices. Either go voluntarily or be forced out as allowed under the university's policies and procedures.

Chancellor Shain knew that if Dr. Allen refused to go, it would take time, but in the end, he would be rid of him.

THIRTY-SIX

On November 27, 1979, at 11:00 a.m., a hushed silence fell over the courtroom. Judge Franklin Stuart Elmore, in a flowing black robe, seated himself on the bench.

"Please be seated," he said.

"Case number 79-CR-71, United States of America versus James Allen called for sentencing. May we have the appearances," the bailiff called.

As attorneys for the prosecution and defense responded, Judge Elmore looked at hundreds of people, elbow to elbow, in every pew. He was pleased. "Wonderful," he thought as he spied reporters in the first row. His Honor shifted his gaze to the defense counsel as Robins finished announcing himself.

"Is there a statement you wish to make on the defendant's behalf concerning the matter of sentencing?" Elmore asked.

"There is, Your Honor," Robins replied.

"Very well,"

"Your Honor," Robins began, "this morning I intend to refrain from a discussion of the evidence which has been presented. I should like to focus on the question of the appropriate punishment to be handed down by this court, considering first the defendant's character as reflected in his personal life and in his record of professional employment. Second, to consider his explanation of, and his attitude toward, the offense, and third, to consider the punishment he has already suffered."

As Robins stood at the lectern, extolling his client's virtues, Allen sat at the defense counsel's table with his eyes closed. He knew his family was in the second row behind him and feared they would soon hear the worst: prison. Kessler had told him to prepare a statement and be apologetic to the court. It could lower his jail time, and he had done as his lawyer had advised. He would read it verbatim, but in his heart, he knew it was a lie. He was innocent.

The mention of his name caught his attention. "Dr. James Allen is clearly not a man who is driven by financial self-interest," Robins said. "That is quite evident. One need only speculate as to the financial fruits that a man of his intelligence, drive, and intensity might expect in the private sector. How then can his behavior in these criminal matters be reconciled? Your Honor! We must acknowledge that there can simply be no clear excuse for Dr. Allen's action. It is my sincere belief that not even Dr. Allen can explain why these things happened."

"Not true! Not true!" is what Allen wanted to shout. He had the urge to jump up on the defense table, face the people who packed the courtroom and scream, "I can explain it! I can explain it! I swapped money! I stole nothing! Nothing! I'm innocent!"

But a deep-rooted fear held him to absolute silence. Worse than pleading guilty was the thought of going to prison, living behind bars, and being raped by stronger men and beaten if he showed resistance. Better dead than to lead that kind of life.

Dr. Allen turned his head to Robins, who was standing tall, looking up at His Honor. "In retrospect," Robins said, "taking time to reflect, James Allen clearly recognized the sheer stupidity and criminality of his acts. Looking back at those acts, they are even more incomprehensible to Dr. Allen than they are to us, but they are acts with which he must live with the rest of his life. The toll this matter has taken and will continue to take on James Allen extends well beyond the reach of this court. Dr. Allen's family and friends have noted the profound physical and emotional effects this matter has had on him. They have described the signs of aging on his face, the graying in his hair, and the loss of weight. The effects of admitting his guilt before his university students, associates, and colleagues have been devastating. The effect of admitting these offenses before his loved ones is inestimable. Your Honor, the prosecutor has implied in his letter to you of November twenty-first that an example should be made of Dr. Allen. He said that the crimes Dr. Allen committed are difficult to uncover and that they must be deterred by a more severe treatment than usual. Today, Your Honor, I also ask that an example be made of Dr. Allen, but I do so with a different idea in mind. James Allen can be an example of this court's compassion. If there ever was an individual worthy of that compassion, it is he. James Allen stands before you as a man who is truly remorseful. That is evident throughout these proceedings. He has been cooperative with Mr. Tuerkheimer, with the grand jury, with Mr. Herje, and with this court. He has come forward and admitted his guilt. Now James Allen seeks only the opportunity to continue his important work, giving the court his solemn assurance that his conduct shall never be repeated. It is the court's duty to determine a punishment

CHAPTER THIRTY-SIX

that is just. We have submitted for the court's consideration what we believe are constructive proposals that would be alternatives to a traditional form of punishment. We hope these will be considered. But whatever determination this court makes, we ask that you construe the criminal actions of James Allen as having been an aberration in his behavior, a blemish on what is otherwise an unparalleled record of service to mankind. Your honor, on behalf of James Allen, we ask for a second chance. Thank you, Your Honor."

"Thank you, Mr. Robins. Mr. Tuerkheimer, is there a statement you wish to make?"

"A very brief one, Judge. Your Honor, Dr. Allen is not charged with being a bad researcher or a lazy person or anything of that sort. He was charged with and pleaded guilty to being a thief. It isn't the kind of theft where you walk into a candy store and take a candy bar off the rack. That's an instantaneous, impetuous thing. It's a theft the nature of which involves a series of acts in terms of the submission of documents that contain false and fictitious information. He didn't have to steal to bring food onto the table for his family. I suggest he did it because he felt the rules didn't apply to James Allen. I submit the real explanation for the conduct before the court is a man who thought he was almost entitled to the money by virtue of all the other things he had done, whether we like it or not. There may be other people who feel they are in the same status. I think these other people will be concerned as to their own behavior when the court imposes whatever sentence it imposes. Thank you."

"Thank you, Mr. Tuerkheimer. Mr. Robins, is there any other statement that you might wish to make in light of Mr. Tuerkheimer's remarks?"

"No, Your Honor, but Dr. Allen would like to make a statement."

"Yes, Dr. Allen. I intended and now do turn to you to ask whether there is anything you wish to say to me directly before sentence is imposed. You may speak from the table there if you wish."

Dr. James Allen sat at the table, aware of absolute silence in the courtroom.

"First," he began, "I would like to say that I am experiencing the most difficult and traumatic period of my life. In addition to being involved in federal litigation because of my misuse of federal grant funds, the university has relieved me of my responsibilities for grants amounting to $500,000. This means I no longer have control of the research program I developed over the past eighteen years. Secondly, because of his matter, the university administration has informed me that my tenured professorship may be in jeopardy. The university has discouraged me from submitting additional grants, which are the lifeblood of my research program. I have seen my thirty employees look at me and say, 'What is going to happen?' I am seeing things that I cherish gradually disappear before my eyes. I do not know if there is any way our research program can be salvaged. Because of my actions, I have jeopardized one of the most timely and productive research programs in the world. I would like for the court to take into consideration that I am extremely sorry for having misused federal funds, thus creating immense legal and administrative problems. I have shamed my family, my university, and my state. I am sorry for what has happened, and I promise it will never happen again. I hope the court will realize the suffering and anguish I have gone through this past year, and through its generosity, will allow me to return to my laboratory or some other worthwhile endeavor."

"Thank you," Judge Elmore said.

Tuerkheimer rose and approached the lectern.

"Yes, sir?" Judge Elmore asked.

"Your Honor, just so the record is complete, I want to indicate to the court that I received a receipt from HEW, the audit agency, to the effect that the $892, which is the subject of the four counts, has been repaid by Dr. Allen by check dated November twenty-sixth."

As Judge Elmore began talking, Dr. Allen stared at the floor, listening to his heart hammering away at his rib cage. He knew that he would soon learn if it would be prison or freedom. The judge went into a lengthy commentary about issues in the case. He considered two aspects that allowed for an imposition of some punishment, questioned the nature and extent of the penalty so as to deter others, and concluded that the punishment would not be overly severe.

His Honor was ready. "It is the court's judgment," he said, "that on counts one, two, three, and four the defendant is fined the sum of $4,000, with the fine to be paid by December thirty-first of 1979. In addition, the imposition of sentence as to imprisonment is suspended, and the defendant is placed on probation for a period of six months."

With no further questions from either side, His Honor adjourned the court. Anita Clark, a reporter for the *State Journal* flew out of the courtroom. She had a story. And early the following morning, news trucks dropped off bundles of papers at newsstands, stores, and other news outlets. Newsboys rode their bikes up and down streets and threw papers at front doors.

CHAPTER THIRTY-SIX

The reading frenzy was on again for that day. A large, bold headline proclaimed, "Professor Gets Top Fine in Grant Theft."

The article summed up the highlights of the courtroom proceedings. It reported on an interview with Frank Tuerkheimer, who reported that a federal grand jury was continuing to investigate misuse of federal funds by other University of Wisconsin faculty members. It concluded by reporting that Chancellor Shain would not comment on whether any further action would be taken against Dr. James Allen. Under university rules, there would have to be a meeting between Dr. Allen and Shain before action could be taken.

What the public did not know, nor did Dr. Allen know, was that the wheels had already been set in motion to remove Dr. James Allen from the university.

THIRTY-SEVEN

It was 2:00 p.m. The phone was ringing. Dr. Allen sat idly at the kitchen table with his face to the window. He was still in pajamas, unshaven and unkempt. He had done nothing but mope around the house, thinking. What will happen now?

The phone kept ringing. Finally, he lifted himself up, shuffled over to the other end of the table, and lifted the receiver from the wall.

"Yes?"

"Hi, Doc," Frank McCarthy's voice had a melancholy tone.

"Hi, Frank."

"You sound down, Doc. Can we talk some?"

"Nothin' to say."

"Have you been reading your mail?"

"No point."

"I sent you a copy of an article. It's kinda long, I'll read it for you. Are you sitting down?" Allen eased himself into a chair. "Okay," he said.

"Well, here goes. The article starts by talking about you and your problem. It goes on to say, 'Considering that Dr. Allen is only one of two researchers who will be testifying in the 2,4,5-T and Silvex battle against Dow Chemical, the timing couldn't be better for Dow. Using Dr. Allen's personal misfortune, Dow's lawyers told an EPA judge that Allen's overall credibility and integrity is suspect in light of his recent criminal conviction.' The reporter who wrote the article," Frank went on, "slams into Dow. Just listen to what this guy has to say. 'I remember Dow withholding scientific studies from the public on the harmful effects of dioxin; of testifying publicly that dioxin causes no more than chloracne in their workers while their medical director told scientists of other serious problems. I remember Dow barring unionization of their plants in order to avoid complying with safety regulations; of poisoning the waters and destroying the aquatic life of the Tittabawassee, the Chippewa, and the Saginaw Rivers near their Madison plant. I remember Dow knowing of high levels and harmful effects of dioxin

CHAPTER THIRTY-SEVEN

in their products for at least twenty years before the government forced them to lower the level. I remember Dow manufacturing and exporting deadly dioxin products to Vietnam and shifting the blame to the U.S. government for misusing it. These things mentioned certainly do not raise any questions regarding Dow's overall credibility or integrity. After all, they have not been criminally convicted!'

"Doesn't that hit Dow between the eyes, Doc? I'm hoping it fires you up! You've got to start fighting for your job and your research."

"In point, if Shain wants me out, I'm out."

"My guys tell me you can fight him for years before he forces you out."

"I'm too tired to fight."

"Would you do me a favor, Doc?"

"What?" Allen said as he closed his eyes, wishing he could just fall into a deep hole and disappear.

Frank was adamant. "Read your mail! See what people have to say! The same kind of mail is going to the chancellor's office! Maybe it will help!"

Allen shook his head. "I don't think so."

"We need you, Doc," Frank replied anxiously, "hang in there!"

"I'm doing my best, Frank."

Frank's remarks awakened a spark of curiosity in Dr. Allen. What were people saying? Carting three days of mail and newspapers up to the bedroom, Allen piled it on the bed, propped himself up with two large pillows, and picked up the top newspaper.

Whitney Gould of the *Capital Times* had a great deal to say. Some of the remarks jumped out at Dr. Allen.

"Although Allen avoided jail," Gould said, "it remains to be seen whether he will be able to carry on his work at the university. Shain is believed to be inclined toward outright dismissal. But he has been deluged with letters from scientists and environmental groups around the country urging that Dr. Allen be retained because of the value of his research in toxic chemicals." A faculty colleague said, "I can't believe this is the biggest crime that happened in the last year. And I am alarmed at the prospect of a guy getting destroyed by an $892 misappropriation."

But another article pointed out that the amount of money was not the issue. The issue was that Dr. Allen engaged in activities contrary to law and to the rules under which he received the grant. It went on to say that what Allen did was either very stupid or very arrogant and was not the sort of behavior that reflected on the humility of a scholar.

Dr. Allen agreed. He no longer felt like a scholar. The rules had required that he return unused grant money, not to figure out a way of keeping and using it. He had broken the rules. Saying others had done it was no excuse. He had been stupid, and now he had to pay for that stupidity. Dr. Allen dropped the newspaper on the floor, closed his eyes, and just lay there.

Allen's colleagues and students had carried on with the three final studies. The 50 ppt was nearing completion. The 25 and 5 ppt studies were proceeding well. But no one knew what the future held, especially the graduate students who were working toward their doctorates. The appointment of a new principal investigator had not yet been made, but funds were available until the end of June.

In the midst of uncertainty, Dow Chemical launched an attack on the 50 ppt study. Dow lawyers filed a motion with the EPA, asking for discovery depositions of selected agency witnesses.

"We must question Dr. Allen," they said.

They pointed to Spencer's audit, where deficiencies had been cited. They wanted to examine tissue slides. They argued that Allen's study demonstrated a high number of neoplasms in rats given low doses of dioxin. They claimed the study was flawed by deficiencies in laboratory practice.

"This must be resolved," the lawyers argued. "We have to discuss this with Dr. Allen!" They urged the administrative law judge to force him to talk.

In the midst of swirling pressures on Dr. Allen and his colleagues, Chancellor Shain read and answered mail. Letters from all over the country asked him to retain Dr. Allen. Even letters from members of Congress, including a letter from Al Gore Jr. from the fourth district of Tennessee.

It said, "Give full weight to Dr. James Allen's valuable scientific contributions in your reconsideration of his position at the university. As you undoubtedly know, Dr. Allen has made significant contributions to science and to the country through his work and his willingness

CHAPTER THIRTY-SEVEN

to participate in the public policy arena. Such participation is an essential part of the public decision-making process, which has become increasingly reliant upon arguments from technical and scientific evidence. I base my recommendation of Dr. Allen's accomplishments on the opinions of people whose judgment I trust and with whom I work closely. In no way do I condone Dr. Allen's reported improprieties, which I am told came to light during a recent investigation. Thank you for your consideration."

Following the reading of Representative Gore's letter, Shain dictated a reply.

He said, "Thank you very much for your letter about Dr. James Allen. Your comments will be considered carefully."

But Chancellor Shain knew that ten weeks earlier, on October 19, 1979, he had already decided. He had already taken away all responsibilities from Allen. He had already decided that Allen would never again be in charge of research. He already had decided. Allen had to go.

A letter from Dr. Henry Pitot, director of the McArdle Laboratory for cancer research and a member of the university's faculty, praised Allen's accomplishments.

"I have known Dr. Allen since the early 1960s," Pitot said. "His early studies on the morphologic changes seen in rodents and primates given PCBs as viewed by the electron microscope were among the first such studies reported and have since been corroborated by others. More recently, I have become aware of Dr. Allen's studies on dioxin. I believe his laboratory was the first to demonstrate the carcinogenicity of this material, thus demonstrating that it is an extremely potent carcinogenic agent in rodents, orders of magnitude more effective than aflatoxin B, one of the most powerful carcinogenic agents known. This work has now been reproduced in several laboratories, including our own."

The flood of mail did not influence the chancellor's decision. He started the disciplinary proceedings that would lead to Dr. Allen's dismissal. But on January 17, 1980, Chancellor Shain opened a letter from Dr. Allen: "I am hereby resigning from the faculty of the Department of Pathology, the faculty of the Department of Food Microbiology and Toxicology and the scientific staff of the Regional Primate Research Center, effective June 30, 1980."

Dr. Allen asked for time to supervise five doctoral candidates who would soon complete work necessary for their PhDs, to assist other graduate students in finding other professors to supervise them, to assist his staff in finding other positions, and to attempt a transfer of his research facilities elsewhere.

Chancellor Shain dictated an immediate reply. "I accept your resignation. This letter is formal notice to you that disciplinary proceedings under Chapter 9, Faculty Policies and Procedures are terminated."

On January 18, 1980, Chancellor Shain issued a joint announcement under his and Dr. Allen's name, notifying the world of the resignation. Back home, Dr. Allen felt numb, listless, and had no desire to get out of bed. He was highly self-critical and blamed himself for putting his family through hell. He pushed food away at every meal and began losing weight.

As Christie sat on the edge of the bed, his somber mood reminded her of the night he contemplated suicide. She decided to take a leave of absence to be with him, but this only brought on more agitation.

"How will we manage?" he asked. "After paying a $4,000 fine, our savings have dwindled and bills keep coming. How will we manage if you stay home and babysit me?"

"College tuitions are paid for the year," Christie replied, reaching for his hand. "Our savings will last for almost two years. You will find another job, and we can move. I can get a nursing job anywhere. We'll do fine."

"Another job is like starting life all over."

"We can always go home. You love the family farm, and your folks want you to come. Farming is a good life. It would do us both good to breathe fresh air again."

Christie's line of reasoning made sense. He squeezed her hand and turned on his side to look at her.

"I've done hard work before," he said, "and I enjoy farming. I also have my degree in veterinary medicine, but it has been so long. I forgot a lot."

"We don't have to decide anything right now. If you are up to it, help your students. They need you. Meanwhile, we can plan. Come downstairs, have some breakfast. You just can't lie around like this."

Madison, Wisconsin, February 5, 1980. Ben Rowley, president of Dow Chemical, swung into action. He was in his office in the Bennett Building and quickly dashed off a

CHAPTER THIRTY-SEVEN

letter to Douglas Castle, the EPA administrator. "The Dow Chemical Company urges you to terminate the current emergency suspension of 2,4,5,-T and Silvex," Rowley said, "and to withdraw the recently issued hearing notices pertaining to the non-suspended uses of pesticides. Such action is long overdue."

Rowley went into a lengthy discussion about the Alsea, Oregon, studies being discredited, about an EPA scientific panel favoring continued use of Dow's products, about the panel's recommendations that the EPA's hearings be terminated, and about the EPA's case resting heavily on the work by Dr. Allen.

Rowley then charged ahead. "The EPA should never allow (nor can Dow ever condone) regulatory actions based on Alsea or other faulty or discredited studies, especially when EPA's actions have such far-reaching consequences for the use and regulation of chemicals in society. Now is the time to call a halt before, in its blind march forward, EPA not only wastes enormous resources, but more importantly, forever blemishes its reputation for scientific objectivity. For it is better to accept the suspensions issued last March as an unfortunate aberration than to set a uniquely stringent standard for 2,4,5-T that neither can nor should apply to other pesticides or chemicals in the future."

Rooke's last paragraph blasted Dr. Allen. "In the long run," he said, "the cause of science (not to mention EPA's reputation among independent scientists) is seriously damaged by the course that EPA has followed in this case. As noted in a recent *Lancet* editorial on 2,4,5-T, the polarization spawned by campaigning toxicologists such as Dr. Allen inevitably discourages and prevents constructive work. Such polarization will dissolve only if EPA and the affected parties apply rigorous scientific standards rather than rely on extraneous, non-scientific considerations in the regulation of pesticides and toxic chemicals. This is a classic case of just that problem. For as *Lancet* so succinctly observed, 'it is a waste of effort, resources and credibility to cry wolf about 2,4,5-T when there is no wolf.'"

Dr. Allen was in his car, wrapped in a heavy overcoat, looking through the passenger's window at the Baptist church on the other side of the street. Snow swirled around the tall white columns. They reminded him of the church he had gone to as a child. He remembered his father sitting in an easy chair in the living room reading the Bible. He remembered his baptism at the age of twelve. He remembered his mother telling him of her grandfather getting a doctorate of divinity from Oxford. He remembered his wonderful grandmother, who told him Bible stories at bedtime.

As he sat in the car with his gloved hands in his lap, he had a longing to go inside the church. He hadn't been in a church for years, and suddenly he recalled words from the past: "God is your refuge and strength."

How did such words come to mind now, decades after he had totally ignored them? What would God think of him after so many years? And how could he now ask for help? God would ask, "Where have you been? Where have you been?"

But God was merciful, and Dr. Allen got out of the car, hurried across the street, and up the wide concrete steps. He took hold of the black, metal handle of the ornate, wooden door, opened it, and went inside. A dim light illuminated the front pews while the back rows were cast in darkness. The light, however, clearly outlined a high-domed ceiling that occupied the center of the church. The color of the red carpeting became more apparent as it ran down the aisle to an elevated pulpit. And the wall beyond the pulpit, Dr. Allen saw the cross holding Jesus Christ. He felt safe and peaceful.

Dr. Allen sat in the last pew. In the quiet of the darkness, he bowed his head and prayed.

"Oh, God, where are you? Did all this happen because I threw myself into my work and forgot about you? Please forgive me. Who will now be there for those innocent people, like in Alsea or Love Canal? What about Vietnam veterans, and their families? Who will be there for them? It seems so unfair. Is there a greater plan for all that's happened? Will I ever understand?"

With shadows enveloping him, Dr. James Allen remained in the pew, wondering about the future.

THIRTY-EIGHT

Verlin Belcher was pissed. The VA was giving him the runaround!

"They're treating me like shit!" he grumbled to a phone booth on a street corner in Gary, Indiana, as he went inside. He tried closing the folding door, but it refused to budge.

"Damn it!" he yelled, pushing it harder, trying to force it shut.

The door creaked in opposition to the rude handling of its lower hinge. It refused to submit. So Verlin finally surrendered, leaving the door partly open. He picked up the receiver, dropped coins into a slot, punched in numbers, and waited.

He was fuming. A thirty-gram chunk of fat had been cut out of his belly without a problem. But now he was having one hell of a time getting the VA to tell him how much dioxin was in that chunk of fat.

"Agent Orange Victims International," a familiar voice said.

"Hi, Frank. It's me, Verlin."

"Hi, buddy! How ya doin'? What's up?"

"I need help. The VA is handin' me a lot of crap, and I'm mad as hell. I swear I'll blow one of the bastards away."

"Verlin, remember! No violence."

"I know. That's why I'm callin'."

"What's going on?" Frank asked.

"I volunteered, right? I gave 'em a piece of fat, right?"

"Right," Frank said, letting Verlin blow off steam.

Verlin continued without hesitation. "They're now handin' me a lot of bullshit. I called the head honch, Lee, twice. He's the doc in charge. The first time, Lee tells me the biopsy was back but he could not give me a number 'cause of somethin' called a validation. It wasn't done yet. He said I had more dioxin in me than was called for. He said the VA wanted to follow me for life. He said, 'You're an important piece of medical information.'"

"What does that mean?" Frank asked.

"Ya got me," Verlin replied. "But a few days later I got a call from a Dr. Levinson, who said somethin' about the numbers being coded and that I should pay no attention to what Lee told me."

"What a crock," Frank said.

"It is a crock!" Verlin yelled. "Lee says one thing. This other doc says somethin' else. Now the VA ain't gonna follow me for life. I'm no longer an important piece of medical information. What kind of shit is this?"

"The VA just doesn't give a damn," Frank replied. "They never do. Call Lee again."

"I did! The second time I called," Verlin went on, "Lee said the validation was done, but he wouldn't give me my number. He gave me an average number for all the guys, but I want my number. I'm entitled to it! I got a lot of dioxin in me, but Lee wouldn't tell me how much. He began handin' me bullshit about not knowin' the significance of numbers and told me to stay in touch with Hines Hospital."

Although Frank was angry too, he spoke as calmly as he could. "It's a lot of bureaucratic crap, Verlin. Just keep your cool. I'll take it from here."

"I'll try, Frank." Verlin clicked off.

As Verlin turned to leave the booth, the partly open door jabbed his belly and made it difficult for him to leave the booth. He grabbed the side of the door at the open end with both hands and pushed it back and forth angrily. The door teetered unsteadily as its hinges pulled away and came crashing to the ground. Verlin stomped on it and walked away.

Frank McCarthy was mad. Sitting on the settee, hands laced behind his head, he gazed at the M-16 in its plastic trophy case on the wall. The sleek, black, automatic rifle seemed to talk to him. "Remember Tung Lap, when you charged through the jungle?" it said. "You were always on the attack. Remember when you were blown up in the middle of an ambush? Remember the shrapnel flying every which way?"

"Hell no!" Frank answered silently. "How could I remember shrapnel? The ambush, yes. It was horrendous! But I was soon out of it! The next thing I knew, I was in a hospital. My head was in bandaged, and I was hurting all over."

Frank remembered waking up one morning with blood on the side of his penis. A small piece of shrapnel had poked its way to the top, piercing skin. He threw on clothes, wolfed down

CHAPTER THIRTY-EIGHT

a donut while on the run, and drove to the VA Hospital, but the four and one-half hour wait in the reception area drove him crazy as he watched vets on crutches and legless guys in wheelchairs.

When the VA doctor finally called him, blood had seeped into his shorts and a dark red stain had spread into the crotch of his pants. Frank tried to tell this to the doctor, but he merely scribbled a few words on paper and directed Frank to a specialist.

After seeing the blood, the specialist said, "I'm a shrink. I can't help you with that." He referred Frank to another specialist.

Frank found the bathroom, dropped his pants and shorts, grabbed the piece of shrapnel with the tips of two fingers, and pulled. As it moved upward, Frank ripped it out, screaming and swearing.

"Fuckin' bastards! Cocksuckin' assholes!"

Blood gushed onto his pants, down his leg, and onto the floor. Frank glared at the tiny, damned piece of shrapnel and threw it at the mirror on the wall. It hit with a clink, dropped into the washbowl and down the drain. Grabbing a handful of brown paper towels from a shelf, Frank wrapped them around his penis, pulled his clothes up, and stormed out of the bathroom.

"You motherfuckin' bastards!" he screamed, striding down the hall, letting everyone hear. "You damned sons-a-bitches!" he yelled into a doctor's office and at staff in the reception area. "I could bleed to death, and you'd take your damn time watchin'!"

At times, Frank had nightmares about the whole thing. He'd wake up dripping wet, wondering if he had heard himself scream. Now the VA was handing Verlin the same kind of shit. What could he do?

Doc was on the VA Committee, maybe he could help. Frank reached for the phone on the card table and quickly dialed Allen's number.

"Dr. Allen," came a tired voice.

"Hi, Doc. How're you doin'?"

"I'm tying up loose ends, Frank. Time to move on."

"Yeah," Frank replied, wondering if he should trouble his friend. "I was going to ask a favor, but you've got enough on your mind."

"No. Go ahead, ask."

"Would you try getting Verlin Belcher's fat biopsy report? Dr. Lee won't give it to him."

"If the VA won't give it," Allen replied, "you can bet it's high. I don't think they'll give it to me. They don't even send me a notice of their meetings anymore."

"That sounds like the VA," Frank replied. "Just a bunch of lousy bastards. I'll ask for it under the Freedom of Information Act. If they still refuse, I'll ask Victor Yannacone to intervene."

"I'm willing to call Lee and give it a try," Allen replied. "He'd probably treat you badly because of what's happened. I don't want you to go through that. I'll take care of it."

Dr. Allen sighed, wishing he could do something but realizing he no longer had any influence with VA officials or even with the university where he had spent a lifetime.

"How's Verlin doing?" he asked.

"It's rough. He has a lot of medical problems and no answers. His anger could take over someday, and he could create a mess."

"I'll pray for him," Allen said. "It's the only thing I can really do."

"Pray for all of us, Doc."

"I do that every day, Frank."

"Yeah...well, you're one of the few who do, Doc. When you leave Madison, let me know. I'll ask Bull to get you a stretch-limo and escort you to the airport. You can leave town like a VIP. I can see all the papers with photos of a white-stretch limo, two motorcycles in front and two in back. People will have somethin' else to talk about."

"I like it, Frank."

"You got it, Doc, take care."

After hanging up, Frank sat staring at his beautiful M-16. He loved it. Though empty, his baby could quickly take on twenty rounds. He remembered the sound of automatic fire, clipping away at a furious pace, mowing 'em down. The gun had given him strength and the feeling that he would survive. For some reason, it still gave him that feeling. Frank lifted himself up. "Better get busy," he thought. "Gotta help Verlin before he goes off half-cocked."

THIRTY-NINE

A SPRING SNOWFALL BLANKETED NEW YORK. DRESSED ONLY IN ARMY BATTLE FAtigues, Frank McCarthy trudged through the snow, oblivious to the cold. Sudden gusts kicked up a whirlwind of white flakes, swirling it around him. But Frank only tightened his hold on the handle of a shopping bag, blanching the knuckles of his right hand. His body was numb and his feet felt like heavy blocks of ice. But it didn't matter. He could easily deal with it, but he found it harder to deal with the pain inside him. It far surpassed the effects of the cold.

On reaching a ten-story, yellow brick building, Frank walked down snow-covered steps leading to his Bunker. The clinking of bottles against one another, the wind, and the crunching snow under his shoes were the only sounds on a deserted street.

Once inside, Frank rubbed his hands together, blowing on them to warm his stiff fingers. Pulling off his wet shoes and socks, he stared at his pink feet objectively. They were frostbitten. So he rubbed them hard to get the circulation going.

He could feel the pins and needles in his fingers as he unloaded his shopping bag, carefully setting each of seven bottles of Bushmills Irish whiskey on the card table in front of the settee. They were his treasure, his route of escape from the sadness that had overwhelmed him. For the first time in his life, Frank planned to really get drunk. In fact, bombed would be a better word. And why not? Pain and anguish had welled up into an unbearable knot in his chest. He had to do something to ease the grief. He just couldn't take it anymore, and alcohol would definitely help.

His buddy, Lenny Laviano, was dead. Cancer had eaten him away at the age of thirty. Frank was with him in the hospital for ten straight hours, crying quietly, holding his hand, and watching him slip away. The burial was in Frankfort, a tiny upstate New York village. As the casket was lowered, Frank thought about other close friends who had been more like brothers. They too had left him. He was alone now and felt entitled to getting stoned. But Frank had never consumed hard stuff. A Schlitz or two had been his limit.

But as he had inched his way up and down the aisle of a liquor store, beer was out of the question. He wanted something with a quick punch, and the choices were endless. One ad grabbed his attention, an import from Ireland. "The World's Oldest Whiskey Distillery," it said. For Frank, the word "oldest" meant long-lasting. And he wanted a long-lasting stupor, a perfect way to tune out for a while.

"Why so much? Having a party?" the cashier had asked.

"No," Frank replied, "just thirsty." He picked up his change, grabbed the shopping bag, and strode out of the store.

Now Frank sat on the settee with a tall glass of Bushmills in hand. Taking his time, he picked up ice cubes from a silver bucket and dropped them into his glass. It became whiskey on the rocks. In half an hour, Frank was on the speakerphone talking to a fellow veteran.

"Hiiiii guy," he said, "c'mon over."

"You're drunk, Frank. Let me talk to Lenny."

Frank momentarily recoiled at the mention of his friend's name.

"Lenny's dead. He's dead, do ya hear me! We buried him." He raised the glass to his lips and chugged down more of the awful stuff.

"When...?" his friend asked.

"We buried him today. Dats why I'm gettin' plastered." A long pause followed.

"Gettin' drunk ain't gonna help. Did ya get the VA minutes about Verlin?" The friend sounded concerned.

"I don' know. I got lotsa mail. Piles."

"When you sober up, read it. The VA is givin' our guys a real shaft job. Dr. Lee admitted finding high levels of dioxin in Verlin's fat and won't release the information. You know and I know they're gonna try to cover it up. Somethin's got to be done."

Without waiting for a reply, the friend slammed the phone down, and Frank downed another slug of whiskey. It tasted better. It no longer gave him a jolt as it hit bottom. He glared at the stack of mail on the table in front of him, some having fallen to the floor. He didn't like picking it up. He didn't feel like reading. In fact, he didn't feel like doing anything...just drinking. So he downed another whiskey just as the speakerphone sounded.

CHAPTER THIRTY-NINE

He stared at it, reached out, hesitated, and clicked it on. He leaned back and waited, holding an empty glass.

"Hello?" a familiar voice said.

No answer as Frank tried to figure out who it was.

"Hello, anyone there?" came the voice again.

The familiar inflection finally registered. "Hiiii, Doc."

"Should I call back?"

"No! Talk to me nowww," urged Frank. "Glad to have someone on the other end."

"I'm sorry, Frank. This is not the time to burden you with my problems. Get some sleep, I'll call in the morning."

"Nooooo, Doc! Don' go. I wanna talk."

"I'm getting ready to leave town, Frank. There's too much going on, and I see no reason for staying at the university till the end of June."

"What's goin' on, Doc?" Frank asked, leaning forward, picking up a bottle, and with a wobbly hand, pouring out more whiskey.

"I'm being hit with subpoenas. Dow wants all the data from all of my experiments, starting with the 500 dioxin study. They even want data from the 5 ppt study, even though it was recently started and there's not much data. And Dow is pushing hard to get it. The EPA is helping them, and they are about to drag me into court."

"Whoa!" Frank replied. Although inebriated, he understood the gravity of the situation.

The 50 ppt dioxin study was crucial to Yannacone's suit. The Vietnam vets could lose their case if Dow succeeded in destroying the low-level dioxin studies. Frank knew Allen's work could become worthless if it was released prior to being published in a scientific journal. Peer review by three independent scientists prior to publication was standard practice. If they accepted the study, only then would it become valid.

Frank tried hard to think clearly. "I'll tell Victor," he said. "He'll know what to do. But pleeez, don't leave town."

"No reason to stay," Allen replied. "I can't do research. When my former colleagues asked me to stay on as a consultant, ACR kicked up a fuss. The dean and I sent a letter to the university's attorney, trying to smooth things over, but it's not going to fly."

"How d'ya know?" Frank asked.

Dr. Allen heaved a deep sigh. "It's no use. HEW sent a letter to Bob Erickson, who is in charge of research at the university. It said they wanted the studies to continue, and they would fund it, but the university will not give HEW the information needed to continue the studies. As far as I'm concerned, it means the university has decided to let the research go down the drain. That's exactly what Dow wants. They don't want the results to come out because it could help destroy the pesticide and herbicide industry."

Frank wasn't listening. The empty glass had slipped from his hand and fell to the floor. His head had fallen back on the settee. Dr. Allen was waiting for some kind of reply.

"Frank...Frank! Frank!" Dr. Allen exclaimed. There was no answer.

FORTY

Dr. Michael Gross glanced at the photo on his desk: six smiling grandchildren in front of a yellow brick bungalow. They held up a sign saying, "We Love Grandpa." That photo meant more to him than all the prestigious documents and photos covering his office walls: diplomas, membership in societies, honorary awards, certificates of commendation, congratulatory letters from world leaders, and photographs of Dr. Gross and notables in the world of science.

The scientific community viewed Dr. Gross as a man who approached his work with a high degree of thoughtful deliberation, a man of composure, a gentle and kindly man. But today, Dr. Gross was angry. He had just experienced a taste of the inner workings of the VA bureaucracy. They had attacked his findings as to the amount of dioxin in fat samples from Vietnam veterans, and his reputation was at stake.

The VA had hired him, thinking that with the passage of time, dioxin would never be found in these fat samples, but when he found high levels and had his results confirmed by the EPA, which used a different method of analysis, Dr. Gross felt secure in submitting the results to Dr. Lyndon Lee, who was in charge of the VA project.

Dr. Lee and his staff checked into Chicago's Hilton Hotel, full of enthusiasm about Gross's findings. They praised his work and applauded his accuracy. Discussions were held about veterans with very high dioxin levels. These vets had a history of intense exposure to Agent Orange. One served in an army helicopter crew, handling and spraying the chemical, never having been given protective gear. He ate and drank from contaminated utensils, had skin contact with Agent Orange, and inhaled the stuff. From May 1969 to May 1970, his exposure resulted in a dioxin level of 23 ppt, and a full report was sent to Dr. Haber at the VA central office in Washington, DC.

Dr. Haber received the report with great satisfaction. His superiors had been waiting. Political leaders of both parties had been waiting. Dr. Haber received the report and found it highly commendable. A report was then sent to the VA deputy administrator, and Dr. Gross was congratulated for a job well done.

As he thought about all this, his thoughts were suddenly interrupted when a young lady poked her head into his office and said, "Would you like one of my sandwiches?"

"Strawberry jam and cream cheese?" Gross asked.

"On white bread," came the reply.

"Love it! If not for you, I would wither away. Remind me to change your job description. When a secretary feeds her boss, she should automatically be an executive secretary with an increase in salary."

"I'll buy that," she replied, walking in and handing her boss a sandwich wrapped in cellophane. "Enjoy," she said.

"Thank you. By the way, that's why I leave my door open, so you'll come in and feed me." She laughed and left.

Chewing and licking jelly off of his lips, Dr. Gross leaned back in his soft, cushioned swivel and thought again about the VA bureaucracy. They had sent him the minutes of the latest advisory committee meeting. At that meeting, Dr. Lee reported that the dioxin results had been tabulated and that they were accurate. Lee talked about veterans who showed dioxin levels of 3 to 57 ppt.

Dr. Gross could still recall the words of Dr. Kearney, who jumped in and said, "I don't mean to preach to you, that is not my intention. But I am concerned about the sensitivity of what you have just said."

Gross could not remember Dr. Lee's reply. He put his sandwich down and picked up a yellow manual from a stack on his desk titled "Transcript of Proceedings." He leafed through to page seventy-eight and read.

Dr. Lee: "Nobody is more sensitive than I to the fact that this is a very delicate area."

Dr. Kearney: "As soon as you release these numbers, everyone will attach significance to them. I warn you, once they are released, they will have great significance."

Dr. Moore: "If you send the sample to another laboratory and they come up with the same number, it means they are following the same cookbook procedure, doing the same things and perpetuating the same errors."

Dr. Lee: "On the contrary, the EPA used a different technique."

Dr. Kearney: "My caution here is that remarks you have just made will probably end up in the *Washington Post* by the end of the week. And I expect they will be in *Science* next month."

CHAPTER FORTY

Mr. Young: "What's troubling me is the call I got from an upset veteran Saturday morning who said Dr. Lee and he had spoken and there was more dioxin in his tissue than was called for. After that conversation, he was asked if the VA could follow him for the rest of his life because he was an important piece of medical information. He agreed. A few days later, he received a call from Dr. Levinson and was told that the information was coded and he should disregard the previous call. Can someone please recount the statements surrounding the phone call to Verlin Belcher about a month ago?"

Dr. Lee: "I would be glad to follow that up. I've had two phone calls from that particular gentleman, who lives near Gary, Indiana. His initial call asked if the biopsy was back. The answer was yes. We didn't know what the validation report might be and therefore had nothing to tell him. The second time he called back, we had validation. We gave him a number with the caveat that we didn't know the significance of these numbers. I asked him to be good enough to stay in touch with his hospital of origin so they could follow him."

Dr. Murphy: "Did you give him his number or just a number for the group as a whole?"

Dr. Lee: "I gave him a number for the group as a whole."

Dr. Hobson: "It is very easy to create the impression of being secretive about this business. We are not secretive. It is the same reason a doctor doesn't tell his patient he has pernicious anemia until he has a chance to check it out. We are not trying, nor do we intend to conceal it from these people one minute longer than necessary, but we need to be sure of what we are talking about. On the other hand, they have to realize that the mere presence of a substance in fat or in any other part of the body does not in and of itself constitute a disease."

Dr. Gross stopped reading. "Hogwash!" he thought. "Everyone knows dioxin will kill!" He closed the VA manual and threw it at the wastebasket in a corner of the room. He could feel the frustration gnaw at him as he leaned back and propped his feet up on his desk.

Why did the VA report bother him so deeply? It came down to this. He hated deception and dishonesty. The VA was trying to say that the amount of dioxin in fat didn't matter. So what if the amount was high! It proved nothing, according to the VA. But Dr. Gross knew it was a lie. An outright lie! He was an expert in his field, and the world knew it. The VA knew it. Yet in spite of the praise they initially bestowed on his work, they were now saying his work proved nothing. And he didn't like it.

"You have been caught with your pants down," Gross muttered, shaking his finger at the VA manual in the wastebasket. "You've been exposed! You are trying to wiggle out of your responsibility. Shame."

Dr. Gross told himself to calm down. He knew he had work on his desk that had to get done. But the report on his work to members of Congress by VA Administrator Max Cleland bugged him.

"We have made an effort," Cleland had said, "to find out whether it is possible to detect and measure dioxin in the body fat of veterans exposed to Agent Orange. The thirty-three fat samples were tested by an independent university-based chemist who used the most sensitive method known to detect and measure dioxin. The method is still experimental and difficult to use. The results of the analysis show that seven of twenty veterans with Vietnam service had dioxin in the small amounts of 3 to 89 ppt in their fat. Six others had smaller amounts and seven had no detectable dioxin at all. The three air force officers who worked extensively with Agent Orange had 3 to 4 ppt in their fat. EPA scientists, using a different testing procedure on eight duplicate samples, have confirmed these results. We can only say there is a method to detect and measure small amounts of dioxin in body fat, but that it is difficult to perform. Further, it requires an operation. Accordingly, this test, while a potentially valuable research tool, is not a practical diagnostic procedure."

"Humbug!" Dr. Gross said to the photograph of his grandchildren. "What does he mean 'small amounts?' Eighty-nine ppt is huge! Massive! My God, 89 ppt will kill! How can Cleland say, 'It's experimental, difficult and not practical'? I do it routinely. This idea about needing an operation is pure baloney! I don't need thirty grams of fat! I can do it with a simple needle biopsy."

Dr. Gross turned to his work on the desk, but he just wasn't in the mood. He could not stop thinking about the VA turning his work over to the Office of Technology Assessment for their critical review and comments. And as he had predicted, they too were critical of his work.

One member said, "It is difficult to determine whether the results have any significance."

Another said, "The report shows there is much room for improvement."

CHAPTER FORTY

The chairman of the group wrote a letter to the VA. He had the audacity to report, "In summary, the authors clearly fail to demonstrate they are measuring dioxin. Until there is reliable data of this sort, any attempt to correlate service exposure, degree of exposure, current clinical health, etc., is unwarranted."

Dr. Gross understood why the VA had taken a machete to his work. They had to have a reason to stop doing biopsies. They now knew that dioxin could be found in body fat years after exposure, and they could no longer hold onto the belief that it would not be found. They were running scared. Dr. Gross also held the strong opinion that the VA would soon slam the doors on doing biopsies. And if they did, it would hide the truth temporarily, but the scientific community would plod on. And one day, the truth would reappear.

One week later, Frank McCarthy was in his Bunker raising hell on the speakerphone. He was livid. A VA telegraphic message sent to all VA hospitals touched a raw nerve. He was no longer drinking. One bottle of Bushmills had been enough.

"This is VA garbage!" Frank hollered. "Lenny was right. Taking out a few of them would send the right kind of message. How long are we supposed to sit on our asses and let those bastards get away with this shit?"

"Cool it, Frank," one of his guys said. "You can't go off half-cocked! You must remember our AOVI motto of dignity, self-respect, and solidarity. You represent us, and you're supposed to set the example."

"Yeah, yeah, I know," Frank replied.

"Let me do it my way, Frank. I know Paul Merrell of *Stars and Stripes*. Everybody reads that paper. I'll ask him to write an article about the VA's new policy. The power of the press may not get fast results, but it's the best weapon we have."

Frank knew his buddy was right. "Go ahead," he said.

One week later, Frank was in his Bunker, sitting on his settee with a Coke and a slice of pepperoni pizza. The *Stars and Stripes* newspaper was spread out on the table in front of him. Chomping into pizza, Frank's gaze was riveted on Paul Merrell's article. He read each line slowly, feeling that someone had finally captured the heartaches of his buddies and put it down in an unforgettable way.

"What would you say if someone walked up to you, pointed a gun, pulled the trigger, seriously wounded you, and when you called the cops, you were told there was no scientific evidence that your injury was caused by the gun even though the bullet was recovered? Vietnam vets are being told exactly that. What happens when people are exposed to large quantities of 2,4,5-T is abundantly clear from studies on the industrially exposed. Now we are being told that even though the government aimed that chemical weapon at us, it went off, and we have exactly the same symptoms as reported in the industrially exposed, and dioxin has been removed in veteran's fat tissue, we're accused of being emotional about the issue.

"Think of it! We know what the gun was! We know who fired it! We know when and where it was fired! We have the doctors' reports, and we have the bullet. Yet the VA says there is no evidence of human harm resulting from the use of Orange, except for a slight skin rash. The VA says bring us a study demonstrating with statistical, epidemiological evidence that Agent Orange was the culprit, the gun. In other words, can you imagine the reaction if the police told the gunshot victim that he should prove, with a competent epidemiological study, that gunshots kill? The truth is there is no way to scientifically prove that a hole in your chest did not spontaneously appear ahead of the bullet. Or that something other than the bullet didn't do the damage and then vanished, leaving a hole for the bullet to rest in. Should we accept the scientific burden of proof that Dow's Agent Orange poisoned us? Or should we instead insist on a 'reasonable man' standard of evidence. Let us talk to our fellow men, to a jury of our peers. The only things you need to prove it was Agent Orange that has damaged you physically are your own medical records and the studies on industrial exposure. Let us say it loudly in the halls of Congress."

Frank reached into the Pizza Hut box and lifted out another slice. He thought about the article. It was great! He thought about himself, a guy with a temper. A guy who had lost Lenny and other friends. He needed someone who would work toward the dream of having a foundation where veterans could take care of their own. It was the most important thing he or anyone could ever do. But to do that, he had to stay alive.

If he was ever stupid enough to charge into the VA building with his M-16, to take out a few, there would always be more bastards to take over. He therefore needed someone

CHAPTER FORTY

who could help him control his own emotions. It would not be right for him to go down in a burst of gunfire in a VA building.

God had kept him alive in Vietnam. And God was keeping him alive even now, while his brethren were dying from cancer. There had to be a reason. He had to remember that fact when his emotions flared and tried to take over his ability to reason. It would have to be God's decision whether he lived or died. He had to remember that.

FORTY-ONE

Dr. Allen was in his office cleaning out his desk. His hand reached to the back of the center drawer. It was empty. The entire desk was empty. He had already emptied the filing cabinets, and nine large boxes on the floor held years of fond memories. One box on top of his desk held odds and ends that had been with him for seventeen years, useless items no longer needed by anyone. His son, Chris, would soon pick them up, load it into a rental U-Haul, and haul it all out to his home.

"I can't remember a single time in my life when I felt so...empty," Allen said to himself.

He felt that his life was over. It was as if he had died. And in addition to destroying his career, Dow's attorneys hounded him. They demanded his data from the 500 ppt dioxin study down to the 5 ppt study. Since the 500 ppt study had already been published, Allen turned over the data from that study. But Dow's attorney wanted more. They wanted the raw data, including the data found missing at the time of Rickey Marlar's death. Their demand was loud and persistent. And Dr. Allen had to wonder if Dow knew it was impossible to produce that data because it had been stolen. If so, he would then have to conclude that Dow had arranged for the murder of Rickey Marlar.

As far as the 50, 25 and 5 ppt studies, they had not yet been completed. An abstract of the 50 ppt study was available, but that data was being put into a paper for submission to a scientific journal. It could not be released until after publication. The 25 and 5 ppt studies were in their early stages. Results were not in and to release any of it before being peer-reviewed would prevent publication. In essence, releasing the data prematurely would destroy the studies. Dow wanted it anyhow. They asked, and Judge Finch immediately issued subpoenas to Allen and his colleagues demanding the data.

Robert Aberg, an attorney in private practice, suddenly materialized and was available to assist the small band of researchers. Aberg let it be known that the subpoenas would not be honored. He filed a motion to quash the subpoenas. Oral arguments were

CHAPTER FORTY-ONE

heard, and the motion to quash was granted in part. It was also denied in part in that Judge Finch ordered that the 50 ppt data be turned over.

The researchers refused. An impasse had arisen. So Judge Finch referred the matter to the Justice Department. Representing the government, Justice sided with Dow. And they wanted to force the researchers to abide by the subpoenas and to produce the data. So Justice carried the case to the U.S. District Court and instituted proceedings.

Dow's attorneys moved in. They joined forces with the government in support of enforcement and submitted evidence demonstrating the relevance of the subpoenaed data to the EPA proceeding. The case was assigned to Barbara B. Crabb.

Although the issue of Allen's data was now in a federal court, the EPA hearings proceeded on schedule. Dr. Lennart Hardell was flown in from Sweden.

"My colleagues and I have just completed a study," Hardell said under oath, "and we found that exposure to dioxin was associated with an elevated risk for soft tissue sarcoma and malignant lymphoma."

Dow brought in one of their scientists, Dr. Perry J. Gehring, and had him take the witness stand.

"Dioxin produces carcinogenic effects at sufficiently high doses," he said, "but the dioxin in 2,4,5-T and Silvex are safe for their intended uses."

The EPA then said that dioxin had been observed to cause cancer in animals, and that dioxin also injures or kills animal embryos. The EPA then told of people who were exposed to exceedingly small amounts of dioxin and then developed cancer and / or abnormal pregnancies.

"These predictions are borne out by epidemiologic data that indicates that humans are susceptible to the same kinds of effects as test animals," the EPA testified, "and that workers exposed to dioxin have a greater risk of cancer of the stomach and other organs. Also, the adverse reproductive effects in test animals appear with increased frequency in humans who were exposed to dioxin as compared to those who were not exposed."

An endless parade of witnesses marched in to either support or shoot down the EPA's position regarding the ban on 2,4,5-T and Silvex and the call for cancellation hearings. The EPA had been forced to adopt that position by the overwhelming public pressure that pointed to the similarity between Allen's and the Alsea findings.

As the EPA hearings continued in Washington, DC, Victor Yannacone and his team of lawyers swept into Madison. They joined Aberg in the U.S. District Court and filed as a petitioner and as intervenors against Dow and against the USA.

Yannacone claimed the subpoenas violated fundamental rights and scientific privileges and represented an unwarranted attempt by Dow to discredit the scientific work by Dr. Allen and his colleagues before the work had been completed. Victor went on to voice the interests of Vietnam vets in the ongoing dispute.

He said, "The veterans have an overriding scientific, medical and proprietary interest in protecting the integrity of such work as it may have bearing on the outcome of its class action suit already filed. The veterans are entitled to intervene as a matter of right under Rule 24(a)(2) of Fed.R.Civ.P. since they have a significant overriding interest in the subject matter of this action."

As legal battles stormed on, Dr. Allen stayed home. Sitting on the verandah steps one day, he stared out at his farm, wondering about the future. Christie was reading *Business Week*. She nudged him.

"Listen to this," she said. "Dow has budgeted a huge amount of money for the defense of 2,4,5-T and Silvex. It could be in the tens of millions. Imagine spending that kind of money." Christie shook her head in disbelief.

"They take in seventeen billion a year," Allen said glumly. "They can buy anything." Christie looked at her husband. "Can they buy the university?" she asked.

"Who knows?" Dr. Allen replied.

From the tone in his voice, Christie knew he was depressed again. It was to be expected. His life's work was over. He was a convicted criminal. His dignity and self-respect had been taken from him. What could she possibly say to ease the terrible pain he was in? She wracked her brain and said the best thing she could think of.

She wrapped her arm around him. "Things will work out. We're healthy, and we have each other. Our boys are doing well, and they want to work their way through school. Chris is going into agriculture and wants to live here and take care of the farm. If you don't find another job, your parents have a place for us back home. Things will work out."

CHAPTER FORTY-ONE

"Easy to say but tough for me," Allen replied, looking away from his wife. "When I was on top, everyone was my friend. Now that I'm down, only a few stand by me. I feel like a pariah, a leper, and it hurts."

Christie tried to keep her voice upbeat. "Your six months probation is almost up. We can leave. You won't have to put up with it anymore."

The phone was ringing. Christie lifted herself up and hurried inside. Allen's thoughts remained on a future filled with emptiness and uncertainties.

"It's Frank," Christie hollered from the kitchen. Allen went inside.

"Hi, Frank."

"I know you're going through hell, Doc, but if it'll make you feel any better, you can bet that the government and Dow ain't gonna get your data, Yannacone said so."

"I don't care anymore, Frank. I'm leaving. All the years of hard work have been a total waste. I wonder what my life has been all about."

Frank worried about his friend and wanted to help.

"I know the feeling, Doc. I too wondered what life was all about in Vietnam. I saw buddies blown apart. Some died in my arms. I still hear them crying, 'I don't wanna die.' Some looked at me with fear in their eyes, knowing they would die. And yet, in spite of my living with death at my heels, I kept charging through the jungle, firing like a madman. And I did come home."

Allen broke in. "You were lucky."

"Maybe, Doc. But fifty thousand guys didn't come home. And as hard as we tried, we couldn't force them out of their jungles. In their jungle, they were king. And in your scientific world, Dow and the government are kings. It is hard to dethrone the king, Doc. It's like the lion. He will always be king of the jungle. And when he roars, all you can do is run like hell."

Allen nodded. "I guess I never really had a chance once they ganged up on me."

"You might be right," Frank answered strongly. "But I'm not willing to give up. I'm still gonna try to kick some ass. I'll talk to Bull and ask him to start a quiet investigation. I don't care how long it takes. It could be a waste of time, but what the hell? What's life about anyhow? We're here one day, and gone the next." Frank paused, wondering if his pep talk was having any effect on his friend. "As long as I'm around," he went on, "I'll keep charging through the jungle like a damn fool."

"I wish I could stay and do something," Allen said, "but there's no job for me here. I have to find work elsewhere."

Frank understood what it was like to have the world collapse around you. He had gone through a similar feeling when Lenny and Paul died.

"I understand, Doc. You gotta do what you gotta do. But when you're ready to blow town, let me know. I talked to Bull. He and his guys will escort you to the airport. You will have a limo. No charge."

"Thanks, Frank," Allen said gratefully. "Let's stay in touch. It's hard to find a friend like you. You're one of the few I have left. When your case goes to trial, let me know. I will be there."

FORTY-TWO

Sunday, April 20, 1980. Chris was in blue coveralls, standing barefoot on the verandah, his hand in the air, waving good-bye to his parents. As he listened to the hum of the limo's engine, he still couldn't believe they were leaving him totally on his own to care for their home and farm. He was going to miss them. The white stretch limo came alive and slowly backed out of the driveway. Chris kept waving, already feeling sad and alone.

Four red Harleys were waiting on the road. Four men in black leather outfits and black helmets were gunning their motors. They were ready. The sky was clear, and the yellow-orange sun had already started its climb above the distant horizon.

The limo gleamed in the sunshine, straightened itself and prepared for its motorcycle escort. A young man in a black chauffeur's uniform fingered a button on the inside of his door and the window slid down. He leaned his head out, touched the brim of his cap with one finger, signaling Larry "The Bull" McKitrick. Engines roared as they sped away, two red Harleys in front and two behind the white stretch limo.

Dr. Allen and his wife turned to the rear window and looked at Chris, his hand still in the air. They looked at each other, and for the moment, neither of them knew what to say. It was the first time they had separated from Chris this way. They would live in North Carolina, on the family farm, and their youngest son would stay and care for the eighty-acre farm in Wisconsin. There was a finality about the separation, not only from Chris but from their home…and more. They knew their life in Wisconsin was over and a new one was about to begin. But the new one had not yet been charted.

As the procession raced forward, a farmer on a tractor stood and waved. An oncoming car slowed and the driver craned his neck to catch a glimpse of the passengers, but he couldn't see through the dark windows. A brown and white Collie at the side of the road sat on its hindquarters and watched them pass. A driver up ahead quickly pulled off the road onto a weeded patch of ground and allowed them to go by.

Dr. Allen saw none of this. His thoughts had drifted to North Carolina and the family farm, living with his folks and starting a new life. His spirit was low and anxiety high. It seemed so hopeless at his age.

Before leaving, Christie convinced him to wear his cowboy duds. It usually made him feel good. This one extravagance was something he cherished. But this time, the white, ten-gallon hat and leather boots didn't do a thing for his mood. Sensing his despair, Christie moved closer and took her husband's hand.

"Maybe we should have a drink," she said. "Look! There's Kahlua."

Christie immediately regretted mentioning the coffee liqueur. It was what he had put in his coffee before testifying before the grand jury, and she did not want to bring up unpleasant reminders.

"It was nice of Frank to do this," Allen murmured, "he's about the only friend I've got left."

"I'm sure you have more friends than you realize," she replied, leaning her head on his shoulder.

The soft buzz of the phone sounded from the cradle in front of them. Dr. Allen hesitated until he saw the driver nod.

"Hello?"

"Hi, Doc! How's it feel to live in luxury for a while?" Frank's voice was reassuring.

"Frank, this is so kind of you—"

"I called to say keep your chin up. There's a big world out there, a million things to do. I know it's hard right now, but you'll find a niche. And you might be happier away from the university."

Allen shook his head. "I'm fifty-four, Frank. Nobody will hire me. I applied to a few universities, and they knew all about me. It was the same with governmental agencies. I've been blackballed."

"They did a real number on you, Doc. And they're trying to do more. Dow is attacking you at the EPA hearings and the District Court."

"How much more can they do, Frank?" Allen asked incredulously.

"A lot. My guys tell me that Dow is trying to destroy all of your publications."

"Impossible," Allen replied softly. "They've been peer reviewed and accepted."

CHAPTER FORTY-TWO

"True, Doc. But here's what Dow's attorneys are saying to Judge Finch at the EPA hearings, and I am quoting, 'There are compelling reasons to require full scrutiny of Dr. Allen's work. Toxic PCBs have been found in tissue from test animals in Dr. Allen's 500 ppt monkey study, raising serious questions about the reliability of any of Dr. Allen's work. In addition, Dr. Allen's general credibility is impugned by his recent admission of guilt involving the theft of government funds.'"

"How can they get away with that?" Allen replied with a rising tone of anger.

"Victor said, 'For the purpose of attacking the credibility of a witness, the Federal Rules of Evidence allows a lawyer to cite for up to ten years a conviction involving dishonesty or false statements.'"

"Ten years! That's unbelievable! Will I be allowed to testify before the EPA?"

"I don't know," Frank said, swallowing hard, wishing he could be more reassuring.

Christie sat tight-lipped, watching her husband's growing agitation.

"What about my testimony for you? Dow can make the same claim!"

"Victor has a list of scientists whose work supports yours. A reasonable jury will have to look at the facts."

"My lawyers never explained any of this. What a fool I've been!" Allen exclaimed.

"You are not a fool, Doc. Naïve, yes. But you've been up against powerful forces. They have unlimited resources and can do whatever it takes to win. They are ruthless and without conscience."

"Tell Frank the latest," Christie chimed in, "about Cartwright and Aberg."

"Hi, Christie!" Frank hollered. "What does she mean by the latest, Doc?"

"Remember the missing data?" Allen asked, "when Rickey Marlar was found dead?"

"Uh huh."

Dr. Allen paused, and let out a deep sigh. "Just before we left, I got a call from the legal affairs office. Aberg was there telling them there was no missing data."

"Whaaat?" Frank was taken aback.

"That's right! Aberg said there had been no data, that it had never been gathered before the experiment began."

"Where did he get that crap?"

"Cartwright and Androtti reported it to Aberg. That's what I was told. They were my students. My students! Why would they say this?"

"What would that do to the 500 dioxin study, Doc?"

"I don't know. I sent the university a letter, explaining that the missing data had been collected by a student who died. I pointed out that Cartwright and Androtti not only went over the manuscript when it was being prepared for publication, but they have written subsequent papers that required knowledge of the data they now claim never existed. I don't understand it!"

"Sounds fishy to me, Doc. That experiment is one of the strongest reasons the EPA had to justify the discontinuation of 2,4,5-T. It's also important for the Vietnam veterans who were exposed to Agent Orange."

"That's right," Allen exclaimed. "And it's vital for—"

"Ya know, Doc," Frank interjected, "I've said it before and I'll say it again. This entire affair is a well-orchestrated conspiracy. How in the hell did Aberg suddenly get involved? He helped Burek and Bell, the Dow employees who went over your 500 dioxin study over a year ago. Aberg let them use his office. Now Aberg is back. Who is paying him? He is in court, supposedly fighting for your former colleagues, but they're not paying him. And he sure as hell ain't helping them out of the goodness of his heart. Bull checked up on him. He's a graduate of the university's law school. And as far as I'm concerned, the university is using one of their own to help Dow."

Christie had been listening and thinking about what was being said.

"Frank!" she said. "I am so glad that we are getting out of this crazy mess."

"It's more of a crazy mess than you realize," Frank replied. "There's somethin' going on at the EPA that tells me the hearings are really over. Maybe not officially, but they have decided to call it quits. One of my guys sent me a copy of a letter from Professor Dougherty to Dorothy Patton, an EPA attorney. He's a chemist at the Florida State University. The first sentence of the letter tells it all. Dougherty said, 'Thank you for informing me of your decision to remove me from the witness list for the 2,4,5-T and Silvex cancellation hearings.' Dougherty is a researcher, an expert on fertility, and he was prepared to give the EPA evidence that dioxin made Vietnam veterans sterile. Victor will use him in our suit against Dow. But the fact that they dropped him is enough to tell me that the EPA is winding down."

CHAPTER FORTY-TWO

Dr. Allen shook his head in disgust. Christie sat tight-lipped and watched Bull, his buddies, and the chauffeur coordinate the movements of their vehicles smoothly, in unison and with precision. She saw familiar high-rise university buildings. The traffic became heavier. The limo began to slow as they approached the airport.

"We're coming to the airport, Frank," Christie said. "Mr. McKitrick is absolutely marvelous. We thank all of you."

"And we would do anything for you, for Bull or any of your guys. We can never repay you or Bull for the friendship you two have shown."

"It works both ways, Doc. I'll talk with you in a few days. Bull will have something to say to you at the airport. He is speaking for our entire organization. Remember! We have an army out there, and I'm one who doesn't believe in surrender. They have to kill me before they stop me. It's not yet over, Doc. Take care."

"So long, Frank."

The caravan wound its way toward the departure area. Police waved them on, not knowing who was in the limo. Taxis and cars pulled over. People stared. The limo finally came to a stop and the chauffeur hopped out, hurried around to the other side, and opened the door. Dr. Allen and Christie eased out of the limo. Bull and one of his guys had already unloaded the luggage and were checking it in curbside.

Dr. Allen and Christie waited. Bull came over, his black helmet in his left hand, tickets with attached luggage receipts in the other. He gave the tickets to Christie, then locked eyes with Dr. Allen.

"Frank asked me to check out everything that's happened to you," he began. "I will do just that. I'll do it quietly. It will be a new experience for me, but I learn fast. I'll report to Frank, and we will see where it leads us. But wherever it goes, do me a favor."

Dr. Allen was moved by Bull's sincere commitment.

"Anything," he replied.

"Don't lose heart." Bull put out his hand for a handshake.

Allen took his hand and said, "Do me a favor."

"Anything," Bull replied.

"Can I give you a hug?"

233

For a moment, Bull seemed flustered. But the next moment found them with their arms around one another. Bull's helmet fell to the ground. Fighting off tears, Christie picked it up and held it out to Bull.

"What about me?" Christie said.

Bull smiled. He handed the helmet to Dr. Allen and gave her a big hug. "Thank you," she said.

Bull looked into Christie's eyes and said, "Take care of him."

FORTY-THREE

June 4, 1980. AOVI board members filed out of the Bunker and up the steps. Frank closed the door behind them. They left with seething emotions. Anger! Outrage! Many wanted to return to the days of Vietnam. To fight! To deliver a message to Dow, to the government, and others who destroyed Dr. Allen. The people who destroyed Allen could destroy their suit, which was now before Judge Pratt.

Frank joined this small group who favored plan B. He argued for a motion to change the organization's motto. To hell with dignity, self-respect, and solidarity, he reasoned. How can we have self-respect if we sit on our asses, watch it happen, and do nothing?

The board unanimously accepted the idea that Allen's downfall had been a conspiracy. It began with the death of Rickey Marlar and the missing data, stolen by whoever it was who killed Marlar. The 500 study and all other studies coming down the pike threatened to destroy the pesticide and herbicide industry. Dow could not allow it to happen.

Dow had continued the pretense of helping Allen. They supposedly were analyzing his tissue samples for dioxin. However, Dr. Kociba, a Dow scientist, told of high PCBs in tissue samples in a letter to Cartwright. Dow was never asked to analyze for PCBs because Dr. Allen did it himself. He had been doing it for years.

Kociba's letter was a ploy! It created a record! Had Kociba sent the letter to Allen, there would have been an uproar. Dr. Allen would have wanted to know why Dow had done something they had not been asked to do. He would have wanted to review Dow's findings.

Even though the board had no proof at the moment, they accepted the idea that Dow and the government had arranged to plant Kathryn Anderson in Allen's office. Her job was to poke around, find something or create something that would raise hell for Allen. In less than two months, Anderson found what she was looking for, made damning allegations, and quit. She was then shipped out of town and could never be found. The damage was done, and an audit of Allen's records followed.

Dr. Spencer was ordered into Allen's lab to audit a rat study. Dr. Allen wasn't there, nor did he know Spencer was coming. Cartwright showed him around and assisted with every detail. Had Allen been there, Spencer would never have gotten into the lab. It was unheard of to suddenly appear, walk into a laboratory and conduct an examination without a prior request and without justification. There had to be a reason for his coming. That reason was demonstrated by the scathing and highly critical report about Allen's laboratory practices that Spencer issued to the EPA, which turned it over to Dow.

One month later, Dow employees Drs. Burek and Bell appeared unannounced. Allen was away. People knew when Allen was away. Burek and Bell reported to Aberg's office, and again, Cartwright gave them every assistance. He carried Dr. Allen's slides, photos, and records to Aberg's office, including a microscope and other equipment needed to examine the 500 ppt study. One year later, their report surfaced. It contained statements about high PCBs totally unrelated to the 500 study. It tied in with the Kociba letter that falsely reported high PCBs. All of this was Dow chicanery to do Dr. Allen in.

Kathryn Anderson had pointed a finger resulting in Dr. Allen's conviction. That conviction, Kociba's letter, Spencer's report, and Burek and Bell's report were being used by Dow's attorneys at the EPA hearings to destroy Allen's reputation and his life's work.

The strategy worked. And the final nails in Allen's coffin were being hammered into place in the U.S. District Court in Wisconsin.

"I'm mad as hell," Frank said to the board. "Some of our guys, dying of cancer, can invade the courtroom during the EPA hearings and kill some of those bastards."

But Muriel Reutershan shook her head. "That will accomplish nothing," she argued. "Others will take their place. And...it would give us a black eye. We can't afford bad PR. It would destroy our organization." It was difficult for her to keep her composure, so she tried to speak calmly, "Don't you see, Frank?"

Frank could not obtain a two-thirds vote to change the long-standing motto, and he was pissed. When the board left, Frank sulked. He popped open a Schlitz, downed it with one gulp, and threw the can forcefully at the wastebasket. In it went. He eyed the Bushmills Irish whiskey, reached up, and took a bottle down from the top of the

CHAPTER FORTY-THREE

fridge. He was tempted to open it, but his previous misadventure with the delicious beverage came to mind. He did not want another hangover. So he put the bottle back.

Frank walked over to his M-16 on the wall, opened the display case, and gently lifted the weapon from its moorings. He stroked the steel-gray barrel, touched the stock, and fingered the trigger. It felt good holding his baby again. Should he carry out plan B on his own? He put the gun back, wondering.

The phone rang. Frank glared at it as if an enemy had suddenly invaded his Bunker. He clicked on the speakerphone and leaned back on the settee. "AOVI," Frank said with an obvious disdain for conversation.

"It's me. You sound like something's wrong."

"Hi, Bull," Frank replied, lifted slightly out of his moodiness by the sound of his friend's voice. "I'm outta sorts. I don't like Dow getting away with all the shit they've been pullin'."

"I've got some good news, Frank. Judge Crabb ruled against Dow. They can't get the 25 and 5 ppt dioxin studies. Victor and his boys did a good job protecting Allen's work. Dow will appeal, but I think the Seventh Circuit will go along with Crabb's decision."

"That's good. What about the 50 ppt study?" Frank asked.

"ACE doesn't get it until the paper is published. By then, the results will be official. And Allen's paper will help us when our case goes to trial. Have you talked to him?"

"No, I didn't have anything good to tell him."

Excited, Bull banged his fist on a table and said, "You do now! I found someone at the university who's willing to dig for information. He's on his way to my office. Should be here soon. If it's the last thing I do, I'm going to find proof of who did what to get rid of Dr. Allen."

"What's it costin' ya?"

"A couple hundred a month."

"I'll tell, Doc."

Frank hung up, and in seconds he was again on the speakerphone. Christie answered. "Frank! This is a pleasant surprise."

It pleased Frank knowing Christie enjoyed talking to him.

"How's everything?" he asked.

"Not bad. Jim's parents are helping us survive. We're living in a farmhouse built before the Civil War."

"Well I'll be darned!" Frank replied, surprised that such a house still existed.

"I love it!" Christie said, making herself comfortable on a kitchen chair. "His folks left their furniture in it when they built a new house. All we had to do was move right in. It has eight rooms and four fireplaces. It's been modernized and is really quite lovely."

"Hey, that sounds terrific. Tell me, how's Doc?"

Christie sighed. "He's working like a horse, sixteen hours a day. He's become a farmer and...it's been good for him. It keeps him from thinking, at least while he's working. I'll let him tell you about it."

"And what about you? Have you gone back to nursing?"

"I'm retired, Frank. Before we left Madison, Mr. McKitrick told me to take care of him and that is what I'm doing. Right now, I've got an apple pie in the oven. Come on over and join us for dinner. I'll feed you so well, you'll never want to leave."

"I'll take you up on that some day," Frank replied. "I would love a good home-cooked meal."

"That would be lovely. Do you realize we've never met face to face? It would be a treat if you would be our guest. You could stay for as long as you want. Have you ever tasted cold mountain spring water?"

"No...can't say I have."

"What about looking out of every window in our house and seeing the high peaks of the Smoky Mountains?"

"Sounds beautiful," Frank replied. He knew he could use a change of scenery. His Bunker windows, looking out onto a dreary street, were for the birds. "But tell me," he asked, "where did you learn to be a farmer's wife?"

Christie laughed. "I grew up on a dairy farm in Pennsylvania. I know a lot about being a farmer's wife. I can even raise crops."

"Sounds good, Christie. Tell me, what's Doc raising down there?"

"Burley tobacco. It's the main cash crop in North Carolina. It's hard work for most of the year, and the way Jim's doing it, it's even worse. He won't use pesticides, insecticides, fungicides, or herbicides. He's doing it the way they did it years ago...with a hoe. I'm so proud of him."

CHAPTER FORTY-THREE

"Does he have help?"

"The best, our son Jim. He was an engineer with the Atomic Energy Commission and quit his job at Los Alamos. He came here two months ahead of us and is spending time with his father, something he's rarely done. The two of them are finally getting to know one another after all these years. Oh! Hold on, Frank! I hear them coming."

Frank could hear the happiness in Christie's voice when talking about Jim and his son. Maybe some good would come out of the whole mess. After several moments, Allen's voice came through, warm and upbeat.

"Hey, Frank! How are you?"

"Fine, Doc. I hear you're getting a real workout on your farm."

"Lord, yes," Allen replied with a chuckle. "I can do hard work. I learned it as a kid. We didn't have help and were too scotch to pay the high price of farm labor. If we couldn't do it ourselves, it didn't get done."

"It must be nice to have your son with you," Frank said.

"Frank!" Allen replied thoughtfully, "I never realized what I was missing. Since coming home, I've grown closer to everyone: my son, mother, father, and my wife. We have time for one another. It feels good working with my son, sitting down with the family and just talking without feeling rushed. Even though I'm working long hours, it's different than before. Christie comes out with cold lemonade and we sit on the ground, talking for as long as we want before I go back to hoeing. This is a whole new life for me. And you know what? I love it!"

Frank sensed the satisfaction the new lifestyle gave his friend.

"Christie tells me you're growing tobacco. What's it like?"

"It's a year-round job. My son prepared the tobacco bed before I came down."

"Tobacco bed? What's that, Doc?"

"Well...first, he piles wood and brush several feet high, ten feet wide, and several hundred feet long. Then he burns it, and the heat sterilizes the ground. This cuts down on the disease problem. But in late August and September, the real backbreaking work begins. The plants will get cut near the ground, and five or six plants will be strung on a stick, each load weighing eighty to a hundred pounds. Once we haul these sticks into the barn, we hang them at different levels. And lifting those sticks over our heads to the top tier is the most grueling job I've ever done or ever could do. By the time I'm through, I will be totally exhausted."

"I'm exhausted just listening to you, Doc," Frank quipped. "Anyhow, I've got a bit of news from Bull. He's starting an investigation and wants you to know he'll keep digging until he finds out who did what to get rid of you."

Allen swallowed hard and didn't immediately reply.

He finally said, "When I'm busy all day, it's not bad, Frank. But when I wake up at night, the pain is still there. I cry. Imagine! A grown man like me crying. I don't think I'll ever get over it. All the years of work. Building a reputation. Then watching it all slip away. Like you once said, Dow and the government really did a job on me."

Dr. Allen paused to wipe away a tear, then took a deep breath.

"Tell me," he said, "did Dow finally get my data?"

"They didn't get anything, Doc. But Dow is still hammerin' away at you at the EPA hearings. One of my guys said you're scheduled to testify June twelfth. That's eight days from now."

"Me! Testify! That's news to me! I was never asked!"

"Maybe you were, Doc. Maybe the request was sent to the university and they never told you about it."

"Could be."

"It's just another piece of information that might serve you well when Bull pieces everything together. Someday, I think you'll be able to sue the hell out of those bastards."

"I'd like that, Frank, more than anything. It bothers me to think I was so close to proving my theory about dioxin. So close...so close."

Frank understood Allen's frustration. He too had that feeling from trying to get VA benefits for his guys, many now dead.

"When our case goes to trial, Doc, Victor will show the court a Dow document proving that your theory was correct. Dow knew and still knows there is no such thing as a safe level for dioxin."

"When's your case going to trial, Frank?"

"Don't know. It's draggin.'"

"Well...when you need me, just holler."

CHAPTER FORTY-THREE

"Holler? We'll come and get ya."

"One other thing, Frank. What happened to Verlin's fat biopsy?"

"The VA still won't release his number. But Victor took it to court. He thinks we'll get it."

"Let me know what happens."

"I'll bring the news in person. I'd like to see what it's like livin' on a farm. And I wouldn't mind a home-cooked meal."

"The guest room will always be ready, Frank. And I know you'll love Christie's cooking. I'll call Bull and invite him too. It would be nice having both of you."

"Sounds good, Doc."

As they hung up, both men shared a feeling of gratitude, realizing that each had discovered what they knew was a real friend as well as a brother-in-arms.

Meanwhile, Larry McKitrick was determined to prove that Dr. Allen had been falsely accused and falsely convicted. His gut told him the whole thing had been a massive conspiracy. He wanted proof. For a small monthly stipend, he acquired the services of a university employee who agreed to do anything for a buck. He was a steward in the union who had connections. Connections meant clout, and clout meant power. And with power, there wasn't a damn thing this steward couldn't find if it existed.

"I don't want anyone to find out," the steward said as he seated himself in Bull's office.

"No one will," Bull replied. "Refer to yourself as mole. Use only a public phone."

"What are you looking for?" Mole asked.

"Start with Kathryn Anderson," Bull said. "Hired in August of '78 and quit less than two months later. Everything you can find out about her, and while you're digging, keep a sharp eye for anything you come across that has to do with Dr. James Allen."

A roll of tens, held firm by a rubber band, came out of Bull's hip pocket. Bull stuffed it into the steward's shirt pocket. With a toothy grin and a handshake, the steward knew he had a nice deal.

FORTY-FOUR

University officials demanded an investigation into Dr. Allen's missing data. It was carried out by three of the most respected, most prestigious professors on the faculty: James Crow, Elizabeth Miller, and Philip Cohen. They wasted no time.

They talked with Allen's colleagues who helped author the published paper. They asked for and received a written statement from Allen. They studied photographs and examined master records at the Primate Center. Huddling together, Crow, Miller, and Cohen reached a conclusion on September 26, 1980.

They said, "No action should be taken at this time to alert either the journal editor or the public with regard to concerns about the possible lack of authenticity of some of the data. The death of Mr. Marlar does not permit us to question the person whom Dr. Allen stated was the collator of the clinical records. But the authors appear to be in agreement that the interpretation of the data is a reasonable reflection of the experimental observations."

Dr. John Smith, dean of the medical school, was in his office. He read the report and accepted the recommendation. Everyone understood that the report would be held in confidence. For several weeks, nothing more was heard about it until a rumor surfaced. Then university phone lines began buzzing.

"Did you hear...?" one secretary asked.

"Yes, I heard," came the reply.

"Is it true?"

"I'll check with Mabel."

"And I'll call Gladys, she should know."

By noon, word had gotten out. Chancellor Shain had refused to follow the committee's recommendation. He absolutely wanted the EPA to know that the authenticity of some of Allen's data had been questioned. And he wanted the journal editor to know. On December 2, 1980, he dashed off a letter to the Honorable Edward B. Finch, administrative law judge at the EPA.

CHAPTER FORTY-FOUR

The chancellor said, "On August 28, 1980, my office was orally informed by counsel [Aberg] for Abigail Androtti and John Cartwright, two of the co-authors of the study, that there were questions regarding the authenticity or accuracy of certain data reported in the published paper summarizing the study's conclusion. Whether they affect the conclusions or not, we consider this a serious matter. It was my conclusion that the university has a responsibility to promptly address the allegations and determine their accuracy."

The chancellor told of the investigation and attached a copy of the committee's report. He made no mention of the fact that the journal editor decided, based on the committee's findings, that no further action was necessary as far as he was concerned. Chancellor Shain also made no mention of the fact that when Androtti and Cartwright reviewed the draft of his letter to Edward Finch, they pointed to inaccuracies and suggested corrections, but the chancellor ignored their suggestions and sent the letter as drafted by the university attorney.

Meanwhile, Mole loved gathering all of this university scuttlebutt. He rode around campus on a golf cart picking up information. Parking was never a problem. He would find a spot between parked cars or in a corner of a building. Many times, he didn't have to stop. He'd roll across a lawn, see his contact, reach out for an envelope, and keep right on going. Today, he moved past the horse barn, went on to the Memorial Library, and then Bascom Hall. He now had three pieces of new information and drove off with a smile of satisfaction. He headed for a public pay phone because he never forgot Bull's warning about using university lines.

Mole dialed a number. "Let me talk to Bull."

"Hold on," came the reply.

"Yeah," Bull said.

"It's me, Mole. I got somethin'."

"One of my guys will pick it up," Bull replied.

Frank McCarthy loved receiving information from Bull. He was in his Bunker, sitting on the floor, his back against the settee. He had a smug grin on his face as he held and read documents in his hand. They were from Bull, and they told an intriguing story. He wanted Doc to know and phoned him. The phone was ringing, ringing, no answer. A half-hour later, no answer. An hour later, no answer. Where was he? They couldn't all be out in the field on Sunday, working their tails off. Finally, at twelve-thirty, Frank got through.

"I was in church praying for you, Frank."

"Me and my guys could use a little help from above, Doc. Our suit is just marking time. It seems as if we need a miracle to get the court system moving. Anyhow, I called to tell ya about information I got from Bull. The university has a one-page form on file about the Anderson gal. It's got her name on it, but no address and not much of anything, not even her Social Security number."

"That's really something," Allen replied. "How does anyone get hired without a Social Security number?"

"That's the sixty-four dollar question, Doc."

"To think I never checked her out."

"I'm also sending you copies of two letters," Frank continued. "One about the investigation of the missing data and another showing Dow and the government coughing up a lot of dough for research at the university. As far as I'm concerned, that's why the chancellor had no hesitation in getting rid of you. Anything for a buck."

The reminder of being dumped brought tears to Dr. Allen's eyes.

"Everyone needs money, Frank. But it's how you get it that counts. I was raised with the old-fashioned idea that you worked for it, and you were ethical in getting it. If Bull finds proof that the university sold me down the river for a few lousy bucks, I'd be tempted to take the bastards to court. Because of what's happened, I can't get a job."

"You'll make money on that tobacco, won't you?" Frank asked.

"Only the good Lord can answer that. If everything is perfect, we should have about three thousand pounds of tobacco per acre. Fifteen acres means forty-five thousand pounds. At a buck eighty a pound, that's eighty-one thousand a year, not counting expenses. If you consider the time we put in, it comes to about fifty cents an hour. If conditions are bad, we could lose the entire crop and make nothing."

Frank did not realize that Dr. Allen and his family lived day to day, working their tails off, always with the knowledge that they were in a precarious situation.

"How would you live if the crop went bad?" Frank asked.

"It would be rough for a while. My parents would help, but thank God I have a veterinary degree to fall back on. I'm relearning veterinary medicine after all these years."

CHAPTER FORTY-FOUR

"That sounds great, Doc, but isn't it hard to pick up again?"

Allen smiled. "You know the old expression, Frank. Where there's a will, there's a way. I'm helping a local vet just for experience. And it's been some experience. Last week, we walked two miles at night to a cow in an infested briar patch. She couldn't deliver her calf. It was having a problem in the birth canal. So we did a C-section using flashlights."

Frank was impressed. "Surgery at night in the bushes, using small flashlights? How'd you two pull that off?"

"With difficulty. It took a couple of hours. And I have to tell you, I was exhausted. Large animals are hard work. And there are times when it is dangerous."

"You are something, Doc. Where do you find the time?"

"You know me, Frank. I'm a workaholic. With raising tobacco and all, I'm putting in sixteen hours a day, seven days a week, and I'm still going to church on Sunday."

Frank shook his head with disbelief. "How's Christie holdin' up?"

"She loves it! Not working nights opened up a new world for her. She cooks and bakes and enjoys being a farmer's wife. When I start a veterinary practice, she is going to be there with me. The animals will have a caring nurse."

Frank knew he could use loving attention too. He had not received any for such a long time. He had almost forgotten what it felt like.

"I'd sure like to visit you guys," he said softly.

"Plan on it. Make it happen," Allen replied.

"I wish it were that simple," Frank answered. "When Paul and Lenny were alive, it was easy to get away. Now I'm busy all the time answering calls from our guys. So many need help, and our resources are so limited. That's why I can't wait for our case to go before a jury. We are hurting for money."

"How much are you suing for?"

"Forty five billion."

"Wow! How did Victor pick such an astronomical number?"

"It's not as much as it sounds," Frank replied. "When Paul died, Victor Yannacone took the suit and organized it into many class action cases."

"That was brilliant," Allen said.

"It sure was. Paul and Lenny represent all vets who died from cancer as a result of Agent Orange. Kay Laviano, Lenny's wife, represents all widows who lost a husband. Muriel, Paul's mother, is another class action case for all mothers who lost a son. Two of our guys represent all Vietnam vets who are sick because of Agent Orange, and their kids is a class action suit for all children born with deformities and defects. Each class action has to be tried separately. And when you think of hundreds of thousands of people being killed or damaged by dioxin, forty-four billion suddenly looks small. But it would be an enormous amount for a nonprofit foundation. We could do a lot with that kind of money."

"Yannacone is putting in a lot of time. Who's paying him?"

"No one. I still marvel at his generosity."

"That is really nice," Allen said.

"It sure is. When I first talked with Victor, he looked over the case and felt we could win. I will never forget his words. He said, 'These chemical companies are evil people. They did an evil thing to you. We're going to take them to court and hold their feet to the fire.' Since that first day, he's been taking money out of his own pocket. Victor is our champion. He is uncompromising and not afraid of any judge. I never met anyone like him. We'd kill for him and...even die for him."

"I'm impressed," Allen replied. "But let me ask you something. Right now, Victor is fighting to keep my data out of Dow's hands. I'm not paying him. How can he work for nothing?"

"If he wins, Dow might have to foot the bill. It's up to the judge."

"How long does Victor think it's going to take?"

"Well, here's the rundown. The class action was filed January '79. Victor immediately went on the attack by talking to the news media. He stirred up a lot of public sentiment for our guys and their families. Dow tried like hell to get the case dismissed. They also filed a motion to shut Victor's mouth. In August of '79, George Pratt, the District Court judge, denied all motions to dismiss and ruled in favor of allowing Victor to speak out."

"Interesting," commented Allen.

Frank excitedly went on. "Dow then tried to destroy the class action suit. They wanted our guys to file in their individual states. This would have fragmented the large group into

CHAPTER FORTY-FOUR

smaller groups all over the country. Luckily, in November of '79, Pratt said no. All suits were to be filed in federal court."

"Judge Pratt is on your side, Frank. That's half the battle."

"Yeah. I think Pratt is terrific. But Dow is always looking for an angle. Two months later, they dragged the government into the case. They charged the U.S. government with being reckless in the use of chemicals. Dow pointed out that herbicides were made according to government specifications and that the government used Agent Orange in far heavier concentrations than had ever been used in this country."

"From the documents we've seen, Frank, that's true. What else is Dow saying?'

"They're claiming the government knew more about the dangers and risks and hazards of Agent Orange than they did and that they were prohibited from putting warning labels on shipping containers. They are also saying the government failed to instruct, failed to protect, and failed to treat veterans exposed to dioxin."

"That's amazing!" Allen shouted, holding the phone tightly. "They finally admitted that Agent Orange was a danger during the Vietnam War! When it comes to saving a buck, Dow is ready to tell the truth and stick it to the government."

"Dow and their cronies are not going to stick it to anyone, Doc. They thought they were clever in trying to stick it to Uncle Sam but it backfired. Dow knew Judge Pratt had given Victor a real challenge. In order to prove a legitimate claim, Victor had to show that Dow knew more about the dangers of Agent Orange than they revealed to the government. What Dow knew compared to what the government knew was extremely important to Judge Pratt."

"Did Victor do that?"

"He sure did. That's where discovery came in. Dow had to turn over thousands of secret and confidential documents. Some dated back to 1957. They showed what Dow knew even back then. So Judge Pratt allowed the case to continue."

Dr. Allen marveled at what he had just heard, nodding his head, but before he could comment, Frank had more to say.

"Pratt made marvelous rulings. In January of '80, he ruled that videotaped testimony would be admissible. That meant veterans who died could talk to the jury. This was a great victory for us. One month later, Pratt allowed six hundred fifty Australians who served in Vietnam to join the class action. Since then, Dow has been able to stall for time with a lot of legal maneuvering. We were supposed to go to trial in September of '80, but we're still waiting."

"I see why Yannacone is your champion," Allen said. "I wish I'd had him defending me."

"We were lucky to find him, Doc."

"I sometimes wonder about luck," Allen replied. "Is it luck? Or was it meant to be? Why do things happen the way they do? Maybe there's a higher power up there. There might be a wisdom behind what we go through in life. And maybe, just maybe, we'll understand it some day."

Frank smiled on hearing his friend speak so philosophically. Maybe his friend was starting to heal.

"I'll say amen to that, Doc."

FORTY-FIVE

A YOUNG MAN IN A BLUE PINSTRIPE SUIT AND A WHITE BUTTON-DOWN SHIRT MADE his way along a crowded street in Washington, DC. He held three white envelopes close to his chest as he sidled between a group of elderly women. There was no return address on any of the envelopes. Up ahead, a U.S. Postal Service box stood flush against a gray, stone building. The young man dropped the letters into the open slot.

Three days later, editors of Madison newspapers opened the anonymous letters. The area erupted into its accustomed reading frenzy. Headlines tore into Dr. Allen's 500 ppt dioxin study. Reliability was questioned, authenticity of data was questioned, and the committee's report was proof! Chancellor Shain's letter to the EPA clearly demonstrated the university's position on Allen's work. It was suspect and viewed with disfavor. It was a serious problem that had to be dealt with.

The Associated Press picked up the news. Within twenty-four hours, the defamatory remarks had spread like wildfire. Dow's attorneys used it to their advantage. They hammered away at the EPA hearings, determined to prove that Allen's work was even worse than anyone had ever imagined. They pulled out the Burek and Bell report that had been completed fourteen months earlier. They waved it before Judge Finch as additional proof that Allen's research was worthless. Absolutely worthless!

"Dow's review shows, inter alia," they said, "tissue slides were missing and record keeping was severely deficient. No pathology was performed on any of the control monkeys, and many of the 500 ppt monkeys showed high levels of PCBs. The toxicity in the monkeys could be due, at least in part, to PCB contamination. Nowhere have Dr. Allen and his colleagues made any attempt to determine the source of PCB contamination, nor is there any evidence that they considered the PCB problem in reporting their results."

Although Dow's attorneys failed to obtain data from the 50 ppt monkey study, they pointed to Spencer's audit of the 50 ppt rat study and severely criticized Allen's laboratory practices.

"Dr. Allen improperly used control animals from a different study. Tissues from control animals were not properly examined. Tissue slides were lost. Study animals had been disposed of."

Dow was trying to show that Spencer's findings and the Burek and Bell report proved that Allen's work was flawed and had to be looked upon with contempt and therefore cast aside.

Edward W. Warren, another Dow attorney, didn't fare as well in the U.S. District Court in Madison. Judge Crabb ruled against Dow, denying them access to Allen's data, citing academic rights. Warren tried to overturn Crabb's decision by appealing to the Seventh Circuit Court of Appeals, but suddenly, before the three-judge panel could render an opinion, the appeal came to an abrupt end.

At the EPA hearings, Dow's attorneys moved to exclude from the EPA record all reference to Dr. Allen's 50 ppt study. If approved, they would no longer need the data. They also moved that the subpoena duces tecum against Allen and the other scientists be vacated. Dow no longer wanted to question any of them. Dorothy Patten, the EPA attorney, asked that Dow's request be granted. Judge Edward B. Finch allowed both motions. This action automatically terminated Dow's appeal before the Seventh Circuit. And on March 10, 1981, the *Capital Times* had another story: "The EPA has dropped federal court action aimed at forcing the University of Wisconsin to release the results of dioxin research being done on campus."

In announcing its decision, the EPA cited the possibility of substantial irregularities in studies conducted in 1978 and 1979 by former pathologist Dr. James Allen and now being completed by Allen's former assistants. The EPA also pointed out that the university's own claim of lack of confidence in the studies raised questions about the reliability of data from the study. The EPA then terminated the cancellation proceedings. Dow had won. It was business as usual.

The chain of events was watched closely by all governmental agencies. Very quickly, the university and Allen's former colleagues were notified that the National Institute for Environmental Health Sciences had terminated all research funding. All animals had to be removed from the Primate Center, and every project had to be closed down.

The Veterans Administration then distributed a two-volume report to researchers throughout the government and the scientific community. It was a compilation of world scientific literature on Agent Orange and other herbicides used in Vietnam. It covered twelve hundred documents spanning more than twenty years. JRB Associates of McLean, Virginia, compiled

CHAPTER FORTY-FIVE

it under a contract for the VA, mandated by Public Law 96-151. Volume 1, pages seven and eight, attacked Dr. Allen.

It said, "The EPA found that the monkeys used in the studies by Allen and Schantz had been exposed to PCBs in a previous experiment and the results of the dioxin experiment have not been generally accepted by the scientific community."

Not everyone agreed. Abigail Androtti was furious! She sat in Linda's office pecking away on the old fashioned Remington.

"I've been involved in this research from the start," she wrote. "I know the EPA did not find that monkeys had been exposed to PCBs in a previous experiment because they were not. The EPA was given all the data from the 500 ppt study and they know the animals had not been on any previous PCB study. Neither the EPA nor anyone else was given data on the 50 ppt study. Therefore, in addition to the fact that these animals were never on any previous study, no one had the background or documentation to substantiate the claim cited in your firm's publication as being attributed to the EPA. The statement regarding the general non-acceptance of the results from these dioxin experiments is puzzling and damaging to the research and the researchers involved. The plethora of dioxin data from other laboratories substantiates our findings and it does not seem logical that your statement accurately represents the feeling of the scientific community. Above all, this statement is opinionated and cannot be substantiated and has no place in a publication financed by the federal government. The political and volatile nature of the herbicide situation dictates responsible assessment and investigation of any material that is to be published. This includes publication of research, as well as reviews of literature. Since the report was prepared wholly and exclusively by JRB Associates, your firm is responsible for the above non-referenced statements. I therefore request your documentation as to the source of the EPA findings and the means by which your firm accepts such information. The consequences of publishing undocumented and inaccurate information could be devastating to continuing research. In general, publication of such fabrications offers the persons involved little or no rebuttal in the public forum and provides a chilling effect on the research and the researcher. I am hoping you will expedite your compliance with my request to document for me your informational source for the erroneous statements in your report."

Three weeks later, Abigail read the reply from James F. Striegel of JRB Associates.

He said, "I assume you are aware of the concerns that have been expressed concerning Dr. Allen's research. Since we have now concluded our contractual activities concerning the review of the literature on the Vietnam herbicides, I have forwarded your letter to Dr. Shepard at the Veterans Administration."

Mole rode his golf cart all around campus. He knew that as a steward in the union, he had every right to visit members, to inquire about complaints, to interview non-members, to gather information, obtain opinions, and ask for documents, and he knew who to talk to when he wanted to prove that a mere suspicion was a solid fact. He enjoyed this new line of work, and he knew that Bull needed him and the money was good.

After talking with Abigail Androtti, he hopped onto his golf cart and headed for a public pay phone.

"Bull McKitrick," said a familiar voice.

"It's me. I got a pick-up," Mole said, glancing over his shoulder as had become his habit.

"My guy'll be there in an hour."

"Fine."

Four days later, on a blustery Saturday afternoon, Frank McCarthy was in his Bunker, sitting on the settee with Karen Riley, scrutinizing the organization's financial books. As treasurer, Karen worried about every bill.

"We can't afford it, Frank!" she exclaimed. "I don't care how you feel."

"Toll-free calls are a must," Frank argued. "Our guys don't have money. They can't pay for long-distance calls."

"I know, but when Victor filed suit against the VA, our numbers jumped. We have thousands of new members, including wives and children. Our phone bill keeps climbing. We either raise more money or get rid of the phone."

Frank knew she was right. He also knew that without a toll-free line, his guys would be unable to cope with all of their problems and miseries. They had to talk to family and friends.

"Money, money, money," he said, "all we need is money. I'll beg on the streets, I'll open up a thrift shop. I'll do anything. The phone stays. Did you see the number of kids we have on file? Kids with birth defects. Close to sixty-four thousand! We must keep the toll-free line open."

CHAPTER FORTY-FIVE

"I've seen the poor dears. It breaks my heart, but we need money." Karen paused and wondered aloud, "What about asking Bull?"

"I can't. He's given so much already."

Karen agreed. If not for Larry McKitrick, most of the bills could not have been paid. And even now, he was paying $200 a month more to dig for information that would help prove Allen's innocence.

"Anything new on Dr. Allen?" she asked, looking up from the pile of bills in front of her.

"Yeah," Frank replied. "I have to call and fill him in on it."

"Call now," Karen said. "I'd like to listen and say hello."

"That's long-distance. Are you gonna pay for the call?" Frank knew he'd made his point.

Karen smiled and waved him away. The speakerphone was on the card table in front of the settee. Frank reached out and dialed.

"Hey, Doc!" Frank said, motioning Karen closer. "I'm with a friend of yours who wants to say hello."

"Hi, cowboy!" Karen chimed in, her face aglow.

"Well, hi there yourself. This is a real treat," Allen replied with obvious delight. "Two of the nicest people I know."

"Flattery will get you everywhere, cowboy!" Karen said. "How's the sci-fi collection doing? Any new ones?"

"I stopped collecting. I donated the entire collection to the local library. They were happy to get it."

"Have you been getting all the news, Doc?" Frank asked, pulling the speakerphone to his end of the table. Karen sat back and listened.

"It's been in the local paper," Allen replied with a disheartened tone, "those stories make me look bad."

"Bull's working on it. He dug up a letter from Aberg to the EPA. Aberg reported that everyone voted not to testify, and that included you. This helped destroy the cancellation hearings. Aberg's been friendly with Phil Davis, a Dow attorney. Calls him Phil. He's been sending Phil a copy of everything."

"It infuriates me, Frank, Aberg speaking for me. Phil Davis and his lawyer buddies throwing mud at me. It never seems to end. I think this bad publicity will hurt your case if you use me to testify."

"As I said before, Doc, Yannacone will handle it, don't worry."

"When's your case going to trial?"

"We're still waiting," Frank replied, eyeing Karen, who was looking at the bills. "There always seems to be a snag," Frank went on. "Judge Pratt was promoted to the Appellate Court and can't handle the case anymore. The next judge in line is Jack Weinstein. I'm told he's an okay guy. I was also told that Dow is gonna try to get some of Pratt's decisions changed. They'll do anything to stall for time."

Dr. Allen remembered an article in *USA Today*.

"I read that Victor Yannacone dragged the VA into your class action suit."

"He sure did," Frank said, leaning back on the settee. "He named Max Cleland and his cohorts as defendants. Up until now, no one's ever been able to sue the VA. They've been exempt. But Victor knew about the Second Circuit's federal common law decision, whatever that is. He charged the VA with permitting unlicensed doctors to practice medicine on Vietnam vets!"

"Really?"

"Yeah, it's incredible. They've been using high doses of mind-altering drugs, burying Agent Orange claims and violating the Constitutional rights of veterans, and a lot of other crap."

"Every time you talk about Victor," Allen said, "I realize how different my life could have been with a different lawyer. I still get so mad at myself for going along with Kessler and Robins."

"It's ancient history, Doc. What's important is tomorrow."

"I guess so," Allen said dejectedly. "Thanks for calling, Frank. I appreciate your letting me know what's going on. Take care, Karen."

As soon as Frank clicked off the speakerphone, it rang. Frank reached out and flipped the switch back on.

"Agent Orange Victims International," he said.

"It's me, Bull. I'm sending you a letter from Cartwright to a friend. It talks about Phil Davis, a Dow attorney. This guy was given all the data from the 500 study, but he wasn't satisfied."

Frank was puzzled. "Whaddya mean?"

CHAPTER FORTY-FIVE

"He wanted substantial raw data not associated with the study. This would've had to include the data that was missing at the time of Marlar's death. Dow knew it was missing. It was in all the papers. All this hullabaloo about the missing data was used to clobber Dr. Allen. It makes me wonder more and more about Marlar's death, and I'm going to try to find out more. Just wanted you to know."

Before Frank could answer, Bull hung up.

FORTY-SIX

No Bull Security, Inc. had a reputation for efficiency and dependability, and McKitrick's men were dedicated to these principles. They were also loyal. They enjoyed their work and earned good pay. Business was good.

At first, Bull was happy with the status quo. But as he became involved in the Allen investigation, he began toying with an idea. The idea became more fascinating every time Mole delivered information. Bits and pieces came together. This gave him clues that pointed the way to other areas of investigation. The challenge of proving Allen's innocence became an ongoing preoccupation. Bull decided to put in more time as a private eye.

"I'd like you guys to run things," Bull said to his two top men.

"Anything you say, boss," said one while the other nodded.

In twenty-four hours, white index cards were pinned high on the walls of his office, all in a straight line, three feet apart. The top of each card held the name of a person, block lettered in black ink.

Bull pushed away from his desk and rolled his swivel to the center of the room. He twirled around slowly. The names of Rickey Marlar, Kathryn Anderson, John Cartwright, Abigail Androtti, Burek and Bell, Henry Spencer, Bill Kessler, Jim Robins, and Frank Tuerkheimer looked down at him. Other blank cards waited patiently for additional names.

Bull eyed the line to the phone jack as it slithered across the floor to the top of his desk. He did not like it and decided to call AT&T and to have them install a jack on the floor under his desk. He looked at the small stack of documents on his desk.

"We're in business, by God," he said to himself.

Ambling over to his desk, he fingered the top document, picked up a roll of Scotch tape, took several steps to Kathryn Anderson's card, and taped the document to the wall. Bull backed away, pleased at the arrangement. He liked having information out in the open. He could study it. He could walk around the room and think about fitting bits and pieces of information together. Grabbing his swivel, Bull pulled it back to his desk, sat down, grabbed the phone, and dialed.

CHAPTER FORTY-SIX

"AOVI," the voice said.

"It's me, Frank. Just wanted to check on your progress."

"The word's out. Our guys will copy everything with Doc's name on it and anything else that seems suspicious and send it to you."

"Are all the bases covered?"

"We are one short. We need a guy in VA's central office, but there's no job opening right now. We'll stay on top of it. The best we can do is tape record all committee meetings and get copies of minutes from old meetings."

"How did yesterday's VA taping go? Can you hear everything?"

"Our guy was in the last row of the spectator's section and picked up every word. Hold on. Listen."

Bull leaned back, swung his legs up, and planted the bottom of his boots against the edge of his desk.

"The first guy you'll hear is Senator Berning from Illinois," Frank said, pushing play.

A voice boomed into Bull's office.

"Thank you, Dr. Shepard. We of the Illinois Agent Orange Commission appreciate this opportunity to appear before you and share some of our views with you. We in Illinois have been much concerned about the plight of the Vietnam veterans in our state, and obviously throughout the United States. Many of us in Illinois have the feeling like one of our southern Illinois farmer friends, who one day for the first time visited a zoo. He stood there for quite some time looking at that tall, long-neck thing. A giraffe. He turned around on his heel and spat. He said to his wife, 'Hell, there ain't no such animal.' That's about what we felt was the attitude of the federal government and the VA about the Agent Orange problem. Now let me hasten to point out that I'm not interested in criticizing or attacking. But we in the Illinois legislature represent all of our citizens. And we feel there's been too much delay in facing up to a problem of huge dimensions. Studies are necessary and should be continued. However, I remind you that while you and I are talking, men and women are suffering and dying. They are dying now with little or no help from their government. All too often, they are treated with abuse and contempt by the VA, according to the testimony we've received in duly convened Agent Orange Commission hearings."

Frank pushed stop. "Not bad," he said, "you can hear everything."

"Is this gonna help our court case?" Bull wanted to know.

"Victor thinks so. Keep listening. Berning is really putting the VA on the spot." Frank pushed play. Senator Berning's voice rang out, full of conviction.

"We in Illinois have been concerned about the lack of concern on the part of the well-being, yes, the very life of our Illinois Vietnam veterans, who really are typical of veterans all over this nation. I have a question that arose as a result of a conference of all state commissions. Inasmuch as the scientific studies are projected to continue for anywhere from a year to five or six or seven years, and since decisions affecting people, now suffering, will require a political determination, our question is simply this: if we assume a positive political posture, and if congressional members individually of our states as well as collectively appeal to Congress, will the VA passively refrain from attempting to interfere or block our efforts? We would like to know if we can approach Congress and not be running into bureaucratic blocks."

Frank pushed the stop button.

"Now you're gonna hear Shepard's reply," Frank said excitedly. "It proves that all the crap we've been getting is coming down from the top. We've known it all along, but now we have proof."

Frank pushed play.

"Senator Berning, you better than I are aware of the political implications involved," Dr. Shepard replied with a hint of irritation in his voice. "I think the only thing I can really say is that when legislation is proposed by Congress, it is sent on to the appropriate agency for comments. This is a fairly complex process in many instances and requires, I would say, the corporate wisdom of an administration such as the VA. I think we have to look at the language of the legislation before we could make any comments on it."

"Let me challenge that for just a minute," Senator Berning said politely. "We wouldn't want you to look at the language of a bill, we want you to look at the concept. In other words, help now versus a determination of possible help, one year, five years, ten years down the road. The VA, to whom a bill might be referred for comment, could either bludgeon it to death or just passively accept it." Speaking strongly, Berning continued on, "We hope

CHAPTER FORTY-SIX

that the conviction of those of us who represent the various state commissions is beginning to make itself apparent to you. This is going to be politically resolved. And it's going to rise or fall, to a large extent, on the degree of acceptance or resistance by the people who influence Congress."

There was a slight pause, as if Shepard was giving careful thought to the reply.

"I don't feel comfortable speaking for the administration," he finally said.

Frank pushed stop.

"There's a lot more on that tape. Other people are talking. It shows how the VA is giving us the shaft and violating their own regulations. Victor thinks the court will agree. Maybe this tape will help turn things around."

"I'd sure like to see it happen," Bull replied. "At least we've finally got 'em going to court. Maybe it will help us get every damn piece of correspondence between Shepard and that JRB kiss-ass company in McLean, Virginia. I'd lay odds they sucked up to the VA when they put that manual together."

"Why shouldn't they? The VA paid them big bucks to put it out! That four-line lie about Doc's work havin' high levels of PCBs was put in without proof. Who else but the VA would've thought of such a thing! I'd like to finger those bureaucratic bastards."

Bull agreed. "Me too. They mailed that lie to scientists around the world, and it helped destroy Allen. Ask Victor to send an FOIA letter to the VA, asking them for any and all correspondence between the VA and JRB. Who know, we might strike oil."

"Okay," Frank said. "Oh, by the way, the VA finally answered the FOIA on Verlin. We got his numbers. His fat was tested four times, and it was loaded with dioxin."

"How's he doin'?"

"Not good. Just like a lot of our guys."

"Yeah," Bull replied. "What's new on our class action case?"

"Only rumors. This new judge might hold somethin' called fairness hearings. A lot of hush-hush about it, but somethin's goin' on. Victor is tryin' to find out more. So far, nothin'. I'll call ya when I know."

Almost immediately, after hanging up, his hand still on the receiver, Bull's phone rang.

"No Bull Security," he said.

"It's me, Mole."

Bull waited. He thought Mole had another pick-up, but for five seconds not a word was spoken.

"Yeah," Bull said, "have ya got somethin'?"

"Nothin' 'bout Allen," Mole replied with some hesitation.

"Well....?" Bull asked with an attitude that demanded a reply.

"Well," Mole began, "you're payin' me two hundred a month to dig up stuff on Allen. What if I find juicy stuff on the VA? Would I get a bonus?"

Bull didn't like it. "Don't start getting greedy with me," he roared. "You'll give me anything and everything you find for the same two bills or I'll cancel the whole deal."

Mole knew he should have kept his mouth shut. "Don't get mad," he replied apologetically. "I'm just askin'."

"What've you got?"

"A letter from the American Federation of Government Employees to all VA employees."

"Yeah?" Bull said, waiting for more.

"The VA issued a circular giving themselves the right to silently monitor phone calls between VA employees and veterans without anyone knowing. The American Federation called it Gestapo-type tactics."

"Why is the VA doing this?" Bull asked testily.

"They released fat biopsy numbers. They know guys will be screaming for benefits because of high numbers. They also know that benefit counselors are sympathetic to our guys and don't want these counselors recommending benefits and creating problems for the VA."

"One of my guys will pick it up," Bull replied, slamming the phone down and fuming over Mole's attempt to shake him down for a few more bucks. Bull did not like doing business that way. He would have to learn how to uncover information on his own and get rid of Mole. But for now, he needed him.

Bull mulled over the VA's latest action. It coincided with the release of fat biopsy results. That damn agency would never consider doing such biopsies again! He needed as much proof as he could get to clearly show that the VA wasn't favorably inclined toward

CHAPTER FORTY-SIX

veterans. Such proof could go a long way in winning their case against the VA. He needed Allen's help, so he picked up the phone again.

Christie, in coveralls and a large straw hat, was in the back yard kneeling on the ground, dropping seeds into a furrow and covering it over with dirt. Hearing the distant ring of the phone, she hurried inside.

"Mr. McKitrick! What a nice surprise. I hope you're calling to say you've accepted our invitation to visit. I know—"

Bull hurriedly interjected. "I appreciate the invite, Christie. And as soon as I can make it, I'll be there. But right now, I've got a job to do. Is Dr. Allen around?"

"Hold on, he's in the barn."

Christie scooted out the front door as if she was off on one of her runs. In moments, she and her husband were out of the barn, he trying to keep pace with his wife. Allen had gradually acquired a degree of physical fitness. Between laboring on the farm and his work with the local vet, he had shaped up and felt good about it.

"Hi, Bull," Allen said, slightly out of breath.

"It's nice hearing your voice, Dr. Allen. How're ya doin'?"

"Oh, moving along. The tobacco crop is doing well, and I'm planning to open an animal clinic. I finally got my vet's license. Working with the local vet helped shape me up. Yesterday, a mare went into labor and I delivered a foal."

"How's that vet going to feel when you're his competitor?"

"Oh, I wouldn't think of being a competitor. I'm opening up in Weaverville, a nearby town. They need a vet."

"I know they'll get a good one. I called to ask a favor."

"Anything, Bull."

"Do you know Dr. Gross, the man who did the biopsies?"

"I met him once."

"Would you ask him to write the VA and offer to do fat biopsies at no charge? I'll foot the bill, whatever it is."

"I'll ask him, but you must know that the VA asked all of their physicians not to order a fat biopsy without permission from VA central office in DC."

"I know, but Yannacone is suing the VA along with the chemical companies. The more proof we have showing the VA doesn't give a damn about Vietnam vets, the better. I'm sure they'll say no."

Dr. Allen was glad he could finally do something for Bull.

"I'll call Gross today," he said.

"Would you also ask him to send me a copy of his letter and the VA's reply?"

"Sure will."

"One other thing," Bull said, "something I've been wanting to thank you for."

"Thank me for?"

"Yeah. Do you remember what you asked for when we said good-bye at the airport?"

Dr. Allen's brain raced back in time, trying to remember.

"No," he replied, "can't say I do."

"You asked for permission to give me a hug."

"Yes, I remember that."

"Well, it was very special for me. I'll never forget it. People always want something from me. Something that'll benefit them in some way. No one ever asked for permission to give me a hug. In fact, no one ever hugged me except my momma."

"Really?" Allen asked, amazed at how such a kindhearted man would have grown up without an abundance of affection.

"It's true," admitted Bull sheepishly. "Papa always said hugging was for sissies. He used to holler at Momma when he caught her huggin' me. But I liked being hugged. When you and Christie threw your arms around me, it reminded me of Momma. I really appreciated that hug, and I want you to know that."

"So when are you coming for a visit?" Allen asked light-heartedly. "There are more hugs waiting for you."

Bull smiled. "I'll surprise you one day. Right now, I've got too much to do. I gotta prove your innocence. I wanna find out how those bastards did you in. I also gotta help our guys."

"Would you do me a favor?" Allen asked in an offhanded manner.

"Name it."

"Would you stop calling me Dr. Allen? My wife and my friends call me Jim."

CHAPTER FORTY-SIX

Bull laughed. "Sure, Jim. But tell Christie to stop calling me Mr. McKitrick. It's Bull or Larry."

"I'll tell her. And Bull, thanks for trying to prove my innocence. It's a terrible feeling knowing I have a criminal record and knowing I've put a blot on the family name. I never dreamed that I'd be blackballed by universities, government agencies, and private industry. And even worse, knowing I've been abandoned and shunned by the scientific community is an agonizing feeling. I would give anything to clear my name and to have the criminal record expunged. When I die, I could never face my ancestors. They would have every right to send me straight to hell."

Bull could feel the suffering in his friend's voice. He knew the answers were out there, somewhere. But being another Sam Spade was not going to be easy.

FORTY-SEVEN

Spring 1984. Delays, delays, and more delays. Although filed in January 1979, the veteran's suit against the chemical giant and the government had not yet gone to trial. There had been over five years of wrangling between dozens of attorneys and the court. Attorneys for veterans, attorneys for chemical companies, and attorneys for the United States government. Judge Weinstein listened to never-ending arguments.

When Dow and the other defendants named the US as a third party, the Department of Justice argued that the United States could not be held liable for negligence for injuries resulting from service in Vietnam on the basis of sovereign immunity. There was an appropriate remedy available to individuals who sustained an injury, namely the Veterans Administration's compensation system. The case against the United States was then dropped, but attorneys continued to find reason for delays.

Judge Weinstein had had enough. He told both sides there would be no more delays. He told them the case was going to trial whether ready or not. He set a date for jury selection and told the attorneys to be ready. On the first day of jury selection, word filtered down that a settlement had been reached. The amount was not to be in the billions, but millions. To be exact, it was $180 million, the largest settlement of its kind in American history. But Dow and the other defendants demanded a stipulation. They simply would not admit to liability or wrongdoing.

Frank called an emergency meeting of AOVI's board of directors. He and Muriel sat quietly on the settee. Jane sat alongside the card table, ready to take minutes.

Members trudged down the stairs and piled into the Bunker. They were grim.

Nobody spoke. Nobody went into the kitchen for refreshments. They just found a spot on the floor, dropped down, and waited. Frank took a deep breath, saw that the door to the outside had not been closed, and thought it best to leave it open. Those who wanted to get up and walk out could do so.

"Let's start," Frank said. "A few of our guys ain't comin.'"

CHAPTER FORTY-SEVEN

"None of us should have," one voice hollered from the middle of the pack as he locked eyes with Frank. "How could you sell Yannacone down the river? He took on our fight when nobody gave a hoot about us! He's been our champion! And not once has he asked anyone for a dime! How could you betray him?"

"Yeah, yeah," came mumbling from others on the floor.

Frank looked at Muriel, hoping she would jump in, wanting her to defend him. She had a feisty way of convincing members that there were always two points of view to every issue. But Muriel sat stone-faced.

"I didn't betray Victor," Frank hollered. "Victor betrayed himself! He was uncompromising. He wouldn't budge an inch. When Dow and the other chemical companies offered to settle out of court, Victor said no. The other law firms went to Weinstein and gave him an ultimatum. They told the judge that either Victor's power over the lawsuit be taken away, or they would stop funding the litigation. Those guys have put up millions! They wanted to talk settlement. They just wanted to talk. They were offered $180 million. As far as I'm concerned, that is something to talk about. I don't agree with Victor. I love him, and I'd be willing to die for him, but I see him as a wild man. We've got tens of thousands of kids out there with birth defects. They need help! With $180 million, we can build a foundation. That's what I told the judge."

A second voice from the floor hollered, "Victor said he could win this case and maybe get billions. That's what we've been suing for! Billions!"

"Yeah," the first voice said. "The damn judge put the other law firms in charge, and I blame you, Frank. You sided with those bastards. When you told the judge you were in favor of the settlement, he thought you were speaking for all of us. Who the hell are you to speak for me or anyone else without asking?"

There were a few more "yeahs" from the group. Some heads nodded in agreement. One member at the back of the room, sitting beneath the M-16, stood up and looked at it.

"Hey, guys!" he said, "there are a lot of angry vets out there who are threatening to whack Frank. And I'm hearin' some scuttlebutt that Victor will be next. This bickering will get us nowhere. It's only good for Dow. I happen to agree with Frank. Our first consideration should be the kids. How long should they have to wait for help? The families have no money, no insurance, nothing! They're hurting bad! If Victor and those radical vets want their day in court, let 'em start a separate suit! I'm in favor of grabbin' the $180 million and startin' a nonprofit foundation."

Muriel knew this was the place to jump into the fray. She straightened her back and lifted her chin.

"I've got something to say," she said. "Most of you knew my son, Paul. You know why he sued. He knew he was dying and wanted to make a difference. He saw suffering. He saw the kids. He wanted to help. The VA didn't give a damn and he knew that nobody would lift a finger to help. He started his own suit and asked for $10 million. He wanted every vet to sue for at least a million. He talked and dreamed about a foundation." Muriel's voice rose with indignation. "You should be glad we've been offered money! You should be glad we can start a foundation! You should be glad veterans will get help! You should be glad for the children! How can you even think of going to trial? What if we lose! What will happen to the children if we lose?"

Muriel turned to Frank and took his hand.

"I remember that day in the hospital," she said, "the day before Paul died. You and Lenny were there. Paul talked about a foundation that would help everyone, especially the children. Both of you promised to carry on. And I want to thank you for keeping your word, for trying to make Paul's dreams come true."

Tears started to run down her cheeks. She threw her arms around Frank, buried her face on his shoulder, and hugged him. She kissed his cheek, sat back with her head down, sniffed, and dabbed at her eyes with the backs of her hands. She looked at no one. She listened to the silence around her, waiting for someone to speak.

Hundreds of letters poured into the U.S. District Court. Judge Weinstein, a tall, thin man in his sixties, sat in his chambers, his black robe draped over his burgundy, leather chair and his white shirt open at the collar. He looked at stacks of mail on his desk and knew he was in for a long weekend. He reached out, took a long, white envelope from the top of the stack and opened it.

A mother wrote, "We strongly support the recent proposal. We have a nine-year-old daughter who was born with a slanted right eye and no lower lid. There was no cheekbone under that eye, just cartilage. She has a deformed right ear, no visible canal, and a blocked left ear canal. Sounds cannot reach her. She also has a stunted lower jawbone and a very high palate.

CHAPTER FORTY-SEVEN

Her speech is distorted. She's had surgery straightening her eye, and a cheekbone was formed from grafts taken from her skull and ribs. This January, she will be having surgery on her lower jaw. Thanks to the wonderful people at Agent Orange Victims International, along with Tom Condon, a newspaper reporter, a fund was started for my daughter's medical expenses. This support has been mainly from unknown individuals. There are so many other children who have not been as fortunate as our daughter. We pray to God for the best possible outcome for this proposal. People need this money for their children's operations. They should not have to worry about money. There is enough to worry about when your child goes into the hospital."

Judge Weinstein sat long into the night reading letters. He wanted more input. He wanted testimony from both sides, those in favor of and those against the settlement. He wanted testimony from children. Everyone had to be heard. They all had to have a say before he arrived at a final decision, before he approved the out-of-court settlement.

He published a legal notice entitled, "Notice Of Proposed Settlement Of Class Action in re Agent Orange." The notice announced hearings to be held in five cities between August 8 and August 24, 1984. The terms of the settlement were given, as well as instructions for those who had not yet filed a claim. The deadline for filing was October 26, 1984.

The first fairness hearing was held in Brooklyn from August 8 to 10, 1984.

One veteran took the stand as Judge Weinstein looked on. When it was obvious that he found it difficult to speak, Weinstein looked down from the bench.

In a fatherly tone of voice, he said, "There's nothing to be nervous about. Just look up here and talk to me. Tell me your story."

The veteran, not once taking his eyes off the judge, said, "I had things wrong with me, but I never connected it with Agent Orange until I learned I had cancer in my eye."

He then told how he lost that eye.

He went on to say, "I could not support my wife and two kids on $300 a month disability pay. Our families have kept us alive."

He fought back tears, looked down and became silent.

Weinstein waited a few moments and gently asked, "Are you in favor of settlement or against?"

"In favor," he replied through his tears. "Thank you, Your Honor."

Another veteran told a rambling tale of how Vietnam had left him crippled emotionally. He was unable to get along with friends or family, unable to have a relationship with a woman, unable to hold down a job. It was obvious to the judge that he had never been able to say those things to anybody. As he struggled through his story, Weinstein listened without interruption until he was done.

"Are you for or opposed to the settlement?" the judge asked.

"Opposed."

"Opposed," Weinstein repeated it for the record. "Thank you."

And so it went for three days. Some in favor of settlement, others against.

On August 14, veterans, wives, and children crowded the entrance to the Federal Building in downtown Chicago. It was too early to enter the building, but a line had already formed. Some sat on the sidewalk in army green fatigues and combat boots, their backs against the building, talking loudly. Others were in military uniforms bedecked with ribbons. Some were casually dressed. Wives and children stood nearby. Several of the women drank coffee from a Dunkin Donuts Styrofoam cup. One small boy held his mother's hand while her other hand was busily engaged with a chocolate donut, pushing it into her son's mouth, watching him bite off a piece, chew it and gulp it down, then bite off another piece.

Another small boy with a stump for an arm was in the lap of his father, who was on the ground having a heated discussion with another veteran. The two had opposite points of view. One wanted to settle and argued for it. The other disagreed.

At 10:00 a.m., police officers opened the doors, and all began filing in. A bank of elevators carried them to the twenty-fifth floor, where another line inched its way into the courtroom. Security was tight. The hearings were about to begin.

Judge Weinstein, in a flowing black robe, entered through a door behind the bench. After a brief, inaudible consultation with the court clerk and the court reporter, he spoke to the hushed silence of a packed courtroom.

"I would like to talk with all of you," he said, "but as you can see, it's impossible. There just isn't enough time. I would welcome your letters, and I promise to respond to each of you who choose to write to me."

CHAPTER FORTY-SEVEN

Judge Weinstein then asked the clerk to call the first speaker. A veteran started his testimony with a soft voice.

"I flew a chopper," he said. "I volunteered. I can live with the consequences of my actions even as I sit here dying of cancer."

He suddenly rose, looked out at the hushed courtroom, and pointed a finger. His voice became loud and angry.

"But my wife!" he shouted, "the last miscarriage nearly killed her. She nearly bled to death."

Other stories followed. Veterans dying of cancer. The lives of families torn apart. Endless suffering. Children with birth defects. Heartless doctors in VA hospitals who turned ailing veterans away. Extreme financial difficulties. Some at the brink of starvation. Many favored settlement. Others wanted their day in court. They wanted the world to know what they had endured and what had happened to them. They wanted the chemical companies and the government brought before the court of public opinion. They wanted justice for themselves and their families. Especially the children.

As Judge Weinstein listened to each speaker, he remained compassionate and calm. He had a kindly manner, and it was readily apparent that he had a great deal of sympathy for the veterans and their families. One black veteran pointed to acne scars on his face.

"This rash," he said, "started in Vietnam. I watched that spray come down. Nobody said it would hurt me. Now nothing makes it go away. It only gets worse. After the rash, my heart began to beat fast. I would break out in a sweat. I almost could not breathe. I began to shake all over and was put in a hospital. They discharged me even though I was a mess. The pain in my stomach, the vomiting and diarrhea, and all the other problems landed me in Lucerne General Hospital in Orlando. I was vomiting blood. I had a nervous breakdown. I would find myself wandering alone, not knowing where I was or where I was going. It's been hard on me and my wife. We wanted children, but my sperm count is so low, we cannot have kids."

As he went on, Weinstein did not interrupt him.

When he finished, the judge asked, "Are you for or opposed to the settlement?"

"I'm opposed."

"Opposed," Weinstein repeated for the record. "Thank you."

A veteran's wife took the stand.

"I can't believe there are people here that want to accept the settlement," she said. "For God's sake! In Vietnam, you never left a buddy behind. You'd always go back for your buddies. Don't abandon them now!"

The next speaker hobbled to the witness box leaning on a cane.

He turned to the judge and said, "You know, Your Honor, me and my buddies talked a lot about the settlement. None of us care about the money. But we do care a lot about what happened to us. We want a trial. We want everything to come out. Our lawyers got a lot of Dow's secret documents. They tell the truth! Not the hogwash ACE has been handing out to the public. If there's no trial, these documents go back to Dow. The truth will be hidden. No one will know. I'm against the settlement for this reason."

Other speakers followed. Some were adamant in wanting a trial. They wanted their day in court. They knew that Dow's secret and confidential information would prove how deadly Agent Orange was. Some speakers said they needed the money.

The last speaker of the day was the thirteen-year-old son of one of the veterans. He had difficulty expressing himself. In bits and pieces, he told what life was like being born with physical and mental handicaps. He haltingly explained how he couldn't run, play, or do things like other kids. How he was behind in school. He then began to cry. His feelings overwhelmed him as tears rolled down his cheeks. He hunched forward with loud, shuddering sobs. His small body shook. He could not go on with what he wanted to say. His mother led him from the witness stand, put her arms around him, and held him as he cried on her shoulder. There was silence in the room as men fought back tears.

By the end of the day, it seemed as if a majority wanted to go to trial. It was reported that the number against settlement had even been higher in New York. If the trend held, the case would probably go to trial. The next hearing would be in Houston, Texas. Then Atlanta, Georgia. Then on to San Francisco. After that, Weinstein's decision would be a matter of time.

FORTY-EIGHT

When Dr. Allen finally decided to strike out on his own and open an animal clinic, he was extremely apprehensive. What if he ran into a problem he couldn't handle? What if an animal died? What then?

"You'll do fine," Christie reassured him. "You've been working with your friend long enough. You've handled emergencies well. You're just a worrier."

"I'm fifty-seven," Allen said, reaching for his wife's hand. "I'm getting old. It's hard starting life over. What if something goes wrong?"

"Stop with the what-ifs already! What if everything goes well! What if you build up a wonderful practice? What if you learn to be happy again? Be optimistic. Forget the past."

Dr. Allen attempted a half-hearted smile.

"I know you're right. It's just that...I'm scared."

Christie squeezed his hand.

"Haven't we always been a team, honey? I'll be there with you. I'm a good nurse. You'll see, we'll have fun."

One bright Saturday morning, Dr. Allen and Christie piled into their pick-up truck and drove to the nearby town of Weaverville. As their vehicle toured the community, Christie was impressed.

"It's beautiful," she said. "Look at those homes. They are on acres of green grass with rolling landscapes. And those flowers and trees...I like this town."

Her husband also liked it. "It's a calm, peaceful place," he said. "I'll head toward the mall. There's a store for rent."

Driving along in silence, Christie hoped and prayed everything would work out. Her husband needed a break. Something to make him feel useful again.

"There it is!" Christie said excitedly.

The pick-up veered to the right and climbed a short incline into the mall parking lot.

Pointing to a vacancy sign in a corner of the mall, Christie said, "That's ideal. I can hardly wait to go inside. How exciting!"

"I like it," Allen said.

He angled the white Chevy pick-up truck into a parking stall and came to a stop.

In one hour, the vacancy sign went down. Over the next three weeks, carpenters, painters, plumbers, and other workers pounded and painted the wooden structure into shape. Delivery men drove into the mall, lifted crates off the backs of trucks, and moved them into Allen's new clinic.

Twenty days after signing a two-year lease, a bold black-lettered sign, forty-eight inches long, was nailed firmly in place below the edge of the roof. It announced the new addition at 9 Tri-City Plaza: Weaverville ANIMAL CLINIC

Even before the new veterinarian moved in, the townspeople of Weaverville, North Carolina, began talking. They gossiped on park benches, in the barbershop, and at PTA meetings. They spoke over a cup of coffee and while waiting in line to check out at the Supermart. The rumor mill ground away at Allen's reputation. Dreadful stories.

Even though the townspeople came to the Plaza, no one came to Allen's clinic. Months went by. And still no one came. The Weaverville residents continued taking their pets to a neighboring town.

One day, an emergency arose. An elderly gray-haired lady hurried toward the Weaverville clinic. The tinkle of the bell sounded as she opened the door. In her arms was a limp and unresponsive brown and white tabby. She thought it was dead.

Dr. Allen took the animal in his arms and hurried to a back room. Christie sat beside the woman in the waiting room trying to comfort her. In less than an hour, Dr. Allen was back, cradling the tabby in his arms. He handed the cat back to the lady. She hugged and kissed it.

"My baby, my baby," she cooed as the cat licked its paw.

A week later, another emergency. A father, his son, and daughter rushed up the four wooden stairs and into the clinic. The father carried a kennel cab that held a brown spotted mongrel that had been hit by a car. Eight days later, the trio was back.

"Penny," the boy and girl gleefully shouted as Allen carried their pet into the waiting room.

CHAPTER FORTY-EIGHT

He put the dog down on the floor. It ran around the room, looked up at the youngsters, barked, and happily wagged its tail.

Other emergencies followed. Allen's reputation grew. It wasn't long before his animal clinic buzzed with activity. Christie loved putting on her white uniform and being a nurse again. She enjoyed her new role of receptionist, secretary, surgical assistant, and chief consultant on any and all matters. The schedule grew. The days became hectic. All went well.

Christie knew that any day now, her husband would receive a call to come to New York to testify. They both expected the veterans' case to go to trial, and she had already packed his bag. The attorneys had arranged for Allen to pick up his ticket at the airport. But on May 14, 1984, in mid-afternoon, he received a call. He stood behind the receptionist's desk, his left hand in the pocket of his starched white lab coat, his right holding the phone tight to his ear.

"Dr. Allen, I'm calling for the law firm of Schlegel and Trafelet. Your testimony will not be needed. The case was settled. I want to thank you for your willingness to assist us."

Allen stood there holding the dead phone. Christie, who was seated, looked up at him and knew from the look on his face that he was not at all pleased with the call. He slowly put the phone down, lifted it, punched in numbers, and again held it to his ear.

"Hi, Frank," he said, "just got a call telling me the case was settled."

"Yeah," Frank replied solemnly, not knowing whether to be happy or not. "For $180 million."

"That's a nice sum, Frank. Aren't you happy?"

"I don't know. Yannacone's upset with me. A lot of the guys wanted a trial. I don't know, Doc. I've got mixed feelings. Money is accruing $61,000 a day in interest, and the lawyers are pleased. But the bastards should be. They're already hollering for their fee, and they expect to get a third. Sixty million!"

"That's a big piece of pie!" Allen replied, taken aback at the amount.

"Sure is, Doc. But Judge Weinstein will decide what they get. He seems favorably inclined toward us vets, and he likes the idea of a foundation. He knows about the 161,000 kids out there who need help. I hope we can finally get started."

"I'm truly happy for you, Frank. But in a way, I'm disappointed at not being able to testify. I really wanted to. I wanted to shoot down Dow's claim that there is no biologically plausible way to explain how dioxin causes cancer."

"Are you saying there is?"

"I was saving it as a surprise. A few researchers out there still talk to me. A group at UCLA has been working on a project since 1976. They finally found a gene called Arnt. They've shown how chemicals like dioxin get into the cell and cause the genetic damage leading to cancer. I would have enjoyed blasting Dow with that one."

"If Yannacone is still suing the VA, Doc, he'd want that info. It would help shoot down the VA's crap about no connection between dioxin and what our guys are dying from."

"Whaddya mean if he's suing the VA? Don't you know?"

"No, Doc. He and I had a falling out. I opted for settlement. So did other law firms. But Victor wanted to go to trial. He would not give in. The other law firms went to the judge and had Victor removed as the lead attorney. They took away his power over the suit."

"Don't the two of you talk?"

"Not really. There's a lot of hard feelings between us. I feel bad about it, but I think I did the right thing. The kids need help. Now we have money. Now we can start a foundation! It's a dream come true, Doc."

"I agree," Allen said. "Kids should always be the priority. I wanted to testify to get even with Dow, but that's really stupid. That's my gut talking, not my head. There is no way for me to get even. The whole affair ended a long time ago, but I can't seem to put it behind me. It still hurts."

"Have you talked with Bull lately?"

"He called about a month ago. He's really something. He has a man full time in the library going over old newspapers stored on microfiche. He's looking for everything ever printed on the Rickey Marlar case and found some interesting articles. The coroner came out with a statement in 1979 saying that if he had to do it over again, he would rule the cause of death as unknown instead of accidental. Another article told of the coroner being gunned down and killed in Madison. Bull's been trying to get the official reports on the Marlar case and finally found the coroner's report and the autopsy report in the State Historical Society archives. But the police reports were not there."

Frank nodded, thinking about his recent conversation with Bull.

"He told me about those police reports. He was really pissed when some gal at the Madison Police Department told him Marlar's records were destroyed. She said they computerized

CHAPTER FORTY-EIGHT

everything in 1981 and all the old stuff was trashed. But don't lose heart, Doc. I know Bull. He'll never give up. The only way you can get even with Dow and all the others is to have the truth come out. And Bull is the one person who can find it."

"It's hard not to lose heart, Frank. These feeling will not go away. I still wake up at night and they are there. It's hell knowing I have a criminal record."

"Doc, remember when you said there must be a reason for everything?"

"I remember."

"Remember when you said that someone up there is sitting with a deck of cards ready to deal?"

"Uh huh."

"Well, I agree with you," Frank said firmly. "The world is not just a random helter-skelter mishmash pot where things are thrown in without rhyme or reason. Everything gets dealt out in the end. Someone once said the mills of the Gods grind slowly but they grind exceedingly fine. You'll see! Someday the truth will come out. Someday you will understand."

"I hope so, Frank. I sure hope so," Allen said.

FORTY-NINE

Larry McKitrick was in his office, grinning incredulously. He felt like a newly anointed king, and the pampered feeling was enough to make him giddy. When had people ever treated him so well? His new leather, high-backed executive chair wrapped around him. What a rich looking thing. Not at all like his old wooden swivel, that squeaky old relic he had used for years.

Bull had arrived at work that morning, preoccupied with the Allen investigation. As he opened his office door, a room full of men shouted, "Happy birthday!" The sudden eruption of shouting and clapping startled him. Two men on either side of him motioned him to the center of the room where sixty-nine employees stood shoulder to shoulder, obviously hiding something. He slowly approached the group with a grin on his face. They broke rank and revealed what stood in the middle of the room.

Bull stood transfixed. Turning his head to his men, he acknowledged their gift with a nod of gratitude. His group smiled joyfully and watched as Bull lowered himself into his new swivel, obviously delighted by what they had bought him. The executive furniture with an IBM computer and a laser jet printer was fit for a corporate CEO. But what fascinated Bull was all the buttons on a highly sophisticated phone positioned on top of a burgundy credenza. And on the floor next to the credenza was a matching wooden wastebasket, too elegant for trash.

"Thanks guys," Bull said sheepishly.

They all murmured heartfelt replies, giving Bull a high-five or shaking his hand. "Just to let you know how we feel about you," said one employee.

After a few minutes of camaraderie, the happy bunch departed. As they closed the door behind them, Bull reflected on how fortunate he was to have such a cadre of men who were like brothers—loyal and dedicated to the business he had started so long ago. Bull knew he could spend as many hours as he wished on the Allen investigation, and they would carry on.

Bull also knew that with Frank's help, a large network of Vietnam veterans was in place in almost all areas of the country. They had jobs in federal agencies, and many held membership

CHAPTER FORTY-NINE

in the American Legion, Disabled American Veterans, and in every other veteran organization. Doctors, lawyers, police officers, congressmen, senators, and even a few convicted felons serving time in correctional facilities had joined AOVI and were part of Bull's network. Bull called it "people power." They gathered information, and Bull stuck all of it on his wall and memorized it. He knew every lead he was pursuing and every lead that had come to a dead end.

Bull lifted himself up and went to a sidewall. The card at the top said "Kathryn Anderson." He selected one of the documents. It said "United States Marshals Service." Bull lifted up page one, and for what seemed like the hundredth time he read the two-line statement on page two: "Final determination that a witness qualifies for WitSec protection is made by the U.S. Attorney General. The decision is based on recommendations by U.S. Attorneys assigned to major federal cases throughout the nation."

Bull again mulled over this seemingly innocuous information. Frank Tuerkheimer was the U.S. Attorney in the Allen case. It landed in court in 1979. The Anderson gal did her thing in '78 and disappeared long before Allen's head was on the chopping block. If she was given witness protection, how did it happen? She wasn't a major federal case, and Tuerkheimer would have had nothing to do with it. It would have been arranged months before Allen's records were audited, months before the $892 irregularity was found, long before Allen was charged with theft. If she was in WitSec, someone other than Tuerkheimer would have put her into it. That could be important in proving the conspiracy theory.

Then again, was Anderson really in a witness protection program? And if she was, could she have been put into it without Tuerkheimer's input? No one had yet answered these questions. The Marshall's Service would neither confirm nor deny that Anderson was in WitSec. A real dilemma.

Bull strolled over to another card on the wall. He loved this one. Robert Aberg. Many letters and documents easily proved his tie to the university and easily showed how he helped Dow. Also how he lied about Allen when he wrote to the EPA, with a copy to Dow's attorneys, saying, Allen voted not to testify.

"Yeah," murmured Bull. "A real scumbag."

But one thing was missing. How could he find Sue Zeck, a woman who knew what Aberg had in mind?

Allen told Bull that she had called one day, saying, "Aberg is your enemy. He's trying to destroy you."

But Allen could do nothing. He had not hired Aberg. The man suddenly appeared and became involved with Allen and his staff after Dow demanded all of his records.

But Sue Zeck had information about this man. And Bull had tried to find her. Her maiden name was Tyson from Toledo, Ohio. Mother's name was Ann. She had a brother, Scott, who was found in Fostoria, Ohio. But a letter to his home went unanswered. One of Bull's contacts called her ex-husband in Madison, but he did not know where she was.

A search on the Internet failed to find her. None of his guys could find her. Another dilemma. Nevertheless, Bull enjoyed sleuthing. It was a challenge. It required thinking and analyzing and making speculations with some kind of plan to prove true or false. It required a detailed knowledge of the archives at the university where documents lay buried in twenty-three thousand cubic feet of space in underground chambers, housing millions of documents. Two vets employed at the university had an intimate knowledge of how to find information. He no longer needed Mole.

"You're fired," Bull said one afternoon, promptly hanging up the phone, not wanting any discussion from someone who had tried to shake him down for a few extra bucks.

Bull learned that if anyone at the university had documented information on Allen, it would eventually go into the archives. It was state law. All documents and papers had to be put there when a state official retired. The University of Wisconsin was a state school. Every upper echelon person was a state employee, including the chancellor.

Officials not from the university put their papers in the State Historical Society. That's how he found the coroner and autopsy reports on the Marlar case. Bull loved this state law. It made finding records easy. The only drawback was the waiting for an official to retire. But he was a patient man. After Vietnam, waiting was unimportant. A trivial thing.

Bull backed away from the Aberg documents and walked back to his elegant desk and leather chair. "Cool," he thought, "but easy to scratch if I throw my feet up, especially with these boots." Suddenly, he had a yen for his old, beat-up relic.

Bull curiously examined the gadgetry on his new phone. The handbook next to it would teach him about the special features. But right now he had to call Frank.

CHAPTER FORTY-NINE

Frank was in his Bunker, sitting on the settee. He held a glass filled with ice cubes and a dark liquid. Nasty stuff. A bottle of Bushmills stood on the card table in front of him. The phone rang, jarring Frank's ill-humored solitude. He looked up with no intention of answering. Taking a swig of Bushmills, Frank listened to the damn thing ring and ring.

"Damn it," said Frank, wishing it would stop.

It was as if someone knew he was home and demanded he answer. He chugged down more Bushmills and finally could no longer stand listening to the continuous ringing.

"Yeaaah?" Frank said, and it was obvious that his woozy voice was filled with despair.

"Put the damn booze away, Frank. It ain't gonna help."

Frank thought it was already helping.

"I don't know 'bout that," he replied. "At least I'll get some sleep."

"But you'll wake up with a hangover," Bull replied, wondering why Frank was feeling down.

"Fuck it. At least, I'll sleep. Why'd ya call?"

"I'm sending you a letter Dr. Gross sent to the VA. He offered to do fat biopsies for free. Naturally, the VA said no. It'll help Yannacone with his suit against them."

"Nothin's gonna help," Frank replied angrily. "All the friggin' suits will go on for years. We'll be long dead before it's over. Join me. Have a Bushmills on the rocks. It'll take your cares away."

"Frank!" Bull's voice was commanding, cutting through Frank's apathy. "Get hold of yourself, damn it."

Frank frowned, not giving a damn what Bull said. "Give me ten reasons why," Frank replied.

Bull held the phone tightly and hollered back, "I'll give you one reason why! Only one! Weinstein ruled in our favor. He made it clear that what's at stake are the lives of sick veterans and sick kids. He made it damn clear there's a need for programs and services for entire families. And he agreed to the idea of a trust fund, a foundation! That's what we wanted. That's what we've been fighting for, damn it. Get hold of yourself!"

Bull was pissed with having to plead with Frank.

"What the hell's with you?" Bull asked.

"You haven't heard the latest," Frank said in a monotone, gulping down more booze.

"What?" Bull asked, swinging his black boots onto the credenza, not giving a damn if it got scratched.

"The lawyers appealed some of the rulings."

Bull waited for more while Frank guzzled more Bushmills.

"Frank!" Bull shouted. "Talk to me! What rulings are you talking about?"

"Well," Frank slowly began, "Yannacone appealed. His guys want a trial. All the other bastard lawyers appealed because they want more money. I don't know if they want forty or sixty million, but Weinstein is givin' those guys a good swift kick in the ass. They are gettin' next to nothin' or maybe nothin'. I vote nothin'. The case now goes to the Second Circuit Court of Appeals."

"So why in the hell are you getting drunk? The ruling was in our favor."

"Ohhh, it was a wonderful ruling. But the Second Circuit is a buncha fat-assed politicians. They never did like us. It'll then go to the Supreme Court. That bunch don't give a hoot about us. Those men in black robes will drag their asses for years. And all the while I'll take calls. I'll listen to stories. Vietnam vets dyin' from cancer. Kids not makin' it because of this or that reason. I should've listened to Muriel. She told me we couldn't afford the toll free number. She told me to get rid of it. We can't even pay the phone bill. Can ya see the pickle we're in? Come on over...have a drink on me."

FIFTY

FRANK'S FORECAST WAS CORRECT. WHEN HE PREDICTED "THOSE MEN IN BLACK robes will drag their asses for years," he never realized how long a wait it would be. And he never dreamed that those men in black robes, that august body known as the Second Circuit Court of Appeals, would go far beyond the issues they had been asked to consider. The results were devastating.

Victor Yannacone did not want to settle. He represented veterans who demanded a trial, and he adamantly believed they deserved one. He filed an appeal.

The Plaintiff's Management Committee, the group of lawyers that wrestled control of the suit away from Yannacone, wanted more money for their services than Judge Weinstein would allow. They too filed an appeal.

Both appeals lay dormant for years. But the day finally arrived. On April 7, 1987, the Second Circuit handed down a ruling: "There will be no trial. And no more money for the lawyers." The court upheld the terms of the settlement with certain exceptions. Wives and children were dismissed from the suit for lack of jurisdiction. With a bang of the gavel, the Second Circuit destroyed the trust fund. There would be no foundation! No nonprofit charitable corporation where people could donate money or a wheelchair or crutches or anything else that might lessen the pain and suffering of veterans and their families. With another bang of the gavel, the black-robed men instantly created a Veteran Payment and a Class Assistance Program. Both programs would gobble up $180 million plus $77 million in accumulated interest.

The Bunker was packed. Frank and Muriel were on the settee facing the entire board. They were stunned by the sudden, devastating announcement. It was unexpected and heartbreaking. And they just sat there digesting the unexpected news.

"Why?" a voice finally shouted from the back of the room.

Frank slowly replied, "The Second Circuit said lawsuits cannot be initiated to create foundations. They are initiated to distribute money." His voice then rose, "The bastards then had the audacity to say that Vietnam veterans were not capable of making impassioned decisions necessary to run such a foundation."

Muriel was livid, but she reined in her anger.

"How could they say that?" she asked, almost in a whisper. She turned to Frank and loudly said, "Judge Weinstein formed a board of directors to run the foundation! Thirty-two Vietnam veterans! Distinguished men, Congressman Bonier, a lawyer from the *New York Times*. All the others. How could they say these men couldn't make impassioned decisions? There must be an appeal!"

The Second Circuit ruling was appealed. But in June 1988, the Supreme Court upheld the lower court's decision without review and without comment.

Later the following morning, Frank was still in bed, awake but out of sorts. He was fed up with everyone and everything, especially the phone. Every time it rang, he would look at the ceiling and swear under his breath.

"Fuck it," he'd say.

Frank would then roll on his side, pound the pillow and close his eyes until the damn thing stopped ringing. He was tired of listening to calls for help, knowing he had nothing to give. But it would ring again. This time, disgusted with the situation, he swung his legs off the bed and grabbed the phone off its receiver. He could no longer tolerate the constant ringing and decided to tell everyone to stop calling.

"Yeah?" Frank grumbled.

"Good morning," Dr. Allen said.

"Oh! Hi, Doc."

"I heard the news, Frank. I'm sorry it didn't work out."

"Me too, Doc. I feel bad for all those people out there, especially the kids who will get no help. Those Supreme Court sonsabitches, I'll hate them forever. How in the hell could they refuse to review the case? How could they refuse to comment?"

"I don't understand it, Frank. Even though I'm ignorant of the law, the Second Circuit's ruling was a disgusting display of prejudice against Vietnam veterans."

Frank's head was throbbing.

"It sure was, but we've gotta live with it. We've gotta move on and do what we can do. I'm waiting to see what Judge Weinstein goin' to do."

CHAPTER FIFTY

"What are his choices?" Allen asked as he sat at the kitchen table with his face to the window.

"Not many," said Frank as his right hand massaged his forehead. "Here is how it works. We have $257 million. The Second Circuit allowed $52 million for programs and services to vets and their kids if Weinstein agrees to run it. There's no precedent for a federal judge overseeing and distributing money. He would have to do it for years! As for the rest of the money, we're being forced to blow it! Give it away!"

"I don't understand."

Frank rubbed the back of his neck.

"Those old bastards with their majestic robes spelled out the eligibility criteria. It's outrageous! In order to collect something, a vet has to be dead or totally disabled. If a guy is dead, his wife and kids get $350 to $3,400. If a guy is totally disabled, he gets $12,880."

Frank stood and paced up and back. He was so damn mad.

"Just imagine, Doc, putting a price on the life of a veteran. How can anyone decide that? And when it comes to the guys who are totally disabled, they collect from Social Security. They can get along without that money. To top it all off, since they're collecting Social Security disability benefits, they have to declare that lump sum as income and give some of it back. How's that for a solution to the national debt?"

Dr. Allen shook his head.

In a slow, deliberate voice, he said, "One hundred eighty million down the drain. What a tragedy. You could have had a foundation. That is how the March of Dimes got started."

Dr. Allen was disgusted.

"You know, Frank," he said, "I often think about getting a law degree. It is so important to know something about law. Judges and lawyers, the entire judicial system, they have so much power over everyone and everything. I've learned the hard way. You can't rely on other lawyers. You have to rely on yourself."

Frank piped up, "True...true, Doc. But why work your tail off getting a law degree? You have a nice practice. You're doing well. You've told me you're happy. Why bother?"

There was a long silence.

Dr. Allen finally let out a long sigh and said, "Yes and no. I'm making more money than I would ever have made at the university. I love my work. Christie and I have never been closer or happier. I've grown close to my parents and my son, Jim, who runs the family farm. We recently bought four hundred more acres of land right next door. None of this would have happened if I stayed at the university. And yet I have this empty feeling. I enjoyed research. I enjoyed doing something important, making a contribution. But I let it slip away. And the past still haunts me...real bad sometimes. And it's painful thinking about my criminal record, pleading guilty to something I did not do. I often look back and see how stupid I was. It hurts. And I don't like carrying this knowledge to my grave."

As Frank listened, he slowly stretched his neck, trying to ease the tension.

When Doc finished, he said, "Bull's still working on it. I haven't talked to him in a while. Let's hang up. I'll call, and he'll connect us up on his fancy new phone. We can have a conference call and find out if he's found anything new."

Larry McKitrick was in his office, fingering his keypad. He was online with AOL, typing information into the find-a-person box, still trying to locate Sue Zeck. His private line buzzed. He turned to his credenza, glanced at his caller ID, saw it was Frank, reached out, and flicked a switch.

"Hi, Frank. What's up?" Bell said as he continued staring at his computer screen.

"How about a conference call with Doc? He's moody again."

"You've been moody too, Frank," retorted Bull.

"Can't help it, you know why."

"Like I've said, Frank, you gotta take it one day at a time. That dough will last for ten years. Why worry about it now? Just charge ahead, like in Nam."

Frank conceded. "I guess so. Plug in Doc, he needs a pep talk."

Bull punched number six on his phone pad. In moments, they were all connected.

"Before we start talking," Bull said, "thank Christie for the wonderful apple pie."

"She keeps sending pies to you guys, hoping you'll pay us a visit."

"Some day, Doc," Frank said. "When all this work goes away."

"How about you, Bull? Your men can take care of things. Treat yourself to a getaway."

CHAPTER FIFTY

"Not now, Jim," Bull replied. "I'm looking forward to the day when I can sit with you and Christie and show you proof that the whole damn thing was a conspiracy. Then I'll come."

Dr. Allen said nothing, wondering if that would ever happen. Although he wanted Bull to keep digging for information, it was hard to be optimistic after eight long years. Nevertheless, he talked with his friend as if that get-together would someday become a reality.

"I'll pray it happens soon, Bull. Any new information?"

"You bet," Bull said with a proud lift in his voice. "I can now prove that Spencer testified falsely about high levels of PCBs. And I just got hold of a document telling me that Spencer gave this information to the World Health Organization."

Dr. Allen was excited.

"What kind of document tells you that?" he asked.

"A notarized affidavit from Dr. Kociba. If it isn't true, he could be charged with perjury. If it is true, Spencer could by the guy who helped spread false information to the scientific community."

Dr. Allen nodded in agreement, amazed at how past events began falling into place.

"Maybe that's how that false four-line statement got into the JRB manual," Allen said.

"Could be," said Bull. "That's one of the strategies they used to destroy your reputation. But one thing is clear as far as I'm concerned. It ties a Dow scientist to an EPA employee. It shows the government working with Dow for your destruction. In my book, that spells conspiracy."

"I remember Kociba," Frank quickly chimed in. "He e-mailed Cartwright that letter about high PCBs. And he was supposed to check only for dioxin. Right?"

"You got it, Frank," Bull replied. "The PCB strategy worked well for Dow. But besides Spencer, other people were involved."

"Like who?" Allen asked.

"Certainly the university official who allowed Spencer to come on campus!" Bull explained. "And the EPA official who signed for Spencer's trip to Madison. And I still wonder about Cartwright. Why was he so helpful when people barged into your lab unannounced?"

Dr. Allen still wondered about the answer to that question. He sat at the kitchen table, his left hand clutching the phone tight to his ear while the fingers of his right hand drummed the table. He was astounded by what he had just heard. It was all coming together. And he clearly began to see the picture. But what could he do after so many years?

FIFTY-ONE

Prior to the Second Circuit's decision, Judge Weinstein had put in place a thirty-four member board to run the foundation. He did so with the belief that a nonprofit corporation was a forgone conclusion. It had never been an issue. The vets needed it, and everyone wanted it. But when the ruling came down from the upper court, Weinstein knew that the idea of a foundation had gone up in smoke. He would have to accept the responsibility of overseeing the Class Assistance Program spelled out by the Second Circuit.

His pencil carefully circled twelve names from the defunct thirty-four member board. He now had a twelve-member advisory board with himself as its head. They would use $52 million as best they could to provide for needy veterans and their families.

"Hallelujah!" Frank exclaimed. He was jubilant when he learned he had been selected as a member of the advisory board. He dialed Muriel. "I'll have a say in dishing out money to the kids," he excitedly said.

Muriel too was excited. "I'm so glad. Thank you God," she said with upturned eyes.

Frank's priority had always been children. It was what he and Lenny and Paul had talked about. Frank felt energized. He was off and running. For the first time, he would be able to directly affect the lives of people who had no money and no insurance.

A boy in Texas with a 5 percent chance of living was flown to and treated at Sloan Kettering. He lived. A girl in Pennsylvania was born with a right arm that ended as a stump below the shoulder. She was given a prosthesis and in time used it well. A young girl in Ohio couldn't walk. Her bones had not developed properly. She was given hip braces and learned to ambulate on her own. Some birth defects were impossible to correct. A girl in Wisconsin was born with one leg bent over the other one. She had deformed hips, stunted thighs, no calf parts on her legs, and one leg longer than the other. She was put in a body cast with a board between her feet, her legs spread apart and feet turned out. A year later, surgery was performed. A plate was put in the shorter leg and then taken out. Problems remained.

CHAPTER FIFTY-ONE

The most common birth defects were learning disabilities. Somehow, those Agent Orange chemicals had disrupted connections in the brain. Children were doomed even before they were born. The advisory board approved grants to learning disability organizations that then provided services. Lives were significantly altered. Still, a number of children could not be helped. A twelve-year-old boy lay dying in an upstate New York hospital. He had struggled for three years against a deadly disease. His bone marrow stopped making platelets. When the platelet count dropped to a very low level, blood could not clot, and the boy hemorrhaged.

The boy's father had been drenched by Agent Orange in the Vietnam jungles and blamed himself for his son's affliction. He had donated blood platelets to his son, Jason, every other day. But in 1989, two days before Christmas, Jason suffered a brain hemorrhage and lapsed into a coma. On Christmas day, he opened his eyes, gazing at family who stood at his bedside.

"God touched my face," Jason said to Jenny, his nine-year-old sister who leaned against the bed, her hand on his pillow.

"Was it nice?" Jenny asked, looking tenderly at her brother.

"Yes, very nice," Jason replied, reaching over and touching her hand.

That evening, Jason died. Doctors were ready to hook him up to life support. But Mom and Dad shook their heads.

"No," they said in unison. "We want him in heaven with God."

Frank dwelled upon every death. It troubled him immensely. He wondered if anything could have been done for Jason had there been a foundation years ago, when he first came down with the dreadful disease. Frank's heart ached as he stood in his Bunker, watching snowflakes coming down on the slushy street just beyond his window. The ringing of the phone interrupted his thoughts. Dropping into his favorite spot, the cushioned settee, he flicked a switch.

"Agent Orange Victims International," he said, "can I help you?"

"It's me, Frank," came the familiar voice.

"Hi, Bull." Frank was not in the mood for conversation.

"What's wrong?" Bull said. "You sound down."

"One of our kids died last night."

"Anything I can do? Does the family need anything?"

"No, they're holding up better than me."

"What can I do for you?"

"Give me a foundation. Some day, we're gonna run out of money."

"I've thought of that," replied Bull. "And I'd like to toss out an idea."

"Go ahead, toss," replied Frank, resting his head on the back of the settee.

"Remember the letter Gross sent the VA about doing free fat biopsies?"

"Yeah."

"Nothing came of it. It's the same for a lot of other things we uncovered, like the study the VA sat on. The one proving that marines in Vietnam had a 110 percent higher death rate from one kind of cancer as compared to the normal population and a 58 percent higher death rate from another. Covering up that study was in violation of the law. They also covered up other things. We thought all this info would play well in our suit against the VA, but it hasn't. That suit seems to be dead in the water."

"Yeah, yeah," Frank replied. "We've been through this before. The big guys beat up on the little guys...what else is new?"

Bull pushed on, knowing Frank would grab on to a new idea.

"What about giving a grant to the Veterans Legal Services Program? They're a good bunch of guys. They could file a suit for Vietnam vets and show that the VA has set too tough a standard of proof for vets claiming injury from Agent Orange. They could show that the VA screwed our guys by not givin' 'em compensation they really deserve. Whaddya think?"

Frank came alive. "I like it! The court can look at numbers. They tell a story! Only five vets got benefits. Five out of 33,272. The judge would see it! And he'd have to agree that those VA bastards have been screwin' our guys for years."

"Right," Bull replied. "Just think, Frank. The VA might be forced to rescind every case where they denied a claim. They might have to give our guys over $400 million in back compensation."

Frank sat upright. "Did I ever tell you you're a genius, Bull? A real genius."

"I don't think you ever told me that," Bull replied with a chuckle.

"Well, you are! And that's what I keep telling Doc about you."

Bull laughed and said, "I want you to promise me something, Frank."

CHAPTER FIFTY-ONE

"What?"

"Some day, I'm going to visit Jim and Christie, to show them what we found. I'd like you to come with me. We can spend time on the farm, enjoy home-cooking and just relax. They've been inviting us for years. We deserve a vacation."

"You got a deal. Why don't we get Doc on the phone?"

"Hang on," Bull said, putting Frank on hold and punching in numbers.

Dr. Allen's voice came on line.

"Hello?"

"Merry Christmas, Jim," Bull called out.

"Merry Christmas, Doc," Frank chimed in.

"Well, goodness gracious, this is a surprise. Merry Christmas to both of you," said Dr. Allen, sinking back in a cozy chair in his living room.

"Is Christie around?" Bull asked, drumming his fingers on his desk.

"Hold on," Allen said, hollering, "Christie!"

"I'm on!" she exclaimed as she sat on the side of the bed holding a shoe.

"Hey, Christie," Bull called out, "thanks for the cookies."

"Ditto for me," Frank chimed in, "they were great."

"Our two best friends," she replied, sliding her foot into a shoe.

"How nice of you to call. And on Christmas Eve. It's so sweet of you. As far as the cookies go, I do send you treats now and then to remind you to visit us. Right now," she went on teasingly, "there's a lovely turkey dinner in the oven waiting for two men like you."

Bull let out a hearty laugh.

"Some day, Frank and I will be knocking on your door, Christie. We might like it so much, you'll never get rid of us."

"You can't scare me, Larry McKitrick," she retorted with a toss of her head. "Try us! We can use both of you down here. We will even adopt you! Legally. You can sit around all day and eat apple pie. And if you're good, I'll put chocolate ice cream on top of it."

"How can we possibly turn down an offer like that?" Frank replied. "It means early retirement. No more work.

"I don't know about that no more work part," Christie said, shifting her position on the bed. "You might have to do a little somethin' now and then. At least for a while...until Jim finishes school."

"School!" Frank and Bull exclaimed in unison.

"It's Christie's fault!" Allen joked, jumping into the conversation. "The one thing she had to agree to before we were married was that I could go to school as long as I wished and she'd support me. Ask her! Go ahead, ask her!"

Christie stood up, smiling. She ran her hand over the bedspread, smoothing away wrinkles.

"He's right, boys," she said. "Naïve me. I never realized what I was letting myself in for. Fifteen years after we were married and with four kids, Jim was still going to school. Now, he's back studying law."

"But Jim," Bull was perplexed, "what about your animal clinic and farm?"

"You don't understand," Allen quickly explained. "I'm not physically in school. I do it by mail. It's a correspondence course from the William Howard Taft University in California. It's quite demanding. After a full day at the clinic, I study late into the night. I don't have time for the farm anymore. Luckily, my son Jim takes care of it. All I do is help him unload bales of hay and stack 'em in the barn."

"I don't know how he does it," Christie said. "Sometimes, he's up all night."

"Everyone knows I'm a workaholic," Allen went on. "For a law degree, I am willing to put in whatever time it takes." His voice grew more passionate. "I want to understand the law! I've got to know if my lawyers did right by me. I don't care if I sleep or not. I've got to know!"

The emotional outburst was unexpected. Christie was sorry she had brought up the subject. Frank felt bad for his friend. Bull felt that the damn investigation was taking far too long. He would have to try harder, put another man full-time on the job. Dig like hell for information. It would also be a good idea to hire someone to interview everyone involved in the ugly affair, especially the lawyers. But Bull felt certain that the lawyers would refuse to be interviewed.

FIFTY-TWO

Frank McCarthy and the AOVI board threw a party. They invited the entire block. The simply had to whoop it up because they had been victorious.

When Bull tossed out the idea of trying to force the VA to pay compensation to Vietnam veterans for war-related injuries, Frank jumped on it. He brought it before the advisory board and they loved it. A suit was filed on behalf of the Vietnam Veterans of America. Court wrangling between attorneys did not last long after Judge Thelton E. Henderson of San Francisco saw that only five vets out of 33,272 were granted benefits by the VA.

"The VA's approach to granting compensation has been radically different from what Congress ordered," Judge Henderson said. "The agency has made it almost impossible for a veteran to prove his case. And in Agent Orange cases," the judge went on, "the VA has not followed its own regulations. They have abandoned the requirement that a ruling must be made in favor of the veteran where there is any doubt about the connection between military service and illness."

It was a victory for tens of thousands of Vietnam veterans. They had been denied $400 million in benefit claims for illness due to Agent Orange exposure. Until Judge Henderson ruled, they could not get one red cent. But now they would get it all. Every dollar! They had cause to celebrate.

Frank knocked on every door in his block and invited everyone. On Sunday afternoon, with the sun high overhead, a Vietnam vet dressed as a clown stood on the walkway, motioning for people to walk down to the Bunker. Waving a colorful, flapping hand, he yelled to a group of kids in the park across the street.

"Come join the party," he said, "food and drink for everyone."

They hurried toward him, laughing at his bulbous red nose, yellow and red streaked smiling face, and yellow wig with long curls hanging down. After they crossed the street, the kids pulled at his baggy clothes and mimicked his gait as the long red rubber shoes slapped the concrete with every step.

The clown waved his arms at passing cars and held his hands in the air like a prizefighter who had just won the heavyweight crown. He whistled at everyone walking by, urging them to walk down the stairs and into the Bunker. He didn't care if they lived on the block or not. The world was welcome.

The Bunker had wall-to-wall people milling about. The place hummed with conversation and bursts of laughter. A radio played soft rap music in the background. Long tables against two walls held heaping platters of food: meatballs and spaghetti, hamburgers and hot dogs, potato salad, and cole slaw. Dill pickles, olives, relish, and mustard stood in open jars at one end of the table. Assorted cakes, pies, cookies, and homemade brownies drew people to the other end.

Frank McCarthy served as bartender, moving to and from the kitchen, replenishing supplies of soft drinks, beer, and orange juice. A round aluminum bucket was constantly running low on ice cubes. On every trip to the fridge, Frank would cast an eye at the Bushmills. He was tempted to put it on display along with the other beverages, but Muriel caught his gaze and fixed a stern eye on him. It was as if she could read his mind. The Bushmills stayed on top of the fridge.

The speakerphone rang.

"Where's the phone?" Frank shouted above the din. Someone on the settee hollered, "Over here, Frank!"

Frank had been waiting for a call from one of his guys in DC. As he sidled through the crowd, he thought how strange it was, calling a Congressman one of his guys. Frank grabbed the phone, put it to his ear, and covered the other ear with one hand.

"Talk loud," Frank said, "we're havin' a party. Lots of noise."

As Frank listened, he smiled broadly.

"That's great! I'll let everyone know. Thanks."

Putting the phone under the settee, Frank wondered how to get the crowd's attention. There was nothing to stand on and everyone was busy eating, drinking, and talking. Some were moving in rhythm with the music.

Frank edged his way toward the wall that displayed his M-16, his baby. Motioning for a husky vet with broad shoulders to follow him, they pushed their way to the wall. Frank whispered in his buddy's ear and was instantly lifted and held so his head almost touched the ceiling.

CHAPTER FIFTY-TWO

"Everybody! Everybody!" Frank shouted. "I'd like to say something."

The room gradually became quiet except for soft background music.

"Turn the music off," someone called out.

The radio clicked off. Absolute silence prevailed. People looked at Frank, somewhat amused at the way he was being held up.

"Thank you," Frank said. "I've got wonderful news. Something I thought I'd never see. Besides doling out the $400 million to thousands of our guys, the VA will no longer be able to turn down claims for benefits any time they want to. Congress took it out of their hands. They ordered the VA to contract with an independent agency that will look at scientific evidence. From now on, the National Academy of Sciences will decide what's service-connected and what's not."

Frank's voice rose to a crescendo.

"The National Academy will be our voice! They can be trusted! From now on, the Academy will decide whether a disease is service-connected or not!"

Frank hesitated and was about to go on, when he saw Muriel giving him the eye. He was about to say "not those sonsabitches that run the VA."

But instead he said, "Not the VA."

Frank was glad he hadn't spoken impulsively. The entire block and others were listening. It was good having Muriel around. She kept a reality check on him. But how the hell did she know what was on his mind? He looked back at her and saw the faint smile. He smiled back and winked. Close to midnight, Frank found himself on the floor sipping a Coke, his back against the settee. He felt tired and had no desire to clean up the mess he was looking at. As he wondered about cleaning it up in the morning, the phone rang. Frank reached under the settee, pulled the phone out, and stuck it to his ear.

"Who's callin' this late?" Frank asked.

"Who wants to know?" the familiar voice teased back.

"Hi, Bull! What're you doin' up so late?"

"Couldn't sleep. Too many things to think about."

"Yeah, I know. I'm always thinkin' about who to dole out money to and how it will all be gone some day."

"Take it one day at a time, Frank. And when you give it away, make that money do miracles for the vets and their kids."

"It was a miracle getting $400 million. And a miracle having the Academy take over. It was your idea, Bull."

Frank paused. He thought about all that had happened since Bull tossed out the idea. It truly was a miracle.

"You're quite a guy, Bull. I thank you from the bottom of my heart."

"Don't get mushy with me, Frank. I never learned how to handle compliments. They make me uncomfortable."

"I know. But I'll say it again. You're quite a guy. Look at what you're doin' for Doc. That's really special."

"That's why I called, Frank. Would you ask your guy at Justice about getting a copy of Jim's testimony before the grand jury in '79?"

"Isn't that classified as secret?" Frank asked.

"Maybe not. Just ask."

"Okay. What's up?"

"It's hard to believe, but I don't think Jim was indicted by the grand jury. I talked with the clerk of the U.S. District Court here in Madison, and she has no record of an indictment. She referred me to the Federal Records Center in Chicago, where Jim's records are stored. I've got copies of everything. There was no indictment. Nothing was ever handed down."

"Then why did he plead guilty? And why was there a plea bargain? What the hell was that all about?"

"I don't know. I'm not a lawyer. But I'd like to see Jim's testimony. If he told the grand jury what he told me, it seems as if there would have been a mitigating circumstance. The grand jury may have realized there was no actual theft, no actual walking away with money in his pocket. Maybe that's why they didn't indict him. If that is true, it seems reasonable to say that the U.S. Attorney would've known this. And if he knew, Allen's lawyers should have known. The whole thing bothers me. And I must check it out."

"I'll talk to my guys in Justice," Frank replied, putting his Coke can on the floor. "Maybe we can pull off another miracle."

FIFTY-THREE

December 31, 1996. Frank McCarthy was drunk again. He was in his Bunker in army battle fatigues, slouched down on his settee, resting on the end of his spine with his legs stretched out in front of him. He studied a half-filled bottle of Bushmills in his right hand and a certificate in his left. He tilted the bottle to his lips and gulped down a mouthful. He held the document out in front of him, but all he could see was the official gold seal in the lower right corner. He moved it up and back to bring it into focus. His head wobbled as he squinted and peered at the award from Judge Jack B. Weinstein. He held it away a smidgen and was finally able to read it.

"Frank McCarthy, a member of the Agent Orange Class Assistance Program Advisory Board, who without compensation has assisted tens of thousands of veterans and their families, is discharged from further duties at the end of the litigation with the gratitude of the court."

Frank tossed the document in the air, aiming it at the table, but it sailed off to a side and dropped to the floor. He tilted and emptied the bottle, then dropped it on the floor next to the document. Leaning his head back on the settee and closing his eyes, Frank was still able to dimly think about his dilemma. What would he do now? For eight long years, he and others had been able to improve the lives of veterans and their families. These were people with no money and no insurance. All total, 101,000 kids were helped. But now there was no more money. So the advisory board was out of business.

Frank felt helpless, so utterly alone. How would he manage without the support of his great friend! Paul and Lenny were gone. And not long ago, the gal who had helped with all of her heart, Muriel, had passed away. As he thought about these friends, the speakerphone startled Frank. He lifted himself to a more upright position, edged forward, and with a wobbly hand, flicked a switch.

"Yeaaah?" he said.

"It's me, Frank. Why the booze?"

"Hi, Bull. There's nothin' more for me to do, so I'm bein' sent off to Florida. It's retirement time, and since there's nothin' more for me to do, why not booze it up?"

"You can be a real pain in the ass," Bull retorted. "Just because there's no money, there's a ton of work to do and you don't have to go off half-cocked. The organization is still in place, and we have sixty-eight chapters."

Frank snorted. "Hah! That takes do-re-mi, Bully Boy. No one's gonna give us that kind of dough. Us guys are still outcasts, bums beggin' for a handout. I don't know why all you guys bought me a house in Florida. It cost a bundle! Better to give that dough to someone who needs it."

Frank leaned back again, feeling as if he were drifting off.

"Frank! Listen to me! Try, even though you're drunk! Are you listening?"

"Yeaaah, I'm listenin.'"

"Now listen hard. You're fifty-two. You've given your life to vets, to their families, and their kids. We love you. I love you, you crazy nut. Our guys in the office had an idea and talked it over. Everyone agreed to kick in a few bucks for that log home in Florida. It's our way of saying thank-you."

"Yeaaah, right," grumbled Frank. "You're puttin' me out to pasture."

Bull felt frustrated, but he continued talking, trying to reason with his friend.

"You're not listening, Frank! Now...listen!"

"I'm listenin.'"

"The organization has a new name, right?"

"Uh huh," Frank said. "Vietnam Veterans Agent Orange, Inc. I like the Inc. It's short and sweet. Sounds like a hiccup. Inc., Inc., Inc. Doesn't it sound like a hiccup?"

Bull felt like hanging up and calling back later when the effects of the alcohol had worn off. But he could not hang up on his friend.

"Frank!"

"I'm listenin,'" Frank said softly.

"You've done more for Vietnam vets than anyone. Because of you and the advisory board, the VA was forced to kick in $400 million for claims they had rejected. They were forced to pay benefits for nine different diseases, from chloracne to cancer. The National Academy is studying

CHAPTER FIFTY-THREE

kids with spina bifida, and if what I'm hearing is correct, they are going to say that there is a connection between Agent Orange and birth defects. You and the board have done miracles."

Frank shrugged off the compliment.

"Then why am I bein' put out to pasture?"

"You're not, damn it!" Bull shouted.

"Dooon't swear. Dignity, self-respect and...and...what's the motto? I forgot."

"Solidarity," Bull replied.

"Yeaaah. Solidarity. All for one and one for all, right? Then why am I bein' moved to Oviedo, Florida? I like it here in my Bunker."

"Would you be open to a deal?" Bull asked, still determined to reason with Frank.

"What kinda deal?"

"Our organization needs an office in the southeast. You know that. We have thousands of vets down there who are sick and need a warm climate. They know and respect you. They'll listen to you. If we can hit on a plan to raise money and have a foundation, it would help them. You are still president of the organization. You can fly up and back for board meetings..."

Bull paused, waiting for a reply, but Frank said nothing.

Bull went on, "Look at the benefits. You will own a spacious log home where vets can meet. It will have a well-equipped office with a computer. You will be able to network with all our guys around the country. If you don't like the place, you can always move back."

Frank was still troubled by the loss of his Bunker. It was his home.

Frank said, "But the board's gonna move the main office to Darion, Connecticut. Where would I move back to? Darion?"

"That's what the guys want," Bull replied. "Jimmy Sparrow lives in Darion, and he will be running that office. What's the big deal?"

"Well..." Frank cleared his throat. "It's just that...I like it here."

Bull took a deep breath and let it out slowly.

"You might like Oviedo. It's near Disney in Orlando."

"Yeah, sure. Me and Mickey Mouse. Ha, ha."

Bull knew Frank was softening.

"Is it a deal?"

Frank hesitated for just a moment.

"I guess so...how am I gettin' to Oviedo?"

Bull smiled, relieved that Frank would stick with the organization. They needed him.

"A Mayflower truck will be there day after tomorrow. They will wrap and pack everything."

"Not my Bushmills," Frank cried out.

"That too," Bull replied. "Two board members will drive you all the way. You take things too much to heart, and I want you to stay sober."

"When are you gonna visit me?" Frank's tone had changed.

"Soon," Bull said, glancing at his watch. "I'm about to wind down the Allen investigation, and you and I can plan on visiting him and Christie."

"I'd like that," Frank murmured.

"Good. I'm going to hang up now. You get some sleep and...happy New Year."

"Yeaaah, you too. And...thanks."

Frank sat back and marveled at the fact that, just minutes before, he had felt so alone, even lost. With one phone call from Bull, he had come alive. He was given a continued reason for living. And, by God, he felt not only alive but confident. He knew he was needed.

FIFTY-FOUR

The day had finally arrived. After eighteen years, seven months, and eight days, Larry "The Bull" McKitrick and Frank McCarthy accepted the long-standing invitation. Christie felt a wave of pure exhilaration as she studied her face in front of the bathroom mirror, brilliantly lit from above by a horizontal row of frosted bulbs. Frank and Bull were coming! They were really coming! And she had to look her best.

With fingers of one hand, she stroked her skin. The lotion and toner had cleansed it, and the moisturizer softened it. She should have been pleased. But as she examined her forehead, cheeks, and chin in the mirror, she frowned at the small irregular discolorations. Age spots! Leaning forward over the white marble vanity, she was aghast at the crow's feet in the outer corners of both eyes. She hated getting old! She thought back when everyone told her she looked like Ingrid Bergman. So long ago. On stepping back a few feet and assessing herself in her white terrycloth robe, Ingrid was nowhere to be seen. Christie knew she had work to do.

An arsenal of makeup, including lipstick, face powder, mascara, eye shadow, hair spray, a moist sponge, red nail polish, a nail file, and a small cache of perfumery all flew out of drawers and a vanity cabinet.

With painstaking attention to detail, Christie began making herself up. Smoothing on the foundation, she dabbed at crow's feet with the sponge. Lines began to fade. Soon, they could hardly be seen. "Thank God for makeup," she thought as she checked her improved look in the mirror.

As she continued her transformation, she wondered if her husband would be reasonably presentable. A shower and a shave was a certainty. A dash of aftershave lotion was not. Jim had changed over the years. Suits and shirts and ties were no longer important. Shined shoes were a thing of the past. A pair of socks was worn at least two, sometimes three days in a row. The one thing he had always cared for, his white ten-gallon hat and shiny, blue, high-heeled leather boots, were in a closet, high on a shelf, gathering dust. Beneath Jim's outward appearance of self-denigration, there were on occasion faint glimmers of his former self. But they were fleeting and hard to discern.

Christie remembered how handsome Jim was when she first met him. She could still see him holding a stack of newspapers under his arm. How he had insisted on receiving three cents before giving her one of the dailies. She smiled at the memory. Eons ago. Her smile faded as she thought about the facade he had put on before the family. With all of his current problems, he wanted everyone to believe he was happy. But the family knew better. He was the only family member with a criminal record, and it still bothered him. They saw it in his eyes, in his frequent visits to the gravesites of his ancestors, begging their forgiveness for putting a blot on the family name.

Christie felt helpless. She was unable to encourage her husband to talk about it, so she tiptoed around it. Ignored it. And explored a variety of unemotional topics, trying to get Jim involved in something other than work. Nothing helped. Nothing caught his interest until two years ago, just before his sixty-eighth birthday.

"Let's buy him a horse and a saddle," said their son, Chris. The family agreed.

Christie remembered the astonished and pleased look on Jim's face when she called him into the barn. He stood frozen to the spot as a beautiful white horse with black spots lowered its head and nibbled at a pile of hay on the floor. Jim loved the Apaloosa.

Every Saturday, he'd slip into his blue jeans and boots and go horseback riding. Not on a neighbor's farm as he did in the past, but on his own land and on his own horse. The strong and agile steed trotted up and down steep, wooded trails, sheltered by pine, oak, and walnut trees. Along one stretch of land, he'd pull on the reins and stop. Allen and his Apaloosa looked down at family burial plots. The horse would let out a whinny as if saying hello.

There were times when his beautiful steed would swing its legs along a gravel-covered trail and carry him upward to the top of a mountain. His mountain. He would sit in the saddle transfixed and look down at a lush green valley, at the rise and fall of land, his land. He would sit and stare at Gabriel's creek from that height. The creek was a black line running through his land. He sat there often, but always alone. He preferred it that way.

"Stop thinking so much," Christie said to the mirror as she checked herself over. Color in cheeks, nose not shiny, no smearing of the mascara, red lipstick just right. She patted her gray

CHAPTER FIFTY-FOUR

hair down and held her hands out for inspection. Nails filed and red polish perfect. A quick dab of Chanel #5 behind one ear. Not bad, she thought.

Christie hurried into the bedroom, knowing she had better not dilly-dally in getting dressed. Jim was waiting. With the gathering darkness, she knew the drive to the Asheville airport would take longer than usual. Bull and Frank would be landing at 10:45 p.m., and she wanted to be there before they landed.

Metal light posts anchored in concrete surrounded Pizza Roma's asphalt parking lot, illuminating three hundred feet of the surrounding landscape. Rows of parked cars clearly announced that the restaurant was packed. Across the road, the Chevron station had a regular stream of customers filling up. In the midst of it all, two red Toyota pickup trucks suddenly appeared, one vehicle following close to the other, heading away from Mars Hill. Dr. Allen was in the lead truck, checking the rearview mirror and making certain that Christie was behind him.

Dr. Allen hated driving at night. His vision had gradually deteriorated over the years, especially at night. He would drive slow, and once on the highway, he'd hug the right lane. He did not want to become separated from his wife.

The headlight from his truck pierced the darkness. Up ahead, a white sign. A black arrow pointed to the right; Highway 19 / 23 South was nearly upon him. He turned down the entry ramp with Christie almost tailgating him. They eased into the flow of traffic and picked up speed, allowing other cars to pass them by. Both Dr. Allen and Christie settled back, knowing they would soon come to highway 240 West. From there, it was nine miles to Interstate 26 East and then almost a stone's throw to Airport Road.

Allen's mood was buoyed by the coming of his friends. His only friends. They were the only two people who had not abandoned him after the trouble broke. It was true that they needed him because he had been scheduled to testify on their behalf. But after the out-of-court settlement, their friendship continued.

Larry "The Bull" McKitrick had promised to conduct a quiet investigation regardless of how long it took. He was determined to dig up facts. He wanted to know exactly how his friend had been done away with...and by whom. So Bull kept plodding along in search of the truth. But Allen knew that as far as he was concerned, hope for the truth had gradually faded long ago.

Dr. Allen stopped reminiscing. Leaning forward, he fixed his gaze on the highway up ahead. Traffic was veering off in different directions and a green sign was up ahead and hard to discern. Peering at it hard, he followed the arrow pointing to 240 West and checked the rearview mirror. Christie was right behind him as he eased into the middle lane, settled back, and relaxed his grip on the steering wheel.

His thoughts slipped back to the past. What did Bull find out? What good would it do? It couldn't alter the facts. He was a convicted criminal. He would carry the disgrace to his grave.

Interstate 26 East was near. He moved over, hugged the right lane, and checked the mirror. Christie was on his tail. She hadn't lost an inch of distance between her vehicle and his. Airport Road would be the next exit. Almost there.

The runway was surrounded by a veil of darkness. A row of white lights on either side of the runway stretched into the distance. The silhouette of a plane with its twinkling wing and taillights descended from the sky. With its nose slightly upward and its wheels down, it touched the ground with the grace and majesty of a golden bald eagle in full control of its landing.

Frank McCarthy was behind Larry Mckitrick as they inched their way down the narrow aisle, following a line of passengers. Frank had a green knapsack strapped to his back. Bull held the handle of a black duffel bag as he moved down the aisle. They neared a stewardess and the flight captain, who stood up front, smiling at passengers as they departed.

Bull stepped out and waited momentarily for Frank. They followed the crowd up the gentle incline toward waiting friends and relatives. Bull craned his neck, looking at people waiting at the open door. There they were! Standing side-by-side, smiling. They looked older than Bull had anticipated, but he recognized both of them. Jim was good-looking, but he seemed thin and…worn. His dark slacks and baggy green sweater were so different from the crisp blue jeans he had worn when last seen. And where was his ten-gallon hat? And the boots? Jim's appearance had definitely gone downhill. And his lined face gave evidence of stress over the years. But Christie! She was a stunning elderly woman. Done up well. The soft periwinkle blouse and the matching button-down sweater contrasted nicely with the daisy print skirt.

Christie and Jim suddenly had both hands in the air, waving, sidling their way to the open door, smiling, and eager with anticipation. Bull and Frank were smiling also as they stepped into the gray, carpeted terminal.

CHAPTER FIFTY-FOUR

"Where's my hug?" Bull called out, dropping his duffel bag and encircling his friends with both arms.

For the moment, there was joy for all of them as they hugged and greeted one another, then chatted as they took long strides toward baggage. Christie found it difficult to keep up. She was shorter than the others, so she took small, rapid steps and momentarily had the urge to jog, something she had not done for years. But she thought better of it and continued holding onto her husband's arm, wishing they would slow down.

As they moved along, men, women, and children turned and stared. They were startled by the muscular man in a black leather jacket with twinkling blue eyes and only one ear. The man next to him had on army green fatigues with medals pinned to his left breast pocket. Along with his matching cap and sturdy, black boots, he looked as if he had just returned from a war.

"Who's going with who?" Christie asked as she stepped onto the down escalator. Jim quickly explained, "Since we don't own a car, we each came in a pick-up truck. How about if Frank rides with me and Bull can go with Christie? Is that okay?"

"Sure," Bull replied as Frank nodded his agreement.

"Christie and I will pull our trucks up to the front door and wait. When you get your luggage, come out and toss it in back and hop in."

Christie kept a reasonable distance behind her husband as her truck came down the ramp and picked up speed on Interstate 26 West. Traffic was light, and she did not have to stay as vigilant as she had en-route to the airport.

"It's about time you paid us a visit," Christie admonished Bull jokingly. "I thought I'd never be able to show you what a good cook I am."

Leaning his head back on the cushioned backrest, Bull smiled.

"I've known that for years," he said. "Your apple pies and cookies told me everything."

"Well..." Christie replied, keeping her eyes on Jim's truck, "that was only dessert! You and Frank are in for a real treat. The Queen of England never tasted beef Wellington the way I make it. And my lobster tail and aged filet is something you will never forget."

"Sounds like you want to fatten us up," Bull said.

"Oh, fiddle-de-de. You're as muscular now as you were eighteen years ago. Not an ounce of fat. I have to tell you, Larry 'The Bull' McKitrick, you are a very impressive hulk of a man.

The little gray around your temples gives you a distinguished look. And I must say, you don't look a day older than when I last saw you."

Bull sat upright and glanced at Christie.

"Well...thank you," he said.

Christie pushed on. "Do you remember the last thing you said to me on Sunday, April 20, 1980, just before you left Madison?"

"I'm impressed! What did I say?"

Christie spoke softly. "Take care of him. That's what you said. I remember."

"I remember too. How's he been doing?"

Christie shook her head. "He's still a workaholic, seven days a week. He takes part of Saturday and Sunday off, but he'll go nowhere. No vacation. No social life. Nothing. He goes horseback riding every Saturday, but he rides alone. The past still bothers him, and it bothers him deeply. He has occasional nightmares and cries out from his sleep, asking for forgiveness. He despises himself for damaging the family name."

"It's a tragedy what they did to him," Bull replied.

Christie glanced at Bull but quickly returned her gaze to the road. "They? Who are they?"

Bull did not immediately reply.

He finally said, "That's what Frank and I are here for. We know who did what to Jim. We also know how and why."

Bull's remarks filled Christie with a bit of hope. She had long ago given up on the idea that Jim could be helped. She was resigned to living out her remaining years with her husband's never-ending nightmares, with his sense of guilt and self-chastisement.

"Will it help if he knows?" she asked.

Bull sensed Christie's resignation and her despair.

"It depends," he replied with a matter-of-fact tone. "Once Jim knows everything, there are things he can do. But it will be his choice. We'll have to wait and see."

FIFTY-FIVE

It was early morning, seven days before Christmas. A tall evergreen stood in a tree stand in a corner of the Allen's living room. Bull and Frank were on their knees hanging silver tinsel on the lower branches. The varnished, hardwood floor contrasted nicely with the colorful tree.

Dr. Allen sat in a wicker rocker at the far end of the room, admiring the decorations. He gazed at the crown of the tree and followed the strands of tiny, blinking white lights as they draped down to the lower branches.

"What about more lights near the bottom?" Dr. Allen asked.

"You got it, Doc," Frank said.

"How about more candy cane in the middle?" Allen went on. "The red striping will add more color, more contrast with the green of the tree."

"Sounds good, Doc," Frank called out. "Do you think we need more tinsel? More glitter?"

Dr. Allen ran his gaze from top to bottom, contemplating the question.

Bull chimed in. "Whaddya think, Jim? Do we need more glitter?"

"Nooo...I don't think so. No," Allen replied.

Bull opened boxes. Red, green, yellow, and white ornamental bulbs added more color to the tree. It was really shaping up, and Dr. Allen loved it.

"Sure is a tall one," Allen said. "One more inch, and there'd be no room for the star on top."

"I haven't done this since I was a kid," Bull said, sitting back on his haunches, grinning broadly. "I remember that fragrant aroma."

"The tree does smell good," Frank agreed, "but I also smell food, and I'm beginning to wonder how much work we have to do before someone feeds us."

"I heard that, Frank McCarthy," Christie hollered from the kitchen. "When you taste my cooking, you'll do any chore I give you to get another mouthful. In five minutes, you gentlemen will see what I mean. So wash up like good little boys and make yourselves comfortable on the front deck. Today, we are dining outside."

The wooden deck stretched away from the house a full twelve feet. It ran the length of the house and was protected by a pitched roof with an overhang. Decorative wood fencing guarded an edge that overlooked a long stretch of tall pines. A pond could be seen beyond the trees. And green fields covered the distant landscape as far as the eye could see. At one end of the deck, a large, round, picnic table, covered with a white tablecloth, beckoned. It had an inviting look and boasted place settings for four. Proudly displayed were colorful plates with gilded rims, matching side dishes, cups, and saucers. It contrasted beautifully with Christie's best stainless silver. White napkins and tall glass goblets added an extra touch of class.

Although the table setting was for a party of four, there were two large pitchers of fresh-squeezed orange juice, Pyrex platters of scrambled eggs, dark-brown sausages, crispy bacon, and fried potatoes. Hot buttermilk biscuits lay nestled in a basket covered with a red cloth, while apple fritters and cinnamon buns were piled high in a matching basket. Two sticks of butter and black cherry jam stood ready on a dish in the corner of the table. The feast was waiting to be devoured. And to wash it all down, two thermos containers steaming Irish Creme coffee.

"It's about time we were fed," Frank said, "but how many others are coming?"

"Oh, fiddle-faddle," Christie replied, waving him away. "You need some meat on your bones."

They poured juice, passed the platters around, filled their plates, and began eating.

"Mmm, good," Frank said, chewing a mouthful. "If you feed us like this, we'll never leave."

"It's beautiful out here," Bull said, working his fork into eggs and potatoes. "It's December, and here we are sitting in pajamas, robe, and slippers."

"We don't have winters," Allen chimed in, holding a half-filled glass of orange juice. "Look below, through those trees. That pond never freezes over. And those cattle grazing in the distance? We never put them in the barn. The grass is green all year round. It is nice around these parts."

"It's more than nice," Christie said, "it's heaven. You two will retire some day. Move down here. Jim and I will give each of you two acres. No charge."

"That's quite an offer," Bull said, dabbing his mouth with a napkin and pushing his empty plate away. "Who knows? But right now, I would like to start telling you about some of the things we have learned these past years. I can prove there was a conspiracy against you. I know

CHAPTER FIFTY-FIVE

who did what to bring you down. And I know why. I've been examining letters and documents for years. It's all etched into my brain."

Dr. Allen pushed his plate away. Christie pulled the top of her green lounging robe tight to her neck and just sat there. Frank still shoveled food into his mouth.

"Let's start with the Anderson gal," Bull said, pushing his chair away from the table and crossing his legs. "She appeared in your lab on August 14, 1978, and resigned fifty-one days later. Who hired her? That's the first thing I wanted to know. My contact went to Carla Raatz, the director of personnel at the university. The only record on file was one sheet of paper with the gal's name on it. There was no address, no date of birth, no Social Security number, no back-ground information, no last place of employment, no references, absolutely nothing. My contact asked, 'Who hired her?' The bottom of that one sheet of paper has a line requiring the approval of the Department of Pathology. Beneath that line was the date, May 17, 1978. Miss Raatz said it was the date signed off by the department. My contact pointed out that the name, S. L. Inhorn, had been printed and not signed. He wanted to know why the man in charge of Pathology hadn't signed his name. It was a requirement for hiring anyone. Carla Raatz didn't know. There were all kinds of dates at the bottom of the form. That made it look as if something had been going on since May 17, 1978. But none of it made sense. There was one signature for the dean. It was signed on June 28, 1978. That signature gave the impression that the dean agreed with Inhorn's decision to hire this gal. But Raatz pointed out that on June 28, 1978, the Personnel Office had just received the position vacancy. How could anyone approve a job that had just been listed as vacant?"

Allen nodded. Christie sat stone-faced. Frank had just finished his second apple fritter and was washing it down with coffee. Bull reached out for a pitcher, poured orange juice, and took a swallow.

He then asked, "Who hired her, Jim?"

"I don't know. I assumed she'd been hired by the department."

"Who interviewed her?" Bull went on.

"I don't know that either," Allen replied.

"What's amazing," Bull said, "was the fact that no one knew anything about her. She materialized like magic. Dr. Abigail Androtti, one of your former students, confirmed this. She said, 'That was the strangest hiring. One day, she suddenly appeared.' There was no job posting. My contact talked with Dr. Androtti a number of times, and I learned that after the trouble started, your colleagues wondered if Kathryn Anderson had been a plant."

"Everyone knew it was a state requirement for all jobs to be posted. Only someone higher up could've done this."

"I know," Bull said. "Carla Raatz claimed the job had been posted, but when asked for proof, there was none. Former Dean Smith agreed to a taped interview. My contact put the facts before him: no background information, no Social Security number, and so on. He was told that people viewed her as a plant and that she had used the sexual harassment and other charges as a reason for her resignation."

"What did he say?" Christie chimed in with a show of irritation.

She still harbored strong feelings toward that...that woman. Bull looked at Christie, knowing his remarks had opened up old wounds.

"The former dean said, and I quote, 'I wasn't aware she hadn't been hired in the usual way. There is strict protocol. Not posting is highly unusual.' When asked to comment on the sex charges, he said, 'I was not convinced that those charges were solid.' The dean's remarks are very important in light of other facts."

Frank nibbled on a strip of bacon. Christie stared at the napkin in her lap, knowing she had almost lost her cool. Dr. Allen sat on the edge of his seat, arms folded across his chest, waiting for Bull to go on.

"Would you folks like to take a breather?" Bull asked, aware of the need for the new information to settle in and for Jim and Christie to feel more at ease.

Christie glanced at her husband. He shook his head.

"Okay, let's move on with a question. Why are the dean's remarks important?"

Christie responded. "There was no proof of sexual harassment. He should know! He conducted the investigation!"

"Okay," Bull seemed satisfied with the answer. "If there was no sexual harassment, why did Anderson make such outrageous allegations? What purpose did it serve?"

"It gave her a reason for quitting!" Christie replied emphatically.

CHAPTER FIFTY-FIVE

"True, but more than that."

Allen laced his hands behind his head and looked upward. Christie shook her head.

"Well," Bull began, "here's how it added up for me. The FBI had been on Jim's tail for years. That's a fact. Jim was always on the go, taking trips and talkin' to people about research. There were expenses: plane fare, hotel, food, whatever. Expenses were paid for out of grant money. The FBI checked into every penny spent. They talked to everybody as a way of looking for the slightest irregularity. Any kind of misstep would become something to latch onto. They were out to get you, Jim. On May 30, 1978, you gave them the opportunity. They saw you and your son, Chris, in Telluride, Colorado. When you got home three days later, you filled out a travel expense report. You asked for reimbursement for yourself and Chris. The money was to be taken from a training grant that belonged to Walter Hargraves, one of your students. The paperwork made its way through university channels, and within weeks, Hargraves received a check with his name on it. Two weeks later, he endorsed it to you. He knew you would replace his grant money from your discretionary account when he was ready to attend a scientific meeting. You deposited that check in the bank and by the end of July, the FBI knew they had you. Two weeks later, on August 14, Anderson showed up, and with access to your records, she found what the FBI wanted, and then she quit. With the help of a university employee named Janet Morgan, a letter surfaced. A story was concocted about sexual harassment along with embezzlement and fraudulent activities. She claimed you were criminally cavalier in the way you spent federal grant money. It all makes sense when you follow the timeline."

Christie glanced at Jim, who still sat with his hands laced behind his head.

"Then why did she need sexual harassment charges?" Christie asked.

Bull nodded. "It gave her a reason to quit and allowed for an attack on Jim's character. But most important, the FBI had a reason to bring in auditors to check Jim's records. Linking sex charges to the spending of grant money on women was a pretty neat way of tearing Jim to shreds. The newspapers had a field day. The charges made Jim out to be a womanizer and a thief. That gal was supposedly a victim. But interestingly, the paper kept her name secret. In fact, one article said, 'The *Capital Times*, at the woman's request, has agreed not to use her real name or new address.' They called her Liv. And every time the newspaper wrote about Liv, they lambasted Jim."

"Tell me about it," Dr. Allen said angrily. "I once had the idea of becoming a hermit and hiding out in a cave at the Wisconsin Dells."

"And," Bull went on, "after your conviction, Benjamin Civiletti, the U.S. Attorney General, awarded that woman a plaque for fighting white-collar crime. This took place in a federal courthouse in San Francisco in an unpublicized ceremony. To the best of my knowledge, the only newspaper to publish it was the *Capital Times* and the reporter was Rob Fixmer. He was still calling her Liv. If that ceremony was unpublicized, who called it into the *Capital Times*? And why was it called in all the way from Frisco?"

"I remember those articles," Jim said, "they kept the heat on. They made me want to crawl in a hole and die."

"That's right," Bull said. "Those articles kept fannin' the flames. I tried to get more information. My contact wrote to Justice for confirmation of that award. They replied, and I quote, 'A search...has revealed no records responsive to your request.' Now, let me ask what for me was a fascinating question. I know they gave her an award on September 23, 1979. Why were there no records at the Justice Department?"

Dead silence prevailed. Christie's eyes opened wide as she turned to her husband. All he did was shrug. Frank stopped eating and slouched down with his head on the back of the chair. Bull waited, glancing at Frank, who was unusually quiet.

"Nobody? Okay, here's what I have," Bull said. "One of my guys picked up a rumor. After Anderson resigned, your staff suspected that this gal was placed in a witness protection program. My guy tried to check it out under the Freedom of Information Act. He wrote to Justice, and his letter was referred to the U.S. Marshal's Service. Their reply said, 'The Marshal's Service is unable to confirm or deny your request for information on Kathryn Anderson, as either action would constitute an unwarranted invasion of privacy and could enable persons to identify and endanger the lives of confidential sources.' I think Justice had no record on Anderson because the slate had been wiped clean. She had a new name! Kathryn Anderson had disappeared from planet Earth. That's why I haven't been able to find her all these years."

Christie shook her head. "Unbelievable," she muttered to herself.

CHAPTER FIFTY-FIVE

"Now let me ask another question," Bull said. "If Witsec, also known as witness protection, was created to prevent people from getting killed, why would Justice put that gal in such a program? No one was threatening her life, unless that gal had ESP," Bull added jokingly.

He turned to Christie, fixed his gaze on her, and continued joking.

"Christie! Did you ever consider going after this gal with a butcher knife?"

Christie smiled broadly at the thought of it.

"I would have. Believe me! I would have, if I could have gotten my hands on her."

Bull nodded. "It's easy to see that she still stirs you up. But joking aside, do you have any thoughts as to why she was put in Witsec?"

Christie looked puzzled. Dr. Allen shook his head.

"Frank!" Bull exclaimed, "do you know?"

Frank sat upright in his high backed chair.

"A piece of cake," he said. "That gal was put in WitSec to keep her away from people. She's probably a chatty little thing, and if someone got to her, she could sing like a birdie and tell all."

"That's right," Bull agreed. "One more question, Frank. Anderson filed charges against Jim in October 1978. The *Capital Times* carried the story. Then she disappeared. In October of '79, Jim was convicted. He agreed to leave the university June 30, 1980. In spite of his leaving, Anderson was in Frisco in 1980 getting a plaque. The *Capital Times* carried the story about the award and rehashed the past. Why did the paper rehash the whole thing? Why did someone want to keep the heat on Jim?"

Frank shifted in his seat, trying to find a comfortable position.

"Another piece of cake," he replied. "Doc was convicted, but he was still at the university. His research was still goin' good with the department head in charge. But someone wanted Doc to go down the drain. The newspaper acted like a pressure cooker. So someone increased the heat, waitin' for it all to blow."

"Right again. I've got no more questions, just a comment, and we can call it quits for now. If Anderson was a plant, the university had to be involved. If she was given a plaque and put in Witsec, the Justice Department had to be involved. That ties the university to Justice. For me, that spells conspiracy. Our next talk will dig a little deeper into Justice. And I will also tie the university to Dow. How about passing one of them cinnamon buns? They look good."

"I'll make more coffee," Christie said, lifting herself up.

"Not for me," Frank replied, spreading his hands over his empty cup.

"Oh, fiddle-faddle," Christie replied. "Most of the food is still on the table, and you'll need something to wash it down. I'm determined to put meat on your bones. You are too skinny."

Frank rolled his eyes upward, wondering what Christie was planning for lunch.

FIFTY-SIX

Bull and Frank strolled toward the barn. The scent of straw and horse manure intermingled with the country air as they neared a massive wooden sliding door that was slightly ajar. A chestnut filly with large friendly eyes stood looking through the narrow opening. She lowered her head, threw it back quickly, moved back one step, and stomped her front hoof on the straw-covered floor. It was as if she was inviting the visitors in.

"She's a beauty," Frank said. "I love that reddish brown color. Push the door open a bit, let's go in."

"I don't know," Bull replied. "She's a frisky thing. Might run off. I'd sure hate to chase her down. Let's wait for Jim."

"Here he comes," Frank said. "I don't believe it! He's carrying two bananas. We just finished lunch. That Christie is somethin' else."

"Don't sweat it, we can feed it to the horse."

"She wouldn't let me out the door," Jim said, coming close and handing his friends Christie's latest offering.

"Does that horse like bananas?" Bull asked.

"I don't know. That's my son's horse."

Frank peeled the bananas, moved near the open space, stretched his arm into the barn, and held the fruit in the palm of his hand. In an instant, the bananas were gone. Frank smiled as he watched the horse chomp away at the tidbits.

Bull grinned. "What would Christie do if she caught us?" he asked.

"Nothing to you two. I'm worried what she'd do to me for letting it happen."

Frank looked around for a trash bucket. "Where can I throw the peel?" he asked.

"Drop it on the barn floor," Jim said. "My son will be cleaning up all that manure. He'll get rid of it."

Frank looked at Dr. Allen with eager anticipation.

"Can I ride her?" he asked.

"It's up to my son, Jim. He's away with his wife, but he'll be calling in. I'll ask. Maybe we can all go riding. I have an Appaloosa, and Jim's wife has a mare that happens to be the mother of that beautiful horse you're looking at."

"Sounds good," Bull replied. "Why don't we walk and work off some of the food? We can also talk."

"I'd like that," Jim replied.

"It's nippy out," Frank said. "Bull and I have leather jackets. Are you going be warm in that thin sweater?"

"I'm okay," Jim replied. "Let's head toward the pond. It's a beautiful place. And peaceful."

The trio made their way along a winding dirt path with foliage on either side: green shrubs with brown leaves scattered on the ground, tall pine with its greenery intact, oak and walnut trees with branches hanging down and holding onto a vast supply of yellow leaves. Bull gazed up at the branches and reminded himself about the information they had already talked about.

"Any questions on what we covered this morning?" Bull asked.

"I was wondering," Jim said, "you tied Anderson to the university and to the FBI. Why did the university do this to me? I brought in a half-million a year. The university took 20 percent off the top for administrative fees. That's a hundred grand a year. Why would they want to hurt me?"

"I asked that question, and after years of digging, I found the answer. The university and Dow formed a kind of partnership in 1934. Henry Dow began funding small projects at the university. This became big time after Willard Dow and the university's Board of Regents signed off on an agreement that created an industrial fellowship in agricultural chemistry and agricultural bacteriology. From that time on, the marriage between the two became rock solid. My contact uncovered documents that show a constant flow of big bucks from Dow to the university."

Amazed, Jim asked, "Where did you find this?"

"University archives," Bull replied, "the one on State Street, and also in the Steenbock Library on Babcock Drive. They hold millions of documents on shelves from floor to ceiling. It's massive."

"I've heard of it, but never had reason to go there," Jim replied.

CHAPTER FIFTY-SIX

"Those dungeons gave us a lot of information, including proof of what they did to you. For example, I have a letter that explained why the university and its legal staff threw you to the wolves, as you once pointed out in a fax to one of my contacts."

"I'd like to see that letter," Jim said.

"It's in my office, but I also have it up here," Bull replied, tapping his head with the tips of his fingers. "That letter said, and I quote, 'On July 10, 1980, attorney Aberg sent a letter to one of your former colleagues.' This researcher was embroiled in a battle with Dow and the EPA. And she wanted legal assistance from the university. Aberg pointed out that the university was receiving a substantial amount of grant money from Dow and the government. Aberg said the University would find it difficult to help because of these grants."

"How much does the university rake in a year?" Jim asked.

"Don't know. My contact talked with Andrew Wilcox, who runs the university's foundation. We got a copy of their 1995 income tax return. It showed a total of over eighty-seven million. That tidy sum was contributed by government and public support. My contact tried to find out how much money came from Dow. Wilcox said it was confidential. However, when I think about Aberg's letter and the tax return, I'd guess that Dow and the government kicked in somewhere in the high millions. So you see, Jim, your hundred grand was chicken feed."

Allen shook his head with disbelief.

"How stupid can one person be!" he exclaimed. "Here I am, seventy years old, and I still think like an idiot. I'm so damn naïve, I...I just want to scream! I always thought a hundred grand was a fortune. I always wondered why the university would throw so much money away. But to them it was peanuts! Nothing but peanuts!"

Bull and Frank glanced at one another and took Jim by an arm.

"Jim," Bull said, "I'm sorry for being so blunt."

"Oh no!" Jim replied, raising his voice. "Don't be sorry. You are helping me see the light. I need more of this. Be blunt! Tell it straight out! Did you know I once thought about killing myself over this?"

Dr. Allen remembered that night so clearly.

"Christie told me," Frank replied. "I told Bull."

Bull decided to change the subject.

"The pond is up ahead. It's all downhill from here on. Wow! Look at those large hills off in the distance!"

"They are not hills," Jim replied. "They are part of the Smoky Mountains."

"Are there fish in that pond?" Bull asked, somewhat relieved at the change in topic.

"We stock it...and let the kids in town go fishing."

"That's nice," Frank said. "So why is there an electrified fence around your property?"

"Poachers used to come here and hunt wild game in the wooded areas. The animal population began to go down. So my son, Jim, spent two years putting up that fence. It keeps poachers out and our cattle in."

Frank was curious.

"What kind of wild game do you have here?" he asked.

"Squirrels, rabbits, deer, a lot of wild turkeys, and black bears."

"Black bears!" Frank exclaimed. "What if we're on horseback, riding, and a black bear suddenly rises up on its hind legs in front of us? What do we do?"

"You best turn your horse and run like hell," Jim replied, smiling at Frank's concern.

"Has anyone ever run into a bear?" Bull asked.

"Not that I know of, but there are animals worse than bears. They are called people."

Bull did not respond. He wanted to avoid talking about the past for the moment. His friend had become emotional, and it was easy to see that it didn't take much to bring out the anger, the pain, and the suffering of the past.

"Why don't we head back?" Bull said. "I'd like to spend the rest of the day exploring the town of Mars Hill. There's a place called Pizza Roma. Frank and I are taking you and Christie out tonight."

They began trudging up the incline, walking in silence, each lost in thought. Bull wondered if Jim would ever be up to the task of trying to right some of the wrongs of the past. It might be difficult, but records of his conviction could possibly be expunged. Libelous statements put into print could possibly be retracted. If not, Jim could sue those who libeled him. Jim could also contact a judge in a Wisconsin federal court and point to false statements made under oath. He could do other things, but would he?

CHAPTER FIFTY-SIX

Frank thought about his friend's emotional outburst and wanted to do something to ease the pain. But what?

Dr. Allen wanted to know everything. He wanted to understand. Most of all, he wanted forgiveness from his ancestors and peace of mind.

"Bull," Jim said, "in less than a day, you have shown me a connection between the university and the FBI. Is there a connection between Dow and the FBI?"

A long pause followed. Bull walked on with his eyes to the ground, thinking. Seeing a polished stone, he swiftly kicked it high in the air with the tip of his boot. It landed between two pine trees. As they walked on, Bull glanced at Jim.

"I've had some dealings with the FBI," Bull finally said. "When I kicked that stone, I pretended it was an FBI man stooping down. It felt good bootin' him in the ass. To answer your question about a connection between Dow and the FBI, I'd rather wait until we talk about Rickey Marlar and the missing data. We've had enough for one day. We'll talk again tomorrow."

FIFTY-SEVEN

Dr. Allen's Toyota pick-up truck rolled to a stop in front of the Mars Hill Barber Styling Shop. Allen and Frank eased themselves out of the front cab while Larry McKitrick hopped down from the back.

David Metcalf, owner of the shop, was sitting on a blue Naugahyde chair in the waiting room. Its age was readily apparent from the white stuffing peeking out from under the seat. Metcalf, in a green, striped shirt, was relaxing with the morning paper. He looked out the window and saw Dr. Allen with two strangers, one of whom had his hand on the red and blue striped barber pole. Metcalf stared at the other man dressed in black and marveled at the bulging muscles. His jaw dropped when he saw the man had only one ear. He folded the paper, put it on the chair next to him and stood up as they walked in.

"Good morning, Dr. Allen," he said. "Who are your friends?"

"Dave, I'd like you to meet Larry 'The Bull' McKitrick and Frank McCarthy. Larry wants a haircut."

"This way, gentlemen," Dave said, escorting the trio to the other side of a partition where his son, Tim, was shaping up the red beard of a huge man of at least four hundred pounds.

Dr. Allen and Frank took seats along a wall and watched Bull ease himself into the barber chair. Dave whipped out a fresh, white sheet from a cabinet beneath a shelf, covered Bull from his chin to below his knees, and pulled two ties together behind his neck. He then broke out a pair of electric shears from an open cabinet and began buzzing away.

"You really need a haircut," Dave said as clumps of black hair fell to the floor. "Probably had your last one, oh...I'd say about eight or nine weeks ago."

"Not bad," Bull replied. "Ten weeks ago. How'd you guess so close?"

"I've been barberin' goin' on forty years. I can tell a lot about people just by lookin' at their hair. I can tell quite a bit about you."

Bull was amused by this interesting man.

"Do your thing...show me," Bull replied.

CHAPTER FIFTY-SEVEN

"Well," Dave began, "you comb your hair straight back, parted in the middle, and it's all slicked down. You're the kind of man who doesn't fool around. No ands, ifs, or buts. No tomfoolery. The all-business type. Once you make up your mind, you go for it."

Bull was taken aback.

"How about my friend?"

Dave tossed a quick eye at Frank, still buzzing away at the nape of Bull's neck.

"Well," he continued, "he handles his hair different. Parts it on the side. Puts a little wave in it, but it's been flattened by that army cap he's holding. He doesn't need a haircut right now, so he's the kind of guy who tries to look good for other people. You, on the other hand, don't give a hoot about what people think. So you just let it grow until it becomes unmanageable."

Dave stopped buzzing because Bull suddenly shook from laughter and couldn't sit still. Jim, Frank, Tim, and the bearded man smiled. After a few moments, the laughter subsided.

"You're good," Bull said. "What does Jim's hair tell you?"

"Well...his hair is different from the way it used to be. I noticed the change when he came back to these parts years ago. It used to have a vibrant look, full of life. He took nice care of it. But he let it go downhill. I suspect it was because of all the trouble he had."

Dr. Allen took a deep breath and let it out slowly, then studied his hair in a mirror behind Dave.

"You know about Jim's trouble?" Bull asked.

"Young fella, this is a small town," Dave replied. "Everybody knows everybody, and we know when one of our own is in trouble. Our town then rallies 'round and does what it can. Why sure, I know about the trouble Dr. Allen had years ago. But none of us believed any of it. He's been one of us since he was born."

Bull looked at Jim and said, "Is it okay to talk about things here?"

Dr. Allen shifted his gaze to Bull and came alive.

"Absolutely," he replied.

"Is it okay with you, Dave?" Bull asked.

"Fine with me, as long as you don't move in the chair."

"Okay. Any questions, Jim, about what we've covered?"

Jim laced his hands behind his head and reflected a moment.

"Yes. You tied the university to the FBI through Anderson. You said the FBI wanted her there and the university let her in. How can you be so sure?"

Bull began to turn his head to look at Jim before responding.

"Don't move!" Dave said.

"Well," Bull began, "do you remember how the university treated this gal?"

"No, can't say I do."

"Do you remember Dean Smith asking a committee to investigate her charges?"

"I remember that," Jim replied, nodding and remembering his anger. "What you probably don't remember is that the university paid her unemployment benefits even though she wasn't entitled to them because she had not worked six months. And the only way she could have received benefits after her resignation was due to employer misconduct. By paying her before the investigation had even begun, the university was saying that you were guilty as charged."

"Yes, by golly, I do remember," Jim replied.

Dave put the shears on a shelf, picked up a scissors and a comb, and began trimming. He had been listening to every word.

"Sounds to me like this gal was given special treatment," Dave said.

Bull turned his head a fraction of an inch. He wanted to say something to this interesting barber who understood the depths of human behavior.

"Don't move," Dave ordered as he combed and snipped at hair on top of Bull's head.

"Dave," Bull said, "let me tell you about a memo to the chancellor. It told him that the payroll office was instructed to pay that Anderson gal benefits with no questions asked. It also told him that Joyce Traynor, a university employee, was one of the authors of the letter to Dean Smith. That's the letter that made all kinds of allegations against Jim. It triggered the whole mess. Think of it! The university helped put that letter together. If that doesn't tie the university to that gal, I don't know what would."

"Sounds to me," Dave interjected, waving his scissors around, "like maybe the whole thing was a frame. Why else would someone at the university help put a letter like that together?"

"You've got it, Dave," Bull went on, "that letter really tied the university to Anderson and the FBI, who were probably calling the shots."

Jim blurted out, "If they wanted to get rid of me, why didn't they just kill me?"

CHAPTER FIFTY-SEVEN

Dave stopped snipping and said thoughtfully, "They could of. They must've had reasons." "They did," Bull said. "They couldn't afford to kill you. Your work would have lived on. Someone would've picked up the ball and run with it. They had to make your work look like trash."

Everyone in the barbershop became silent. Dave cleared his throat and firmly said, "Hold still," while snipping at the side of Bull's head.

Tim, Dave's son, finished with the bearded man, who got up and lumbered out of the shop. Tim then slid into the barber chair. He had been captivated by the conversation and wanted to hear more.

Dave combed Bull's hair, slicked it back, and parted it in the middle. He too wanted to hear more. So even though he was finished with the haircut, he decided to keep Bull in the chair. He began working the scissors and comb at the back of Bull's head, snipping off miniscule and imaginary bits of hair.

"Did you know, Jim, that the FBI was following you long before you ever heard of Kathryn Anderson?" Bull asked.

Dr. Allen closed his eyes, trying to retrieve a memory. "The FBI talked to me in 1978. Dr. Tung, the health minister from North Vietnam, came to the US and I had dinner with him. Before he arrived, an FBI man came to see me and wanted to know why he was coming. I told him we were going to exchange scientific information about Agent Orange. That was it, and I never heard any more about it."

"After that," Frank chimed in, "they could have been following you around."

"The FBI did more than just follow you, Jim," Bull went on. "After Rickey Marlar died in '77, they questioned your staff. I was told that the questions were aimed at trying to pin a murder rap on you. Two years later, the FBI questioned Dr. Billy Jack Bauman, the pathologist who autopsied Marlar. They asked him the same questions. Why would the feds try to pin Marlar's death on you? Why were the feds even involved in the death of a young man from a small town like Middleton?"

Dave hovered over Bull, holding the scissors and comb in the air as if he hadn't yet finished.

"Yeah, I remember reading about the Marlar thing," Dave piped up. "Isn't that when somethin' was missing?"

"Data was missing," Jim said.

Dave rolled his eyes toward the ceiling, fascinated by his own thoughts.

"Could the FBI have killed that young man?" Dave murmured.

"Could they have taken the data?"

Bull glanced at Dave, then at the white sheet still covering him.

"Am I finished?" he asked.

Dave pulled himself into an upright, straight-backed position, still holding the scissors and comb in the air.

"You are finished when I take the sheet off. First answer my question."

Bull tossed a glance at Jim, who was smiling. Frank sat back with an amused look. Bull shrugged and said nothing.

Finally, Bull said, "Well, if you must know, I have proof that Dow's attorneys had some of Jim's data. It wasn't the data found missing at the time of Marlar's death, but it was from the same experiment."

"If they had one piece," Dave replied, "they could've had more. Right?"

"They could've," Bull replied. "And that data could possibly tie Dow to the FBI. But that story is for another day. Right now, Jim's going to show us the town. So if you'd be so kind as to take this sheet off, we'll be on our way. How much for the haircut?"

"Eight dollars," Dave said, wishing he could hang onto these men and continue the conversation.

Bull took out his wallet from a back pocket, took out a ten spot, and pressed the bill into Dave's hand.

"Keep the change," he said.

Dave watched as Jim, Frank, and Bull made their way out the door and down the street. Bull waved to this fascinating barber, who stood looking out the window. Dave waved back and had the urge to bolt out the door and leave the barbering to his son. But in the forty years he'd been there, not once did he fail to be available for barbering. He was not about to start now.

"That's our volunteer fire department," Jim said, pointing across the street. "And up ahead is the Mars Hill Baptist Church. That is where Christie and I were married."

CHAPTER FIFTY-SEVEN

"Not many shops on Main Street," Bull said. "Where do you go if you have a taste for ice cream?"

"Turn left at the corner," Jim replied. "Mars Hill College is a block away. We can get ice cream at Spilman Hall."

The three men walked in silence for a while, each deep in his own thoughts. Bull was the first to speak up.

"I like that barber," Bull said. "He's sharp. I could easily agree with him about Dow having that missing data. But having it doesn't mean they lifted it. The FBI would more likely know how to pull a job like that."

"Sounds logical to me," said Frank, pausing while Bull and Jim looked at a display in a shop window. The trio walked on.

Bull picked up the conversation.

"The FBI can barge into anything at anytime in any place they want. And when they come knockin' on a door, it means trouble. People are afraid even if the questions are about someone else. One of my contacts told me about your former secretary and a former colleague who are both still afraid. Imagine! After twenty years, they're still afraid. Why?"

"I don't know," Jim replied.

"I'll tell you why," Frank said. "Your friends know that your enemies have long memories and long arms, and they can reach out anytime. I remember investigators following Paul and even taking pictures at the cemetery after he died. They followed me and the rest of the board. We were afraid. We never knew what to expect. They finally backed away when Yannacone called Dow's attorneys and told them, in no uncertain terms, that if they didn't stop following us, he would give the order to kill Dow executives. Then and only then did they stop following us around. People are afraid when they can't predict the future. Like when we patrolled the jungles in Nam, not knowing where the enemy was, not knowing if we would live or die."

"Frank!" Bull said. "Jim wasn't afraid, because he never knew what was going on. He didn't know the FBI had invaded his personal life by questioning friends and associates. He did not know Dow had him followed, or that Dow recorded what he said at scientific meetings and then plotted against him. He didn't know that Dow fabricated stories about his research. He didn't know until it was too late. There's so much to tell. It's best we do it a little at a time."

They walked in silence and came to a giant oak, its branches reaching high. In front of the tree, bold black letters on a fifteen-foot by three-foot red brick wall proudly proclaimed: "MARS HILL COLLEGE Founded 1856."

"Hey! That's a neat looking school," Frank said. "There's a sign over there, Spilman Hall. Let's forget all this stuff for now and enjoy some ice cream."

FIFTY-EIGHT

Late that evening, Bull pulled open the sliding door in the living room and stepped out onto the deck. Frank and Jim were right behind him.

"The chairs might need brushing off," Christie called from the kitchen. "One second, I'll be right there."

"I'll do it!" Jim replied, taking a bath towel from a hook on the cedar siding of the deck wall.

He wiped four padded chairs facing the dim outline of trees and branches below. The moon, hidden behind clouds, left the night sky in total darkness except for a few shimmering stars. Low-level lighting on the deck came from a forty-watt bulb in a fixture on the deck wall.

Dr. Allen sat down and crossed his legs, swinging one foot. Frank sat next to him and munched on a walnut. Bull dropped into a seat and plucked a cigar and lighter from an inside pocket of his jacket. Seeing this, Jim hurried back into the house for an ashtray, returned quickly, and handed it to Bull.

"Mmm, this is the life," said Frank. "Peaceful...nice."

Bull flicked on the Zippo, put the flame to the cigar, and inhaled deeply. The end of the cigar began to glow. He blew a smoke ring into the air and watched it rise until it slowly pulled apart and disappeared.

"I never smoked these things," Bull said, "until one of my men handed me a cigar and urged me to try it. I found it relaxing."

Bull inhaled and blew another smoke ring.

"Would you like to try one, Jim?"

Jim shook his head.

"How about you, Frank?"

"No, thanks."

"I've never smoked," Jim said as he sniffed at the aroma of cigar smoke. "It sure smells good. We grew tobacco for a while but stopped when publicity came out about teens who got hooked on nicotine. My conscience would not let me grow it anymore. The only thing we now grow is alfalfa hay."

"The cows must love that," Frank said. "But getting back to the cigar, what does one of 'em cost?"

"This is a regular Monte Cristo," Bull replied. "It's nine-fifty."

"For one?" Frank shouted.

"If you think that's expensive," Bull went on, "a Monte Cristo Desartes is over fourteen bucks."

"You're burning up money," Frank replied disapprovingly.

"Not really. A box of twenty-five lasts over a year. I am getting older...so I indulge myself now and then."

"Can an old lady join the gabfest?" Christie asked as she stepped onto the deck.

Without waiting for anyone to reply, she pulled a chair over and sat next to Bull. A pleased look splashed across her face.

"I want to thank you and Frank again," she said. "When UPS rang my bell this afternoon and held out a beautiful basket of fruit and chocolates, I thought he had the wrong address. It was sweet of you two to send it."

"It was Frank's idea," Bull replied. "I only obeyed orders and had it shipped. It should've gotten here ahead of us. But you can never be sure just before Christmas."

Frank tossed a walnut into his mouth and tried to be nonchalant about who deserved credit for the gift.

"It may have been my idea," he said, "but Bull picked up the tab."

Christie smiled at the way each of them tried to shrug away the gift they'd sent her. It was as if each of them was uncomfortable to openly admit to tenderness and generosity.

"Well, I love both of you," she said, "and tomorrow I will make you a luscious, mouth-watering beef Wellington, something you will never forget."

"I can vouch for that," Jim said, "but I would like to get off the topic of food and get back to what we were talking about."

"Fine with me," Bull replied, then puckered his lips and blew another smoke ring. He tapped his cigar, allowing the ash to fall into the round metal tray. "Before we start, any questions?"

CHAPTER FIFTY-EIGHT

Christie said, "I have one. Isn't it strange no one knew anything about Kathryn Anderson? You'd think she would have made friends with someone who would know something about her."

Bull nodded. "Sounds logical, but I have a statement from Dr. Androtti saying this gal had no friends."

"But," Jim interjected, "I still don't understand why they bothered to give her a plaque."

Bull took a long draw on his cigar and blew four small rings.

"How about taking that one, Frank."

Frank stood up to stretch, put one hand on the deck's railing, and gave thought to what he wanted to say.

He finally said, "It's this way, Doc. That plaque allowed for another story in the *Capital Times*. That story fanned the flames at the university and gave the chancellor something to point to when he got rid of you. It was the same old stuff as before, but it served as a reminder. More importantly, this plaque served as a membership card to an elite club. This gal now saw herself as an FBI agent. Cloak and dagger stuff. She was sworn to secrecy. A code of ethics had to be followed. Loyalty was a must. The only thing Anderson had to do now was keep her mouth shut. That's how I see it."

"One more question," Christie said, turning to Bull.

"Shoot," Bull replied, puffing on his cigar.

"Joyce Traynor helped prepare that letter charging Jim with those lies. Did you ever question her?"

Bull shook his head.

"Couldn't find her," he said. "My contact faxed the personnel director a letter, asking about Traynor. There was no address, no phone, nothing. She just disappeared like Kathryn Anderson."

"Why did the government give me $500,000 a year for research if they were against it?" Jim asked.

"Tell him, Frank," Bull said.

Frank lowered himself into his chair. He remembered his discussion with Bull.

"It was for the same reason Dow gave you dioxin and analyzed your tissues for free. You were less likely to see them as an enemy, and it was easier for them to keep tabs on you. When the government funded your research, you had to send them reports. And when they saw how close you were to uncovering the truth about dioxin, a plan was mapped out and they moved in. If you had found funding elsewhere, and if you could have done your own dioxin analyses, they never could have touched you. You never would have been convicted. And Dow would never have been able to say that your tissue samples were contaminated with high levels of PCBs By supposedly helping you, it gave them the opportunity to get rid of you."

Dr. Allen heaved a heavy sigh. And Bull broke into the conversation.

"You walked into a political minefield, Jim. Let's cover one more point and call it a day. As you know, I've been trying to get a copy of your records from the FBI under the FOI Act. I first asked on September 16, 1997, and J. Kevin O'Brien replied ten days later, and I quote, 'Your daytime phone number is not required but could assist the FBI's efforts to promptly respond to your request.'"

"That's bullshit," Frank spoke up, his voice brimming with anger. "Why a phone number?"

"I don't know," Bull replied, "but I gave him Jim's number. They could've found it out anyhow. But the important thing was O'Brien's remark about responding promptly. Since that time, my contact called again and again, and he always gets the same baloney. Three or four months ago, he talked with a Miss Hawkins. She knew the law required the FBI to respond within twenty days, but she claimed they had a backlog."

"More bullshit," Frank said. "They told you that a year ago."

"I'm afraid that's gonna be their answer for as long as we live," Bull said, putting out the stub of his cigar and leaving it in the ashtray.

Christie had been listening intently and suddenly flared up.

"How can they do that? It's against the law!"

Bull tossed Christie a glance and saw the fire in her eyes.

"I know," he replied. "We tried to deal with that a year ago when the FBI director didn't respond. My contact wrote to Janet Reno. He sent the letter certified, asking for help. Three days later, Kevin O'Brien replied. He handed us a line about being busy and ended his letter by asking for understanding, assuring us that the FBI would process the request in due course."

Christie sat back, aghast at the political maneuvering.

"Where do you get the patience to put up with all that?" she asked.

CHAPTER FIFTY-EIGHT

Bull laughed. "That's funny," he said. "Me! Patient! When I first started out on this crusade, I did not have much patience. Frank can tell you. I'd call him in the middle of the night and let it all out. But I learned. A private eye has to plod along with infinite patience...and perseverance. I picked it up along the way."

Christie shook her head. She was angry.

"It doesn't seem to help with the FBI."

"That's true," Bull replied as he looked up at the sliver of moon in the black sky. "I know the FBI is stonewalling. We received a letter from them, telling us the original request was one of many thousands still pending. They wanted to know if we still wanted Jim's records. They said, 'If we do not receive a response within thirty days from the date of this communication, we will conclude that you are no longer interested and close your request immediately.' It was again J. Kevin O'Brien, the same guy who asked for Jim's daytime phone number...the one who said it would assist the FBI in responding promptly."

"How do you deal with something like that?" Jim asked, wondering how long Bull would go on with his case, knowing it could last forever.

Bull sensed Dr. Allen's discouragement.

"We're trying," Bull said. "When you told O'Brien you still wanted your records, I decided not to trust him or anyone at the FBI. It took thirteen days for their letter to reach you. Isn't that amazing? If it took a little longer for your reply to reach O'Brien, the original request for your records could have been terminated. If you then kicked up a fuss, the FBI could say you didn't respond in time."

Christie muttered an expletive under her breath. Bull ignored it and forged ahead.

"My contact put a letter together with attachments, including your latest reply to O'Brien. The letter summarized everything since your first request went out. He pointed to the possibility that the FBI would close your file if your latest request did not reach them in time. My contact told O'Brien that he did not trust his office. He pointed out that based on their replies, you could be dead by the time they released your records. He asked O'Brien to inform him of appeal rights and talked about a possible court action."

Christie's face brightened. She seemed pleased by that possibility.

"What did O'Brien say to that?" she asked.

Bull harrumphed his disapproval.

"It's unbelievable! When the FBI learned we were headed for court, they suddenly had time to search for Jim's records. That's what they said, and they also said they had no file on Jim, no records at all. My contact replied with a laundry list, showing how the FBI followed Jim, who they talked to, how their men came to Jim's office and read him his Miranda rights, and so on and so on. My contact told the FBI he knew they had records on Jim and again asked for information on where he could file an appeal."

"I...don't understand something," Christie said hesitantly.

"What?"

"Well...if Jim asked for his records, it seems to me the FBI should be dealing with him. Records are private. And with all due respect to you, Bull, why would the FBI reply to anyone other than Jim?"

Bull smiled. "Jim sent the FBI a notarized letter, giving them permission to contact me and for me to act on his behalf."

Christie was sorry she had asked the question.

"Oh," she replied. "What can you do if they don't turn Jim's records over to you?"

"That's up to Jim. He can forget about it, or he can go to court and fight. By law, he is entitled to his records."

"I wonder why they won't let go of them," Jim said.

"If I had to make one guess," Bull replied, "those records tell a hell of a lot. And the FBI intends to keep it under wraps. If my theory is correct, there might be information about Anderson and about how she was planted in your lab. And there could also be information about Rickey Marlar's death. Those records might even tell who killed him."

"Sonsabitches," Jim said angrily as he stared into the black sky.

"It's only speculation," Bull said, "but it makes sense to me. We can talk more about it, but we've all had enough for now."

FIFTY-NINE

It was late Sunday morning. Church had let out. Mars Hill residents made their way to the parking lot, bade farewell to friends, and went about their business.

David Metcalf was in Ingles pushing a grocery cart into the fruit section. He wheeled it around shoppers and stopped in front of a display of newly arrived bananas. Pushing aside a green bunch and lifting out beautiful, yellow bananas, he held them up, examined them, and was satisfied with his selection. Suddenly, he became pleasantly excited. There in front of him, not more than twenty feet away, the man with one ear was sitting in the café with Dr. Allen and the other guy. Dave tossed the bananas on top of his groceries and hurried to join them.

"Good morning!" he said, parking his cart in front of a large window facing the parking lot. Without waiting to be asked, he dropped into a vacant chair at the table. "Great seeing you again. Okay if I join you guys?"

Bull, Jim, and Frank looked at one another. Frank smiled and turned to the friendly barber. "What goodies are in your cart?" Frank asked.

Turning a quick glance at his groceries, Dave seemed flustered.

"Would you like a banana?" Dave asked.

Frank hesitated, then said, "I better not. You haven't paid for them yet."

"Oh...that's right!" Dave exclaimed.

Bull and Jim were amused. Frank reached out and slapped Dave on the knee.

"Join us," Frank said.

Dave beamed. "Thank you," he replied, settling back in his seat and turning to Bull. "Did I miss anything?"

"Not really. We just started with Jim asking a question. Do you remember when we talked about the FBI trying to pin a murder rap on him?"

"I remember it well," Dave replied. "That's when they talked to his staff and to Dr. Billy Jack Bauman, the pathologist who did the autopsy on Rickey Marlar. That's when the FBI asked questions as if Dr. Allen had killed his own student."

Bull was amazed! "Fantastic!" he said.

Dave did not reply, but merely sat there with eager anticipation.

"Well..." Bull gathered his thoughts and said, "Jim tossed out a very good question. He reasoned that if the FBI wanted to pin a murder rap on him, they would've planted evidence at the crime scene, and he would've been arrested. The feds are good at things like that. Jim wanted to know why the FBI was trying to make him out to be a murderer in 1979 when they could have had him convicted in '77 when Marlar died."

Dave nodded, agreeing with Dr. Allen's reasoning.

"I think," Bull said, "that early on, nobody ever thought of pinning a murder rap on Jim. The plan was to befriend Marlar, get to know him well, and when the 500 study was done, kill him, and steal the data. Only later did the FBI think of trying to stick it to Jim. So they went around looking for some way of doing it, but were up against a brick wall."

"Why would they want the data?" Dave asked.

"The 500 ppt study began to prove that small amounts of dioxin would kill. Dow and the government knew what Jim had found and knew they had to stop him. If data was missing, they could claim it was never there to start with, that Jim falsified his results and could not be trusted to do an honest experiment."

But Dave demonstrated that he had done his homework on Dr. James Allen.

"Their claim would have been laughed at!" Dave replied. "Dr. Allen had over two hundred publications. They were reviewed by scientists and were accepted."

"But," Bull replied, "if Chancellor Shain was able to force Jim to resign, it would have ended his research."

"He should not have resigned," Dave said. "He should have put up a fight!"

"Maybe so," Bull said, "but eventually, he would have lost. The chancellor had the power to force him out."

Dave edged his chair closer to the table, happy to be part of the inner circle.

"And when I say power," Bull continued, "I mean real power. He joined the Department of Chemistry at the university in 1952, became departmental chairman in '67, vice chancellor in '70, and chancellor in 1977. Shain had and still has strong ties to the chemical community. One tie is to the Olin Corporation. He joined their board of directors in 1982, and upon

CHAPTER FIFTY-NINE

retirement from the university, joined Olin as corporate vice president and chief scientist. On retiring from Olin in 1992, he continued on as a member of the board. Dave, why am I telling you all this?"

"There's a reason," Dave replied without hesitation, "but only you have the answer."

Dr. Allen and Frank got a kick out of Dave's one-on-one conversation with Bull, who was highly amused. Bull liked this barber who was quick on his feet and enjoyed sparing with him.

"You are right, Dave. I do have the answer. The Olin Corporation makes chloralkali products and caustic soda. Dow also makes these chemicals and, in fact, is the world's largest maker of chlorine and caustic soda. This is used in the paper and pulp industry. These industries have always allied themselves with Dow on the issue of the safety of dioxin. These industries depend on the spraying of chemicals in forested areas to enhance the growth of trees. Agricultural products depend on these chemicals. Agribusiness and the Department of Agriculture have a reputation for siding with Dow in promoting the use of chemicals that contain dioxin while claiming low levels are safe. Since the chancellor was closely allied to Olin, he could have been inclined to view Jim's research findings as a threat to his company."

Dr. Allen squirmed in his seat, obviously uncomfortable at what he had just heard.

"No wonder the Ag people never liked me," he said. "I can also see why the chancellor was never friendly toward me."

Dave sat quietly, thinking and nodding his head ever so slightly. He understood.

"You were rocking the boat," Dave said, looking at Dr. Allen.

"He sure was," Bull said. "The chancellor was pro-chemistry, and Jim's work was close to creating havoc for a chemical empire. Leaders of empires like that belong to the American Association for the Advancement of Science, and they often support Dow's point of view. Chancellor Shain was a member of that prestigious group."

"It's easy to understand why the university brought Dr. Spencer to my lab," Jim said. "And why they told Cartwright he had to assist him. And later told Cartwright he had to assist Drs. Burek and Bell. But what I've never understood is why Cartwright didn't call me before he allowed it to happen. He was one of my students. He should've never let these men into my lab without first asking me."

Dave glanced at his cart.

"Excuse me," he said. "I bought ice cream. It's melting. I'll get something and dish it out. Okay?"

"Sounds good to me," Frank replied.

"Don't talk till I come back."

Dave scampered away, heading toward the aisle for Styrofoam bowls and plastic spoons.

"I never met a barber like him before," Bull said.

"You'll never meet another one," Jim replied. "He's one of a kind. Everyone goes to his shop. He soaks up information like a sponge. He knows just about everything about everyone in this town. Ah, here he comes."

Dave was breathing hard as he dropped a package of plastic-wrapped bowls, a box of plastic spoons, and an ice cream scooper on the table. He eased over to his cart, reached down between Motts applesauce and Shredded Wheat, and pulled out a quart of Ben and Jerry's Chunky Monkey ice cream. He opened it and put the tub in the center of the table.

"Help yourself," Dave said, dropping into his seat. "It's okay with the manager. He knows I'll pay for it."

"Mmm, good" Frank murmured.

"Where were we?" Dave asked.

"Jim wanted to know why Cartwright assisted Spencer and Burek and Bell before calling him," Bull replied.

"Was Cartwright strong enough to say no?" Dave asked.

"Absolutely not," Bull said. "When my contact asked Cartwright why Spencer was allowed in, he said he had no other choice. He explained that the university attorney brought Spencer to the lab and told him it was legal. My contact checked with the EPA and learned that in 1979 there was no legal way for Spencer to get into the lab. The Good Laboratory Practice regulation that allowed this to happen didn't go into effect until 1983. My contact interviewed Spencer. He said the university invited him in. He received his marching orders from Diana Reissa, a section head at the EPA. In my opinion, it was at the request of Dow. But he would never have been able to enter Jim's lab without the university's say-so. In a few days, you will see how Spencer's audit, orchestrated by a government agency, the university, and Dow, helped destroy Jim's reputation as a scientist. Let's take a breather and finish the ice cream."

CHAPTER FIFTY-NINE

"I'll be right back," Frank said. "I gotta go."

Dave picked up his bowl, put it to his lips, and tilted it. The ice cream flowed like thick malted milk. Jim pushed his bowl away. Bull slurped it down with relish just as he saw Frank coming back. Frank seated himself, slid the tub of Chunky Monkey to his side of the table, and scooped out another bowl.

"A few words about Burek and Bell," Bull said as he continued, "they arrived at the university on March 25, 1979, and reviewed the 500 study. Cartwright assisted them all day as they poured over Jim's slides and data in Aberg's office. In a letter to a friend, Cartwright claimed that 'legal matters mandated the honoring of this request.' Abigail Androtti told my contact she was against giving the data to these men, but that Aberg and the university's attorney had agreed that the information had to be released. They told her the study was funded by tax dollars and this made it public information. She said, 'There was no other choice.' She also thought there may have been a subpoena, but could not remember. There couldn't have been a subpoena! My investigation showed that Dow's first subpoena was issued February 1, 1980. Burek and Bell arrived at the university almost a year earlier. My contact located Dr. Burek at West Point, Pennsylvania, and called him on June 25, 1997. He no longer worked for Dow. He remembered his visit to Aberg's office and confirmed that there was no subpoena. Burek told my contact, and I quote, 'I recall one time I had a meeting. I was in a room with sixty lawyers from around the world. Everybody was involved. The government, the university, and business.' Burek wanted to check with Dow to see if it would be alright to talk. He told my contact to call back. The next call went far better. He had not heard from Dow but was willing to talk anyhow. He explained that the lawyers worked out an arrangement, and he and Dr. Bell were given the assignment with permission from the government, the university, and Dow. This admission clearly smacks of a conspiracy. I began to study and think about every piece of paper on my wall. I examined everything over and over again. It seemed reasonable to conclude that Marlar's death may have been part of this evil cabal. This is how I see it. The bottom of page one of the Burek and Bell report says, 'The original gross and histopathologic data sheets were not provided, but we had copies of these sheets which were sent to us from the law offices of Kirkland and Ellis in Washington, DC, just prior to our trip to Madison.' These data sheets came from the same study

335

where data was missing. It's amazing that Dow's attorneys had it. Where did they get it? It was not from a subpoena."

Dave eyed Bull for several seconds.

"Well," he said, "if you're pretty sure no one gave it to him, then someone must've stole it."

"I think so," Bull said. "The FBI would be able to arrange for this. If true, it would put the FBI in bed with Dow."

Christie suddenly arrived, pushing a grocery cart into the café.

"Good morning, Dave, or should I say afternoon. I hope all of you have had a nice chat. I've finished shopping and am ready to check out."

Jim, Bull, and Frank eased themselves up from their chairs. Dave sat there, not wanting to separate himself from his new friends.

"When will you be back in town?" he asked.

"I don't know," Jim replied. "But before we come back, I'll give you a call. But what about your barber shop?"

"It's time I had a few days off now and then. Tim can take care of it."

"Okay, I'll let you know."

"I'd like that," Dave said. "If we meet here, the refreshments are on me. Chunky Monkey or anything else. And I'll volunteer to get rid of the trash and clean the table like I am going to do it right now."

"Sounds good to me," Frank replied.

SIXTY

The shadows of early evening began to fall around the Allen farm. Frank was in the barn perched atop a bale of hay, arms around his knees. "The air smells better here than in the city," Frank thought as he looked through the open doors into the corral. He enjoyed watching Bull and Jim trot their horses around the ring. "They both look so carefree...does 'em good," he mused. As Bull and Jim dismounted and headed back toward the barn, Frank realized he hadn't been depressed once since coming to the Allen home. "I feel more alive here," he thought, wishing this vacation could last forever. He couldn't remember ever feeling so relaxed. Frank eased off the bale of hay and stood waiting for his friends.

"You guys look great," Frank said as the horses came into the barn with Bull and Jim holding the reins.

The Appaloosa nuzzled its nose against Jim's arm as if inviting him to take another trot around. The chestnut filly that Frank had wanted to ride poked its head out from a nearby stall. Frank was tempted to open the lower door and let it out. It wasn't right for that horse to be cooped up just because he was too tired to ride.

Bull and Jim quickly removed the halters, bridles, saddles, and stirrups, cast them aside, and grabbed a handful of hay.

"Frank," Bull said, "how about helping us rub down the horses?" Frank grabbed some hay and began rubbing.

The Appaloosa turned its head toward the chestnut filly and whinnied softly. The mare flapped its bushy tail against its backside as if brushing a fly away.

After the rub down, Jim took two blankets from a hook on the wall and tossed one to Bull. They covered the horses and walked them out of the barn into the corral. They walked the horses one lap around and back to the barn.

"Do you know how to curry?" Jim asked, tossing a rubber comb to Bull.

"I think so. The comb is moved in small circles in the direction of the hair growth, right?"

"Right," Jim replied.

Frank's curiosity demanded an explanation.

"Why's that?" Frank asked.

"It loosens hair and stimulates blood flow through the skin," Jim replied.

Frank watched his friends work the comb with rapid movements while the horses stood still, apparently enjoying the grooming. As Jim started to curry the hindquarters, the Appaloosa turned away from the comb, took several steps toward the open stall, and nuzzled its nose to the nose of the chestnut filly.

"Hey," Frank said, "you might be having another horse around here, Doc."

Jim shook his head. "That would be a true miracle. I had him castrated."

"Why did you do that?" Frank was upset. "A beautiful horse like that! You had its balls cut off! It's not fair."

The Appaloosa turned its head and looked at Frank.

"I think he agrees with you," Jim said. "He's an intelligent horse. He's also strong and agile. He would go crazy if he smelled that mare in heat. He'd tear the barn down or destroy anything in his way to get at that mare when the time came."

"I don't care," Frank replied. "It is not fair."

"Frank's got a soft heart for anyone maimed or crippled," Bull piped in. "He's seen more than his share."

"Sorry, Frank," Jim said.

"No need to be sorry, Doc. Don't mind me. Why don't we take a rest? I'm tired."

"Good idea," Bull replied as Jim nodded.

They hopped onto bales of hay, their feet dangling down, touching the ground.

"I'm tired too," Bull said.

Jim looked at Bull. "Something's been troubling me. Are you too tired to talk now?"

"No, go ahead," Bull replied.

"Once the university got rid of me, why didn't my work go on?"

Bull thought for several moments, then explained.

"As you've seen, with the university's help, Dow could do anything. And they did."

Jim chimed in, "They could do anything because I was so stupid!"

CHAPTER SIXTY

"Look, Jim, don't be so hard on yourself," Bull replied. "You were up against pros. Even after you were forced to resign, Dow still wasn't satisfied. They wanted your work out. Dean Smith wanted your work out, but he was willing for you to be a consultant to your staff. But Dow's attorneys kicked up a fuss. They weren't about to let it happen. And even when the National Institutes of Health wrote to Robert Erickson, the man in charge of research at the university, and told him they wanted to continue funding your research and even asked for an appointment so they could talk with him and get a thumbs-up, Chancellor Shain stepped in and quashed the whole deal. The point I'm trying to make is how easy it was for Dow to do any damn thing they wanted to do with the chancellor on their side. No one could have saved your research. In a letter to my contact, Dr. Androtti summed it all up in a nutshell. She pointed out how she and others struggled to keep the research going. How for a while the studies moved forward. But she ended her remarks by saying that her biggest disappointment was not being able to finish the work and publish it for everyone to see. And then she said how happy she was to have been a thorn in the side of those people who expected her and her colleagues to go silently into the night, as she put it."

Dr. Allen still felt the pain.

"Even though Dow had the clout to force me out," he said, "it was still my fault. If I had been more alert about who or who not to trust, this never would have happened. And if I had never swapped money, this never could've happened. I let everyone down. Myself, my staff, my students, and all the people who depended on me. I still wake up at night with nightmares, knowing I let it slip away. It's so sad...so sad."

SIXTY-ONE

December 21, 1998. A red Toyota pick-up truck rolled to a stop in the northwest corner of the Allen farm. Larry McKitrick's hair flew wildly about as he hopped off the back of the truck. Dr. Allen held his hair with one hand as he opened the door and poked his head out from the driver's seat. Frank eased out from his side of the truck with his army cap tight to his head.

Trees swayed as a gusty wind whistled through the thickly wooded area. Jim, Bull, and Frank made their way to a small clearing surrounded by tall pine trees. Ensconced among the pines, the three men looked down at gravesites where five generations of Allen ancestors lay buried. Three sites bore engraved markers. The others held sizeable rocks at each end of the gravesite.

"I wanted you to see this," Jim said, flicking strands of hair from his face. "These are my ancestors. I often come here and talk to them. I ask for forgiveness. Do you think that's crazy?"

"Not at all," Bull replied. "They could be listening. You never know."

"Why only three markers?" Frank asked.

Dr. Allen remembered his childhood and what his mom told him.

"In the early days, the family had no money for fancy burials. All they did was wrap their kin in cloth or put 'em in a bag and lay them to rest."

Frank was puzzled. "How do you know who's buried where?" he asked.

"You don't. Nobody kept records, or if they did, they're long gone."

"What about those with markers?" Bull chimed in.

"The one on the left is my great-great-great-grandfather. He fought the battle of Bunker Hill. Next to him is his grandson, Colonel Lawrence Allen. He commanded the 64TH North Carolina Regiment in the Civil War. The other is John, another grandson who fought in the Civil War. My mom said, 'The family put up markers because these men were heroes and the family was proud.' It took sacrifice to buy fancy headstones in those days, but that's what they did for these three."

CHAPTER SIXTY-ONE

"Your parents died a few years ago. Where are they buried?" Frank asked.

"Cremated. That's what they put in their will. I felt real bad about it, but...like it or not, I had to honor it."

"What's in your will?" Bull asked.

"My spot is over there," Jim replied, pointing to a large pine tree, fifty feet away. "I chose that shaded spot because it overlooks the entire farm. I'd like to keep an eye on what's going on."

"Why so far from your ancestors?" Bull wanted to know.

Jim seemed flustered by the question. He looked at the brown leaves on the ground and found it hard to reply.

"Well...I...I don't belong in the family plot. I've put a blot on the Allen name."

"C'mon, Doc!" Frank exclaimed, "how can you be so hard on yourself? And for no reason!"

"No reason!" Jim replied, "look at those three markers! Look at my ancestors! They were people who fought! People who were willing to sacrifice their lives for what they believed in. Look at me! I believed in my work, but I let it go down the drain without putting up a smidgen of a fight!"

Dr. Allen's eyes brimmed with tears as he felt a wave of frustration wash over him. He was the black sheep in the family and he always would be...unless his name could be cleared. Bull shook his head. He lowered himself to the ground, his back against the bark of a sturdy pine.

"Sit," he said firmly. "Let's talk."

Frank and Jim chose a tree. They all sat facing one another. Bull looked up at swaying treetops, gathering his thoughts.

"Jim," he began. "I've said it before, and I must say it again. When I finish explaining everything, you will be able to fight back if you want to. It's not too late to right some wrongs."

"With all due respect to you, Bull, I find that hard to believe."

"You find it hard to believe now, but by the end of the week, you will understand exactly what happened. Then you will see how you can fight back."

Jim pulled his knees up, consulted his fingernails, and decided on frankness.

"After all these years, I don't believe there's a thing I can do. And even if I could, I'd be fighting the same people who put me in this position. They are still out there, as strong and as powerful as ever. But if you show me a way, I'd give it a try."

"Fair enough," Bull replied. "Let's talk more about the missing data. It will show how, once again, the university and Dow joined together to destroy you. The data was missing in 1977 when Marlar died. Three years later, on February 1, 1980, Dow's attorneys issued subpoenas demanding data from the 500 study. You gave them everything, but they wanted more. They wanted all the raw data. Dow's attorneys kept pounding away without let-up. They decided to ask Dr. Androtti about it and subpoenaed her. She told Aberg, who was supposedly acting on her behalf, that there was no missing data, that pre-experimental platelet counts had never been done. Her remarks caused a monumental explosion to say the least. If her statement was true, it would have meant that the data in the published paper had been falsified, that the entire study was a fraud. Your reputation was at stake. Aberg carried this information to the chancellor and the dean called you in. You pointed to the published paper. The data was there. You explained that Rickey Marlar had gathered that data, put it together in final form, and included it in the paper as it was being prepared for publication. Dean Smith appointed a committee to investigate. They examined everything and talked with everybody who had anything to do with that study. They reported back to the dean on September 26, 1980."

"I was long gone by then," Jim said.

"I know," Bull replied, "but the committee reported that the authors of the paper agreed, the conclusions of the study were valid. All of the researchers, including Androtti, agreed with the findings. The committee recommended that no further action be taken to alert either the journal editor or the public with regard to concerns about the possible lack of authenticity of some of the data."

"What still bothers me," Frank said as he held the stem of a leaf and twirled it between his fingers, "is what the chancellor did in spite of the recommendations."

"I'll buy that," Bull said. "I have two taped interviews. One from Dean Smith and the other from Chancellor Shain. Smith said he followed the recommendation and took no further action. When the chancellor was asked why he didn't abide by the committee's recommendation, he said he was in China and he claimed that the vice chancellor, the dean, and the legal staff handled most of the administrative responsibilities. Nevertheless, he was told that the letter to the EPA was inaccurate and damaging to the 500 study. And when one of my contacts called and told me he found a copy of that letter in the university's archives and that the signature

CHAPTER SIXTY-ONE

was that of the chancellor and not the vice chancellor or someone from legal affairs, that was clear evidence as to who out to do Dr. Allen in."

Jim sat spellbound as the story unfolded. He leaned his head back against the tree and looked upward. Bull saw the look on his face and knew he was angry. Bull wanted him to be angry, to be charged up. He wanted him to fight.

Bull continued, "I had information from Dr. Androtti that the university attorney had drafted the letter for Shain and gave it to the chancellor and John Cartwright for review. Androtti pointed out that paragraph three was not correct and had to be changed so as not to raise doubts about the conclusions of the study. She also pointed out that the committee had no doubts about the validity of the study, and even though Shain admitted that the committee had a strong reputation for objectivity and integrity, he had not followed their recommendation."

"Why didn't Shain follow the committee's advice and leave well enough alone?" Jim asked.

"It's obvious. By sending that damaging letter to the EPA and to Kirkland and Ellis, Dow's attorneys, he was siding with your enemies. Imagine! Sending that to your enemies!"

"How does anyone fight the chancellor, someone with all that power?"

"It's hard," Bull replied. "Look at what happened when his letter arrived at the local newspapers in March 1981. Those envelopes had no return address other than a Washington, DC postmark. And it made headlines, remember? 'Ex-UW prof's research in doubt.' The article tore into you! Bad-mouthed your work! Dow had additional ammunition, and they used it against you at the EPA hearings. It was one more bomb used to destroy you. The hypocrisy of the whole thing really got to me," Bull went on, all fired up. "The newspapers reported that the university officials were puzzled over who had mailed copies of the documents to the media in plain white envelopes with no return address other than a Washington, DC postmark."

"It must have been Dow's attorneys," Jim said, "Kirkland and Ellis were in DC."

"I'd bet on it," Bull replied. "But picture a university official, whoever that was, talkin' on the phone to the *Capital Times* reporter, scratchin' his head and sayin', 'I'm puzzled. I'm truly puzzled. I wonder who could have sent those letters to your paper.' He surely knew that the information was sent to Dow's attorneys in DC, so why all the puzzlement? What a lot of bull."

"Too bad the reporter didn't mention names," Frank said.

"Too bad," Bull agreed. "The newspaper only said 'university officials.'"

"It makes my blood boil, knowing the chancellor took it upon himself to create a commotion about the missing data," Jim said.

"What about Androtti?" Bull asked. "Why did she say what she said in the first place? She started the whole thing."

"I don't know," Jim replied. "But if I had to make a guess, I'd look at all the events swirling around her: people invading our lab and doing audits, me being convicted and forced to resign, the students left high and dry wondering if they would finish their training, wondering if they would get their Ph.D.s, Dow's attorneys clamoring for all of the data, the matter being argued in court, the ongoing EPA hearings and then Androtti being handed a subpoena telling her she had to testify. The stress must have been overwhelming and unbearable. She may not have known or may not have remembered that Rickey Marlar had arranged for platelet counts as reported in the published paper. But we'll never know why she did what she did."

"Doc!" Frank asked, "would you explain something? When Marlar died, you knew that pre-experimental data was missing from the 500 dioxin study. When Burek and Bell came to the university, Dow's lawyers had given them different data from the same experiment. Why didn't you know it too was missing at the time you found the pre-experiment platelet data missing?"

"That's because all data put into the paper for publication had to be checked. Pre-experimental went into the paper and on checking, it was found missing. The information Dow's attorneys gave Burek and Bell was not going into the paper and therefore was not checked for. Nobody knew it was missing."

"Jim," Bull said, "Christie asked me to remind you about your clinic. It's one-twenty."

"We better get back," Jim replied. "I told my son, Rob, I'd relieve him for a few hours. He had things to do. I should be done by four or four-thirty. Would you like to come along? You can stroll around Weaverville and see the town."

"I'd like that," Bull said.

"Ditto," Frank said, raising himself from the ground.

SIXTY-TWO

The beef Wellington was a rousing success. Christie left the dirty dishes on the dining room table and followed the others into the dining room. They sat quietly on tan leather chairs, enjoying the satisfaction of a hearty meal. The warmth of the crackling fire added to their contentment. Andirons in the fireplace held three glowing logs with yellow flames reaching up to the bright red glow at the periphery. Frank turned his head to Christie, who was resting her stocking feet on a wooden coffee table.

"I'm stuffed," he said. "That was the best meal I've ever had."

"Glad you liked it," she replied. "The butcher at Ingles had to order that beef special. It took an extra day getting here, but it was worth waiting for."

Bull sat next to Jim on the other side of the coffee table, enjoying the warmth of the fire.

"That's a beautiful hearth," he said. "Those colorful stones give it a special look."

"Jim's folks had it built when they remodeled the house," Christie said.

"What about that clock on the shelf, is it an antique?" Bull asked.

"Probably. It's been in the family for ages. So has that Santa Claus standing next to his sleigh and reindeer."

Bull glanced at Jim and nudged him with his elbow.

"You are dozing off," he said.

Jim opened his eyes.

"I always do in front of a fireplace."

"I think we're ready for bed," Bull replied, "maybe we should call it a night."

Although Jim was sleepy, the thought of learning more about his downfall gnawed at him.

"Let's talk a bit," he said, pulling himself into an upright position.

"I'd like that too," Christie said, "but before we talk about Jim, I'd like to ask Frank a question about the millions of dollars he and his group handed out for so many years."

"What would you like to know?" Frank asked.

"How did it feel giving away all that money?"

"I loved it! It felt good helping those kids. There were so many. But when the money ran out, I got depressed. Bull called one day when I was drunk. Ask him."

Bull nodded. "Frank drowned his sorrows in Bushmills Irish whiskey. It was his tranquilizer. But he should've been happy thinkin' about all the kids he helped. Did you know he was in the rose garden when President Clinton signed a piece of legislation that helped some of the kids?"

"Frank!" Christie exclaimed. "You never told me about that!"

"Well," Frank replied sheepishly, "for me, that was one of our finest accomplishments. When I saw one of our spina bifida kids sitting next to our president, watching him sign that bill into law, I cried. For the first time in our nation's history, the children of veterans received benefits for a birth defect resulting from their dad's military service. The National Academy of Sciences found a connection between spina bifida and Agent Orange. And there wasn't a damn thing the VA could do about it. But I still get mad when I think about all the money running out and all the kids out there who still need help. I'd rather not talk about it anymore."

Christie was sorry she had raised the question.

"Ya know," Bull said. "I think we are all pooped and I'd like to hit the sack and get some shut-eye."

"Mind if I ask one question?" Jim said. "It's been on my mind for years."

"Okay."

"If the family had mortgaged everything and if I had hired a different lawyer, do you think the outcome would've been any different?"

Bull folded his hands in his lap and looked at the coffee table reflectively.

"I don't know," he said, "you were being hammered on two separate fronts. One attack was aimed at destroying you as a person. It made you out to be a thief. The other assault destroyed your reputation. From then on, your publications were seen at best...as highly questionable. If you had a different lawyer, and if you had not been convicted, your enemies may still have discredited your work. It's impossible to say what would have happened. But since you've raised the question, let's take a deeper look at it. Let's start with the grand jury proceedings. I wanted proof that you told them about swapping money. With your permission, my contact tried every which way to get a copy of your testimony. It was refused. An appeal was denied. The letter from Justice talked about the secrecy of grand jury proceedings."

CHAPTER SIXTY-TWO

"Why did you want Jim's testimony?" Christie asked.

"To get all the facts. I was amazed when I learned that the grand jury never handed down an indictment, never handed down anything. I wondered why and reasoned that if the grand jury believed that Jim took money from one pot and put it back from another, they may have concluded there was no theft. And if this was their conclusion, they would not have handed down an indictment. They may have found Jim innocent. But before the grand jury had a chance to hand down a finding, the U.S. Attorney and Jim's lawyer reached a plea bargain. My contact was confused. He could not understand why Jim's lawyer agreed to a plea bargain without waiting for the grand jury's decision. My contact wanted to know if this was common practice. So he put the question to Frank Tuerkheimer, the U.S. Attorney in charge of the case. Tuerkheimer said it was standard practice to prosecute someone who had not been indicted by a grand jury. He claimed that putting the money back was irrelevant to the case. I sent Jim a copy of Tuerkheimer's letter. Jim disagreed with it and pointed out that swapping money should have been the basis for his defense. Jim called it mens rea and said it demonstrated he had no criminal intent to steal federal funds."

"Damn right!" Jim chimed in. He was no longer drowsy. "I worked my butt off to get a law degree and one thing I learned was...there has to be intent before one could be convicted of theft. When I studied law, I saw how Kessler had dropped the ball. I was just plain stupid about law and accepted what he told me. I paid him $15,000 for a job that I could have done no worse if I had been my own attorney."

"I checked up on Kessler," Bull said. "He graduated from the University of Wisconsin Law School and was admitted to the bar in 1975. He practiced corporate, business, tax, and high technology law. Never criminal law. And yet even though he didn't practice criminal law, I have a letter showing that he and the U.S. Attorney signed off on a plea agreement in a criminal case."

"I remember that! You sent me a copy!" Jim exclaimed. "Thinking about it still riles me up. I knew nothing about that plea bargain until late in the game."

"It seemed important to know if Robins had taken part in the plea agreement since he was experienced in criminal law," Bull explained, "and from the information we had, Robins never participated. His signature was not on the agreement. My contact mailed a letter to Kessler and Robins with two attachments—the plea agreement and the allegations Jim made against

Kessler. Kessler didn't reply, but Robins did. He denied all allegations and claimed that with the passage of time, Jim's recollections had been blurred."

Jim looked at the logs in the fireplace. The small flames were struggling to stay alive. He shook his head with a feeling of raw anger and remained silent as he rose, stepped onto the hearth, picked up a fresh log, and placed it on the dying embers. He stood there and watched as tiny flames licked at their new salvation. Jim stepped back and lowered himself into his chair.

"Robins knew Jim's story was being told in a book," Bull went on, "and he threatened a suit should he or Kessler be libeled."

"Would he have a case?" Frank asked.

"I don't know," Bull replied. "But since Robins made the threat, it seemed best to get copies of Jim's records from Kessler so we could see what he had on file. Their records could have told the full story. Jim asked Kessler and Robins to cooperate with my contact, and gave permission for us to get his records. After much effort, Kessler sent him a reply saying, 'The files had been disposed of in November 1996.'"

"How could they sue?" Christie asked. "Without records, it's their word against the author of the book."

"Anybody can sue," Bull replied, "but we found someone who knows a lot. And he wants to talk. His name is Ed Krill."

"Ed Krill!" Jim exclaimed. "He was the university's attorney. What does he know about it?"

"It's late, and we're all tired," Bull replied, "let's pick up on it in the morning."

Jim reluctantly picked himself up. Frank and Bull were already climbing the wide wooden staircase to the loft. Christie stood up and took her husband's hand. She gave it a squeeze and saw that faraway look in his eyes. She knew he was thinking the kind of thinking he used to do years ago when laying out plans for a research project. She wondered what it was he had in mind.

SIXTY-THREE

On again, off again lights on the Christmas tree threw an eerie glow into the living room. The only sound was the ticking of the clock on the shelf above the hearth. The minute hand moved straight down. It was 5:30 a.m. and everybody was sleeping.

Jim was on his side on one side of a king-sized bed, his head on a large white pillow. A checkerboard red and blue quilt covered him from chin to his toes. His chest moved up and down, slow and easy. Suddenly, his breathing quickened. Rapid eye movements beneath his closed lids were followed by beads of perspiration gathering on his forehead. He began to thrash about. Moans of desperation broke the silence. Swearing became profuse, breathing more rapid. His heart raced. He flung himself into a sitting position, his arms flailing in the air. A shrill horrifying scream bounced off walls into the entire house. In seconds, Christie wrapped her arms around him, held him close, and Jim opened his eyes, not yet fully awake.

"Everything's fine, everything's fine," she said, "it's just a bad dream. Relax. Relax."

Bull and Frank popped into the room bare-chested, wearing only the lower part of their pajamas. Christie's hand waved them away.

Two hours later, as the sun started its climb above the distant horizon, they were all on the deck in pajamas, robes, and slippers. They sat around the picnic table sipping Irish Crème coffee.

"You scared the hell out of us," Frank said. "What were ya dreamin' about?"

"I've had that dream before," Jim replied. "I'm in a rowboat...no oars. Water is rocking the boat, and suddenly, I'm thrown overboard. I'm thrashing about trying to swim."

"You're a psychiatric nurse, Christie," Bull said, "what's it mean?"

"It's a Post-Traumatic Stress Disorder. It started with all the trouble, and it's gotten worse lately because his feelings have been stirred up by all the talking."

"Gee...I'm sorry," Bull replied, "maybe we oughta call it quits for a while."

"No!" Jim exclaimed. "We must go on."

"I agree," Frank said, reaching for the coffee pot in the middle of the table. "Let's get it all out. There is no point in putting it off."

Bull put his cup down. "Okay," he said, pushing his chair back, stretching his legs under the table and crossing his ankles. "But before we go on, any questions?"

"Yes," Christie replied, putting her cup down and fingering her robe tight to her neck. "From what you've learned, was there a way for Jim's lawyers to get him off scot free?"

Bull did not immediately reply. He gazed at a tall pine tree near the barn. A gray, bushy-tailed squirrel was scrambling up the tree, stopping momentarily and jerking its head from side to side. It kept on going, scooted up higher, and disappeared into a hole. As Bull watched, Christie's question bounced around in his head.

"Well..." he finally said, "instead of saying yes or no, let me tell you what I've learned. You be the judge. When Jim first talked about having a pot of money that belonged to him to do with as he pleased, I frankly didn't believe it. That is why I tried to get a copy of his grand jury testimony. I wanted to see if he told the jury the same thing. Unfortunately, Justice would not turn it over. But it was important to see if Jim had the means to swap money. I checked with the university. My contact called August Hackbart, director of fiscal. He verified it. Jim received gift funds from the Food Research Institute and the university. It was his money to do with as he pleased. There were no strings attached. My contact called Dr. Androtti. She replied in writing and she confirmed the fact that Jim always grant-pooled, or swapped money as he called it. She told how everyone did the same thing and explained that it was a practical way of getting work done. She told about the spending frenzy when a grant was due to expire. No one wanted to give money back. She said that Jim was not the kind of person to steal. Dr. Androtti would have been a good witness before a jury. If I were a lawyer with this information, I would've deposed other professors to show that they too swapped money. It would have been easy to depose Walter Hargraves. He'd tell about the arrangement he had with Jim for spending the training grant money and replacing it later. He too would've made a good witness. There were other people I could have deposed. I believe a jury would have seen that Jim had no intent and did not steal government funds. He violated NIH rules and regulations, but there was no actual theft. Would this kind of defense have gotten Jim off scot free? We will never know."

Dr. Allen laced his hands under his chin and gazed at the pond in the distance. He remembered the gut feeling he had when his lawyer gave him advice.

CHAPTER SIXTY-THREE

"If I could only turn the clock back," he murmured to himself.

Christie took a deep breath and sighed.

She looked at Bull and said, "You made Jim's defense seem so simple. It's hard for me to understand why his attorneys didn't ask for a jury trial. Could his lawyers have been influenced by the university?"

"I found no evidence of that. But they were affiliated one way or another with the university's law school. My contact talked with Russ Cagle, the guy in charge of a general practice course. He said, 'Jim Robins taught a course in trial advocacy.' Kessler was a graduate of the law school, and Tuerkheimer was a full professor. But all of this proves nothing. His lawyers must have been doing what they thought was best under the circumstances. The thing that bothered me was what I found in Martindale-Hubbell. It's a listing of lawyers and the kind of law they practice. Kessler didn't practice criminal law, and yet he was heavily involved in Jim's case. Robins was also involved, and he had some experience in criminal law. But Jim needed a lawyer well versed in criminal law."

"You mentioned Ed Krill as a possible witness," Jim chimed in.

"He, in my opinion, is the smoking gun," Bull replied. "He was a university attorney and had a ringside seat to all the goings on. My contact found him in Washington, DC and took notes on their conversation. He was no longer with the university. When asked about Dr. Allen, his immediate reply was, 'I know a lot. It's a tragedy what they did to him...I think the penalty wasn't ever close to fitting the crime.... Krill talked about people making a buck, but he did not go into specifics. He ended his conversation by saying, 'Allen was just cannon fodder for the whole process.' Krill wanted to spill his guts, but he needed an okay from the university. He talked about the attorney-client privilege and gave my contact the phone number of Helen Madsen, a university attorney. He wanted a release from the university and from Jim so he'd be free to talk."

"I faxed him my okay right away," Jim said.

"But," Bull replied, "the university didn't. They wanted him to keep his mouth shut. A letter from David Ward, who was now chancellor, said, 'I am unable to accede to your request.' Since it was a state school, my contact appealed to Tommy Thompson, the governor. He also said no. What's interesting is the recent Supreme Court ruling regarding

White House lawyers. Since they are paid by the government, they were not considered President Clinton's personal attorneys and they had to testify before the grand jury. There was no attorney / client privilege, and it seems to me that it could apply to Ed Krill. He was paid by the state of Wisconsin. But it would take a good chunk of dough to pursue this in court. It's too bad. Krill could tell a lot. We would know more about people makin' a buck. We would know more about who was paying who. We would know if the chancellor treated Jim like other professors. Or if Jim was singled out. Shain is on record as saying, 'I was always consistent. We treated such cases severely. In every case, the faculty member resigned.'"

"That's not true!" Jim exclaimed, his voice filled with anger. "I remember the newspaper article about doctors Folkert Belzer and Fritz Bach. They did not resign! Belzer and Bach got letters of reprimand. It was like a slap on the wrist for both of 'em. And what about the rest of the medical school! They had over two hundred doctors! The reporter pointed to big time stuff. They were raking in millions! The newspaper hinted at the possibility of fraudulent billing for Medicare and Medicaid patients. It talked about bills for medical work that had never been done! Did any of those doctors go to jail? Did any of them get dragged into court? Did any of them get kicked out of the university? Did any of them have to start life over? Hell no! They got off scot free!"

"Could be," Bull agreed. "I found nothing to prove you wrong. I even tried to get records from Medicare, but they said the records had been destroyed."

Christie had been listening intently and suddenly seemed perplexed.

"I don't understand why Tuerkheimer was allowed to conduct an investigation against university doctors when he was a full professor at the law school," Christie said. "Isn't that a conflict of interest?"

"That question was put to Mr. Tuerkheimer, but he never answered. One of his letters told of four people going to prison, but none were doctors from the medical school."

"I remember the *Capital Times* article about the medical school," Christie said. "The thing that really stands out in my mind is the one statement that said, 'There were no criminal charges.' With so many doctors and so many things that were reported, it's amazing to me that nothing happened to any of them."

CHAPTER SIXTY-THREE

Frank shook his head. "I'm pissed," he said. "It's clear to me that Doc was treated differently from the others. Krill would've known that. The one man who knew the whole story had to keep his mouth shut. How can we get him to talk?"

"We'd have to go to court for that," Bull replied. "Where can we get a ton of money to hire a good lawyer?"

Christie stared at her husband with an unbelievable thought that started bouncing around in her head.

"Jim!" she exclaimed. "You've got a JD. Couldn't you take it on?"

"Me!" Jim replied.

No one said anything. They sat around the picnic table thinking about this sudden intriguing idea.

SIXTY-FOUR

Later that day, Bull, Frank, and Jim were sipping hot gourmet coffee and munching on cheese Danish in front of the Mountain Java Coffee Shop in Black Mountain, North Carolina. They sat in ornamental green metal chairs around a matching circular table beneath a green umbrella.

It was early morning, and the town was in a festive mood. People strolling by the coffee shop could not keep their eyes off of the three men.

"Do you know the one in army-green fatigues?" a lady asked her friend.

"Never saw him before," the friend replied. "What do you make of that other one?"

"He's something else. Never saw anyone dressed in black like that. Wonder how he lost his ear."

The two women quickly blended into the crowd of happy holiday shoppers who crowded the cobblestone street. It was aglow with banners stretching from one side of the street to the other. One banner held pictures of Santa Claus, his sleigh, and reindeer. Another, a night scene of a boy and girl sitting on a stairway, eyes riveted on a fireplace, waiting for Santa to come down.

Green wreaths laced with tiny white lights clung to telephone poles on both sides of the street. Shops were open, ablaze with lights. Small Christmas trees with colorful ornamental displays stood in front of every shop.

The street had barricades on both sides. Traffic was prohibited. People strolled in the middle of the street, arm in arm, some on sidewalks, eating and talking. Others stopped and stood before windows, admiring beautiful Christmas displays. A group of children and adult Christmas carolers filled the air with song. An elderly man with baggy clothes, colorful paint on his face, and a long black beard stood behind the children strumming a guitar.

"That was good," Frank said, smacking his lips.

Bull put his cup down. "More coffee or Danish?" he asked.

"I've had my fill," Frank said.

"No more for me," said Jim, shaking his head.

CHAPTER SIXTY-FOUR

"Feels good just sitting here," Frank said. "I'm glad we came. It's a nice, relaxing place. But I can't get Christie's idea out of my mind, Doc. Being your own lawyer, getting Krill to talk. That grabs me."

"It would be quite a challenge," Bull said. "You never practiced law, but the best way to start is to jump right in. Might be fun. It's better than sittin' around and thinkin' about the past."

"True," Jim agreed. "I'd have time, now that Rob is out of school. He could take over the clinic. But being my own lawyer is intimidating. I wouldn't know where to start."

"You could get help," Bull replied. "It's a way of fighting back after all these years. Once I tell you everything, you will know what to do to restore your good name and your reputation."

Jim was intrigued by what Bull said, but down deep, he was afraid.

"I'd love that," he said, "but I am getting older. What you suggest could take years."

"Well...think about it," Bull replied. "See how you feel after we're through talking. Right now, I'd like you to understand how your enemies destroyed your reputation."

Frank leaned over and put his hand reassuringly on Jim's shoulder.

"The story will make you mad as hell, Doc. Like it did me."

Jim looked at Bull and nodded.

"Go ahead. Fill me in," he said.

Bull inched his chair back and crossed one leg over the other.

"Okay," he said. "let's talk about PCBs. You know that Dr. Kociba was one of Dow's scientists. Well, he started a little fire on May 8, 1978, in a letter to Cartwright. He claimed he found high amounts of PCBs in tissues from monkeys in the 500 ppt dioxin study. This claim surfaced two weeks after you published your findings in the Federal Register and six weeks after you appeared on the Bill Kurtis TV documentary where you told the world that dioxin was deadly. But as we now know, Kociba's claim was hogwash. Nearly all of the tissues Kociba talked about had nothing to do with the monkey study. Nevertheless, it's important to read Kociba's letter carefully. He said, 'It was presumed some of these samples were collected from monkeys.' Do you see? He knew he couldn't say for sure that the tissue slides were from monkeys, so he used the word presumed."

Jim saw how dumb he had been, how that one word had escaped his attention. He grimaced and slowly shook his head at his own stupidity. Bull knew Jim understood.

"In August 1978," Bull went on, "three months after Kociba ignited that fire, Kathryn Anderson moved into your lab, did her thing, and moved out in October '78. When you started the 25 study one month later, in November 1978, Dow knew the 50 study was going well and that you were getting closer to the truth about dioxin. It was then that plans were made to throw more wood on the fire. One month later, in December, Dr. Spencer moved in and did an audit on Dow's rat study, and in January, he came to your lab and did an audit on your rat study. And it's important to remember that Spencer had nothing to do with your monkey study. Nothing whatsoever! He only did a rat study! Remember that! And I'll show you what he said when he testified in court. But before doing that, I want you to follow a trail."

Jim sat spellbound, looking at Bull straight in the eye. Bull chose his words carefully. He wanted to paint a clear picture.

"On February 28, 1979, the EPA banned 2,4,5-T and Silvex. Two weeks later, you gave a talk in New Orleans on the 50 ppt dioxin monkey study. Five days later, you were interviewed by CBS TV and talked about your findings. On March, 20, 1979, the day you gave your interview, Dow prepared a report on your activities. It proves they kept tabs on you. This report went to Dow scientists and Dow's attorneys. It was then that the PCB claim, started by Kociba, began to move forward. On March 25, 1979, five days after Dow reported on your activities, Drs. Burek and Bell suddenly showed up at the university. Their visit had been agreed upon by attorneys for Dow, the university, and the U.S. government. They moved into Aberg's office, took your 500 study, and fanned the flames of the PCB issue Kociba had started. They wanted you to prove that the monkeys had not been pretreated with PCBs. This demand had nothing to do with your 500 study. It was part of Dow's overall strategy to destroy your reputation. This report bothered me. I hired two independent professionals to evaluate the Burek and Bell report. One had a DVM degree and the other was an MD, PhD researcher, board certified in pathology. I gave each one a copy of the 500 study publication and a copy of the Burek and Bell Report. They both agreed with your findings and pointed out that Burek and Bell talked about things that had nothing to do with your research, nothing to do with your monkey study. Burek and Bell ignored blood findings, including the fact that the monkeys hemorrhaged to death. As far as I'm concerned, the Burek and Bell report was pieced together to go along with Kociba's letter and with what Spencer testified to in court. Each of these

CHAPTER SIXTY-FOUR

men were like land mines, linked together and put into the ground. Dow was getting ready to trigger the switch and blow you sky high."

Dr. Allen stroked his chin and contemplated the chain of events that Dow had set in motion.

"You said there was something I could do to right this wrong, right?" Jim asked.

"That's what I said," Bull replied as he glanced at a group of carolers across the street singing "Silent Night" in front of Howard's Antique Shop.

"It's beginning to get dark," Frank said, "how about heading back?"

"Let's do that," Jim said, "I don't like driving when it's dark."

"We can talk along the way," Bull said.

In twenty-five minutes, the red Toyota pick-up truck was on the highway heading back to Mars Hill. Bull sat up front in the cab. Frank was in the back gazing at the bumper-to-bumper traffic around him.

"I'll make a deal with you, Jim," Bull said.

"What kind of deal?"

"If you agree to be your own lawyer, I'll get someone to lend you a hand. But you must start now."

"It can't hurt to try. Where do I start?"

"You once told me about a former colleague who talked to Charles Kessler about expunging your criminal records, right?"

"It was Dr. Nordstrom, back in...ninety-five or ninety-six. Kessler told her the records were in storage. She said he did not seem interested in pursuing the case."

"Let's start there. Fight to get your records expunged. I'll make a call when we get back. By tomorrow, you will know what to do."

Jim liked it. The idea of fighting back gave him a jolt of something he had never before experienced.

"Once I do that," he said, "what about this PCB baloney that Dow shoved down my throat?"

"Before Frank and I leave, you might know what to do about that too. Win or lose, you'll at least have a chance to give it your best shot."

SIXTY-FIVE

December 22, 1998. It was 8:00 a.m. when the red Toyota pick-up turned onto the Weaverville exit ramp. Frank found the ride smooth as he sat with his back against the rear window of the cab, knees drawn up. But as the truck neared the mall and bumped its way up into the parking lot, Frank quickly put both palms flush to the floor to hold himself steady until the Toyota rolled to a stop.

"This is it," Jim said.

Frank hopped down from the back and looked up at the sign: "Weaverville Animal Clinic."

"Nice place, Doc," Frank said.

The clinic was in a low, red brick building, snugly tucked away between the Beauty Barn to the left and Poppy's Kitchen on the right. Four large windows allowed early morning rays of sunshine into the waiting room, where chrome chairs with padded seats stood against a wall. The aluminum-framed glass door stood four feet to right of the windows and was held firm to the spot by a red brick wall.

"Nice," Bull said. "A fax from my guy ought to be here. When he said he'd get it done, it's as good as done."

Bull and Frank followed Jim, who fingered his key into the lock. They went inside, and the door slowly closed behind them. To the right was the reception area, separated from the waiting room by a rectangular open space in a wood-paneled wall. A clipboard with a sign-in sheet and a pencil lay on one end of a white countertop. Jim poked his head into the space, reached down, and snatched two sheets of paper from the back end of a fax machine on a desk.

"They're here," Jim said, handing them to Bull.

Bull glanced at the sheets, nodded his approval, and handed them back.

"This could help you get your records expunged," he said.

Jim dropped into a waiting room chair. Bull and Frank stood near, their backs against the paneled wall, watching Jim finger each line as he went down the page.

CHAPTER SIXTY-FIVE

Dear Larry:

The attached form has to be signed and dated by Dr. Allen.
Our friend said it was best to make the request pro hoc vice and pro se. This means that Dr. Allen is asking the court for permission to act as an attorney on his own behalf in the State of Wisconsin even though he doesn't have a license to practice law.

The court could say no to pro hoc vice. He therefore suggested that the request also include the words pro se. Since anyone can represent himself even though not a lawyer, Dr. Allen can still bring his case to court.

He has to mail the form to:

> *Joseph W. Skupmiewitz, Clerk*
> *U.S. District Court, Western District of Wisconsin*
> *120 N. Henry Street*
> *Room 320*
> *Madison, WI 53703*

The guys expect you back soon. Don't forget the Christmas party. We've got a lot of VIPs coming. Bring Frank along. Don't let him say no.

> *in re: Expungement of Records*
> *In and for the U.S. District Court, Case No. 79-CR-71*
> *Western District of Wisconsin*
> *Request to Admit Pro Hoc Vice*

NOW COMES the undersigned counsel, James Allen, and requests this Honorable Court to admit him Pro Hoc Vice before this Court for the purpose of expungement of criminal records and to represent himself Pro Se.

The undersigned was convicted of four misdemeanor counts of theft totaling $892 on October 17, 1979, placed on six months probation and fined a total of

$4,000 by the Honorable James E. Doyle. This was the first and only offense ever charged against the undersigned. Since that conviction, the undersigned has demonstrated an exemplary lifestyle and would appreciate the opportunity of presenting his case before the Court.

Dr. Allen holds a MS degree, University of Tennessee, DVM degree, University of Georgia, PhD, University of Wisconsin, and a Juris Doctor, William Howard Taft University, Fountain Valley, California.

*James Allen
Weaverville Animal Clinic
9 Tri City Plaza
Weaverville, NC 28787*

Dr. Allen's spirit soared, but he was nervous.

"Seems easy," he said, "but what do I do if the court gives me permission to go ahead? I don't know beans about expunging records."

Bull knew Jim needed support.

"My friend will spoon-feed you all the way."

Frank too knew that Doc had to be nudged along.

"You'll like bein' your own lawyer," he said, "especially if you force them to retract the false statements they made against you."

Dr. Allen felt overwhelmed at the thought of going into court and doing battle.

"Sure, I have a law degree. But that's a far cry from going into court and getting something done."

"We'll talk more about that later," Bull replied.

Bull wanted his friend to calmly think about being his own lawyer and to allow the idea to settle in.

"Let's finish up with PCBs before we call it a day," Bull said.

"I'll give Dave Metcalf a call," Jim replied. "I promised."

"Fine. I like Dave," Bull agreed.

CHAPTER SIXTY-FIVE

"We can meet him at that Supermart," Frank said. "I think he'll feed us. That's what he said."

In half an hour, Frank, Bull, and Jim pushed through the door of Ingles and headed for the café. Shoppers pushed carts and loaded up on groceries. Displays of red and green apples, pears, oranges, grapes, bananas, and other fresh fruit were nicely lit up by lights from the high ceiling. The enticing fragrance of cinnamon and apple permeated the air in the bakery section. Warm, freshly baked pies in clear plastic containers looked enticing as they lay stacked on a red-checkered, cloth-covered table.

Frank caught sight of a green striped shirt. It was Dave, his hand in the air. He smiled as the trio entered and eased into chairs around the table.

"Good morning, gentlemen," Dave said. "It's nice seeing you again."

Before anyone could acknowledge Dave's greeting, two young ladies in a store uniform appeared. One held a platter covered with Saran Wrap, paper plates, and a packet of plastic forks. She placed it daintily in the center of the table. The other held two cartons of Tropicana Pure Premium orange juice and four paper cups.

"I hope you like it," Dave said. "It's the best cheese in the store. The crackers are French Onion Snackwells and the grapes are seedless."

"Well...thank you," Jim said. "That's real nice of you."

Frank and Bull nodded in agreement. As they ate, Bull continued on, filling in Dave on information he had missed.

"We talked about people who tore Jim's research to shreds by claiming his tissues were contaminated with PCBs"

Dave nodded while contemplating that piece of information.

"It wasn't true, right?" Dave said.

"Right," Bull replied. "This was Dow's strategy. I will now show you how falsehoods were joined to other false statements, and it blew up into one loud bang, destroying Jim's reputation as a scientist."

Bull unzipped his leather jacket, reached into an inside pocket, slid out four folded sheets of paper, and laid them flat on the table in front of him.

"Stand up and crowd around me," he said, "I want to read this. But keep in mind that in January 1979, the EPA sent Dr. Spencer to Jim's lab to do a rat study audit, only a rat study. H had nothing to do with Jim's monkey study. Absolutely nothing! One month later, in February 1979, the EPA banned two of Dow's products because of public pressure. Dow went to court and demanded that the ban be lifted. On April 7, 1979, three months after Spencer did the rat study audit, he testified in the U.S. District Court in Flint, Michigan. Listen to what he said."

Q: Did you participate in the EPA audit of the Allen and Schantz laboratory?

A: Yes, I did.

Q: Did that audit involve review of the monkey study, which was the specific study being discussed in prior testimony?

A: No, it did not.

Q: To clarify matters, were there two studies being conducted by Drs. Allen and Schantz?

A: Yes, there were. There was a 50 ppt and a 500 ppt monkey study.

Q: Was there also a study on rats?

A: Yes, there was.

Q: Which study did you audit?

A: I audited the rat study.

Q: In your opinion, did the audit of the rat study indicate anything with respect to the monkey study?

A: Not to my knowledge.

Q: Dr. Spencer, have you heard prior testimony by Dr. Gehring that referred to PCB contamination with respect to this Allen and Schantz monkey study?

A: Yes, I have.

Q: Was any PCB contamination of the food used in the monkey study found?

A: Yes

Q: To clarify matters, you said there were two studies at different dose levels with monkeys.

A: That is true, yes.

Q: Now, with respect to the finding of high PCB contamination, was this found in the 500 ppt study?

A: Yes, it was.

"How could that man testify about monkeys when he audited rats?" Dave asked with obvious irritation in his voice.

CHAPTER SIXTY-FIVE

"I have no idea," Bull replied. "But he did testify. He talked as if he knew there was high PCB contamination in the monkey study even though he had nothing to do with that study. Read on."

Q: I would like to ask you if you have seen a copy of the letter I'm going to hand you.

A: Yes, I think I've seen a copy of this letter, and I have not read it as a matter of fact.

Q: Where did you see a copy of that letter?

A: I saw a copy of that letter approximately one week ago when I talked to Dr. Allen in Washington, DC.

Q: When you talked to...

A: Dr. Allen.

Q: Could you tell the court exactly what the letter...let's identify the letter.

A: It's a letter from Dow Chemical Company to Dr. John Cartwright.

Dr. Allen became incensed. "That's Kociba's letter, where Dow claimed my monkey tissues had high amounts of PCBs! How in the hell can Spencer say he saw a copy of that letter when he talked to me in DC? I wasn't in DC! I never met the man!"

"Nevertheless," Bull replied, "Spencer's false remarks were now linked to the Kociba letter and to the Burek and Bell report. Dow now had three false statements about high PCBs in monkey tissues. How do you like that for a strategy?"

Dave squinted his eyes, seemingly perplexed.

"I don't understand something," he said. "I'm not a lawyer, but when Spencer said he audited rats and then answered questions about monkeys, why didn't the other lawyer object?"

Bull smiled. "You may not be a lawyer, Dave, but you're right on the mark. My contact interviewed Spencer about that. He admitted he shouldn't have answered questions about monkeys. He also said the lawyers should have objected."

They resumed their seats. Dr. Allen speared a cube of cheddar and fingered a cracker.

"What about this business of seeing me in DC?" he asked.

"We caught him with his pants down on that one," Bull replied. "He gave my contact permission to tape record the interview on March 31, 1998. He was questioned about his claim that he saw you in DC—one week before he testified. That would've been on or before March 31, 1979. Spencer was certain it was you. He remembered you clearly. He described you as

363

having a beard and wearing a green tweed jacket. He said he could still see you with the Kociba letter in your hand. Spencer claimed you were in DC to see Pat Roberts, an EPA attorney. Soon after that interview, my contact faxed Spencer a photo of you. The back of the photo was dated April 1979. More importantly, he also faxed him a picture of you in the *Lodi Enterprise*, a newspaper in a town near Madison, Wisconsin. The date on the paper was May 3, 1979. Neither picture had a beard. And since he claimed he saw you with a beard about that time, he knew his statement was false. To top it off, Spencer was faxed a report that told of former colleagues who had known you for years. None of them ever saw you with a beard."

Dr. Allen was outraged, and his voice rose. "Why did he say it?"

"I don't know," Bull replied. "I only know what his testimony managed to do. It created an official record tying you to the Kociba letter and thus to the idea that Dow had found high PCBs in your monkey tissues. But Spencer knew differently. I've got a letter from that man. It shows he knew the tissues sent to Dow may not have been from the 500 study. But he testified anyhow, and Dow must have loved his testimony. In my opinion, it was part of an overall Dow strategy to build a firestorm about PCB contamination in the 500 ppt dioxin study. It destroyed the study and Jim's reputation as a scientist."

Dave's outrage did not let up.

"What did Spencer have to gain?" he asked.

"Don't know," Bull replied, "but Dow gained a lot when the EPA ban was lifted."

Dr. Allen sat subdued, as if the fatal blow had just been delivered.

"What did Spencer say," Jim asked, "when he learned he didn't see me in DC?"

Bull drummed his fingers on the table as he thought about Spencer's remark on tape.

"Spencer said he must've confused you with someone else," Bull replied.

Frank was just as pissed now as he had been when he first heard the story.

"Spencer never dreamed," Frank said, "you'd come up with photos of Doc showing he never had a beard. But when you did, that guy still had an answer. What a crock."

"He owned up to nothing," Bull replied. "In a more recent interview, he said and I quote, 'I was an innocent little player in the whole thing.' He denied knowing what was going on. But Dow's strategy moved on. Let me show you something else."

Bull fingered two sheets of paper.

CHAPTER SIXTY-FIVE

"This is an affidavit signed by Dr. Kociba on April 18, 1980," Bull said, "notarized and filed in the U.S. District Court in Madison, Wisconsin. It's about PCBs, and it added to Dow's strategy. They wanted all of Jim's data, and Kociba claimed that Spencer went to Geneva, Switzerland, in February 1979 and gave the World Health Organization proof that Jim's monkeys were contaminated with PCBs. My contact faxed the affidavit to Spencer. He seemed outraged by Kociba's remarks and initially denied giving anything to WHO and denied ever seeing any data that told of high PCBs in monkey tissues. Four months later, he changed his story. He said he saw this data when Kociba gave him a box full of data. He again changed his story several weeks later and said he found the PCB data when he was in Kociba's lab and opened a drawer."

Dave vigorously shook his head.

"It's unbelievable," he said, "why did he keep changing his story?"

"I look at it this way," Bull replied. "When someone tells the truth, the story stays the same. Truth never changes."

Dr. Allen was steaming on the inside.

"Can you prove he changed his story?" he asked.

"Absolutely! My contact received permission to tape an interview with him and even encouraged him to submit a written statement. There are notes on the other statements and all of these documents speak for themselves. At one point, he frankly admitted that he never obtained copies of PCB data when he did a rat audit at Dow. When my contact confronted him with his testimony about Jim's monkey studies, he said, 'Why in the world was I talking about monkeys?' But his testimony about PCBs in monkey tissues contributed to Dow's strategy to discredit Jim."

"I have a question," Dave said. "Why was the World Health Organization mentioned? Who are they?"

Bull glanced at Dr. Allen and said, "Do you want to answer that Jim?"

Jim remembered being on one of the working groups for WHO, where he evaluated cancer-causing chemicals.

Heaving a long and heavy sigh, he said, "WHO is an agency of the United Nations. They help the world in attaining the highest possible levels of health. They disseminate information about diseases and environmental sanitation and publish scientific works. WHO would be interested in PCB information because they represent the worldwide scientific community."

Bull turned to Dave. "WHO also took a position on dioxin," he said. "We'll talk about that in the afternoon. But before we call it quits, I'd like to add one more thing about Spencer. This man said and I quote, 'I got sucked in with that statement about high PCBs.' My contact didn't ask what he meant by that, but he did say that Spencer was concerned about his reputation. Let's break for lunch."

Dave did not want his friends to leave.

"Where are you going?" he asked.

"I was thinking of heading home," Jim replied.

"How about my place?" Dave said. "I'm not far from the visitor's center. After lunch, we can sit on their verandah. They have nice wicker rocking chairs and...it's nice out."

"Don't you have to work?" Bull asked.

"My son must run the shop someday. I'm not going to live forever."

As the red Toyota pick-up rolled to a stop on Main Street, Frank had a fit of coughing. He felt chilly. He zipped up his brown leather jacket and held the fur collar tight to his neck. The coughing slowly subsided. Frank wondered if he was coming down with the flu or some kind of bronchial condition from a bug he had picked up. He sat with his back against the cab's rear window holding his fur collar tight to his neck.

SIXTY-SIX

That same day, at 1:30 p.m., Dave led the way up a wooden ramp of the Mars Hill Visitors Information Center. It was a two-story, red brick building with a white door and white wood trim around its upper and lower windows. The front verandah stretched the entire length of the building, its dark-green flooring and white wooden railing contrasting nicely. The pitched roof above the verandah was held in place by round, white-fluted columns. They added a touch of class to an already charming building.

Dave motioned for his friends to follow him toward one end of the verandah, where a grouping of four wicker rocking chairs stood empty. They sat facing one another.

Bull glanced across the street at a line of cars in front of the post office. Frank sucked on a mentholated cough drop. Jim couldn't get the idea of expunging his records out of his mind. Dave rocked up and back, enjoying his newfound freedom and new friends.

"Your wife's a good cook, Dave," Bull said.

"She's always been that way. Her recipes are hand-me-downs from mother to daughter. They go back a hundred years. Everything in this town is tradition."

"Sure is," Jim said, "my ancestors go back to the beginning of Mars Hill. That's why it's important for me to preserve the family farm and its land. It's a matter of pride in one's heritage. Once that's broken, it's impossible to mend."

"I know where you're comin' from, Doc," Frank said, tossing another lozenge into his mouth, "but pride in one's heritage be damned if powerful people gang up on you and make you look bad. You must fight back."

Bull gazed at cars and people across the street, going in and out of the post office. He wondered what he had to do to get Jim fired up, mad enough to he would want to kick butt, mad enough to take decisive action.

"Let's talk about PCBs again," Bull said. "But before we do, it's important to know what Dr. Spencer told my contact. It is downright amazing."

Dave stopped rocking. Resting his arms on the armrests of his rocker, he waited.

Bull began. "Spencer knew about Jim's discretionary account. He knew Jim swapped money. He knew that money had been put into that account by the university. He knew Jim had been given a raw deal. He said, and I quote, 'He got screwed royally because Dow put pressure on the university. They fund the university. That's the whole point, money talks. You think they wouldn't sacrifice Allen in a second?'"

Bull turned to Dave. "Whaddya think about that?"

"I think Spencer knew Dr. Allen was innocent," Dave replied, "and if he knew, so did others."

Frank nodded and said, "Like Ed Krill, who was forced to keep his mouth shut."

Dr. Allen leaned his head back, closed his eyes, and rocked up and back, thinking. He finally straightened up.

"It's the first time in...going on twenty years," he said, "that I've heard someone other than family say I was innocent, but what good does it do? I still have this thing hanging over my head. I've got a criminal record."

"Remember one thing," Bull replied, "if you expunge your records, there will be no criminal record. It will disappear."

Jim did not reply. Bull viewed his silence as an obstacle yet to be dealt with.

"I'd like t'toss out a question about WHO," Bull said. "Why would Kociba sign an affidavit saying Spencer gave PCB info to the World Health Organization?"

No one answered.

"Remember one thing," Bull went on, "Dow was using PCBs to destroy Jim's reputation, to make him out to be a fraud, to make his publications suspect, and if Dow could convince the world that the monkeys died from PCB contamination instead of dioxin, Jim's work wouldn't be worth a tinker's damn."

"Ah," Dave said, "the affidavit carried a story about PCBs. It gave the PCB idea a ring of truth even though it was hogwash. It also gave the WHO information that could be sent around the world. And if you kept that lie travelin' around long enough, it would be seen as truth."

"I said the same thing a year ago in a memo to your contact!" Jim exclaimed.

"I read it," Bull replied. "Then I saw the same thing in Kociba's letter and the same thing in the Burek and Bell report, and then in Spencer's testimony and again in Kociba's affidavit. That lie then went to WHO and from there to the scientific community around the world.

CHAPTER SIXTY-SIX

And my contact found a document showing that WHO sided with Dow when they said, '2,4,5-T with levels of less than 0.1 part per million of dioxin would probably not result in a human health hazard.'"

"Probably?" Dave asked. "Why did they hedge?"

"Because Italy, Sweden, and the Netherlands banned it totally," Bull explained.

"What about the US?" Jim asked.

"The US permitted its use, but a dioxin level was not given. And there's no doubt that Dow influenced this country's position on dioxin. They've got big bucks and can lobby their way into the political system any time they want."

"Lobby or not," Frank said, "Doc would have made a big dent in their bottom line if he could have finished his research. And they knew it."

"Too bad Dr. Allen pleaded guilty," Dave said.

"I was stupid," Jim replied.

The steady honk of a horn drew everyone's attention to the post office parking lot across the street. A white sedan wanted to park. But a dog with a flat black nose and a wrinkled forehead sat on its hindquarters in the middle of a parking space and refused to move. It was as if it was holding the space for its master.

"That's quite a pug," Jim said. "That car can honk all day. That dog will not move. It has guts. Something I didn't have back then and maybe I don't have even now."

"You dwell on it too much," said Bull. "You've let it get you down. I'll show you what Dow's lawyers did. And…if it gets you riled up, I mean mad as hell, you might want to get even. We've talked about a lot of things. Now look at how Dow's lawyers pulled it all together and clobbered you with it. They attacked your credibility by pointing to your guilty plea and your conviction. This threw a dark shadow over you as a person. Then they waved the Burek and Bell report in front of Judge Finch. They painted a picture showing your monkeys being fed PCBs, claiming your monkeys were diseased even before you started your experiment. They then threw Spencer's report into the pot and severely criticized your laboratory practices. They were extremely adept at dancing around the truth. They'd add a word here, a word there, and in an instant, they'd be roasting your hide. For example, instead of saying Spencer criticized your lab practices, they said severely criticized. Instead of saying used control animals, they said improperly used control animals. Instead of saying were not examined, they said not properly examined. They put a spin on everything. But Dow's attorneys could not have slammed into you so hard without Spencer's report. His report is outrageous, and I didn't understand it until a scientist explained it to me."

Dave's eyes were riveted on Bull as he explained.

"Spencer came to Jim's lab and did a GLP audit on rats. This type of audit is never done at universities. It applies only to companies who must register products before manufacturing and then selling them to the public. A GLP audit is done to safeguard public health. Universities don't make products. They do research. Therefore, Spencer should never have done a GLP audit in Jim's lab. Spencer knew that a GLP audit did not apply and still doesn't apply to any university. But he did it anyhow and admitted that Dow's attorneys used his report incorrectly. They took Spencer's report and other reports and used them as a club. They beat Jim over the head with it in front of the EPA's administrative law judge. The picture they painted was of a professor who was inept, a fraud, and morally corrupt."

Frank slid another mentholated cough drop into his mouth. Breathing in the menthol vapor felt good. Jim wondered if he could really do something after so many years. Dave rocked up and back, thinking about the injustice that had been perpetrated against his friend.

"It's not right for people to get away with that kind of stuff," Dave said.

"They'll get away with it if we let 'em," Bull replied. "I hate to see it happen, and my contact feels the same way. He sent Spencer a strong letter wanting to know who told him to go to the university to do a GLP audit, why he did it, and whether or not he ever did a GLP audit at any other university."

"What did he say?" Dave asked.

"He didn't answer all the questions," Bull replied, "but he did say that in his twenty-five years with the EPA, he never did a GLP audit at any other university. Isn't that amazing?"

Dave continued rocking, contemplating the latest revelation.

"Spencer's admission is interesting," Dave said. "This man comes across as someone who... down deep, wants to tell the truth."

"I think so," Bull said. "Spencer told the truth about Dow funding the university and how this put pressure on university officials who got rid of Jim. Dow's pressure really paid off,"

CHAPTER SIXTY-SIX

Bull went on. "The university even helped in closing down the EPA hearings. Look at Robert Aberg, the attorney who supposedly was representing Jim and the other researchers. He did two things. First, he wrote the EPA saying that Jim and all of his colleagues decided not to testify at the EPA hearings. He had the audacity to assure the EPA that Dr. Allen had struggled with this decision and only took this position because of the concern he had about jeopardizing the ongoing work of his colleagues and future research in this area. Then Aberg wrote another letter to Dow's attorneys, with a copy to the EPA. It was about data that Jim and his staff had promised to give Dow. Aberg said that all of the researchers changed their minds. Dow would get none of it. In essence, Aberg told the EPA that no one was going to cooperate with what had been agreed upon during the EPA hearings. This then allowed the EPA to close down the hearings. But Aberg's remarks about Jim and his colleagues were false. My contact proved it. Jim took a trip on April 20, 1980. Aberg's letters were dated April 16 and April 20, 1980. My contact confronted Aberg, showing him that at the time he claimed Jim voted, Jim was in California. Aberg then admitted that Jim didn't vote. He admitted using Jim's name in a letter to the EPA with a copy to Dow's attorneys. He admitted he was speaking for the university, which didn't want Jim or anybody else to testify. And neither did Dow. And it is important to remember that Jim was scheduled to testify in June. Aberg's letters went out in May. The timing was perfect."

"Androtti was also scheduled to testify," Jim said. "Did she?"

"Hell no," Bull replied. "I have a written statement from her saying the university was making decisions for her and everyone else. And it was Aberg who was again speaking for the university. No one ever voted or made decisions as Aberg had claimed," Bull went on, "I even have a letter from Dr. Dougherty, who was about to leave for DC to testify. He received a letter from the EPA telling him not to come. His name was removed from the witness list. Everything was on its way to being shut down. From here on, it was downhill all the way. The EPA hearings did shut down. For Dow Chemical, it was business as usual. But for Jim, it was not yet over."

Everyone was silent. Frank watched the pug across the street as it stood to one side of the parking stall, wagging its stubby tail at the driver of a black Model T Ford chugging its way into the spot. In less than a minute, the Model T backed out with the pug in the back seat, its front paws on the side window.

Dr. Allen was mad, wondering why a man like Aberg had allowed himself to be drawn into such shenanigans.

Dave was amazed at what had taken place, all designed to rid the world of a man and his research. But Dave was also troubled by Bull's last remark. He turned to Bull.

"What did you mean," he asked, "when you said it was not yet over for Dr. Allen? They destroyed his reputation, his work, and everything about him as a person. What was left? Did you expect them to beat him to death?"

"For a scientist like Jim," Bull replied, "dying would be easy. One last breath and it's over. But real death is being shunned by other scientists, being shunned by your peers, being rejected and looked down upon by people who had once looked up to you. That is death for a man like Jim."

"Is that where the World Health Organization came into it?" Dave asked.

"Possibly," Bull replied, "along with the VA and a company in McLean, Virginia, called JRB Associates. The VA hired this company to assess the worldwide literature, all the scientific studies on dioxin. And they did a pretty good job, except for a one sentence inserted in one of their manuals. JRB reported, 'The EPA found that monkeys used in studies by Dr. Allen had been exposed to PCBs in a previous experiment and the results of his dioxin experiments have not been accepted by the scientific community.' JRB used Spencer's testimony about high PCBs to bury Jim."

"Spencer's testimony wasn't a scientific study," Dave quickly pointed out. "Who told JRB to do that?"

"It took a long time to find out," Bull replied. "We couldn't find JRB. But my contact kept plugging away. He talked with Spencer about it because he said he had been a member of the VA Agent Orange Committee and knew that JRB was a fly-by-night company who did the job and then went out of business. Spencer also said the JRB four-line statement about PCBs had been false. For a long time, I believed JRB was gone forever. Until Frank called one day and told me that this fly-by-night company was part of Science Applications International Corporation, a multibillion dollar company that thrives on government contracts."

"Yeah," Frank said as he unwrapped another lozenge, "one of my guys found it in the minutes of a VA meeting."

CHAPTER SIXTY-SIX

"My contact jumped on it," Bull said. "He wrote Dr. Robert Beyster, the CEO of this company, and asked one question. He wanted to know if the company would issue a retraction and a public apology to Jim if that four-line statement was proven false. Beyster turned it over to Jack Friery, their corporate counsel, who seemed willing to investigate the matter. Friery waned more information, and we gave it to him. Friery then found Dr. Striegel, who had been in charge of JRB and who had been long gone from the company. He remembered the whole affair. He blamed the four-line insertion on the VA, saying they wanted it in the manual. Jack Friery then washed his hands of the whole affair. But my contact wasn't about to let him off the hook. He dashed off another letter to the CEO, pointing out that Friery refused to release Striegel's phone number and refused to say who it was at the VA that ordered Striegel to keep the four-line insertion in place. My contact then gave the CEO information that proved the four-liner to be not only a lie, but to be totally inappropriate to Public Law 96-151, the legislation that mandated the JRB study to start with. The legislation called for a scientific study. The four-liner was taken from Spencer's testimony, a legal proceeding. It had nothing to do with the scientific literature. When Friery did not reply, my contact dashed off another letter to the CEO and raised hell with the company. He pointed out that the false statement could not be brushed aside by pointing a finger at the VA. That same day, Friery faxed a reply. He refused to conduct any further investigation and claimed he could not release Striegel's phone number without his consent because of privacy laws in California. He also claimed he had no record regarding the identity of the VA official to whom the matter was referred twenty years ago. My contact didn't ask for a twenty-year-old record. He asked for a name. Striegel clearly remembered the incident, and he also remembered the phone call. Striegel knows who called, and he remembers that name! He has that name and probably told Friery!"

"Calm down," Dave said. "You're letting it get to you."

"Some things still get to me," Bull replied.

"At least we know it was the VA who put that statement into their own manual," said Allen.

"I would not like that to be the end of it," Bull replied. "I'm a Yogi Berra fan. And it ain't over till it's over. I'd like to see the ballgame with Beyster and Friery go into extra innings. My contact has some interesting plans for them."

"Plans?" Dave asked.

"Plans," Bull replied. "It depends on Jim. From what I'm told, he might be able, even at this late date, to go to court and try to force those bastards to retract that four-line statement and to issue a public apology."

"That would be something," Dave replied. "That would really be something."

SIXTY-SEVEN

December 23, 1998, two days before Christmas. Business was brisk at the Mars Hill Barber Shop. Dave Metcalf, although attending to his customers, was out of sorts. He didn't talk much and answered questions with one word answers. But when his new friends pushed through the door at high noon, his spirits soared.

"A cut and a styling," Dr. Allen said, "the way it used to be."

"Good thing you came at lunch time," Dave replied, waving Jim into a barber chair.

Bull and Frank seated themselves and watched Dave unfold a white sheet and put it in place. He worked a handle on the right side of the barber chair, lowering the back of the chair until Jim's head almost touched the sink. He turned on the faucet and fingered a bottle of shampoo and began lathering and massaging Jim's scalp. His fingers worked rapidly as water ran full force into the sink.

"Where's your son?" Frank asked as he leaned back and stretched his legs.

"He went to Ingles to pick up tuna subs. We normally close for lunch, but not for you. I enjoy talking with you."

"Ditto, Dave," Bull replied. "But we're taking the day off. This is a fun day."

"Fun day? What are you doing?" Dave asked as he worked a spray nozzle, washing lather out of Jim's hair into the sink.

"Jim's taking us to Gem Mountain."

"Nice place. One of my customers found a sapphire. Another found a ruby."

Bull was intrigued with the idea of striking it rich.

"Maybe we'll get lucky," Bull said.

Dave turned off the faucet, wrapped a towel around Dr. Allen's head, worked the long handle on the chair, and lifted Jim into a sitting position. Having draped a large towel around his shoulders, he removed the towel from his head, picked up a scissors and a comb, and began working at the back of his head.

"Can I ask a question?" Dave said.

"Sure," Bull replied.

"I've been thinking about what we talked about. Why not sue that billion-dollar company?"

Bull shrugged and was about to answer, but Jim jumped in.

"I'm not interested in money. All I want is a clean record, peace of mind, and to be forgiven for smearing the family name. But if lawyers wanted to sue for money, I would not object as long as they gave it to people who need it. Like Frank's guys and their families."

"Gee, Doc," Frank said, "if that ever happened, it would be a miracle. Our guys still need a foundation. I had my hopes up before, but it came to nothing."

Dave began snipping around the right ear and thinking about what had been said. He moved over to the other ear and looked at Dr. Allen.

Before proceeding with the trim, he said, "If you had money, isn't there something you'd like for yourself?"

Without a moment's hesitation, Jim said, "It's all wishful thinking, and it's not going to happen, but I'd sure like to hire good lawyers and sue every son-of-a-bitch who did me in. I don't know if I'd live long enough to see it all through, but I'd sure like to give it a try. If money came out of it, Frank's wish for a foundation could become a reality. At least something good would come out of all this."

Dave had never heard Dr. Allen swear before, but he understood the anger that had been festering for years.

"I'd like to see it happen," Dave said.

"It's a pipe dream," Jim replied, "but what else do I have? Even if I didn't win, I would enjoy draggin' them through the court and giving them a taste of the hell they gave me."

Dave put the scissors and comb back on the shelf, picked up a blow dryer and a brush and flicked on the switch on the dryer. It began purring. With brush in one hand and dryer in the other, Dave made rapid movements, shaping Jim's hair the way he remembered it years ago.

"It's good hearing you talk like that, Jim," Bull said. "You gotta get all fired up before you can do anything. You could easily prove they damaged you. You were blackballed from every kind of job."

CHAPTER SIXTY-SEVEN

"Tell me about it," Jim replied. "I couldn't get a job anywhere. Universities talked with me, but said no. Industries and all the governmental agencies wouldn't even talk to me. It's a good thing I had parents and a family farm."

"I'd like to ask another question," Dave said.

"Shoot," Bull replied.

"I know Dr. Allen's work was important. I know he made waves. But there must've been other people who did important work. Why did they pick on Dr. Allen?"

Bull lifted himself from the chair. His left foot had fallen asleep. He took a few steps, gently stamped his foot on the floor until the tingling was gone, and again took his seat.

"I'll answer that by first sayin' that no one, and I mean no one, did the kind of work Jim did. They couldn't. There were only two Biotron buildings in the world, and Jim had one of them. During the Vietnam War, the government told the world dioxin was safe. After the war, they said the same damn thing. Dow also pretended dioxin was safe. When Jim began to show how deadly dioxin was, both the government and Dow knew that sooner or later, Jim would find what they both already knew: that even in miniscule amounts, dioxin was deadly. As far as the government and Dow were concerned, Jim had a big mouth. He talked to reporters, was on TV, published his findings in journals and in the Federal Register, checked for dioxin in food, warned people about eating fish caught in the Great Lakes, was on committees, and consulted with foreign governments. I could go on and on. Jim was exposing the U.S. government and Dow for what they really were: evil people who placed money and power ahead of the health and welfare of the American people. The government and Dow had to protect their rear. They had to get rid of big mouth."

"Any other questions, Dave?" Bull asked.

"Will you be here for Christmas?"

"No. We're flying out tomorrow night."

"Will you be coming back?"

"I don't know. Jim and his wife offered to give Frank and me two free acres of land if we move here. But we both have things to do back home. Maybe some day."

Dave fingered the switch on the dryer. It went silent. He laid it flat on the shelf behind him, and with the brush in one hand, he began putting the finishing touches on Jim's hair. He was sorry to see Bull and Frank go. It was difficult for him to say good-bye. He had become fond of them.

"I hope you both come back," Dave said. "I like you, and I know the people of Mars Hill would like you. They would adopt you as their own. It's hard to find people who will stick by a friend and go all-out to help him. That's what both of you have done for Dr. Allen. He's lucky to have you as friends."

Dave held up a mirror in front and then in back of Jim's head. Although Jim appeared to be looking at a beautifully styled head of hair, his thoughts focused on what Dave had said. He was grateful for what Bull and Frank had done. It could never be repaid. And he knew that Bull and Frank wanted him to do something to right the wrongs of the past.

But he was still unsure as to what he could really do. It had happened so long ago, so long ago.

SIXTY-EIGHT

DECEMBER 24, 1998. "GOOD MORNING. HOW ARE YOU GUYS DOING?" JIM SAID, poking his head into the guest bedroom.

"After that trek on Gem Mountain," Frank replied, "I ache all over. I'm not in shape like I used to be."

"You are just getting old Frank," Bull said, "and you know the old expression, 'If you don't use it, you lose it.' You gotta keep workin' out."

Dr. Allen stood in the open doorway watching his friends pack. They'd soon be heading home. But before they left, he wanted to show them his retreat, his very own private mountain.

"Let's go horseback riding," Jim said.

"I'm for that," Frank replied as he put toiletries into his backpack.

"Sounds good to me," Bull agreed as he zipped up his duffel bag.

At a little before noon, Jim, Bull, and Frank were in their saddles, holding the reins in front of them, moving up and down in rhythm with the horse's gait. Jim leaned forward, raised his buttocks out of the saddle, and lightened up on his hold of the reins. The Appaloosa shot forward, swinging its legs along the gravel trail, carrying Jim upward into a stretch of winding, shaded land where tall pines, oaks, and walnut trees dominated the landscape. Bull and Frank were close behind.

Although Frank kept pace behind Jim and Bull, he began coughing and found it difficult to relax. He knew it was important to stay calm and avoid tension. Deviations from proper horsemanship would be transmitted to his beautiful chestnut filly, which might then become erratic in her upward climb. And it could be devastating. So he kept his hands light and steady on the reins and tried not to squeeze his legs against the sides of horse. He shifted his weight back a little to slow the pace. His horse slowed, but Frank still had Bull and Jim in sight.

The white Appaloosa finally reached the top of the mountain, his head high. His rider sat erect. The mare came up alongside the Appaloosa, who had his head turned toward the chestnut filly. When Frank reached the top, he erupted into a fit of coughing. His hands jerked back on the reins, his legs squeezed against the sides of the horse and his heavy boots slipped out of the stirrups. The filly became frightened, reared up on its hind legs, and whinnied, throwing Frank to the ground. Jim and Bull quickly dismounted and rushed to his side. Frank pulled himself into a sitting position, rubbing the back of his head.

"Are you okay?" Jim asked.

Frank nodded and covered his mouth with one hand to cover the cough. Bull looked at his buddy with concern.

"You better check into that cough."

"I'll take care of the horses," Jim said.

After several minutes, a calm prevailed. The filly's head was turned, its large eyes focused on the Appaloosa, who stood alongside her. The mare stood close by, as if chaperoning the twosome.

Jim, Bull, and Frank sat cross-legged on a grassy patch of ground. They gazed down at vast acreage of green land, rising hills, and forested areas. Five tiny buildings dotted the landscape, and a black line ran through the greenery as far as their gaze could carry them.

"That black line is Gabriel's creek," Jim said. "It's named after Gabriel Keith, whose daughter married into the Allen family ages ago."

Bull was impressed with the lineage. "How far back does that go?" he asked.

"Gabriel migrated from Virginia in the mid- to the late seventeen hundreds. He was a land speculator. My great-great-grandfather, Riley Allen, married one of his daughters and was given that farm down there in 1790. It's been in the Allen family over two hundred years. That's why I could not mortgage the farm years ago. It would have destroyed a family heritage and ended a long line of tradition. I couldn't do that to my children and grandchildren and all the Allens to come."

"I understand," Bull said.

Frank sucked on a lozenge, fingered the clasp on his leather jacket, and zipped it all the way up. Picking himself off the ground, he walked over to the filly and stroked its neck.

"I didn't mean to ride you that way. Sorry about that."

The reddish-brown beauty moved its head up and down as if it understood. Frank strolled back and lowered himself to the ground. Bull was already answering a question about the Marlar family.

CHAPTER SIXTY-EIGHT

"One of Frank's guys in Texas checked it out. The Marlar home was boarded up, and it's been that way for years. He got a copy of Rickey's obituary from the Odessa library, and it gave us the name of his daughter and sister. But we haven't been able to locate them or any family member as yet."

"Too bad," Allen replied, "his family was left with the idea that he accidently killed himself."

Bull shook his head. "No way," he said. "My contact talked with Dr. Bauman. He did the autopsy, and the doctor showed him evidence that pointed to homicide. Bauman had the same opinion at the time Marlar died. That evidence was handed over to the police chief in Middleton, but he refused to reopen the case."

Dr. Allen buttoned the top button of his sweater.

"Is there any way of forcing them to reopen the case?"

"It's possible, but the Marlar family would have to pressure the police. And we can't find that family."

Jim stared off into he distance, shook his head, and said, "I still find it hard to believe Rickey was murdered."

Bull shrugged. "Well," he said, "look at the facts. He died when the 500 study had just been completed. Dow and the government knew what you had found. Important data was missing. That missing data was later used by Dow's attorneys to clobber you. And never forget! Dow's attorneys had other data from the same study. They gave it to Burek and Bell before they arrived in Madison. Where in hell did they get it? There's one clue that allows me to make a pretty good guess. That clue is in the Burek and Bell report. When those Dow employees were in Aberg's office, they wanted to know if the data given to them by Kirkland and Ellis was authentic. A phone call was made to Cartwright, your student. And over the phone, without seeing the data, he said it was from the original study. How did he know? He knew because he gave it to Dow. Cartwright, in my opinion, helped to do you in, Jim. He let Spencer into your lab. And he gave Burek and Bell everything they needed to tear your 500 study into shreds. He even carried equipment to Aberg's office. Why was he so helpful? And does he know anything about Marlar's death?"

Jim shook his head. "He was one of Marlar's best friends. He was my student. What would make him do that?"

"Who knows?" Bull replied. "Could be one of several reasons. But the one thing I know is that, according to the police reports, Cartwright was the last known person to see Marlar alive. And according to the police reports, Cartwright lied. When questioned, he said he never slept overnight in Marlar's apartment. When asked the same question on another day, he said he slept over at times because Marlar had asthma and he stayed with him. But nobody ever saw Marlar have an asthmatic attack."

"That's true," said Jim.

"What's also true," Bull went on, "is the fact that Cartwright agreed to take a lie detector test. But the case was closed so damn fast, he never did. And none of the evidence was followed up on. Why? There can be only one reason as far as I'm concerned. I believe the FBI was in on the conspiracy. Why else would the feds suddenly be interested in the death of a twenty-nine-year-old man who lived in a small town like Middleton? Once I accepted the premise that the FBI arranged to have him killed, everything else fell into place. It wasn't just happenstance that the Middleton police didn't dust Marlar's apartment for prints, failed to follow up on leads their own detective reported, destroyed their own police reports, ignored tons of evidenced, and destroyed whatever evidence they had collected. The FBI could have arranged it all. If not for Dr. Bauman, there wouldn't be a police report. He saved a copy and gave it to us. Also, it wasn't just happenstance that the police failed to mention the time factor for the three injections of ketamine, the drug that killed Marlar. The police reported that he received one intravenous and two intramuscular injections. According to Parke-Davis, the manufacturer of ketamine, when given by IV, it takes fifteen seconds for a person to stop functioning normally and another fifteen seconds to be sound asleep. When given through IM, it takes three to four minutes for that person to be sound asleep. The time element was crucial. Marlar could not have done all the things described in the police reports in such a small amount of time. The time element alone would make anyone sit up and pay attention."

"That's true," Jim said. "Ketamine acts quickly."

"Remember another thing," Bull went on, "Cartwright took Rickey to a bar and fed him drinks. They then went to Rickey's apartment. More drinks. When Marlar was found, he had a high blood alcohol level. It shows that he was drunk before he was killed. He would

CHAPTER SIXTY-EIGHT

not have been able to put up much of a fight. And what about the two glasses on the coffee table? One had remnants of a Bloody Mary, and the other was half filled with tea. While Marlar was boozing it up, the other person was drinking tea. Cartwright said he never drank tea. Was that true? I don't think so. And even if he never drank tea, he could have had it, knowing that he wasn't going to get drunk. And I know that the police stopped their investigation prematurely. As far as I'm concerned, the feds moved in and took over. The police had to back away."

Jim saw Bull's reasoning and tended to agree with him and said, "If Rickey was killed because of me—"

"It'll serve no purpose to blame yourself, Jim. You have to look at the big picture." Bull looked Jim straight in the eye. "Look," he said, "the FBI involvement told me that Dow and the U.S. government would do anything to get rid of you. They could not let you go on with your work. Because of you, two of their products were suspended. If they had been cancelled as a result of the EPA hearings, Dow knew that other products were next in line. And it wasn't only Dow. It was the entire chemical industry. The government couldn't let you go on. Their worldwide reputation and billions of dollars were at stake! When Vietnam vets died from cancer, they knew it was from Agent Orange. When kids were born deformed, they knew it was from dioxin. The veterans wanted compensation and treatment for their families and for themselves. But our government would not own up to what they had done to cause the entire mess. Then you came along, upsetting the apple cart and telling the world about dioxin. You were changing and shaping public policy. The environmentalists and the veterans loved you, but Dow and the government were afraid of you."

Dr. Allen felt overwhelmed by the enormity of the situation he had encountered.

"They should have killed me," he said. "Maybe Rickey Marlar would still be alive."

Frank sensed the sadness in his friend's voice. He saw it in his face.

"They couldn't afford to kill you, Doc. You know that. They had to destroy your reputation."

"They sure had a lot of folks helping them," Allen replied. "The Anderson gal, folks at the university, Burek and Bell, Spencer, JRB, the VA, that fancy law firm in DC, that reporter who tore me apart with his articles, the FBI, and others."

Bull smiled. "You just listed a battle-ready army. And you now know what you can do to right some of the wrongs of the past."

Dr. Allen was silent. Frank and Bull were silent. The trees behind them stood tall, their branches high. The light breeze had subsided. The sun was ablaze in all its glory. The white Appaloosa and the chestnut filly were rubbing noses while the mare looked on with what seemed like obvious approval.

Jim turned to Bull. "We better head back. Both of you have to finish packing."

Frank put his hand on Jim's shoulder. "From here on in, Doc, it's up to you."

"That's right, Jim," Bull agreed. "If you decide to go for it, I'll do whatever I can to help."

Dr. Allen nodded. He did not reply. He lifted himself from the ground, not knowing what he wanted to do.

SIXTY-NINE

It was Christmas morning. Dr. Allen was sitting on the side of the bed, sliding his feet into brown, fur-lined slippers. He was tired. The night had been a tug-of-war between thinking and dozing. On the one hand, he had a thriving practice and was doing quite well. He had more money now than he ever would have had were he still a professor at the university. Outwardly, life was peaceful. His grandchildren were a joy. Why should he start fighting battles that had been lost twenty years ago? On the other hand, he was having nightmares again. Down deep, he was troubled. He remembered the past. He had failed to see Dow as the enemy until it was too late, and he had failed to see the government as an enemy. He had failed to fight the criminal charges that resulted in his conviction and failed in so many other ways.

He lifted himself from the bed, ambled into the bathroom, and studied himself in the mirror. Opening a drawer in the vanity, he took out a brush and began shaping his hair the way Dave had styled it. He liked the wavy look, but it did nothing to make him look younger.

"I'm getting old," he said to himself in the mirror. "How many more years have I got?"

He remembered how he looked years ago. Handsome. Vibrant. Full of life and quite often posing as a cowboy. Oh, how he loved walking around campus dressed in blue jeans, a white ten-gallon cowboy hat, and those high-heeled, blue leather boots.

He turned quickly, walked out of the bathroom, back to the bedroom, and opened the closet door. Suits, slacks, and dresses hung from a pole. The first two shelves in front of him had shoeboxes, one stacked on top of another. And up high on the top shelf was his cowboy hat. He reached up, took it down, and stood there looking at it.

"You've seen better days," he said to the hat, brushing away dust with the backs of his fingers.

Memories came back to him, wanting to look like Clint Eastwood when invited at a VA meeting in DC, wanting to walk into that meeting like a cowboy with a gun on his hip, wanting to show his willingness to shoot it out in the old corral. He smiled at these thoughts, but the smile vanished when he remembered going into a Baptist church wrapped in a heavy overcoat, sitting in the darkness of the last pew, and seeing the cross holding Jesus up where a light shone down from above. He remembered his lament to God, asking about the fate of Vietnam veterans and their families, knowing he would no longer be able to help them.

Like a bolt from the blue, it hit him. All of his life, he talked about and marveled at the way his ancestors fought and died for what they believed in. It was something to cherish and believe in. And now it was his turn. It was a time to be a cowboy, a time to fight, no more pussyfooting around. He hurried out of the bedroom and down the stairs. He had to tell Christie. He was going to have his hat cleaned and blocked. It was time to be a cowboy.

EPILOGUE

Frank McCarthy underwent surgery at the Mayo Clinic for an Agent Orange–related lung cancer. He later married and became a minister. There was a recurrence of the malignancy, and he fought it for a number of years before succumbing to the deadly disease. In talking with his wife, Robin, she reported that Frank chose not to be interred at the Arlington National Cemetery. She said, "Frank loved fishing." And when he died on April 16, 2011, he was cremated and his ashes were strewn in the Sebastian Inlet in Sebastian, Florida, where he used to fish.

Dr. James Allen and his wife, Christie, live in North Carolina. He currently practices veterinary medicine, and his wife works alongside him. Dr. Allen obtained a law degree and decided to act as his own attorney to clear his name. He filed a request with the U.S. District Court in Madison, Wisconsin, on March 1998 and asked that he be allowed to appear to present his case for expunging of his criminal records. The court did not reply.

The FBI has consistently refused to release Dr. Allen's records. Initially they said, "It will take years because of a backlog of requests." After the next request, they said, "They may be in a local FBI office." Since Agent Thomas followed Dr. Allen and gathered information from a number of people, a request was made as to the local FBI office that he had been assigned to. The FBI never replied.

Dr. Beyster of Science Applications International Corporation refused to rescind the false four-line insertion in the VA manual by his subsidiary, JRB, even though he was given proof it was false. Beyster blamed the VA for it. Could his refusal be related to the fact that SAIC thrived on contracts from the government? On November 6, 2000, *Stars and Stripes* listed the top fifty defense contractors providing government purchases. SAIC was number eleven.

Dr. Mather, chief of environmental hazards for the VA, also refused to rescind the four-line insertion. He blamed JRB for it and said the VA did not agree with it.

In September 1994, the EPA said, "Dioxin is a more likely carcinogen than was previously thought and is a potential cause for other illnesses in very low exposure levels."

In June 1998, anthropologist Elizabeth Guillette reported dramatic defects in brain function in rural children with long-term exposure to agricultural chemicals.

The Associated Press reported on an article from the *Chicago Tribune*, dated July 17, 1994. It said, "Biological warfare testing posed no threat, army says."

Déjà vu?

ADDENDUM I

THE DISPOSAL OF AGENT ORANGE

DEPARTMENT OF DEFENSE, NATIONAL MILITARY COMMAND CENTER'S UNCLASSIFIED document saying that a decision had been reached to temporarily store stocks of herbicide, now in Vietnam, on Johnston Island until plans for eventual disposition had been finalized. The two-page document was in two parts, one part dated February 1, 1972, and the other January 1972.

McKinney, Congressman Stewart B., in a letter of outrage regarding the burning of 2.3 million gallons of "Orange" in Texas with the question, "If indeed it is too dangerous to be disposed of in Vietnam, why would it be safer to dispose of it within the United States?" The letter is found in the House of Representatives and is dated February 2, 1972.

Sullivan, Congressman Leonor K. "Protest letter to Melvin Laird, Secretary, Department of Defense, Washington, DC, 20301." The protest was regarding the burning of defoliant Orange at the Monsanto Company plant incinerator at Sauget, Illinois. The letter is found in the House of Representatives and is dated February 14, 1972.

Shaughnessy, Colonel, John J., USAF, Chief, Planning Group, Office of Legislative Liaison. A two-page letter in reply to Congressman Sullivan's protest letter to Melvin Laird, Secretary, Deptartment of Defense, regarding the burning of Orange herbicides in Illinois. The letter stated, "The most logical solution could be high temperature incineration..." But it went onto say there would have to be a public forum before deciding on a course of action. The letter was dated February 14, 1972.

Following the Vietnam War, Anne Wilkinson wrote, "Department of the Air Force, Headquarters 1947TH Administrative Support Group, Washington, DC 20330" and issued documents addressing the options for the disposal of dioxin in herbicide Orange, dated July 29, 1981.

Mays, Attorney Richard H. was involved in a case brought on behalf of the EPA against Hercules Chemical Company in Arkansas for improper storage of 2,4,5–T and the contaminant dioxin. A portion of the site had been used to dig two landfill areas for the burial of wastes. It said, "Wastes at the site have escaped and are now threatening the surrounding environment." It said, "Section 309 of the Clean Water Act, 33 U.S.C. 1319 (b) and (d) authorizes the EPA to institute a suit for injunctive relief and civil penalties not to exceed $10,000 per day for violation of Section 301 of the Clean Water Act, 33 U.S.C. 1311 (a).

ADDENDUM 2

CHEMICAL WARFARE: AGENT ORANGE

Truthout Report, August 11, 2011
By H. Patricia Hynes

DURING THE TEN YEARS (1960–1970) OF AERIAL CHEMICAL WARFARE IN VIETnam, US warplanes sprayed more than twenty million gallons of herbicide defoliants in an operation code-named Ranch Hand. In the late 1980s, Admiral Elmo Zumwalt, whose son died after exposure to Agent Orange in Vietnam, found evidence that the US military increased the defoliant's toxicity by spraying "Agent Orange in concentrations six to twenty-five times the suggested rate." Other investigations, including National Archive documents, have shown that Dow Chemical, as early as 1957, knew that dioxin could be eliminated by lowering the temperature and slowing the manufacturing process. But eliminating dioxin would delay production and reduce company profits when wartime production called for rapid, high-quantity manufacture.

According to a memo found during Zumwalt's 1988 investigation, the US government knew of the defoliant's toxicity. Dr. James R. Clary, a former senior scientist at the U.S. Air Force Chemical Weapons Branch, who designed the spray tanks for Operation Ranch Hand, wrote in response to a Congressional investigation into Agent Orange: "When we initiated the herbicide program in the 1960s, we were aware of the potential for damage due to dioxin contamination in the herbicide. We were even aware that the military formulation had a higher dioxin concentration than the civilian version due to the lower cost and speed of manufacture. However, because the material was to be used on the enemy, none of us were overly concerned. We never considered a scenario in which our own personnel would become contaminated with the herbicide."

Former US pilots revealed that they dumped hundreds of thousands of gallons from their planes into forests, rivers, and drinking water reservoirs because military regulations required that herbicide spray planes return to base empty. In this methodical "ecocide," one-seventh of the land area of South Vietnam was sprayed. Arthur Westing, who documented the scale of US environmental destruction in Vietnam, wrote of the strategic ruination of tropical forest canopy and consequent destruction of its biodiversity.

While successive US administrations denied they were employing first-strike chemical warfare in contravention of the 1925 Geneva Convention against biological toxin weapons warfare, over five thousand scientists signed a petition in 1964 protesting the use of chemical warfare agents in Vietnam. Even after military analysis revealed in 1967 that the defoliation program did not advance the war and, conversely, may have been counterproductive by turning peasants who lost their crops against the US and toward the Viet Cong, the government continued using the chemical weapon.

By the end of the war, nearly five million Vietnamese had been exposed to Agent Orange, resulting in "400,000 deaths and disabilities and a half-million children born with birth defects and disabilities and a half million children born with birth defects," according to the 2008–2009 President's Cancer Panel Report. Agent Orange was so extensively sprayed that all of the two million Americans who served in Vietnam are presumed exposed. The Veterans Administration now associates a multitude of cancers, heart disease, type-2 diabetes, neuropathy, Parkinson's disease, and birth defects including spina bifida suffered by veterans and their children. However, it took advocates, their lawyers, and concerned scientists decades of confronting inept and corrupt government health studies to overcome myths and achieve governmental acknowledgement of the human health harm of Agent Orange. Vietnam veterans continue to eke out needed health services from a reluctant government, which still contends that it used the deadly chemicals to protect the soldiers and refuses to accept any responsibility for generations of Agent Orange victims in Vietnam.

ADDENDUM 3

A FINAL WORD ON AGENT ORANGE

MORE THAN THREE DECADES AFTER AGENT ORANGE BECAME KNOWN TO THE American public, it is still an issue of great concern, as demonstrated by an article in the *Los Angeles Times* on July 21, 2011, titled "Buried Agent Orange claim probed in S. Korea."

Using modern tools to penetrate the ground, such as radar, and analyzing water soil samples, investigators in South Korea are searching for clues to a decades-old mystery. Did American soldiers dispose of Agent Orange at a US-run base about 150 miles southeast of Seoul in 1978?

For weeks, a US / South Korean survey team focused on a site at Camp Carroll because tiny amounts of dioxin were found in nearby streams. But South Korean officials say, "The tiny amount of dioxin is too small to cause health problems, such as cancer or birth defects." US officials say they have no evidence or records of Agent Orange ever being kept at the base. But the investigation was launched after a US veteran told a Phoenix television station in May that he and others buried dozens of drums containing Agent Orange at Camp Carroll more than three decades ago.

Radar mapping at Camp Carroll has detected objects that critics believe may be barrels, but US officials say the anomalies could just be differing soil densities. Task force members have yet to decide whether to fully explore the area.

If significant amounts of the herbicide are discovered, experts say, that could affect U.S. relations with one of its closest Asian allies, damaging US claims of being good stewards at scores of bases, many of which they have occupied since the end of fighting in the Korean War in 1953.

Some observers say the presence of Agent Orange could fuel a sense among some South Koreans that the 28,500 troops in the country should begin to withdraw. Many believe the search for Agent Orange should be widened to military bases nationwide.

South Korean lawmakers say they have not been given access to crucial documents. Many say they fear the administration of President Lee Myung-bak, which supports a US military presence, might cover up any negative results in an investigation to determine environmental damage.

"The U.S. military is not opening its reports to the public," said lawmaker Hong Hee-deok, a critic of the investigation. "Koreans are threatened by this, but we have limited access to information, and this is frustrating."

US military officials acknowledge that barrels containing numerous chemicals were buried at Camp Carroll, but they say they were removed a year later. Records show Agent Orange was not among the compounds, they say. "We've been upfront about this," Birchmeier said.

HAVE THEY?

CPSIA information can be obtained at www.ICGtesting.com
Printed in the USA
LVOW131229130313

324070LV00004B/124/P